heart like mine

Center Point
Large Print

**This Large Print Book carries the
Seal of Approval of N.A.V.H.**

heart like mine

Amy Hatvany

CENTER POINT LARGE PRINT
THORNDIKE, MAINE

This Center Point Large Print edition is published in the
year 2013 by arrangement with Atria Books,
a division of Simon & Schuster, Inc.

The text of this Large Print edition is unabridged.
In other aspects, this book may
vary from the original edition.
Printed in the United States of America
on permanent paper.
Set in 16-point Times New Roman type.

ISBN: 978-1-61173-801-8

Library of Congress Cataloging-in-Publication Data

Hatvany, Amy, 1972–
Heart like mine / Amy Hatvany.
pages ; cm.
ISBN 978-1-61173-801-8 (library binding : alk. paper)
1. Stepmothers—Fiction. 2. Stepchildren—Fiction.
  3. Mothers—Fiction. 4. Death—Fiction.
  5. Fathers and daughters—Fiction.
  6. Children—Family relationships—Fiction.
  7. Seattle (Wash.)—Fiction. 8. Domestic fiction.
  9. Large type books. I. Title.
PS3608.A8658H43 2013b
813'.6—dc23
                                          2013001916

For Anna, my bonus daughter,
who filled a space in my heart
I never knew was there.

If it is true that there are as many minds as there are heads, then there are as many kinds of love as there are hearts.

—Leo Tolstoy, *Anna Karenina*

Every heart sings a song, incomplete, until another heart whispers back.

—Plato

Grace

Later, I would look back and wonder what I was doing the exact moment Kelli died.

When I left the house for work that morning, nothing was different. There was no sense of impending doom, no ominous soundtrack playing in the back of my mind warning me that my world was about to change. There was only Victor asleep in our bed, and me, as usual, trying my best not to wake him as I kissed him good-bye.

It was a Friday in late October, and I drove my usual route downtown, taking in the dark silhouette of the Seattle skyline etched against a coral sky. "Good morning," I said to my assistant, Tanya, after I'd parked and entered the building. She was a stunning woman with skin the color of the deepest, richest cocoa who favored brightly hued dresses to show off her abundant curves. "A pre–Weight Watchers Jennifer Hudson," I told my best friend, Melody, describing Tanya to her after I initially interviewed her for the job.

"Morning," she said, so focused on whatever she was doing that she barely looked up from her computer screen. Her long red nails clackety-clacked on her keyboard. Six months ago, Tanya had been living with her two toddlers in one of our safe houses. At the time, she desperately needed to work and I desperately needed an assistant, so we seemed like a perfect match. I'd taken over as CEO of Second Chances the previous fall, honored to take the lead in an organization that began in the early nineties as a simple twenty-four-hour support line for battered women and had slowly grown into a multi-faceted program including crisis response, counseling, temporary housing, and job placement assistance. We'd even opened a thrift shop earlier that year, where our clients had first pick of donated clothes for job interviews and later, when they were ready to go out on their own, entire wardrobes. My job was to make sure that the more practical, administrative aspects of the program, like funding and staffing, ran smoothly, but the real reason I'd accepted the job was for the privilege of helping women like Tanya rebuild their shattered lives.

I set down the latte I'd bought for her at the café downstairs so it would be within her reach, then turned and walked into my office, closing the door behind me. I assumed this would be like any other day. I positioned myself at my desk, booted up my computer, and reviewed my calendar. Other than a couple of phone calls, there was only a staff meeting at two o'clock, so I got busy studying the client files Tanya had pulled for me. It was time to decide if these women were ready to make the transition from our safe houses into a place of their own. Leaving the first home where they'd felt protected was often the hardest step for victims of domestic violence; I made sure we held their hand every step of the way.

I barely looked up from my papers until a few hours later, when my cell phone vibrated in my purse. I reached for it with a skipping, happy feeling in my belly at the sight of Victor's name on the screen. "Hi, honey," I said, glancing down at the ring on my finger. He'd only proposed five days ago and I was still unused to the weight of it, still a little stunned that he'd asked me to marry him at all.

"Can you go pick up the kids from school for me?" Victor asked. His voice was strained and carried an urgency I didn't recognize.

"What, I'm your fiancée now, so I don't even get a hello?" I said, hoping I could tease him out of his seemingly ugly mood. Victor was usually the most easygoing person I knew; I wondered if something had gone wrong at work, if his head chef had called in sick or one of his busers dropped a box of wineglasses. "Is this what it's going to be like being married to you?"

"Grace," he said. "Seriously. I need you to pick them up and take them back to the house. Please."

"What's wrong?" I asked, sitting up straight in my chair. Every muscle in my body suddenly tensed, realizing this wasn't just a case of Victor's having a bad day.

"It's Kelli. Her friend Diane found her a couple of hours ago. She wasn't breathing and . . ." I heard him swallow once, hard. "She's dead, Grace. Kelli's dead."

My mouth went dry. *Kelli. His ex-wife. Oh, holy shit.* All the air pressed out of my lungs; it took a moment for me to be able to speak. "Oh my *god,* Victor. What *happened?*"

"I don't know the details yet. The medics took her to the ER and I guess I'm still listed as her emergency contact on her insurance plan, so they called me. Can you pick up the kids?"

"Of course." I stood up, scrambling for my purse. Panic jittered in my chest, picturing their response to this news. Ava, especially, at thirteen, needing her mother so much, and Max, who was only seven and still had to talk with Kelli before he could fall asleep the nights he stayed at our house. Max and Ava, who didn't yet know that we were engaged. Victor had told Kelli the news earlier in the week, meeting her for a cup of coffee at the restaurant while the kids were still in school. "How'd it go?" I asked when he came home. He pressed his lips together and gave his head a brief shake. "Not great," he said, and I hadn't pressed him further.

"What do you want me to tell them?" I asked him now, already worried that whatever I said would be wrong.

"Nothing, yet. I'll be home as soon as I can, but

12

I have to go to identify her—" His voice broke, and he cleared it. "Her body."

"Are you sure you don't want me to go with you?" I'd never heard him so upset and felt desperate to do something to comfort him.

"No, just get the kids. Please. I'll figure out what to say to them before I get there."

We hung up, and I hurried outside my office. Tanya turned her gaze from her computer to me. "What's wrong?"

"It's Kelli . . . Victor's ex." I exhaled a heavy breath. "She's dead."

Her hand flew to her mouth. "Oh my god!" she said with her eyes open wide. She dropped her hand back to her lap. "What happened?"

"We don't know yet. Victor is on his way to the hospital right now."

"Oh my god," she said again, shaking her head. "I'll wipe your calendar for next week. The staff meeting can wait." She paused. "Do you want me to call Stephanie?"

I nodded, thinking that the best person to cover for me was definitely my predecessor, who'd retired when I accepted the job but still gave her time to us as a volunteer. "That'd be great. I'm not sure how long I'll be out. Thank you."

"Of course. I'll call if there's anything urgent. And let me know if you need anything else."

I left the building with my muscles shaking, climbed into my car, and gripped the steering wheel, trying to steady myself before pulling out of the lot. Thoughts spun in my head; I tried to imagine what life would be like for Max and Ava after they found out their mother was dead. And for me as the woman who, by default, would wind up standing in her place.

The night I met Victor, the idea that I might become the mother to his children was the furthest thing from my mind. In fact, being a mother was pretty much the furthest thing from my mind *any* night of the week, something I tried to explain to my date as we sat in the bar of Victor's popular Seattle restaurant, the Loft. At that moment, I didn't know I was about to meet Victor. I didn't know that he owned the restaurant or that he was divorced with two kids. All I knew was I needed to find a way to bail on this date before it got any worse. Chad was the college frat boy who'd never grown up, some-thing I hadn't realized when we'd messaged back and forth on Match.com and then briefly chatted on the phone. On paper, he was jocular, sort of funny, and had that confident, teetering-on-the-edge-of-cocky demeanor I typically found appealing in a man, so I figured there wouldn't be much harm in meeting him for a simple drink. Clearly, I had figured wrong.

"So," he said after we'd been seated, ordered our drinks, and gone over the usual niceties of how happy we were to finally meet in person. "You don't want kids?" He leaned back in his chair with an odd smirk on his ruddy face.

I was immediately turned off by the blunt challenge in his tone; every internal red flag I had started waving. My online profile did, in fact, indicate that I was focused on pursuing my career more than motherhood, but it was strange that he would lead with this particular topic. I took a tiny sip of the lemon-drop martini our server had just delivered, letting the crunchy bits of sanding sugar that lined the rim of my glass dissolve on my tongue before answering. "It's not so much that I don't *want* them," I said. "More like I'm not sure I'd be very good as a parent." I hoped my neutral response would dissuade him from pursuing the subject further.

"Don't you like kids?" he asked, tilting his blond head at me.

"Yes, I *like* them," I said, repressing a sigh. It was frustrating how many people seemed to assume that I was heartless or unfeeling because I wasn't rushing to become a mother. Men who chose a career over fatherhood weren't automatically considered assholes. They were classified as devil-may-care George Clooney types. And who didn't love George?

"I have a brother who was born when I was thirteen," I explained to Chad. "And I spent ten years helping to raise him before I finally moved out of my parents' house, so I sort of learned firsthand that motherhood really isn't for me." My decision wasn't quite as simplistic as I'd made it sound, but I was already scanning the room for my quickest escape, so I didn't see the sense in delving deeper than that with Chad. The Loft's bar wasn't huge, maybe a total of fifteen tables. The only exit was past the hostess, right in his line of sight. If I excused myself to the restroom, then tried to sneak out the front door, he'd see. I took a big swallow of my drink, hoping the alcohol would smooth the edges of my growing irritation.

"Well," Chad said as he placed his meaty palms flat on our small, wooden table, "I actually believe it's a woman's biological responsibility to reproduce. I mean, honestly, if you think about it anthropologically, your body is really just a support system for your uterus."

My wrist flicked and the contents of my drink splashed in his face before my mind registered it had given the command. Chad sputtered and wiped at his eyes with the backs of his hands as I set the now-empty glass on the table and quickly began gathering my things.

"What the hell is *wrong* with you?" he said, spitting out the words.

I stood, pulse pounding, holding my black leather clutch up off the table so it wouldn't get vodka on it. "Nothing," I said, attempting to take a slow, measured breath. "You, however, might benefit from therapy." Out of the corner of my eye, I saw a tall man with closely cropped, dark brown hair striding toward us from behind the bar. He wore a black dress shirt and slacks, both cut to complement his lanky build.

Chad stood too, and took a menacing step toward me just as the man in black grabbed him by the arm. "Looks like you spilled your drink," he said. I immediately liked him for his attempt at diplomacy, despite my certainty that he had witnessed what actually happened. He appeared to be around my age, midthirties, maybe a little bit older. The threads of silver woven through the hair around his temples gave him a distinguished edge and his olive-toned skin held the slightly weathered look of a little too much time spent in the sun.

"That bitch threw it in my face!" Chad yelled. Every person who hadn't been looking in our direction suddenly was. The buzz of conversation ceased, and the only sounds were the low, bass-driven background music piped in through the speakers and Chad's hoarse, angry breathing.

The man's grip tightened on Chad's arm. "Sir, I have to ask you to refrain from calling this lovely woman names. I'm sure it was an accident." He looked at me with kind, smoky gray eyes. "Right, miss?"

I shook my head. "Nope. I threw it at him. He was being an ass. Are you the manager?"

17

The man shook his head a little, too, and smiled, revealing white, straight teeth and a cavernous dimple in his left cheek. "The owner, actually. Victor Hansen." He released his grip on Chad and held out his hand.

I clasped it quickly but firmly, my greet-the-executive, don't-mess-with-me handshake. "Grace McAllister. Good to meet you. I love this place."

"Jesus!" Chad interjected. His face flamed red and bits of saliva shot out from his mouth. "If you two are done with your little schmooze-fest, I'd like to know who's going to pay for my shirt!"

Victor glanced over at Chad's late-1990s hold-over mustard-yellow rayon button-down, reached into his pocket, and offered him a twenty. "This should cover it. Now, why don't you show some dignity and walk away?"

Chad looked at the bill in Victor's hand but didn't take it, then made a disgusted noise before grabbing his coat off the back of his chair and pushing his way through the bar to the front door, knocking into a few chairs and tables as he went. Outside, he threw a middle finger up in the air behind him as he walked by the window where Victor and I stood.

"Wow," Victor said, tucking his money back in his pocket, "I wonder if his mom knows he escaped her basement?"

I laughed. "Thank you," I said, reaching into

my purse for my credit card. I held it out to him. "I'm happy to pay for our drinks." The other customers stopped looking at us and returned to their own conversations; the comforting background noise of glasses and silverware tinkling filled the air.

"Oh no," Victor said, waving my card away. "Those are on me." He smiled again. "Did you order dinner?"

"No, thank god. Just a drinks date." I shook my head. "Evidently, I need to work on my screening process." *Maybe I should start asking for men's relationship résumés and require at least three glowing references before agreeing to meet.*

Victor chuckled. "Tough out there, isn't it?"

My eyes stole a glance down at his left hand. No ring. *Hmm.* He caught me midglance and lifted his hand up, wiggling his bare fourth finger. "Some detective I'd make, huh?" I laughed again, then reached up to smooth my russet waves.

Luckily, he laughed, too. "So, I'm thinking the least I can do is feed you so the night's not a total loss. Will you join me for dinner?"

My cheeks flushed, and I dropped my gaze to the floor before looking back up at him and smiling. "I'd like that," I said, "but will you excuse me a moment? I need to visit the ladies' room."

"Of course." He pointed me in the right direction, and I walked away slowly, conscious of his eyes on me, making sure not to sway my hips in too obvious a manner, but enough so that he'd notice the movement. In the restroom, I stood in front of the full-length mirror and swiped on a touch of tinted lip gloss. I took a step back and examined my reflection. Reddish, shoulder-length hair, mussed in that casual, I-meant-it-to-look-a-little-messy way that had taken me over an hour to achieve. Pale skin, a spattering of freckles on my cheeks that no amount of powder could hide; green eyes, set evenly apart. A swash of mascara was the only makeup I wore besides the lip gloss. My lips were full enough, and the gloss definitely helped. Being that this was the first date night I'd had in several months, I'd taken the time to go shopping and pick out a flattering pair of dark, boot-cut jeans and a slightly clingy green sweater, both of which made the most of my somewhat average figure. My legs looked leaner, and with the help of a good bra, my chest looked perkier than usual. Overall, not too shabby. I pinched my cheeks for a little color and returned to the bar, where I found Victor exactly where I'd left him.

"All set?" he asked, and I nodded, following him through swinging black doors into the kitchen. As we entered, I hesitated. "Um, do you want me to put my order in myself?"

Victor laughed again, took my hand, and led me over to a high-backed, cushioned red booth off to the side of where the servers were gathered.

"No, I want you to have the best seat in the house—the chef's table." He gestured for me to sit down. "I'll be right back. What were you drinking? Lemon Drop?"

I smiled. "How did you know?"

"Smelled it on your date." He winked, then strode over past the stainless steel counter behind which several cooks were either sautéing, whisking, or artfully arranging wonderful-smelling food on square white plates. The energy in the room was kinetic but slowed down as Victor spoke to one of the male chefs, a hugely muscled and handsome man with startling black tribal tattoos on his thick neck and forearms. He looked over at me as Victor talked, then he smiled and gave me a clipped salute in greeting. I gave a short wave back, briefly wondering how many other female patrons Victor had given this treatment.

Victor headed out of the kitchen—to get our drinks, presumably—so I quickly texted Melody, my best friend. "Weird night. On date number two (I think), same restaurant." She texted back immediately: "WTH? I can't even get *one* date!" I smiled to myself, picturing her curled up in her favorite plaid flannel pajamas, eating popcorn, and watching reruns of *Sex and the City*. "Will explain tomorrow," I typed, pressing send just as Victor returned with two martinis. Dirty for him, lemon for me.

"So," he said, "I hope you don't mind I ordered

food for us both. I know the menu pretty well."

"How do you know what I like?" I asked, taking what I hoped was a dainty sip from my drink.

"Well, I know you don't like stupid men, so I'm already ahead of the game." He smiled. "I'm having an assortment of dishes brought out, actually, so you can sample a little of everything."

"Impressive. Must be nice to be the owner."

He grinned. "It is. So, what do you do?"

I launched into a short description of my career, how after I got my degree in business management, I'd stumbled into a position as a lowly HR assistant and worked my way up through various companies to an eventual directorship for a local medical center. It was there I learned about Second Chances. I told him how I'd been a volunteer with the organization long before I was one of its employees.

"What made you want to give your time there, in particular?" Victor asked, tilting his head a bit toward his shoulder.

"Well," I said, "that's kind of a long story."

"The good ones usually are."

"All right then, you asked for it," I said with a smile. "So, I was in seventh grade when I saw a news segment about this amazing female doctor who traveled the world helping people who'd been affected by all sorts of atrocities—disease, war, famine. Horrible stuff. And I remember being in awe watching her cradle this extremely ill-looking woman, who just clung to her like she hadn't been held so tenderly in her entire life." Tears swelled my throat even then, as I recalled the power of that moment. "I guess that image sort of stuck with me. I sort of promised myself to someday be like that doctor . . . helping those who couldn't help themselves."

Victor nodded and seemed interested, so I continued, careful not to hop up on my soapbox about the political issues surrounding domestic violence, as I sometimes had the tendency to do when I started talking about my job. "When I heard about the work Second Chances did, it seemed like such a perfect way to fulfill that desire. I mean, HR was great for me professionally, but this was an opportunity to help people on a much more personal level, you know?" He nodded again, and I went on, wrapping the details up as quickly as I could. "I enrolled in crisis counselor training to get qualified to take calls on the help line and started using my business contacts to increase fund-raising donations, and discovered I had a real passion for the work. When the woman who started the organization told me she was retiring, I applied for the position and got it. Most of my management experience is in operations and organizational development, so it's kind of a perfect fit."

"I think it's great that you're so passionate about what you do," Victor said, lifting his glass and tilting his head, indicating that I should do the same. "Congrats."

I complied, and we clinked our glasses together lightly. "Thank you."

He took a sip of his drink, then set it back on the table before giving me another smile. "So, I have to ask. What did that guy say to get you so mad?" I gave him a quick recap of Chad's statements about the role of women in relation to procreating and Victor's jaw dropped. "Are you kidding me?"

I shrugged. "I guess he didn't believe me when I told him I've chosen not to have kids."

"Me too," Victor said. "At least, not any more than I already have."

I cocked a single eyebrow and apparently looked as confused as I felt, so he pulled out his wallet to show me a picture of two dark-haired, blue-eyed children—a girl and a boy. "Max is six and Ava is twelve," he said. "They live with their mom, but I see them every other weekend." His voice was tinged with a tiny bit of sadness, and I automatically wondered what kind of relation-ship he had with his ex-wife. In the past, if I were mentally reviewing a man's relationship résumé and it included the word "father" among his experience, I would have moved it to the "no" pile. But it was becoming increasingly difficult for me to find a single man who hadn't already been married or didn't have children, so I attempted to keep an open mind. Just because I wasn't set on having babies didn't mean I wasn't looking to fall in love.

"How long have you been divorced?" I asked, keeping the inquiry light. How recently he came back on the dating market played a big part in my decision about whether or not he was relationship material. I wasn't anxious to be any man's rebound girl.

"A little over two years," Victor said. "We get along fairly well, which is great for the kids."

"Ah," I said, leaning back against the seat cushion. "They're adorable." I realized he was the first person in as long as I could remember who hadn't immediately asked *why* I wasn't anxious to have children as soon as they found this out about me. Another point in his favor.

"They're also enough," he said. "I'm thirty-nine, and I don't plan to have any more." He looked at me, his expression hesitant. "So, does my daddy status mean this is our last date?"

"Date?" I fiddled with the hem of my sweater and issued what I hoped was an appealing smile. "This isn't just the owner of the restaurant making up for a customer's crappy night?"

"I don't think so." He gaze became more determined as he reached over and skimmed the top of my hand with his fingertips. "I'd like to see you again."

His touch sent a shiver through me, and staring into his kind eyes, I felt a twinge somewhere in the vicinity of my belly. *Do I do this?* I hadn't dated a man with children before, but something about Victor felt different. Special enough to think he might just be worth taking a chance.

Ava

After Dad moved out, Saturday mornings were the hardest. Saturdays used to be when he didn't have to get up early and head to the restaurant; Saturdays were when he woke us with the buttery smell of his special homemade vanilla-bean waffles toasting on the griddle and smoky bacon sizzling on the stove. I loved to lie in my bed, breathing in the tendrils of those familiar scents, feeling them wrap around me, warm and comforting as my father's arms.

"Breakfast, kiddos!" he bellowed when it was ready. "Come and get it while it's hot!"

Max would scamper down the hallway to beat me to the table, but I stayed in bed with a small, secret smile on my face, knowing exactly what was coming next. My bedroom door was flung open, and Daddy would stomp over to me. "Is there a sleepy little girl in here?" he asked in a teasing, slightly maniacal voice. "Does she need to be *tickled* to wake up?"

"No!" I'd squeal, my smile growing wider,

scrunching myself up against the wall, pretending to try to get away from him.

"Oh, yes!" Dad said, holding his hands out in front of him and wiggling his fingers like crazy.

"Daddy, no!" I said again, but inside I was thinking, *Oh, yes!*

"It's time to get uh-up!" he said, and then it would come, the dive-bomb of his fingertips to my sides, and I couldn't help but shriek, giggling and laughing and writhing around beneath his touch. "Are you awake yet?" he asked, rubbing the short stubble of his beard against my neck to tickle me more. "Are you ready to come have breakfast?"

"Yes!" I yelled, smiling so wide it almost hurt my cheeks. "Okay! I'm coming!"

Dad kissed my cheek and pulled his hands away from my body. "All right then," he said. "Let's eat!"

Now that he was gone, now that Mama had asked him to leave, Saturday mornings were quiet, empty of any happy laughter. For breakfast we had cereal or toast, and most of the time, I ended up going into Mama's room to wake her up so we wouldn't be late for Max's soccer games. Just last week, she had forgotten that we were in charge of bringing the snack, and instead of just stopping at the store to buy something like any of the other moms probably would have, she'd rushed to bake a batch of cupcakes before we could leave.

27

"Yoo-hoo!" she had singsonged as we finally made our way to the field where Max's game was about to get under way. "Sorry we're late!"

He'd missed warm-up, but as I carefully balanced the carrying case filled with the chocolate cupcakes, Max raced past us to get to where his coach was picking the starting lineup. The mothers of Max's teammates barely turned to acknowledge Mama's greeting. They sat together on the bleachers with heavy plaid blankets over their laps, chattering and laughing at something one of them had said. A group of men stood nearby, laughing and shaking each other's hands; a few of them shouted encouragement to Max and his teammates. Daddy used to stand with those men, talking and laughing, before he moved out. Now he only came to Max's games on the Saturdays we were with him.

I set the carrying case on the table next to the cooler full of water bottles and watched as Mama tried again. She fluffed her hair and put on her best, brightest smile. "Hey there," she said as she walked over to stand next to the group. "Beautiful weather for a game, isn't it?" It was a cold, crisp fall day.

A heavyset woman with black, straight hair turned her head and gave Mama a false smile in return. "Yes," she said, as though stating something incredibly obvious. "It is."

"How's the other team looking this morning?"

Mama asked, shoving her hands into the side pockets of her fitted black leather jacket. The other moms wore Columbia fleece pullovers or earthy-toned wool sweaters. Mama chose tight Levi's and over-the-knee black boots to match her jacket; the other women had on rain boots or closed-toed Birkenstocks. "Our babies are going to show 'em who's boss, right?"

No one answered her. Instead, a few of them covered their mouths and stifled coughs. Mama's chin trembled just the tiniest bit before she sat down on the bottom bleacher and tucked her tiny hands between her legs. I joined her, and she put her arm around me, hugging me to her. I wanted to tell her not to worry—that she was prettier than all those other women. Nicer, too. But I didn't know if I should. If it was good for her to know that I could see the sadness in her eyes when she looked at them—the longing to be made a part of their group. Mama and I were alike that way. She had Diane and I had my best friend, Bree, but that was pretty much it. She looked at those women like I looked at the popular girls at school. Like, *Please, just give me a chance.*

One of the fathers noticed Mama sitting on the edge of the bleachers. He was tall and barrel chested, with sandy blond hair and a goatee. He made a comment under his breath to the other men, and a few of them snickered in response. He walked over to us, propped his foot up on the edge of the bleacher right next to Mama's leg, and leaned on his thigh with his forearm. "Hey, Kelli," he said. "How are you?" His words were slick, as though coated in oil as they slid from his mouth.

Mama gave him a sparkling smile. "Well, I'm just fine, thank you very much." Her voice was bubbly, practically dripping with enthusiasm. "How are *you?*"

"Better now," he said with a wink, and my stomach clenched. I was pretty sure he was Carter's dad, and the husband of the black-haired, heavy woman, who I only knew as "Carter's mom." I didn't like the way he was looking at Mama. I didn't like how hairy his knuckles were, either.

"Honey," Carter's mom called out, noticing her husband talking to us. "Are you watching the game?"

"Carter's not even on the field yet," he said sharply, giving her a hard look. Then he turned his gaze back to Mama, softening it. "I feel like I haven't seen you around much. I was sorry to hear about you and Victor. You two always seemed so happy."

Mama kept her smile bright, but I saw the flash of grief in her eyes. Even after all of this time, she still seemed to miss him. A few weeks ago, she had accidentally set a place for him at the dinner table. "I guess things aren't always as they seem," she said to Carter's father now.

"I guess not," he said with a chuckle. He glanced toward the parking lot. "Is Victor coming today?"

Mama shook her head. "He wanted to, but he's working. He'll be here next week, for sure. It's his weekend with the kids." *He wanted to?* If that was true, it was news to me. I wondered if Mama made that up.

Carter's dad leaned down, closer to Mama. "And what about you?" he almost whispered. "Will *you* be here?"

"Mike!" Carter's mom said loudly. "Can you please get me another blanket from the car? It's colder than I thought out here."

Carter's dad straightened, put both feet back on the ground, and winked at Mama before he looked up at his wife. "Sure thing," he said flatly. He let his fingers brush against Mama's arm as he walked past her, and I saw Mama shrink back.

"He's *gross*," I whispered to Mama, and she turned her head, her lips pursed.

"You hush, now. That's impolite."

"So was he!" I said, maybe a little too loudly.

Mama drew her eyebrows together over the bridge of her nose. "Ava. Watch your mouth. You're too young to be talking like that about a grown-up." She straightened in her seat and then cupped her hands around her mouth. "Go on now, Max!" she hollered as the team ran onto the field. "Push 'em back, push 'em back, waaay

31

back!" She jumped up, shimmied her bent arms, and wiggled her tiny behind.

"Mama," I said, cringing a bit as the other women behind us stopped talking and stared. Acting like that would just make the other mothers make fun of her—didn't she *know* that?

"I think that's a *football* cheer, Kelli," Carter's mom said, and then I saw her roll her eyes. I gritted my teeth, wishing I had something to throw at her. Something sharp and hard that would hurt.

Mama laughed and gave a little shrug. "Oh well," she said, sitting back down. "I never could keep my sports straight. I guess it's a good thing Max is playing and not me."

"Oh yes," another woman said. "What a relief." She had brown hair and a tightly pinched mouth. "Did you remember to bring snacks?"

Mama turned to look at her and nodded. "Chocolate peanut butter cupcakes, fresh out of the oven this morning." She grinned, awaiting approval. I held my breath.

The brown-haired woman frowned. *"Peanut butter?* We can't serve that. Taylor is allergic." She paused. "And Carter is gluten intolerant. Wheat flour is like poison for him. Didn't you review the approved snack list we handed out at the beginning of the season?"

Mama's smile melted away. "Oh," she began, her voice faltering. "No. I didn't realize—"

Carter's mom sighed and stood up. "I can run to the co-op and grab some rice crackers and fruit," she said.

Mama stood, as well. "Please," she said, "let me. It was my mistake."

"It's fine," the woman said as she grabbed her purse. "I'll just go catch *my husband* at the car. We'll go together."

Mama sank back down onto the bleacher, her shoulders slumped. "I'm so sorry," she said to the other women. "I can bring a better snack the next time."

No one responded, and Mama turned away and faced the field. Her eyes were shiny and she held her chin high. I slipped my hand into hers and squeezed it. "I *love* your cupcakes," I said. "They're the best ones."

This morning we were running late again. Except this time it was my fault—I'd spent too much time in the shower, conditioning my hair and carefully shaving my legs. Mama said the hair wasn't thick enough for me to *need* to shave yet, but all the other girls in eighth grade did it, so I begged her to let me do it, too. "They call me *Chewbacca* during gym!" I told her, and she'd relented.

"Ava, hurry up, please!" Mama called out from the kitchen.

"Be right there!" I said, glancing in the full-length mirror on my closet door one last time, making sure that the outfit I'd picked out looked okay. I liked my long, purple shirt and I knew I was luckier than a lot of girls in my class; I could wear skinny jeans and still cross my legs beneath my desk. My dark brown hair was held back from my face with a thin elastic headband, and thanks to the expensive salon conditioner I'd saved up my allowance to buy, it looked shiny and smooth. Still, I found myself wishing for the millionth time that my mom would let me wear makeup. The few times I'd tried to sneak it, using my friend Bree's mascara and lipstick in the bathroom at school, Mama had caught me, even though I thought I'd washed it all off. "You're a natural beauty, love," she said, cupping my face in her hands. "Let's save the makeup for when you actually need it."

I didn't know why she got to be the one who decided when I needed it. It was *my* face. Plus, almost all the other eighth-grade girls at Seattle Academy wore makeup; I was fairly certain that meant I should get to, too. But I'd had enough arguments with her about it to understand this wasn't a fight I was going to win.

Sighing, I grabbed her black boots, the ones she said I could borrow, pulled them on over my jeans, then lugged my heavy backpack down the hall. Mama stood by the kitchen counter, still in her pajamas, which consisted of gray yoga pants and a red T-shirt that looked tiny enough that it might have actually been my brother's. From the back, she looked like a little girl. Her blond hair was pulled into a messy ponytail and she gripped a coffee mug with both hands, sipping from it as she stared out the window into the backyard. It was still dark, but at least it wasn't raining. "I'm ready," I announced.

She turned to look at me with a tired smile, and I noticed that her lips were the same pale hue as her skin, and the spaces beneath her eyes were tinged blue. For the fourth time that week, I'd woken up to the sound of the television in her bedroom in the middle of the night. She still wasn't sleeping. "Hey there, sugar," she said. "You're as pretty as dew on a rose."

I rolled my eyes a little and shook my head but smiled back at her anyway, accustomed to her flowery comparisons. She was prone to silly compliments about my looks. I didn't really feel pretty; I was okay, I guessed, but nothing like my mom, who my friend Peter told me all the boys in my class thought was a MILF because she was blond and thin and had big boobs. I'd nodded, even though I hadn't known what the term meant at that time, so it wasn't until I got home and looked it up online that I wanted to barf. I knew my mom was better looking than some of my friends' mothers, but the thought of the boys wanting to have sex with her made me cringe.

"Do you want breakfast?" Mama asked. "I

made some toast. I could throw peanut butter on it so you'd get some protein."

I shook my head. She knew I didn't like to eat first thing in the morning, but that didn't stop her from trying to feed me. "I can have a granola bar after homeroom." I patted my backpack to let her know I was all set. "Are you working today?" Her job was at a fancy restaurant downtown, the place my dad used to manage before he started his own restaurant. They had met there, and she had to go back to work after he moved out three years ago. She said she liked her job because it was flexible enough that she could drive us to school in the morning and pick us up. She only worked night shifts the weekends we were with our dad.

She shook her head. "Nope. But I took a double shift tomorrow, since you two won't be here. I'm working Sunday brunch, too." She gave me an empty, halfhearted smile then, like she always did when she knew Max and I would be gone for the weekend.

"I'll have her toast!" Max said, piping up from the table, where he was slurping down the last of the milk from his cereal bowl.

"Do you ever stop eating?" I asked, wrinkling my nose at him. "It's gross."

"*You're* gross," Max retorted, lifting his pointy chin back at me.

"Oooh, burn," I said, rolling my eyes again. He was such a little dweeb. I looked at the clock and then my mom. "Can we go? I don't want to be late for homeroom."

"Yes, we should." She shuffled over to me in her slippers and threw her slender arms around my neck. When I was wearing her boots, we were almost the same height. "I love you, baby girl," she whispered. "So much."

"Love you too," I said, hugging her back. She felt fragile in my embrace, her bones like brittle twigs that might snap if I held her too tightly. She was getting so skinny; I could circle her entire wrist with my index finger and thumb and still not touch her skin. She said she ate at the restaurant after her shifts, but her clothes had started looking looser the past few months, so I wasn't sure she was telling me the truth. She'd done the same thing after my dad moved out—no sleep and no food—but Diane made her go to the doctor for some kind of pills and she started getting better after that. I wasn't sure if she was taking those pills anymore.

I wondered if missing her parents had anything to do with how she was feeling now. She had called them last night, but they didn't answer the phone. They lived in a small town outside of San Luis Obispo in California, where Mama grew up, and they'd never even once come to see us, which I honestly thought was kind of strange, considering they were Mama's only family and Max and I were their grandchildren. I guess they didn't even think they could *have* a baby, but Mama was born when her mother was forty-two and Mama said they thanked God and called her their "miracle." And even though they never visited, she still called their house a couple of times a year. When they actually answered the phone, the conversations were always short and her voice got tight and shaky as she spoke with them. Afterward, she'd usually go to her bed-room and cry. I tried not to worry about Mama too much, but she sure didn't make it easy.

I looked over to Max, who was making fun of my hugging our mom with a goofy kissy face and pretending to hug himself. "Max," I said sternly, "go brush your teeth. We'll be in the car."

"You're not the boss of me," Max said as he dropped his bowl into the sink with a clatter. My mother startled at the noise, sucking in a sharp breath, and pulled away from me.

"Max!" she said loudly, then took another, slower breath. She put one hand against the wall, like she suddenly had to hold herself up, then spoke again in a quieter tone. "Brush your teeth, little man, right this instant. Don't make me get the switch." She winked at him then, and he giggled, knowing full well our mother would never hit us. It was a joke she used, to let us know she meant business. Our dad used to say it to us, too, as a joke, but after he moved out, he stopped.

Max raced down the hallway to the bathroom and my mother stared off after him.

"Are you okay, Mama?" I asked, noticing she was breathing a little faster than usual. She kept her hand on the wall, her shoulders curled forward.

"I'm fine. Just a little dizzy, for some reason." She turned her head and gave me a tiny smile, dropping her hand to her side and straightening her spine. "Probably too much caffeine."

I nodded, then looked at the stack of paper on the entryway table—bills, I guessed. Ones she hadn't paid yet. "Want me to help you write the checks tonight?" I asked as we headed out the door and toward the driveway.

"Hmm?" she murmured. "What was that?"

I felt a twinge of irritation. "The bills." I knew my friends didn't help their parents with this kind of thing, but it was something we did together. Mama said it was only because I had better handwriting than hers, but the last time I'd watched her try to do it alone, she started crying, so I offered to fill the checks out and she could just sign them. Max got to put the stamps on the envelopes. We sort of turned it into a game. But when I told my dad about it, the muscles around his lips got all twitchy, and I asked him if it was bad that we helped her.

"She's a grown-up, honey," he said, putting his long arm around my shoulders and squeezing me to him. "You're a kid. You shouldn't have that kind of responsibility."

I shrugged and threw both of my arms around his waist, breathing in the earthy fragrance of roasted meat off his shirt. Some fathers wore cologne; mine wore scents born in a kitchen. "I don't mind," I said. I didn't like feeling that he was criticizing her; I didn't want to get her in trouble.

"I'll talk with her," he said, but I don't think he ever did. Now that they were divorced, they only talked to each other when they had to, and when they did, it was with short, hard sentences that seemed more like weapons than words.

"When are you bringing them back?" Mama asked him when he picked us up every other Saturday. She never did quite look directly at him, either. Her eyes drifted just over his right shoulder.

"Five o'clock tomorrow," my dad told her, sometimes even shifting his feet a little, like he couldn't wait for her to stop moving her mouth. "Like always." He stood in the entryway, not coming all the way into the house while we got ready to go with him.

"Just making sure," my mom would say, her voice quavering a little, and the muscles in my dad's face would tighten even more. It was hard to imagine they ever loved each other enough to get married. I knew they had; I'd seen their wedding picture. Mama dressed in a white princess ball gown, her glossy hair piled on top of her head in messy coils. Daddy tall and handsome in a black tuxedo, feeding her cake and trying to kiss her at the same time. They were laughing.

Now, standing next to our car, as Max finally sped down the front steps and toward us, making a sound like a jet airplane, my mom reached over and clutched my hand. "What would I do without you, baby girl?" She pulled my hand up to her mouth and kissed it.

I smiled at her, my insides shaking, not wanting to say that I sometimes wondered what she might do without me, too.

"Do you have to go to your dad's this weekend?" Bree asked me during second lunch. At Seattle Academy, first lunch was for the kids up through fifth grade; second was for sixth through eighth. Bree and I sat together at a small table by the window, away from the other eighth-grade girls. We each had a big slice of pepperoni pizza and a chocolate milk. That was the best thing about going to a private school—the hot lunches were actually decent. The worst thing was that my brother went there, too. Occasionally, he'd see me in the hallway or when he had recess and he'd wave, do a little dance, and start singing, "Ava-Ava-bo-bava, banana-fanna-fo-fava . . . *Ava!*" I seriously couldn't wait for next year, when high

41

school would start and I wouldn't see that little weirdo until we got home. I loved him and all, but man, could he annoy the crap out of me.

I pulled a piece of pepperoni off the slice and popped it in my mouth. "Yep," I told Bree as I chewed. "Our dad picks us up tomorrow morning."

"With *Grace?*" she said, crossing her eyes and making her lids flutter at the same time. Bree was the funniest girl I knew and wasn't afraid of other people laughing at the things she did, which was part of why she was my friend. She had short, wispy blond hair and wire-rimmed glasses, and she didn't need to wear a bra yet, but she didn't seem to care about being like the popular girls. The girls with really rich parents and their own iPads. The girls who went behind the gym, let their boyfriends feel them up, and didn't care who knew. The girls that part of me wanted to become.

I laughed. "Yes. I keep hoping they'll split up. But it looks like she's staying." Bree's parents were divorced, too, another reason I liked to hang out with her. She got how weird it was to have two houses to live in, two sets of rules, and parents that might have loved us but couldn't stand each other. Her dad was a corporate lawyer, so he had to pay her mom a ton of child support for Bree. My dad gave my mom a check every month, too, but he definitely didn't make as much money as a lawyer. He was a great cook, though, which I thought was kind of a bonus.

Bree didn't say anything more, knowing that my dad's girlfriend was far from my favorite subject. He had met Grace at the end of last summer and waited a couple of months to introduce us, which I guess is better than if he'd made us meet her right away. I knew he'd probably dated other women after he moved out—one time, not very long after he bought his new place, I found a pair of lacy pink women's underwear in his hamper when I was helping him with the laundry. But Grace was the only one he wanted Max and me to get to know, so the fact that she had moved in with him last May didn't really surprise me that much. Mostly, I just tried not to think about the fact that she slept in the same bed as him, which was hard with how many questions my mom asked when we came home from their house.

"Did you have fun with Grace?" she'd ask. "What did she feed you?" When I'd tell her that after Dad cooked, or Grace ordered pizza, we all played Scrabble or watched a movie, her shoulders would fall and her face would look like I'd hit her. I wondered why she didn't get her own boyfriend. She was pretty enough, for sure, and I knew there were a few single dads at our school who would probably ask her out if she did her hair and wore something other than her pajamas to drop us off in the morning. But when I suggested that maybe she could go on a date, too, she waved the thought away. "You and your brother are all the love I need. Your daddy just doesn't like to be alone." *Neither do you,* I'd think. *You just want to be with us instead of a date.* I wondered if something was wrong with her, somehow, since after all these years she still didn't seem to be over my dad's leaving. Which was strange, really, because I knew that she was the one who finally asked him to go. I'd overheard the fight that made him walk out the door.

"Yo, earth to Ava!" Bree said, nudging me with the toe of her Converse. "Come in, Ava! The bell just rang. Time for social studies." She made a face and stuck a finger in her mouth. "Like, gag me with an encyclopedia."

I laughed again, and we cleaned up our mess and headed off to class. On the way, Whitney Blake, whose father owned a chain of organic grocery stores, sidled up next to me. She smelled of citrus and her black hair hung sleek and almost to the middle of her back. Whitney was all sweetness and light to our teachers, but she'd been known to make more than a few other girls in our class cry. I tried not to cross her path unless I absolutely had to.

"How was your lunch, Ava?" she asked, popping her pink gum as she spoke. Whitney liked everyone to know that their family's housekeeper packed organic chicken slices, mixed greens, and some kind of cookie made with agave nectar for her lunch every day, only so

Whitney could toss it all and buy whatever the cafeteria was serving with the credit card her dad gave her to use.

I shrugged one shoulder in response and kept walking, glancing at her out of the corner of my eye, wary of such a seemingly innocent question.

"Did you use your *scholarship* to pay for it?" she continued in a lilting tone as we walked along, pushing against the small throng of other students in the hallway. "You know, my dad gives a lot of our money to those. So, like, my family's sort of making it possible for you to be here."

My stomach clenched as she spoke, my cheeks flushed, and tears pricked the back of my throat. I couldn't look at her. It wasn't a secret that Max and I were scholarship students and that my mom sometimes served meals to the rich parents of the kids in our classes when they went to the restau-rant where she worked. Max was too little to under-stand what people sometimes said about us, but I wasn't. I also understood that having a lot of money didn't just give you nice things, it gave you power. Whitney understood this, too.

"Maybe you should say thank you," Whitney said when I didn't respond.

I couldn't speak. If I did, I might have cried, and that would just have given her another thing to mock.

"Hey, Whitney," Bree said, stepping in to save me. "Maybe you should go make yourself useful and throw up your lunch. If you hurry, maybe your ass won't need its own zip code."

Hearing this, Whitney's normally pretty, unblemished face briefly twisted into an ugly sneer, but she kept her eyes on me. "You should think about trying out for the dance team," she said. "Maybe Mrs. McClain will feel sorry for you as an *underprivileged* student and let you join."

Her gaggle of friends tittered at this, my eyes blurred, and Bree grabbed me by the arm. "C'mon. Let's get to class."

Leaving Whitney and her friends behind us, I let Bree lead me past the few remaining lockers before Mr. Tanner's room, swallowing hard to make sure any remnants of my tears were gone. "Thanks," I said as we slid into our seats next to each other.

Bree smiled, then pushed her glasses back up to the bridge of her nose. "She's a total bitch, so don't listen to her, all right?"

I nodded but still felt the sting of Whitney's words itching beneath my skin. It wasn't like we were poor; my parents paid for some of our tuition, just not all of it. The one thing my mom and dad still agreed on was Max and me getting the best education we could, and Seattle Academy was the best.

"You're not *going* to try out for dance team, are you?" Bree asked.

I shook my head and gave her a closed-lipped smile. My mom loved to dance—she'd been a cheerleader in high school, and it would have made her happy if I did try out, but I knew that getting on the team would mean I'd be away from the house more and Max would have to deal with Mama on his own. He was too young to handle one of her crying sessions when I wasn't there. Even if I'd wanted to join, it just wasn't an option.

I took a couple of deep breaths, the tension in my body relaxing just enough to let me pay attention when Mr. Tanner told us to settle down and began his lecture on women's suffrage. He had only been talking for about twenty minutes when the black phone on his desk rang. He nodded as he listened, thanked whoever had called, and hung up. Only the front office used that phone, so I wondered who had done something bad enough to interrupt class.

"Ava?" Mr. Tanner said, and my belly immediately flip-flopped. "You need to get your things from your locker and head to the office, okay?"

I sighed. "Is it Max?" *That little monster. Mama's going to be pissed if he got in trouble.*

Mr. Tanner pressed his lips together and gave his head a quick shake. Bree shot me a questioning look, and I shrugged slightly, then closed up my folder. Every eye in the room was on me, and I felt my face getting warm again. A few whispers started, but Mr. Tanner shushed them. I slowly put on my jacket and took careful, deliberate steps toward the front of the room. I stopped in front of Mr. Tanner's desk, searching his face for some kind of clue, but there was nothing there. "Is everything all right?" I asked him, and he held my gaze for a moment before dropping it to the floor.

"You just need to go to the office," he repeated, so I walked out the door and made my way alone down the long, quiet hall.

Kelli

It was Monday afternoon, and before Kelli left the house to pick the kids up from school, Victor called and asked her to stop by the Loft. "I need to talk with you about something," he said. "It won't take long. Ten, maybe fifteen minutes, tops."

She knew she wasn't going to like whatever it was he had to tell her. They'd been divorced for several years, but she still recognized the edge in his voice. The first time she'd heard him use it she was nineteen and working as a waitress in the restaurant he managed, eavesdropping as he fired the busboy who'd been caught taking one of Kelli's substantial tips off a table.

"Thanks," she said to Victor later, after he'd escorted the terminated employee out the front door. "I feel kind of bad for him." She under-stood what it was to need money; she shared a tiny two-bedroom apartment with four other girls and was still having a hard time making rent. But she wouldn't steal. She already had enough to feel guilty about—adding theft to the list might have sent her over the edge.

"Don't," Victor said, briefly putting his hand on her shoulder. Kelli's skin tingled and her stomach wiggled. His gray eyes lit up as he grinned at her and she smiled in response. He'd taken a chance on hiring her, considering she didn't have any fine-dining restaurant experience. She didn't know anything about pairing wines with food or what it meant to "eighty-six" an item from the menu when it ran out. Much to the entire kitchen staff's amusement, the first time she'd told the other servers that they were out of salmon for the rest of the night she'd accidentally announced that the fish had been "sixty-nined."

But when Victor interviewed her, she'd batted her eyelashes and pushed out her chest, methods she'd learned were effective in almost every situation for getting what she wanted from men, and it had worked. She could tell Victor was attracted to her, so she played that to her advantage, campaigning for the coveted high-volume weekend shifts and then the best tables in the restaurant— the ones by the window with a view of the city. At first, she flirted with him only to be granted those perks, but after a couple of weeks, she realized she was attracted to him, too. He was twenty-five, good-looking, and kind. He joked around with the employees—he almost made working fun—but he also didn't let them slack off. He'd worked on the line in the kitchen before being promoted to manager just a few months before she moved to Seattle, and she soon learned that he held aspirations of opening his own restaurant.

"I think I might need someone to help me get it started," he told her one night after the restaurant had closed. Everyone else had gone home and they sat together at a small table, a candle flickering between them. She was counting her tips right along with the number of times he smiled at her. "Can you think of anyone who might be interested?"

"Maybe," she said with a slow, suggestive curve of her mouth. She knew how to play this game. She knew how to draw him in and then how to pull back just enough to make him want her a little more. It was a subtle dance, one that came as easily to her as breath. She didn't enjoy using this technique to get what she needed—it made her feel whorish, as her parents had once accused her of being. But with Victor, it was different. She *wanted* him to want her. She liked his sense of humor and how hard he worked at his job. She liked that when he talked to her, he looked her straight in the eyes instead of at her chest. She had a chance to re-create herself here—to leave what had happened in California behind. She could morph into whatever Victor needed her to be, as long as she could find a way to make him love her.

He held her gaze then, the glow from the candle making his gray eyes sparkle. "Do you need a ride home?" he asked, and Kelli dropped her chin down a notch, looking up at him from beneath her long lashes before telling him yes. She knew what this meant. She knew he wanted to sleep with her, and despite her resolve not to get involved with a man for a long, long time, she felt the familiar pull of attraction in her pelvis, and she let him take her hand and lead her to his car.

"I have roommates," she said quietly after he had started the engine. "Should we go to your place instead?"

He turned to look at her. "What for?"

Oh god. Kelli blushed and dropped her eyes to her lap. "Nothing. No reason. Sorry." She couldn't believe she'd been so stupid, thinking he'd be interested in someone like her. She hadn't even graduated from high school. She couldn't. Not after what happened. She'd missed the last half of her freshman year, and when she finally came home the next fall, she was a mess—unable to get out of bed, reluctant to shower or eat more than the bare minimum to avoid starvation. Her parents eventually agreed to let her get her GED through the local community college instead of returning to the school where everyone knew her, but she couldn't help feeling that this wasn't the same as having an actual diploma.

Victor reached over and put his hand on top of hers. "Hey. Don't be sorry. I like you. But I'm your boss, you know? There are rules I need to follow. I have to be careful."

Relieved, Kelli met his gaze and gave him another smile. "I can be careful."

"I'm sure you can," Victor said with a short laugh. "How about I take you on a real date this week? If we feel like it might go somewhere, I can tell the HR rep for the restaurant and just see how things go."

Kelli nodded, pressing her lips together. The fact that he wasn't going to try to sleep with her right away made her like him even more. He was responsible. So mature. He made her feel safe. As they got to know each other over the next couple of months, she began to believe she'd finally found someone who might accept her for exactly who she was. Someone who'd take care of her.

Even now, in some ways, even though they were divorced, he still did. He let her stay in the house his mother had left him so Kelli wouldn't have a house payment and the kids wouldn't have to move. He made sure she got her job back at the restaurant where they'd first met. He paid his child support on time and she never had to worry about the kids' tuition, either. He took care of the scholarship applications. She'd been the one who told him to leave, but she hadn't really believed that he would. By the time she realized her mistake, it was too late. She couldn't find a way to get him to come back. She tried to seduce him, once, after he'd moved out. She'd left Max and Ava with Diane and gone to his new house wearing only a black bra and panties beneath her trench coat, like one of the daring characters she read about in her favorite romance novels.

"Kelli," he'd said, clearly surprised to see her when he opened the front door. "Are the kids okay? Why didn't you call me?"

"The kids are fine," she said. "They're with Diane."

His expression went flat. "Then what's going on? Why are you here?"

She put her hands against his chest and gave him a playful push. "To see you, silly," she said. "I thought we could talk."

Victor sighed. "We don't *need* to talk."

"Are you sure?" Kelli said, quickly untying her coat and flashing him right there on the front porch. She held her breath, waiting for him to take her in his arms, for everything that had gone wrong to be righted.

But he only stared at her, the pity in his eyes too much for her to bear. "Kelli," he began, but she stopped him by closing her coat and shaking her head.

"No, it's fine. I get it." Something went hard inside her then, and shattered. "You've turned into him, you know. Leaving your family like this."

Victor tilted his head toward his shoulder. "Into who?"

"Your father." She spun around and raced down the front steps before he could respond, knowing that she had just delivered what had to be the fatal blow to their marriage. After her saying that to him, there was no way he'd ever return to them. She drove home crying, mortified that she'd believed sex would so easily win him back. What an idiot she was. And in the end, she lost him, just like she'd lost so many other things.

All she had left were her children, whom she adored above everything else. She felt as though they were the only evidence that she was a successful person—they were both smart, were kind, and carried an innate sense of self-worth Kelli had never possessed. She hoped that how she'd mothered them had something to do with this. She wasn't perfect as a parent by any means, but she knew she treated them better than her parents had treated her. No matter what they did, they knew how much she loved them.

She pulled into the parking lot of the Loft, checked her makeup in the rearview mirror, and practiced her smile. Not too big—she didn't want to look desperate. But she wanted Victor to see the girl he fell in love with, the girl he took for long walks around Green Lake, the girl whom, when the single blue line doubled in the restaurant bathroom, he'd gotten down on one knee in front of and asked to marry him. She was only twenty —too young to get married, too young to become a mother—but she felt as though in meeting Victor, the universe was giving her a second chance. The chance to live the right kind of life, be the right kind of person. Victor's own father had left him with his mother when Victor was only five years old; Kelli knew that having a family, being a good father, was the most important thing to him. He would be the father he'd never had. She'd been convinced he would never leave her. But she was naïve to have thought that creating a new life would erase the sins from her past. She was stupid to believe she could outrun the pain.

She wondered what it was Victor wanted to talk with her about today and if he would be distracted by the purple smudges beneath her eyes. The pills she took to sleep worked only sporadically—she found herself needing to take more and more. They hadn't worked at all last night. She'd paced the house like a wildcat, mewling silently as she ruminated on the gaping holes in her life. Mostly, the empty place where a happy marriage should have been. The place where Victor used to stand.

A sharp rap on her window yanked her out of her thoughts and sent her pulse racing. She whipped her head around and saw Spencer, Victor's best friend and head chef, standing next to the car with a gentle smile on his face. She grabbed her purse and opened the car door to greet him.

"Sorry," he said. "Didn't mean to scare you. Just wanted to say hello. It's been a while." He placed a beefy hand on her back and gave it an awkward pat. Kelli found it sad how friends seemed to get divvied up after a divorce, like a couple's book or CD collection. When they were married, she and Victor weren't terribly social—he was always too busy working for them to spend much time with other couples—but when they separated, she realized just how many of her personal connections were through his restaurant. She had Diane, who'd befriended her after Ava was born, and a few acquaintances at her own job, but it was Victor who kept custody of everyone else, including Spencer.

"That's okay," she said. "Great to see you."

"You too." He paused. "You look beautiful, as usual."

"Thanks," she said automatically, though then she pressed her lips together and gave her head a quick shake. She knew he was being kind. She knew she'd lost too much weight to look healthy. Her hair was thinning and even though she was only thirty-three, new lines seemed to carve themselves into her face every day. Diane joked that this was the precise reason she refused to lose the extra twenty pounds she carried. "A little fat plumps out the skin," she said. "Ben and Jerry's instead of Botox."

Kelli glanced at the back entrance of the Loft, then smiled at Spencer. "Can I follow you in, or should I use the front door?"

"Follow me," he said, and they entered the restaurant together. As they walked down the narrow hallway that led into the kitchen, Kelli inhaled the rich aroma of sautéed onions and simmering broth. Victor had taught her to identify the subtle scents in a dish, the underlying earthy breath of mushrooms, the bright tang of citrus. He'd taught her that the ramen noodles she'd always thought were pretty good for pasta were actually just fried and dehydrated dough. He'd taught her the difference between searing a steak and scorching it; he'd shown her the proper method to dress a salad. She remembered the hours they spent in the kitchen before Ava was born, Victor showing her how to bake melt-in-your-mouth biscuits or concoct an aromatic stew. The first time she made a meatloaf for him and misread half a *teaspoon* of salt as half a *cup,* he'd eaten an entire piece anyway, washing each bite down with a huge swallow of water, just to keep her from crying.

"Victor's out front," Spencer said as they walked past the two eight-burner stoves. "I'll go grab him."

"It hasn't been *that* long," Kelli said as brightly as she could manage. "I remember the way." She smiled and patted Spencer on his thick forearm. Almost eight years ago, right before Max was born, she'd helped Victor design the restaurant's layout. She picked out the silverware and wine-glasses, the thick, cream-hued tablecloths to set off the black linen napkins. She felt a pang in her stomach—she wasn't sure if it was hunger or regret—then pushed through the double doors that led to the dining room.

It was quarter to three, smack-dab between the lunch and dinner hours, so there were only a few customers. Kelli moved her gaze over the small bar area and spotted Victor in the corner, where she knew he liked to work. Her breath seized as she took in his handsome face—his dark hair and light silvery eyes. She didn't understand how she had let him get away. And now, there was Grace. Grace with her important job and nice car. Grace who woke up in Victor's bed and touched him in the places he'd promised Kelli would be forever hers.

Victor looked up from his laptop and caught her staring at him. He lifted his hand and beckoned her over, so she took a deep breath, threw her shoulders back, and proceeded to where he sat. "Hi," he said, and there it was. The edge. Sharp enough to wound her.

Kelli sank into the chair across from him and swallowed, trying to moisten her mouth before speaking. "Hi."

Victor raked his fingers through his hair, a gesture Kelli recognized as one he only made when he was anxious about something. "Can I get you something? Coffee or iced tea?"

"My usual would be great," she said, testing him.

He smiled and gestured for the bartender, a short, balding man Kelli didn't recognize. "Can we get a cranberry with Sprite and a hefty squeeze of lime, Jimmy?" Victor asked. "Light on the ice, please." Jimmy nodded, and Kelli relaxed a bit seeing Victor so quickly rattle off her favorite mocktail—one he made for her time and again during both of her pregnancies. He hadn't completely erased her from his mind.

"So . . ." Victor said, turning back to look at her. "How's work going?"

Kelli shrugged. "Fine, I guess. Same old same old. You know." She hated trying to make small talk with him, but this was the level to which their relationship had been reduced. She glanced at her watch. "I have to get the kids at three thirty," she said. "Max has basketball practice at four."

At that moment, Jimmy approached the table and set her drink down in front of her, so Victor waited to respond. "Thanks," she said to the bartender, who gave her a closed-lipped smile and quickly walked away. The sign of a good server, Kelli thought. He picked up on the slight tension at the table and didn't try to engage. That was something Victor had taught her—something he trained all his employees to do. Read the customer and act accordingly. Kelli took a sip from the red straw, then gripped the icy glass with both hands. "What did you need to talk with me about?" she asked.

Victor closed his laptop, pushed it off to the side, and let loose a subtle, but noticeable, sigh. "I have some news," he said. "Good news, really. And we thought you should be the first to know."

We? Kelli thought, momentarily confused, at first thinking he was referring to the two of them. They were the only "we" she knew. And then it hit her. What he meant. She took a measured breath and saw her knuckles go white as she grasped her glass harder. She couldn't speak. She knew what was coming next.

Victor shifted forward in his chair and spoke in a low voice. "Grace and I are getting married," he said.

A sudden buzzing sounded inside Kelli's head, causing her eyeballs to vibrate. The edges of Victor's face went blurry and she blinked a few times to hold back the tears that threatened to fall. She didn't want to cry in front of him. She didn't want him to see how much she hurt. She bit the inside of her cheek and began to nod like an idiot.

"I know this can't be easy to hear," she heard him say as the buzzing began to fade. "I'm sorry, but we thought you should definitely know before we tell the kids this weekend." He paused, searching her face with those kind gray eyes. "Kelli? Aren't you going to say anything?"

She picked up her drink and took a long pull on the straw, just to buy herself some time. She couldn't imagine what he wanted her to say. "Congratulations"? "So happy you've moved on"? Her bottom lip quivered and she bit it, too. Victor saw this and reached out to touch her hand. She jerked away, splashing some of her drink onto the table. "I'm fine," she snapped.

Victor held his hands up, palms facing her, and he leaned back in his chair. "Okay," he said, irritation weaving itself across the lines of his face. She knew that expression well. "Sorry."

She took a couple of shallow breaths. She felt dizzy. Had she eaten that day? She couldn't remember. She straightened her spine and steeled herself as best she could. She didn't want to be the pitiful ex-wife, pining for the spouse who left her. But there she was. She glanced at the double doors leading to the kitchen and saw Spencer's head in the window. He quickly ducked, but she knew he'd been watching them, gauging her reaction. She briefly thought about getting Spencer to sleep with her, just to piss Victor off, but she knew his friend was too loyal to ever do some-thing as horrible as that.

She forced her eyes back to Victor, who was staring at her. "Thank you for telling me," she said in as calm a voice as she could manage. She clasped her hands together in her lap, digging her fingernails into her skin, trying to direct the pain that threatened to overwhelm her somewhere other than her chest. Her lungs felt like they might explode. "Have you set a date?"

Victor shook his head. "It just happened last night. We'll do that after we talk to the kids this weekend."

"Ava's not going to be happy," Kelli said. Her voice was strung tight. "You should be prepared for that."

"How do you figure?" Victor asked, scrunching his eyebrows together.

Kelli gave a small lift to her right shoulder. "She'll think you're trying to replace me." The words slipped out before she could stop them. Passive-aggressive, she knew. He'd nail her for it. Victor wasn't stupid. He'd know Kelli was projecting her feelings onto their daughter so she wouldn't have to claim them herself. It wasn't the first time. It started when he opened the restaurant and was gone so much, leaving her alone with the kids. "Max and Ava miss you," she'd say. "They're starting to forget what their daddy looks like."

"I'm not trying to replace you," Victor said gently now. There he was. The Victor she loved. He dropped his chin and peered at her. "Kelli. Are you okay with this?"

"Of course," she said, a little too quickly. "It's

great. So happy for you both. Are you going to have a baby with her?" Kelli panicked at the thought. It was the one thing she knew she had that Grace didn't—she was the mother of Victor's children. If Grace had a baby, that would be gone, too. She didn't know if she could handle losing one more thing.

Victor sighed. "No." He sat forward again, placing his elbows on the table and loosely linking his fingers. "Please don't tell the kids yet, okay? We'd like to do that."

Kelli nodded and glanced out the window. A young couple strolled by, hands in each other's back pockets, the girl resting her head on the boy's shoulder. Kelli gave a small smile. "Remember that?" she asked Victor. "How we used to be?"

Victor looked in the same direction, taking the couple in. Kelli knew if he remembered her drink, he'd remember that, too. But he stayed silent. They were over; it was done. And there was nothing left to say.

Grace

The night of our first date after meeting at the Loft, Victor drove all the way to my condo on Lake Washington to pick me up, only to turn around and take us back to a Thai place he loved in his own West Seattle neighborhood.

"I have to warn you," he said as we crossed over the high rise of the West Seattle Bridge. "The restaurant is called All Thai'd Up, but I don't want you to think that I'm dropping hints I'm into bondage or anything creepy like that. They just have really excellent curry." I laughed and reassured him I wouldn't make suppositions about his sexual preferences based on his restaurant of choice.

We entered the tiny establishment a few minutes later. The lights were low, the air hinted at luscious notes of garlic and lemongrass, and the walls were curtained in plush red tapestries. The hostess led us to a small table in the corner, where I confirmed by candlelight that Victor was just as handsome as I initially surmised—tonight he wore charcoal slacks and a dark blue sweater that definitely set off his warmer skin tone and gray eyes.

We spent the first part of dinner going over our backgrounds, and I learned that Victor was an only child. "Are your parents still together?" I asked, and he shook his head.

"My father took off when I was five," he said. "And didn't come back. Not cut out to be a dad, I guess."

I nodded, realizing this was something else Victor and I had in common. Only my mother had asked my dad to leave, and not until I'd already moved out myself. "And your mom?"

A shadow of grief flashed across his face. "She had a stroke just after Ava was born. She was only fifty-three."

"I'm so sorry," I said, reaching out to briefly touch the back of his hand.

"Thanks," he said. "I still pick up the phone to call her, you know? When something important happens?" He paused. "I'm always a little shocked when I remember she's gone." He shook his head. "Weird, huh?"

"Not at all," I said, and he smiled.

"Wow," he said, puffing out a breath. "Light topic we've chosen, here. Maybe we should start over?" I chuckled, nodded, and he continued. "So, tell me. How is it that a woman as accomplished and beautiful as you hasn't been snapped up yet?"

I laughed. "Well, I've stayed pretty focused on my career, and I'm getting old and stuck in my ways." I shrugged. "I don't want to settle for anything less than wonderful."

It was his turn to nod. "I can relate to that."

"My best friend and I joke that we just need to find our perfect hat trick," I told him, only to be answered with a confused look, so I clarified. "The exact right balance of physical, emotional, and mental connection with someone."

"Okay." Victor cocked his head to one side and scrunched his eyebrows together, clearly still baffled. "Why is that called a 'hat trick,' exactly?"

I set my wineglass down and waved my hand in

the air a little. "In hockey or whatever, when the same player shoots three points in a game, they call it a hat trick. So if we hit it off with a man on all three levels—mental, physical, emotional—one after the other, *he's* a hat trick."

"Ah," he said, understanding finally blossoming on his face. "You lost me with the sports analogy. I might have to give up my man card for admitting this, but I really couldn't care less about that stuff." His brow furrowed, and he continued hurriedly. "Not about being a 'hat trick.' That's an intriguing concept. But sports. They're not my thing."

"Mine either. I only know the term because of my brother. He played basketball in high school. I was more the studious type." I didn't explain how there was no way I could have been anything but studious. My mother's need for me to help take care of my brother precluded any interest I might have had in sports—or anything else that might have taken me away from the house.

Victor sat back in his seat and gave me a long, slow smile that made me wonder what else he could do with his mouth. "So, tell me, Grace. How do you figure out if someone is your hat trick?"

"Well," I said, "it's highly scientific. They have to meet all three criteria. In the past, I'd date a smart guy who was maybe great in bed but as emotionally available as a rock, so I'd know he wasn't the one. Or one who could debate relevant social issues and express his undying affection for me but was a terrible lover."

At this, Victor laughed out loud, and the other diners paused and glanced over at us. "Sorry," he sputtered. "I guess I'm not used to a woman being so honest about how she picks her men apart."

"Oh, wow," I said, wanting to backtrack immediately. "I don't have a checklist or anything like that." I felt flustered, oddly vulnerable. I paused, wondering if my next question was a loaded one for a first date but wanting to ask it anyway. "What about your ex-wife? Was she your hat trick?"

He leaned forward and rested his forearms across the table, grasping the crooks of his elbows with long fingers. "Well, I'm new to the idea, but I'd have to say no. She definitely was not." His tone indicated he wasn't ready to elaborate, and part of me was glad for it. Men who spoke exces-sively about ex-girlfriends or wives on a first date never came across well. Nor, for that matter, did women who chattered on about their exes. I don't think I was testing him, exactly —I was honestly curious to know more about their relationship. But if it *was* a test, he passed.

Later, he walked me to my door and kissed me softly on the lips. The clean but heady musk of his skin dizzied my senses and turned my joints to mush. "Can I see you again?" he whispered, and I nodded eagerly, thrilled by our immediate, easy sense of connection.

After a few weeks, I slept over for the first time at his house. I woke up to the smell of coffee and bacon in the air, my body pleasurably achy from the night before. *Hat trick. No doubt. Mental, emotional, and physical. And he cooks!* When I opened my eyes, he stood over me with a grin on his handsome face. His dark hair was pressed flat on one side, and his gray eyes twinkled, giving him the look of a mischievous little boy who'd just successfully sneaked several cookies from the jar. "Damn," he said. "You're even beautiful when you wake up."

I crossed my eyes at him and stuck out my tongue, and he laughed. "Let me start the shower for you." He paused. "Or do you want coffee, first?"

"Coffee *always* comes first," I said, propping myself up on my elbows and smiling at him.

"Duly noted," he said, pretending to pull a pencil from behind his ear and write on an invisible notepad.

My smile widened at his silliness, and I felt that incredibly rare emotional spark in my belly. The spark that said, *Oh wow . . . this one's a keeper*. I'd dated my fair share of men over the years, but things tended to end after a certain point, and I suspected it might have something to do with my focus on my career rather than getting married and having children. I found that most men who weren't anxious to be fathers weren't anxious for a long-term, committed relationship, either. There might have been exceptions, but I didn't meet many. This left me with a limited eligible pool of partners from which to choose. Victor appeared to genuinely respect my lifestyle, but I didn't know how to trust that he wouldn't end up expecting me to change somehow, too.

"What if he decides he really wants *us* to have a baby?" I asked Melody not long after I'd spent the night with him. She and I were working together at the Second Chances thrift shop, standing in the back room, sorting through boxes of donated clothes.

"He already *told* you he doesn't want any more kids," Melody said. "You're such a scaredy-cat."

"I'm not scared!" I protested as I pulled out a lovely blue Calvin Klein blouse and laid it carefully on the "keep" pile. These were the clothes in good enough condition that women in the program could pick them out and wear them to job interviews. The "sell" pile consisted of more casual outfits and would be steam-cleaned, then priced to sell in the shop.

"Oh please," Melody said. "You're totally scared." I looked at her fondly. She was tall and thin with long, honey-blond hair, brown eyes, and a wide, easy smile. Clad in black leggings and a sage linen tunic, her body moved with a lithe ease as she worked. She also knew me better than anyone—maybe even better than I knew myself. We'd met in our midtwenties when she had just graduated from massage school. In order to make ends meet while she built up a client list, she temped at the same advertising firm where I worked as a recruiter. One afternoon, we ended up sharing a table at a coffee shop near the office and immediately clicked over a mutual fondness for white chocolate mochas and the cute barista behind the counter.

"What do you think?" she had asked me as we sat down together, nodding toward the hunky employee and lifting a single suggestive eyebrow. "Does he look like a *single*- or *double*-shot kind of guy?" A decade and countless mochas later, she was my closest friend.

I sighed as I looked away from her in the back room of the thrift store, reaching to pull another handful of clothes out of the box next to me. "Maybe you're right."

"Of course I'm right," she said with an impish smirk. "You've got this quiet, orderly life, and inviting in an emotionally available man like Victor, who has two possibly noisy children in his, is totally freaking you out." She paused, taking a moment to shake out the floral skirt she was in the process of putting on a hanger. "Come on. What are you really afraid of? Being happy?"

"No," I said. "That's not it."

"Okay. Then what is it?"

"God, you're pushy!" I exclaimed, throwing a sweater at her. It missed, and she grinned. I sighed again. "I don't know. I guess I'm worried I won't be any good at it. Being around the kids, I mean."

"You were good with Sam," she said.

"That's different. He's my brother. And I only had to help take care of him until he was ten and then I moved out. I might do okay with Max, but Ava is thirteen. I have no idea if I could relate to her at *all*."

"Oh, right. Because *you've* never been a thirteen-year-old girl." I gave her an exasperated look, and she adopted a softer tone. "You won't know until you try. What is it you're always telling me? And what do you tell your clients when they tell you how afraid they are to start their lives over again?"

She looked at me expectantly, her brown eyes open wide, and I laughed, shaking my head at her uncanny ability to use my own words against me. "No risk, no reward," I said.

"Exactly. So I think you should quit your bitching and be grateful that you met a man who clearly seems to adore you. Let the details take care of themselves."

It was good, solid advice, but still, in a weird panic, I canceled on Victor for our date that night. "I'm sorry," I said when I called him. I was

71

supposed to meet him in a few hours for dinner at the Loft. "I'm totally swamped with work."

"It's okay," Victor said. "Can I help?"

I laughed, a little nervously. I wasn't sure if he could tell that I was lying. "That's sweet, but probably not. I have to build a spreadsheet of all the corporate donations Second Chances has received so far this year for our accountant. I'm getting carpal tunnel just thinking about it." I *did* have to build the spreadsheet, but it wasn't something I had to have done that night. Victor said he understood and would call me the next day.

After we hung up, I dropped to my couch, my gaze moving over the sandy earth tones I'd picked for my tiny living room. I loved this space when I bought it. With its coved ceilings and the huge square windows that looked directly out to the lake, it somehow managed to feel both cozy and spacious at the same time. I had decorated with small dishes of shells and smooth stones and hung my favorite black and white photograph of waves crashing against the beach over the fireplace. There were two luxurious cream-colored blankets thrown over the back of my couch and plush goose-down pillows thrown in the corners of it, as well. Everything about the room invited silence and calm. It was safe. Melody was right—I assumed Victor's life was chaotic simply because he had children. But I didn't really know this was true. I hadn't even *met* his children. Backing away from him that night wasn't about him—it was about me and my own fears. It wasn't fair to either of us.

I reached for my cell phone and he picked up on the first ring. "If you need help writing a formula, you have called the *wrong* man."

"I lied to you." I blurted the words before I could lose my nerve. "I didn't really have to work tonight. I'm just scared. I'm so sorry."

He was silent for a moment, and I could feel my pulse pounding inside my head as I waited for him to speak. "What are you scared about?" he finally asked.

"That I'll be terrible with your kids. That I'll have to change everything about my life if this amazing thing we seem to have together goes much further." I paused, trying to steady my pulse. "I'm being stupid. I panicked."

"I don't think you're stupid," Victor said gently. "And I don't want you to change. I want you to stay exactly who you are."

"You do?" The muscles that had been taut beneath my skin relaxed the tiniest bit. *I thought men just said things like that in the movies. I hope he's not feeding me a line.*

"I do." I could hear his smile through the phone. "And I'll tell you something else. I really *like* who you are. Most women I've dated since my divorce were way too anxious to give Max and Ava a baby brother or sister, which is definitely not part of my plan." He paused. "And I understand that kids weren't part of yours. But I think we could find a way to balance things." When I didn't respond, he continued. "It's not like you'd be their mother. That's Kelli's job."

"What would my job be?" I asked in a quiet voice. This felt like a pivotal question, and I held my breath waiting for his answer.

"To be yourself, I hope. Maybe a positive role model for Ava, and a friend to Max, when they're with us." He took a breath. "I don't actually know how it would all work, because I've never been in the situation before, but I think as long as we keep talking and stay honest with each other, we could figure it out. Don't you?"

"Yeah," I said. "I think so." I waited a moment before apologizing again. "I'm really, really sorry I lied to you. That's not the kind of person I am. I don't know what came over me."

"Don't worry. I get it. We just won't make it a habit. Deal?"

"Deal." I hesitated again, playing with the fringe on a pillow. "Do you still want to see me tonight?"

"I don't know," he said with a teasing edge. "Will you be naked?"

I laughed, feeling relieved. "Possibly. Are you going to feed me?"

"Absolutely. I'll see you at seven."

We began seeing each other almost every day,

me coming over to his place more often than he came to mine, not because he didn't like my condo but because my schedule was more flexible than his and I could miss rush-hour traffic over the West Seattle Bridge. He cooked me amazing meals, though he confessed that he was much better at managing a restaurant than being a chef.

"Are you kidding?" I said, trying to keep myself from licking the plate clean of a creamy lemon butter sauce he'd prepared and served over grilled chipotle-spiced halibut. "This is the best thing I've ever put in my mouth!"

"The best, huh?" he said with a sly, suggestive smile. "*That's* unfortunate." I laughed, and he continued. "I started working in restaurants as a line cook when I was a teenager, so I know my way around the kitchen. But I like what I do now more."

"You like to be in charge, then," I said, teasing him. "Control issues, maybe?"

"I prefer to think of it as teamwork-challenged," he quipped, and I laughed again. I knew this was untrue—Victor ran a tight ship at the Loft, but the few times I waited at the bar for him to be done with his day, I saw how he interacted with his staff. He expected everyone to work hard, but he was always right there with them, ready to pitch in, covering for servers and dishwashers alike in a moment of need. I'd seen enough horrible bosses over the years to know that Victor was a great one.

He also turned out to be a really wonderful boyfriend. When I landed a huge corporate donation for Second Chances, he sent me the most beautiful arrangement of orchids I'd ever seen with a card that read: "You inspire me to be a better person." He called when he said he would and lingered when it was time for us to part in the mornings. He made me feel important but didn't smother me. He understood that I sometimes had to take midnight trips to the ER to help a client in crisis. He supported me when I struggled watching yet another woman go back to her abuser, feeling powerless to do anything to stop her. "All you can do is provide the resources," he said. "Whether or not she chooses to use them is about her, not you." I knew this already, of course, but it still helped to hear it from someone other than my own voice inside my head. I was usually the one issuing reassurances to my staff; having someone to do the same for me was new territory.

As we spent more time together, I began to feel better about his status as a father. I still had moments of apprehension, but I quieted them by reasoning that his kids were only with him a couple of weekends a month, so really, more times than not, Victor and I would be on our own. And it wasn't like he was rushing me into meeting them; we both felt we should wait on that until we were more sure of each other. But by then, I was about as sure as I could get.

Kelli is dead. The phrase pulsed through my mind as I drove over to Max and Ava's school. My hands shook and my breaths were shallow and quick. I tried to imagine what Victor might feel in this moment. The ragged grief in his voice over the phone had sparked my own. I couldn't believe she was gone. What could have happened? How is someone there one moment and just . . . *absent* the next? I tried to fight it, but anxiety bubbled up inside me. I didn't know how to get through this moment. I tried to focus on the road, to keep my eyes on the brake lights on the car in front of me, but tears blurred my vision. Not wanting to cause an accident, I pulled to the side of the road and called my mother, overwhelmed by the desire to talk with her. The phone rang and rang. "Come on, Mom," I whispered. "Please pick up." When she didn't answer, I left her a brief message, then quickly called my brother, Sam, next.

"What's up, sis?" he said. I could see him sitting behind his desk at the AIDS Support Center, where he worked as a client counselor, his wiry red hair cropped close to his head, his green eyes bright and smiling. As a child, he'd been called "Opie" by his playmates; today, he still possessed that same nerdy, endearing quality. When he'd come out to me as a teenager, I worried about the difficult road he might face, but as far as I knew, he hadn't experienced any kind of blatant prejudice because of his sexuality and, at twenty-four, was actually in a very happy partnership with a slightly older man named Wade.

My voice rattled in my throat as I told him about Kelli. He let out a low whistle. "Oh my *god,* honey," he said. "That's so *awful.*"

"I know. I'm just . . . blown away." I sniffed and swallowed hard. "And now I'm on my way to pick up the kids and I don't know what to *tell* them. I've never been in a situation like this. I don't know how to act."

"I don't think there's any specific way you *should* act, sweetie." He paused. "You don't have any idea how she died?"

"No," I said, then pushed my lips together to fight a sob I felt building in my throat. "Victor didn't have any details yet and he's the one who should talk to them, but I'm going to *see* them." I paused again. "They're not stupid, you know? They're going to sense something's wrong. I *never* pick them up from school."

"Can you play dumb?" Sam asked.

"Maybe." My throat began to close up again, and I couldn't stop it. The sobs I'd been fighting came hard and fast, filling my chest with sharp, painful edges in every breath. "Sorry," I finally managed to gasp. "I don't know why this is hitting me so hard. It's not like we were friends. But I just . . . I just . . ." I trailed off, unable to find the words to describe how I felt.

"Oh, Gracie," Sam said. "Don't apologize, honey. It's tragic, what's happened. Of *course* you're upset. You wouldn't be human if you weren't. And you love Victor and the kids. You're feeling *their* pain."

I shook my head, as though he could see me, then took a deep breath, only to exhale it slowly. "I'm scared," I whispered. "I'm not sure I can do this."

"Sweetie," he said, his voice swelling with concern. "Think about what you do every day. Everything you handle for your clients. You'll be fine, I *know* it."

I smiled weakly. He was an old soul, my brother. "Thanks, Sammy. I love you."

"Love you too," he said. "Call me when you can."

I hung up, then scavenged for a tissue in my purse to blow my nose. It suddenly struck me that telling the kids about our engagement the same weekend they'd learn their mother had died was not exactly perfect timing. I knew this much about having kids in your life—their needs came first, no matter what. I quickly took the ring off my finger, staring at it again for a moment before slipping it into the zippered compartment in my wallet, suffering a sharp pang of sadness with the act. I prayed it wouldn't get lost.

After another deep breath, I shot a quick text

off to Melody asking her to call me. She didn't respond right away, so I knew she was in the middle of an appointment with a massage client and couldn't answer her phone. Then I pulled back into traffic and drove the rest of the way to Seattle Academy. On the way there, I attempted to give myself a pep talk. Sam was right. I could do this. I could maintain whatever front I needed to with the kids. I was the adult; they would trust me. I'd adopt the same demeanor I'd learned to use when first talking with a domestic-abuse victim—I'd be calm and collected. I'd listen more than I'd speak.

The office was on my left as I entered and I approached the front desk, letting the secretary know who I was and why I was there. She was a plump, older woman with bluish-gray hair the same airy texture as cotton candy. "Mr. Hansen said to expect you," she said, frowning. "It's just so *sad*. I can barely believe it. Kelli was the *best* mother."

I nodded, suddenly feeling impossibly inferior. *Of course she was the best. Of course I could never live up to her.*

"Can I see your driver's license, please?" the secretary asked. "It's our routine security check."

I pulled out my ID and showed it to her, thinking how my license broke me down into such simple parameters: age, height, weight, and eye color. I wondered if this was how the doctors who took care of Kelli defined her when she came in. *Thirty-three-year-old woman, approximately five-one, one hundred pounds, blue eyes.* I flashed on what she might look like laid out on a gurney. Her skin pale and cold. Those blue eyes shut. Not moving. Not breathing anymore.

"Thank you," the secretary said, placing my license back in my hand and snapping me back to the moment. I blinked and tried to erase Kelli's image from my mind.

"Are they still in class?" I asked.

She nodded. "I'll buzz their teachers and let them know to send them to the office." She glanced at the clock above the door. "We weren't sure exactly when you'd get here. Why don't you have a seat?"

Again, I nodded, and I plopped myself into a hard, black plastic chair, anxiously gnawing on my fingernails, a childhood habit that only returned when I was nervous. The air was thick with the scent of stale coffee and the secretary's powdery perfume. A few minutes later, Max entered the office, and I stood to greet him.

"Hey there, Maximilian." I used the familiar nickname his father used, then suddenly wished I hadn't. It was theirs, not ours.

He stopped short in his tracks and stared at me with his mother's eyes. "Why are you here? Where's Mom?"

I smiled. "Your dad asked me to pick you guys

up. We're going back to our house, okay?" It still felt a little strange to call it "our" house, even though I'd lived with Victor for several months now. The kids were only there on the weekends and I wasn't sure they were all that happy to have me be there for breakfast when they woke up. I reached out and put what I hoped was a reassuring hand on Max's shoulder. "He'll be there soon."

"But where's Mom?" Max asked, dropping his backpack to the ground. His brown hair was mussed and a curious expression quickly etched itself across his freckled face. He was small for seven, his frame delicate—almost birdlike—and the top of his head barely reached my chest. "When am I going to get my growth spurt?" he often asked Victor, who was just over six feet tall. "Next Wednesday, three a.m.," Victor always joked in return, and Max would giggle—a bubbly, guttural sound.

"She couldn't be here to pick you up today," I said carefully. "Your dad will talk with you about it when he gets home, okay?" I forced a smile, feeling the stiffness of the motion in the muscles of my cheeks. "Look, there's Ava."

Max's sister entered the office and stared at me, too. "Grace." Her tone was flat. "Where's my mom?" She wore slim-fit jeans, a purple fleece jacket, and knee-high black boots that appeared too big and too grown-up for her skinny legs. I wondered if they were Kelli's. Ava was petite and pretty like her mother, but I could definitely see the shadow of her father in her dark brown hair and the almond shape of her eyes.

I sighed internally, keeping that fake smile on my face, and told her the exact same thing I'd just told her brother. "We can make cookies this afternoon, if you want," I said, desperate to find some way to get them out of this school and into an environment with which I was at least familiar.

"You don't bake," Ava said quietly. *Man,* I thought. *Too perceptive for her own good.* Still, they both picked up their bags and followed me out to my car.

We arrived at our house after a silent car ride, and the kids trudged inside, eyeing me. "When is Dad going to be here?" Max asked. "Doesn't he have to be at the restaurant tonight?" Victor usually worked at the Loft on Friday nights, then picked up the kids from Kelli's place first thing Saturday morning. I knew from taking care of my brother that kids do best when they know what to expect, so both were clearly thrown off by this deviation from their normal routine.

"And why aren't you working?" Ava said before I could respond to Max. "You're *always* working. Mom says so."

I'll bet she does, I mused silently, then immediately chided myself for thinking ill of the dead. "I'm my own boss, so I gave myself the afternoon off," I said, each of my words feeling precariously forced. "What do you guys feel like doing?"

"I'll be in my room," Ava said, and she walked slowly down the hallway. I heard her bedroom door click softly shut. She definitely sensed something wasn't right.

"What about you, Max?" I asked.

He shrugged. "Dunno. Can I watch TV?"

"Sure," I said. I knew he was supposed to read before he plopped in front of *Phineas and Ferb*, but I figured if any day should be one for breaking the rules, it was today. My cell phone vibrated in my purse, and I grabbed for it, thinking it might be Victor.

"What's up?" Melody asked. "Your text was only three words long. Are you okay?"

"Just a sec," I told her now. I looked at Max. "I'll just be down the hall, okay, buddy?" He nodded, then headed into the den. I rushed to our bedroom and locked the door behind me, just in case either of the kids came to look for me. I didn't want them to overhear. "Kelli died," I said breathlessly.

"What?" Melody exclaimed. "Oh my *god*. Are you serious? When? How?"

I filled her in on what I knew, which wasn't much. "And now I'm in the house with the kids and they know something's up." I paused, another sob threatening to take me over. "Well, Ava does. Max is watching TV."

"How long is Victor supposed to take at the hospital?"

"I have no idea. I haven't heard from him yet. I can't imagine it would take too long, but I suppose he'll have to tell them where to take her body and—" My voice broke, as his had earlier, and my pulse suddenly beat in a staccato rhythm. "Mel, I don't think I can do this."

"Do what? Tell them? You don't have to. Victor does. It's your job to support him, and be there for the kids if they reach out to you. That's it." She sighed. "And you guys just got engaged, too. *Geez.*" I'd called Melody immediately after Victor had proposed last weekend, and she'd squealed into the phone, babbling about wedding-dress shopping and finding the perfect venue for the ceremony, but our schedules had been so busy she hadn't seen the ring yet. I wasn't sure I could tell people about the engagement now. *Victor's ex-wife is dead . . . oh, and by the way, we're getting married.*

"That doesn't seem very important all of a sudden," I said. The tiniest part of me felt sad my excitement over getting engaged had been eclipsed and I was totally ashamed of this brief, selfish thought.

"Of course it's important," Melody said insistently. "It's just really shitty timing." She sighed again. "Do you want me to come over and keep you company while you wait? I can cancel my last client."

"That's sweet," I said. "But probably not a good

idea. They'd suspect even more if you were here. I'll call you if I hear anything, okay?" We hung up and I threw myself onto my back on the bed, my gaze traveling the room where Victor and I slept. When I moved in, he insisted I bring everything from my house that I wanted to display and willingly packed away most of his minimal, but clearly masculine, décor.

"This is your house now, too," he said. "I want you to feel comfortable. If you want to paint, we'll paint. If you want new furniture, we can do that, too." The bedroom was the only room where I'd taken him up on his offer, changing his steel-hued color scheme into warmer earthy tones. Together, we picked out a mossy green micro-suede comforter set and an additional dresser to accommodate my extensive wardrobe. I didn't change too much of the rest of the house, since the kids were used to it the way it was. The last thing I wanted was for them to associate losing everything they felt comfortable having in their surroundings with the day I moved in. Since I owned my condo, I decided to lease it for a small profit over selling it outright, telling myself this was a smart fiscal decision instead of a comment on my level of commitment to the man I loved. I put most of my furniture into storage, figuring that we both would eventually sell our individual household possessions and purchase new ones together.

I liked living in Victor's house—a small 1960s rambler on a hillside overlooking the Puget Sound—but what I liked more was waking up to his warm body next to mine every morning. I liked that he made me lunch while I showered to get ready for the day; I liked that he always cupped my face with his hands when he kissed me good-bye. He worked three evenings a week at the restaurant, so I had plenty of time to indulge my craving for alone time or to spend a few hours with Melody. We had a few squabbles over silly things like where to put the stereo and there was always a bit of tension when the kids came for the weekend, but I told myself it would just take time for us all to adjust to a new routine. Most of the time our world felt balanced and I felt at peace.

And then, just last Sunday, he'd taken me to his favorite spot on Alki Beach. The sun was about to set; the sky was streaked with brilliant shades of pink, and a warm, golden light pushed in long streams through the clouds. Seagulls screamed all around us, and a cool breeze blew off the water. When we kissed, I could taste sea salt on his lips.

"I used to come here when I was a kid," Victor told me as we settled on a large hunk of driftwood. He tucked his arm around my waist and I snuggled myself into the warmth of his body. "It was my sanctuary," he continued, "but now *you're* my sanctuary." He stared at me, the evening light glinting off the water and hitting his dark hair, illuminating the sprinkling of silver throughout the scruff of his unshaven beard. After a year together, I had the small, crinkled lines around his eyes memorized; I knew the shape of each tiny fleck of black in his irises, the smattering of freckles that spread out like brown sugar sifted across his nose.

I reached out to touch his cheek. "That's so sweet. You trying to get laid or something?"

He chuckled softly. "No, I'm asking you to marry me." He pulled a black box out of his pocket and opened it, revealing a glittering ring. We'd talked about marriage previously—in theory, really—discussing it as an eventual next step after I moved into his house. But still, the timing of his proposal was a surprise—I wished I'd worn something other than sweatpants, that my hair wasn't whipping around my face like angry Medusa's snakes. Still, I joyfully accepted and felt the kiss that he gave me to the tips of my toes.

The loud jiggle of the doorknob jolted me out of my thoughts. "Just a second," I called out, and stumbled to the door to unlock it, thinking it was likely one of the kids. But it was Victor standing before me, looking bereft in a way I'd never seen him. His usually tan skin was ashen and his dark hair stood on end, as though he'd repeatedly raked his hands through it. His broad shoulders slumped forward and his normally cheerful, handsome face appeared crumpled in on itself. He looked broken.

"Oh, sweetie," I said, pulling him into my arms. He clutched me in a tight embrace, bending down to bury his nose into my neck. His tears wet my skin. "Are you okay?"

He shook his head, then pulled away, staring at me with sad gray eyes. "I just don't know how I'm going to tell them." His voice was hoarse and his chin trembled as he spoke. "The counselor at the hospital said to be as straightforward as possible, without giving them too many details."

I swallowed before speaking again. "Do you know . . . how did she . . . ?" My words were disjointed, trailing off, unsure of the right way to ask what I wanted to know.

Victor sniffed and cleared his throat, looking the tiniest bit more like himself. "They're not sure what happened yet, other than that her heart stopped. They have to run some blood tests, I guess, and they'll know more." He paused. "There was an empty prescription bottle on the night-stand next to her bed."

"Oh *no*." I took a deep breath and I rubbed his back with my open palm. "What kind of pills?"

"Antianxiety. She's taken them before. Mostly because she has trouble sleeping."

Hearing these words, dread twisted in my chest. *Oh god. Victor said she didn't take the news of our engagement very well. What if it was worse than he thought? She was fragile to begin with. What if it pushed her over the edge?* My eyes filled with tears, terrified that I had contributed in any way to her death. I hesitated a moment before asking the next question that leapt into my mind. "Was there a note?"

For a brief moment, he almost looked angry, but then he shook his head again. "I don't want the kids to think that, okay? We don't know anything for sure." His tone was a little sharp, one he hadn't used with me before. He was protective of her, still. I knew he'd played the caretaker role in their marriage—a role he became exhausted of after having to do it too long. I needed to be strong for him now. I needed to not crumble.

"What are you going to say?" I asked.

"The truth. That we don't know what happened. That she lay down in her bed and didn't wake up. I don't think they need more information than that. Not now."

"What do you need me to do?" I caressed his face with my left hand, and he lifted his own up to hold it there. Touching my fingers, he pulled it away from his face.

"Where's your ring?" he asked.

My eyes filled unexpectedly. "I took it off. The kids are going to have enough to deal with. We can tell them later." I searched his face, wiping away an errant tear that slipped down my cheek. "Was that right?"

He rested his forehead against mine. "I love you so much, you know that?" I nodded, then kissed his lips. He took a deep breath, grabbed my hand, and we walked down the hall, bracing ourselves to deliver the news that would no doubt change us all.

Ava

I knew something had to be really wrong the minute I saw Grace standing in the office next to Max. Grace didn't *come* to our school. She didn't make brownies for our bake sales like my mom or chaperone our field trips to the Seattle Art Museum like my dad. The only thing Grace did was work, live with my dad, and drive a car that probably cost more than my mother's whole house, which is something I overheard my mom say once to Diane.

"How much do you think she paid for it?" Diane asked in a low voice, and my mother answered, "Well, it's a *Lexus*. It couldn't have been *cheap*." Then she said the thing about it probably costing more than our house, which I knew couldn't really be true. And even though I was around the corner in the hallway, eavesdropping as they sat on the couch and drank from a box of wine Diane brought over, I could picture the look on my mother's face: her tiny nose all crinkled up and her eyes narrowed, the same way she looked when she accidentally opened a carton of moldy cottage cheese.

"Does Grace have a lot of jewelry?" Mama asked me once when Max and I got home from our dad's house. She was sitting on the edge of my bed as I studied for a history test the next day.

"I don't *know,*" I said, keeping my eyes on my notes. "She has diamond earrings she wears sometimes." At this point, Grace hadn't moved in yet, so I only saw her a couple of times a month. I felt weird talking to my mom about her. She was nice enough and didn't make out with our dad in front of us or anything, which the guy who dated Bree's mom had done the first time he came over. "So *gross,*" Bree said. "He used his tongue and *everything.*" I shuddered at the thought, figuring as long as Grace wasn't doing *that,* I could put up with her hanging out with us.

"What about her clothes?" Mama said persistently. "Are they all business suits and heels?"

Finally looking at her, I shook my head. "It's on the weekend, Mama. She wears jeans and sweaters." I paused. "Why does it matter?"

Mama stood up, fluffed her hair, and gave me a dazzling smile. "I just don't want you to get the wrong idea about what's important."

After she left my room, I considered the fact that it was Mama who seemed to think that

Grace's making more money than us was important. Definitely more than I did. It wasn't like Grace was Whitney's kind of rich—she didn't have a driver or a housekeeper or a tennis court. She just didn't have as many bills as we did because it was just her. Her car was really the only expensive thing it looked like she had. But it wasn't brand-new or anything. Plus, Dad was always talking about how hard Grace worked and how capable and smart she was; I wondered if he said any of that to Mama, so she felt bad about just being a waitress.

"Why didn't *you* go to college?" I asked her not long after Daddy left us, and an odd look popped up on her face. She took a minute before responding, and when she finally did, there was a false brightness in her voice, almost the same way I'd heard her talk to Max when she was trying to pretend he wasn't annoying her.

"School was just never my cup of tea," she said. "I only ever wanted to be a cheerleader. All the silly, meaningless things that just don't matter in the end." Her blue eyes narrowed a bit when she looked at me. "That's why I want you at the academy. You're a smart girl. I don't want you to end up like I did."

I tilted my head and scrunched my eyebrows together. "Like how?"

"Focused on the wrong things in life." She paused and sharpened her gaze. "What's important is in here." She reached over and tapped my forehead lightly with the tip of her index finger. "And in here," she said, placing her palm flat over my heart.

I swallowed and nodded, knowing she wanted me to agree. And I did, to a point, but I also knew that being pretty got other girls things that being plain like Bree or average like me didn't get us. I also thought it was weird that Mama was always telling me how pretty I was, but then practically in the next breath, she insisted being smart was more important. I thought it would be kind of great to be both. I liked school well enough—my favorite subjects were history and English—but I had no idea what I might be when I grew up. Not a waitress, though. I knew that much from watching Mama come home so tired she could barely stand, irritated that the table with the highest bill had only left her a 5 percent tip.

"But you *were* a cheerleader?" I asked Mama, thinking it would be pretty cool if she had been.

"Yes," she said with a frown, not meeting my gaze. "And it didn't get me anything but trouble."

She wouldn't tell me more when I asked her to explain what kind of trouble she meant, but I assumed it had to do with boys. When I was twelve years old, boys in my class were already snapping my training bra in the hallway or trying to brush up against my chest "accidentally" with their hand. Boys were gross and, as far as I could tell at that point, *were* nothing but trouble.

Now, in my room at my dad's house, I could hear the muffled noise of the television from the den. I pulled my cell phone from my backpack and sent my mom another quick text message, asking where she was. I'd sent her one in the car on the way here, too, but she hadn't responded yet, which worried me. She usually answered within a couple of minutes, even when she was working, in case we needed her. When she didn't respond to my second text after five, then ten minutes, a cold, hard spot materialized in my belly. I pushed on it, but it didn't go away. I stared at my phone, squinted my eyes, and willed Mama's name to appear.

As I waited, I lay on my bed—a futon I'd begged my dad to buy because it looked cool but soon grew to hate because it was hard and I didn't sleep very well on it. My walls were painted a pale lime green, and my curtains and blankets were lavender. The same colors as my room at my mom's, which I'd asked for so maybe it wouldn't feel so weird to live in two houses. It didn't work. It still felt weird to come here two weekends a month. I loved seeing my dad but hated having to pack a bag, hated leaving my mom alone, and really hated that Grace got to spend more time with my dad than I did. She was always trying to be my friend.

"I'm going to get a pedicure with Melody," she said to me one Saturday morning. "Would you like to come?"

I shook my head and kept my eyes on the book I was reading. I could be nice to her when she was with my dad, but I didn't see any reason why I had to spend any time alone with her. She was probably just trying to get my dad to think she was greater than he already did.

"Are you sure?" Grace asked. "They have crazy colors like neon orange and green. You can get any shade you want." I threw a glance over to my dad, who stood in the kitchen, watching our exchange over the breakfast bar.

"Ava, it's very nice of Grace to offer to take you to do this," he said. "It's a little rude to not accept."

I sighed and tucked my chin into my chest, burrowing a little deeper into the couch. I didn't care if it was rude. I didn't want to go.

"I'll go!" Max said, piping up from his spot in the recliner across from me. "Can I get black toenails with white skulls painted on them?" I pressed my lips together and glared at him. "What?" he said, blinking at me. "That would be *cool*."

Grace laughed and looked over to my dad, who chuckled and shook his head. "I don't think so, buddy. Grace and Melody want to have some girl time." He paused. "Ava?"

"I don't want to, Dad," I said, pleading. Even

from across the room, I saw a quick flash of disappointment on Grace's face.

"That's okay," she said, backing off. "It's not a big deal. Maybe another time." She smiled at me, and I couldn't help but think how pretty she was. "Right, Ava?"

I gave her a quick nod, thinking, *Fat chance,* but also begrudgingly appreciative that she didn't push things too much with me. For the most part, she gave me the space I needed. Only now she had shown up at my school out of nowhere and she wasn't telling us why.

I sighed and sat up, thinking about the stash of candy bars I had hidden in my closet, wondering if Grace would be able to smell it on my breath if I ate one now. She'd probably tell my dad I'd broken his no-sugar-before-dinner rule. My stomach grumbled and I decided I didn't care. I opened my closet door as quietly as I could, crouching down so I could reach behind a box of Barbie dolls that I didn't play with anymore. I grabbed a Snickers bar and listened for the front door, hopeful my dad had come home, but there was still just the sound of the television. I ate the candy bar quickly, barely tasting the chocolate as it melted on my tongue. I wondered where Grace was. Hiding in my dad's bedroom, I guessed. Or at the dining room table typing away on her laptop, which seemed like her favorite thing to do.

A phone rang in another room—the ringtone

was Grace's, some weird Latin-sounding music. As quietly as I could, I opened the door and snuck down to the end of the hall, where Grace and my father slept. Pressing my ear up against the door, I listened hard, but I could only make out one or two words. She was whispering. Something was definitely wrong. The cold spot grew wider in my stomach, spreading up through my chest, down my arms, and to the tips of my fingers, until I could barely feel them. I walked back to my room; climbed into bed, shivering beneath my blankets; and, like a thousand times before, waited for my dad to come home.

"Do you have to stay at the restaurant so late?" Mama said. She and my daddy were standing in the bathroom, where he had just gotten out of the shower and was now shaving in the steamed-up mirror. I liked the *squeak-squeak* sound his hand made when he rubbed the fogged-up part away so he could actually see his reflection. Max was in his bedroom taking a nap, and I sat in the hallway, my back against the wall and my knees pulled up to my chest, listening.

My daddy sighed. "I can't afford a general manager. It's me, the kitchen staff, and the bartender. That's it. You knew it was going to be like this." Daddy had opened his own restaurant that year, but Mama said it was taking time for it to make enough money so he didn't have to work every day. I liked that he brought us home treats. Sometimes, I even had pasta for breakfast or chocolate cheesecake in my lunchbox. None of the other kids had that, so I thought I was actually pretty lucky.

"Did I?" Mama said, her voice high-pitched and shaking. "Did I know you'd leave first thing in the morning, come home for a couple of hours so your kids will know you still exist, then leave again?" Daddy didn't answer, so she continued, her voice becoming high and squeaky like one of my old baby dolls'. "I didn't sign up for this, Victor. I have to do everything here. The kids, the cleaning, the shopping—"

"It's what we agreed on!" There was a loud clank of something landing in the bathroom sink, and I jumped, slapping my hand over my mouth so they didn't hear my surprised yelp. "We agreed that my opening the Loft was the way to get us where we really want to go. We agreed that you'd stay home with the kids. I know I've been busy, but I really don't understand what you're complaining about. I'm working so hard for us. For our family."

"I miss you. That's all." Mama's voice was so soft I could barely hear her. "I didn't realize you'd be gone so much of the time. I need help."

"What kind of help? What else can I do?" Daddy's voice got quieter, too, and the icky feeling that had started to make me sick to my stomach began to get better. "Kelli, honey. Tell me what you want from me."

"I don't know," she said, but her words were all crackly. "I wish my parents were here. Maybe I should call and ask them to come." She paused and her tone suddenly lifted. "Maybe they've changed their minds."

Daddy sighed. "Sweetie, you haven't seen them in over ten years. They didn't even want to meet their *grandchildren*. I don't understand why you keep letting them hurt you."

"They're my parents," Mama whimpered. "I miss them."

"I understand that. I miss my mother every day. And I'm really sorry to say this, but if yours missed you, do you think we'd be having this conversation?"

A second later, Mama rushed past me in the hall, not even noticing I was on the floor. She was crying. I didn't like how Daddy sounded when he talked with Mama lately. He never used to be mean to her, and now he said things that made her cry. But then, lots of things made her cry. Burned toast, or a messy bathroom. I rubbed her back for her when she got like this, the same way she did for me when I was upset about something, but it didn't help. She cried harder when I touched her. I made it worse.

Now I waited a minute, then crawled into the bathroom on my hands and knees, pretending to be a cat. Mama had allergies so we couldn't get a real kitten; pretending I was one was the next-best thing.

"Meow," I said to my daddy, who was leaning against the bathroom wall, staring up at the ceiling. He looked back down at me and smiled when he heard the noise. "Meow," I said again, pretending to lick the side of my hand and rubbing my face with it, then inched my way over to press my body against his long legs.

"What's this?" he said. "An eight-year-old, brown-haired, blue-eyed cat?"

"Meow," I said. "Almost nine."

He squatted down and cupped the back of my head in his hand. "Here, kitty kitty."

I noticed he still had white foam near his ears from shaving, so I grabbed the towel off the rack and wiped it away for him. "Why don't Gramma and Grampa want to see Mama?" I asked. It scared me to think that my parents could someday not want to see me.

He frowned. "Were you eavesdropping again, young lady? We've talked about that a hundred times. Not okay." He gave the end of my nose a light pinch.

"Sorry," I said. "I didn't mean to. I was just walking down the hall."

"Uh-huh," Daddy said, but winked at me, too, so I knew he wasn't really angry. Daddy never stayed mad at me or Max for very long; Mama was the one who took away TV privileges or sent us to our rooms when we misbehaved. With Daddy, I knew I could get away with pretty much everything.

I tried again. "Are Gramma and Grampa *mad* at Mama? Bree got mad at me once and didn't talk to me for a whole week."

"It's complicated, sweetie. Sometimes grown-ups have problems in their relationships that kids really can't understand."

"Like I don't understand division?"

He chuckled. "Sort of." He grabbed the towel from me. "Now, you need to scoot so I can finish getting ready."

"Do you *have* to go to work?" I asked, carefully searching his face with my eyes. He had brown hair and gray eyes and long, dark lashes. He was the handsomest man in the world.

He gave me a small smile, making his dimple show up. I wanted to stick my finger in it. "I do, kitten," he said. "It's how I take care of you guys."

"But do you have to be gone so long?" I whispered, not looking at him.

He sighed. "As long as it takes to get the business on its feet, baby girl. I know it's hard, but we're a family, and we're going to go through some rough times."

"Mama's tired," I said, still in a whisper. "She cries sometimes, in the middle of the day, she's so tired."

Daddy was quiet a minute, pressing his lips

together and breathing slowly, through his nose. Then he spoke. "I'll take care of your mama, okay, Ava? Don't you worry."

Nodding my head felt like lying, but I did it anyway. I told my daddy exactly what he wanted to hear.

Kelli

When Jason Winkler sat down next to Kelli in Algebra I, she took it as a sign that they were meant to be together. He was by far the cutest boy in the school—everyone thought so. He was tall but not skinny. His dark hair fell over his blue eyes in a way that made Kelli want to reach out and brush it back with the tips of her fingers, then let them slide down the warmth of his cheek. He had a lopsided smile that was almost always accompanied by a wink—Kelli was pretty sure that on the first day of class, he'd smiled more than once at her before sauntering to the back row and plopping into the chair beside her. He was a junior but spent more time at basketball practice than studying, so this was the third time he was taking the introductory class. Kelli was just a freshman and didn't care about that. She only cared that of all the open spots in the room, he picked the one next to her.

"Hey," he said this morning, swinging his head around to look at her. There it was. The smile . . . and the wink. Kelli felt the space between her legs get warm and she blushed.

"Hey," she echoed, tucking the sheet of her long blond hair behind one ear. It was her pride and joy, that hair. Sleek and shiny, not an ounce of frizz or split ends. She spent hours brushing it at night, staring in the mirror, practicing imagined red-carpet speeches into her comb. Her parents said she was vain; she preferred to think of it as optimistic.

"You get the assignment done?" Jason asked as he stretched his long legs out straight beneath the desk and crossed one ankle over the other.

She rolled her eyes. "Kind of. It was totally hard." She hoped he noticed the outfit she'd changed into in the school bathroom—peg-legged Levi's and a tight pink sweater, borrowed from her friend Nancy. They were clothes other girls took for granted, but her parents would have screamed at her for wearing them. Their idea of appropriate clothes for school included two colors, black and white, and one shape—boxy.

"Maybe you need a tutor," Jason said.

She smiled like she knew a secret and raised one of her eyebrows, another thing she'd practiced in front of her mirror. "Are *you* interested in the job?" she asked him. She couldn't believe how bold she was being, but all of the articles she read in *Cosmopolitan* said men liked it when a woman showed confidence. In order to read the magazine, she had to sneak to the library after school, telling her parents she was doing homework. She *was* studying . . . in a way. Brushing up on how to get a boyfriend.

"That's not the *only* job I'm interested in," Jason said, and his friends Mike and Rory, who sat on the other side of him, snickered.

Kelli blushed again—her *Cosmo* textbook had taught her exactly what he meant—but kept smiling as she directed her attention to the front of the room, where their teacher was about to start class. Jason leaned over and nudged her leg with his fist. "You going to the basketball game Friday night?"

She shook her head. Her parents made her go to youth group at their church on Fridays, which was just about the most boring thing in the world.

"You should come," Jason said. "I'm on the starting lineup this week. Maybe we could do something after."

He was asking her out on a date! She forced herself to shrug, knowing boys also liked it if you played just a little bit hard to get. "Maybe," she said. "I'll see if I can."

"Cool," he said.

For the rest of class, Kelli didn't hear a word of what was said. All she could think about was talking with Nancy, seeing if her friend could help her figure out a way to get to that basketball game. Nancy's parents weren't old, like Kelli's. Nancy's mother ran a local coffee shop and loved to tell jokes; her father was a sociology professor at Cal Poly who wore jeans to class just like his students. Kelli's father was a bank manager who wore the same black slacks and white, short-sleeved shirt with a plaid bow tie to work every day. Her mother stayed home, shopping for groceries and cleaning their house, and hadn't worn a pair of jeans in her life. They'd met at church in down-town San Luis Obispo more than thirty-five years ago and quickly married, thinking they'd start a family as soon as possible. Kelli hadn't arrived for another twenty years—something they hadn't expected, having already grown accustomed to a life on their own. Kelli was a blond ball of energy, bouncing into their lives and disrupting the peace. She'd always felt like they didn't know what to do with her. They hoped for a daughter who liked to sit quietly and listen to stories; they had a daughter who raced into mud puddles. Kelli learned to separate herself into two different people—the one they wanted her to be and the one she was. As she got older, the side of her they didn't approve of seemed harder to hide. Now that she was in high school especially, and there were dances to go to and dates to be had. She loved her parents, but she wasn't sure how much longer she could pretend to be the girl they imagined her to be.

Kelli sighed when the bell rang, thinking about how hard it would be to make it to the game on Friday, but gave Jason one last smile, letting her gaze linger on his for a moment, just to keep him interested. "Don't forget," he said, and she nodded, thrilled by the possibility that she might get to fall in love.

Kelli was only six when she realized her parents were different. Her mother would take her to the park after school, but while the other moms and dads chased after their children on the playground, Kelli's would settle on a bench with a book, urging her to go play on her own. The other mothers chatted and laughed together, but Kelli's mom tended to keep to herself. She had a few friends from their church, but none of them had children Kelli's age.

One night, as her mother tucked her into bed and read her a story, Kelli noticed that her mother had wisps of silver strung through the honey-blond locks she had given her daughter. "Why do you have gray in your hair, Mama?" Kelli asked, and her mother leaned down to kiss Kelli's forehead, as she did every night. When she pulled back, she smiled at Kelli.

"Because I'm forty-eight, sweet girl," she said.

"Why doesn't *Janie's* mama have silver hair?" Kelli thought her mother's hair was beautiful, like it belonged to one of the princesses from the fairy tales Kelli loved to read.

"Because I'm older than Janie's mama," her mother said, still smiling. "Most people have babies when they're very young, but your father and I didn't. You surprised us."

Kelli thought about this, knitting her eyebrows together. "Was I an accident?" Kelli's friend Pete had told her about how he overheard his parents talking about *him* as an accident—a baby they hadn't wanted.

Her mother sat down on the edge of her bed and ran her hand along the side of Kelli's cheek. "Absolutely not," she said. "You weren't an accident. You were a surprise. There's a difference."

"What *kind* of difference?"

"An accident is something you didn't want. A surprise is something you didn't realize how *much* you wanted it until it came along."

Kelli had gone to sleep that night feeling loved. It was hard to remember it now, at fourteen, when her parents seemed so far away from her—so impossible to reach. She wondered sometimes if she'd been given to them by mistake. If she was adopted instead of born to them, simply because she was so fundamentally different from them both. She'd always tried to please them—to be quiet and respectful and comply with their requests. She was obedient, accompanying them to church every Sunday, helping her mother clean the house, leaving her father alone in the den so he could read his paper every night in peace. And yet . . . she imagined another family—the one she was meant to live with. Her fantasy mother would laugh more than she scolded; her father would gather her up for a cuddle on the couch, then help her with her homework. They'd have a dog and two cats, and maybe even another daughter so Kelli would have someone to giggle with in her bedroom into the wee hours of morning. She imagined a loud, messy house filled with happiness and love. A house entirely different from the one she lived in now.

She loved her parents, but she knew they didn't understand her. Kelli had big dreams—she wanted the kind of passion she read about in the romance novels at the library. She longed for the rush of attraction, the kind of connection she never saw between her mother and father. They never held hands, never kissed more than a swift, dry peck on the lips. They followed strict routines, waking at five each morning to read the Bible and pray together—something Kelli had begun refusing to do just this year. She wasn't sure she believed everything they believed. She didn't feel Jesus the way they said she should, even though she had asked Him into her heart seven times, just to be sure He took.

Just last Sunday after church, as they'd walked

home together, she'd even been courageous enough to ask her father how he knew there really was a God. He'd looked at her with a cloudy expression, his pale blue eyes narrowing. "I know because I know," he said, and Kelli thought that was a meaningless response. She tried again.

"But how do you *know?* I don't understand how you can believe in something you can't see."

Her father stopped, grabbed her arm, and gave her another stern look. "It's called having faith, young lady. You don't see God, you feel Him. Do you understand?"

Kelli nodded, a little frightened by the grip of her father's hand. He so rarely touched her any- more, it felt foreign. Unnatural.

"Thomas," her mother said, reaching out to pull his hand off of their daughter, and they'd walked the rest of the way home in silence. Kelli's mother recognized her daughter starting to pull away from them—away from God—and she felt help- less to do anything to stop it. All she could hope was that Kelli might learn the error of her ways and come back to them. All she could do was pray.

Kelli thought about that moment all week long as she considered how to ask her parents if she could go to the basketball game. She knew her parents would never let her go. At the beginning of the year, she'd brought up the idea of trying out to be a cheerleader. "Why would you want to flaunt yourself like that in front of everyone?" her father asked.

She'd sighed at the time, wondering how, exactly, she was supposed to answer a question like that. "I was just thinking it would be good exercise," she told him. She loved how the girls looked in their tight red sweaters and short pleated skirts. She loved the bounce of their ponytails and the way all the football players swarmed around them like bees.

He'd looked down at her over the top of his black-rimmed glasses. "You can take a walk," he said. And that was that.

Now it was Friday night and Kelli sat with her parents at the dining room table inside their small brick house. Her mother had made them pasta for dinner—sauce from a jar over mushy egg noodles. "This is good, Mama," she said, even as the bite she had just taken stuck in her throat.

"Thank you, dear," her mother said. Her graying blond hair was pulled into a loose bun at the base of her neck and she wore a black dress sprinkled with tiny white flowers. She looked at Kelli's father. "Thomas? How's your dinner?"

"Just fine, thank you," her father said. He took a gulp of milk, then moved his gaze to his daughter. "How was school today, Kelli?" He wasn't sure how to talk to her lately. She had always been pretty, but now . . . it made him uncomfortable, to see his daughter this way, knowing how men were. What they'd want to do with her. She used to be a skinny thing, with knobby knees and barely any fat on her at all, but her body had blossomed over the last year, her hips rounded and her waist nipped in. But most disturbing to him was the swell of her chest, the way it pushed at the blouses she wore, like it was anxious for the world to notice the change. He wanted to protect her, but he didn't know how. It was hard to look at her now, hard to understand that this was still his little girl.

Kelli nodded. "It was good," she said, then took a deep breath. "There's a basketball game tonight at the gym. All the kids are going." She paused, feeling both her parents' eyes on her. "Do you think . . . would it be okay if I went, too?"

Her mother stitched her thin brows together over her pale blue eyes. "You have youth group," she said.

"I know," Kelli said. "I thought I could miss it just this once. Please?"

Her parents were silent, staring at their daughter. When they were in high school, both of them were more interested in studying than attending sporting events or dances. Thomas wanted to work in a bank and Ruth never had aspirations to be anything but a housewife. He loved the structure of numbers and strict procedure; she loved the time she spent taking care of their home and volunteering at their church. They didn't stray outside of the path they knew their parents wanted them to be on; they never pushed any limits.

Though they were not demonstrative people, they loved their daughter, and up until she'd turned fourteen, they'd assumed she'd simply behave as they had at her age. But sometimes, there were traces of makeup on her face when she came home from school, evidence of misbehavior that she'd failed to wash thoroughly away. Ruth told Thomas this was normal teenage rebellion, that as long as she was coming home at all, they should be grateful. "It could be worse," she said. "Much worse."

They did what they could, of course. Ruth only bought Kelli the most shapeless tops and baggy slacks for her to wear at school. She thought of it as armor against the army of young men who would surely try to have their way with her daughter if given a chance. They kept her busy with youth group and church services; they discouraged the activities that might lead her off course.

"I don't think it's a good idea," Thomas finally said. "Maybe another time, when we can go with you."

Kelli nodded, knowing it was futile to try to convince them. At least she had asked, which was more than she'd usually do. They finished dinner in relative silence, and after Kelli helped her mother clean up the kitchen, her father drove them over to the church. They had Bible study that night, which met in the far corner of the sanctuary while the youth group gathered in the basement.

Her mother kissed her forehead as they parted ways. "We'll see you in a couple of hours," she said, and Kelli nodded, wondering if God would strike her down for telling a lie.

By the time Kelli arrived at the gym, the game was already over. After her parents disappeared around the corner of the church hallway, she had slipped out the side door and walked as fast as she could across town to the school. Halfway there, she hid behind a huge rhododendron bush and took off the stupid blouse she'd put on over Nancy's tight pink sweater, which she'd worn again that day. There was nothing she could do about the black slacks she had on—her jeans wouldn't fit beneath them and her parents would have suspected something was up if she had brought a bag to youth group. She swiped on a bit of red lipstick and took her hair out of the low ponytail at the base of her neck, letting it fall around her shoulders. She hoped Jason would still think she looked pretty. She hoped he might kiss her.

When she got to the school, people poured out of the gym doors into the parking lot and Kelli scanned the crowd for Jason, knowing his dark head would be easily seen. She saw Nancy and beckoned her friend over.

"Oh my *god!*" she squealed. "Your parents let you *come?*"

"Not exactly," Kelli said, then told Nancy what she had done.

"You are going to get in *so* much trouble," Nancy observed, cracking the piece of gum she had in her mouth and fluffing her hot-rollered black curls.

Kelli sighed. "I don't care. I'm sick of never getting to *do* anything."

Nancy's eyes got wide and she smiled, looking just over Kelli's shoulder. "Hi, Jason," she said, reaching over to pinch Kelli quickly on the arm.

"Hey," Jason said, and Kelli whipped around to face him. "You missed the game," he said.

"Yeah." Kelli tried to sound nonchalant. "I had to hang out with my parents for a while."

"That's cool," Jason said. "You want to go for a drive?"

"Sure," Kelli said, her cheeks flushing from more than just her hurried walk to the school. She looked at Nancy. "I'll call you later?"

Nancy nodded, and Kelli let Jason take her hand and lead her to his green truck. *Jason Winkler is holding my hand!* She straightened her spine and lifted her chin as they walked, hopeful she looked natural alongside him. She felt the eyes of the other students on them, and it made her feel important. She knew her parents would be furious with her, but in that moment, it didn't matter. The only thing that mattered was how Jason looked at her as he opened the truck door. Like he wanted her.

"What a gentleman," she remarked with a playful lilt in her voice.

"I try," Jason said, smiling. He shut her door and loped around the truck to the driver's side.

"Where are we going?" Kelli asked as he started the engine.

"I know a spot where we can go to talk," he said. "And get to know each other better."

Kelli smiled and crossed her legs, tucking her hands between her thighs. Her muscles sparked with excitement—she was going to be Jason's girlfriend, she just knew it. "Did we win the game?" she asked, remembering from *Cosmo* how much boys liked it when you asked them questions about their interests.

"Yep," he said, pulling out of the school parking lot onto the main drive of town. "Seventy-four to sixty-two. I shot twenty of those points."

"Wow," Kelli said. "They're lucky to have you."

"*I'm* the lucky one," Jason said. "Look at who's riding in my truck tonight."

Kelli flushed with pleasure and giggled. They were silent awhile, listening to the radio as Jason drove them off the main drag and out of town. A small panicky fire ignited in Kelli's stomach. "I can't stay out too late," she said, keeping her voice light. "My parents don't know where I am."

Jason laughed. "You snuck out?"

"Sort of," she said. She glanced out the window into the dark. "Where are we going, again?"

"Just a spot off the highway," Jason said. "It's quiet and a really cool place to look at the stars."

"Okay," Kelli said, but she looked at her watch. She'd left the church about an hour ago, which meant she had another hour before youth group was over and her parents realized she was gone.

"Chill," Jason said. "I'll get you home . . . eventually." He chuckled, then signaled to pull off the highway onto an unmarked gravel road.

Kelli laughed too, but the sound tumbled out of her on a false note. Jason turned into a spot between two tall evergreen trees and shut down the engine and cut the headlights. Kelli could hear the bright chirp of crickets around them and the distant hoot of an owl. "Wow," she said. "It's really dark. We're really in the woods."

Jason stretched his right arm over the back of the bench seat. "Don't worry. It's my dad's property. It's totally safe." He patted the spot next to him with his left hand. "Why don't you scoot over here? I can keep you warm."

Anticipation sparkled along Kelli's skin as she did as he asked, leaning against him and letting his arm drop around her shoulders. His hand dangled over her right breast, his fingertips just barely brushed the edge of her sweater, and she felt her breath catch in her chest. He was definitely going to kiss her.

"I'm glad you came out tonight," Jason said, pressing his mouth on her ear. His hot breath made her shiver, a reaction she didn't understand. *Why would heat give me the chills?*

"Me too," she said, snuggling a little closer to him. *This is what love feels like,* she decided. He wouldn't have brought her here unless he was falling in love with her. He wouldn't have sat next to her in class or asked her on a date. Maybe he'd had a crush on her as long as she had liked him. Maybe he went home and crawled into bed thinking of what it would be like to kiss her, too.

Bravely, she turned her head so they were looking at each other. *Kiss me,* she thought, and then he did, as though he had read her mind, putting his lips softly against hers. Her entire body began to vibrate and she felt like she might melt right there in his front seat. *This* was what her magazines talked about. This feeling, right here. Kelli never wanted it to end.

Jason set his left hand on the top of her thigh, moving it upward over her belly and onto her breast. He squeezed once, lightly, then again, harder. Kelli squirmed and pulled her mouth away from his. "Hey," she said.

"Sorry," he said. "I can't help it. You're so hot."

He kissed her again, pushing his tongue inside her mouth this time and rolling it around. Kelli put her hands on his chest and tried to get him to slow down. His hands were suddenly all over her, slipping under her sweater, pushing her bra out of the way. His fingers touched her bare skin and she was overcome by that melting feeling again. He took her hand and put it on the zipper of his jeans. She gasped at the shape of him—she knew this was supposed to happen. She knew that when a boy loved her enough, he would want her this much.

Jason groaned as he kissed her, pulling his hands away from her for a minute while he undid his jeans. "I want you so bad," he said. "I love you."

He loves me, Kelli thought as she slipped off her pants and lay down on the seat. Jason pulled down her underwear and pressed his body against hers. She gasped at the sharp pain as he entered her, gritting her teeth and trying not to cry as he pushed once, twice, then shuddered. It was over almost before it began and Kelli wondered if she'd done something wrong. But then Jason kissed her and she let herself believe all was well. *He loves me,* she thought again, and nothing else meant a thing.

Ava

"Ava, sweetie. I need you to come out here." I heard my dad's voice in the hallway outside of my room, and while I wanted to talk with him, a small part of me considered burrowing into my bed and hiding. Whatever was going on, it couldn't be good.

He opened the door. "Ava? Did you hear me?" He walked over to the edge of my bed and put his hand on my back. "I need to talk to you and your brother, okay? Will you come to the living room with me?"

"What's wrong?" I asked, rolling over to look at him. My voice felt like it was strung an octave higher than usual. *I sound like Mama.* "Just tell me."

"I will, baby," he said, and dropped his gaze to the floor. "But come out so I can tell your brother, too."

Feeling like someone had poured lead in my body, I slowly climbed out of bed and walked with him into the living room, where Grace was sitting on the couch with Max. She was still in her work clothes—black slacks and a fancy-looking blue blouse—but she had taken her jacket and shoes off and her red hair was messy, like she'd just gotten out of bed, too.

"Grace," my dad said. "Do you mind if I talk to the kids alone for a few minutes?"

Grace frowned and her eyebrows shot up, but only for a second before she rearranged her face to look like she wasn't surprised. Then she nodded. "Sure. Okay. I'll just be in the den." She stood and walked slowly into the other room, glancing back at my dad with worried lines scribbled across her forehead. I could tell she thought she should stay, but I was happy he made her go into the other room.

Dad sat down with us on the couch, in between Max and me. His skin looked gray.

"What's going on?" I asked again. "Is Mom okay?" My blood pumped so hard through my veins, I felt dizzy.

He took a deep breath. "No, honey. She's not." My dad's eyes filled with tears and I put my hand on my chest to help me stop breathing so fast. I'd never seen him cry before. His words came at me in slow motion—I fought the urge to push them back and clamp my hands over his mouth.

"She got sick," my dad said, reaching out to hold one of each of our hands in his. "Really sick. So fast we didn't even see it coming."

"But she's *okay*," Max said quickly. "She's in the hospital and the doctors will fix her and make her better. Right? 'Cause that's their *job*." The hopefulness in my brother's voice reached in and squeezed my lungs until I thought they'd burst. *Don't say it. Please. Don't say it. Please, please, please.*

"I'm so sorry, Max, but they can't fix her. They tried, but . . ." His voice trailed off a moment before he swallowed hard and almost whispered the words. "Your mommy died today."

Max erupted off the couch and yanked away from his father's touch. "You're a *liar!*" he screeched. "My mom's not dead!" His hands formed fists and the tendons in his neck extended tightly beneath his skin. Dad stood up, still holding my hand; I stared at the carpet, my shoulders shaking. He let go of me and reached for Max, but my brother cringed and leapt backward, as though Dad had tried to hit instead of hold him. Max sped down the hall toward his room, sobbing.

Tears began to stream down my cheeks. My whole body jittered; it felt like an electric current was shooting through it. I couldn't speak. *This isn't happening. This is all just a horrible dream. I'm still lying in my bed, waiting for my dad to come home. I'm going to wake up, and this all won't be true.*

Dad looked at me, helpless, his eyes still glossed with tears. "Grace?" he called out, and she rushed in from the other room, stopping short when she saw me glare at her, then quickly look away. I didn't want her anywhere near me. I wanted her to leave.

122

"Go," she said to my dad, somehow knowing what had happened. She must have been listening from the den; she must have heard everything. It was a small house; it wouldn't have been hard to do. "It's okay."

Max wailed in his bedroom, a high-pitched, keening cry that pierced through the walls. My dad bent down and touched my face, pushing my hair out of the way. "Ava, baby? I'm so sorry, honey. It's so, so sad."

I nodded briskly but didn't look at him. "Is it okay if I go talk with your brother?" he asked me, and I nodded again. I didn't know what else to do. "Grace will stay right here, if you need her. I'll be right down the hall, and then I'll come back." He left, and I sat with Grace in silence for a few minutes. *She knew Mama was dead when she picked us up. She knew and she didn't say anything.* I sniffled a little, then raised my eyes to hers.

"I don't need you," I said. "I *have* a mom." My words were ice. Fury swelled inside my chest, trying to claw its way out up through my throat. Grace remained unmoving, with her hands in her lap. All the color drained from her face and she blinked, but her expression didn't change. She didn't frown, she didn't twitch; she just sat still and spoke in a calm, measured tone.

"Of course you do," she said. "I would never try to take her place. Never. But I can be here for you as a friend, if you want me—"

"Well, I *don't.*" I stood up, arms stiff at my sides, fists clenched, tears still streaming down my face. "I hate you! I wish *you* were dead!"

Grace's green eyes went wide. "Ava—" she began, but before she could continue, I spun around and ran to my room, slammed the door, and locked it tight behind me.

Grace

"I'm nervous," I told Melody when Victor first suggested it was time for his kids to get to know me. We'd been dating about three months. "What if they hate me?"

"They're not going to hate you," Melody said, shaking her blond head and tucking her slender legs up beneath her on the couch. We sat in the living room of her Queen Anne Hill apartment overlooking downtown, sipping mojitos and munching on chips and the fresh fire-roasted salsa she had made for our weekly girls' night in. "The best thing you can do is let Victor take the lead and not push yourself on them."

"Push myself on them how?" I asked, reaching for another handful of chips to dig into the salsa. After cooking for my family when I was a teenager, I'd lost any interest or enjoyment in the task—Victor laughed when I told him my idea of

124

meal preparation as an adult consisted of properly heating up a Lean Cuisine—but my best friend definitely prided herself on her culinary skills.

Melody screwed up her face a bit, thinking before she spoke. "You know. Like being way over the top, cheerleader-friendly with them. 'Rah-rah, I'm your dad's new girlfriend! Yay!' " She waved a couple of tortilla chips above her shoulders next to the sides of her head like they were pom-poms.

I laughed. "So, no back handsprings?"

She smiled and her dark brown eyes sparkled. "Exactly. Just be yourself. It'll take time for them to warm up to you."

She was right, I knew. But Victor hadn't introduced any of the other women he had dated since the divorce to his children, so I felt a deep need to make a good impression. I thought about buying them gifts, the way I would bring a bottle of wine to a dinner party to show appreciation to the host, but I had no clue what they'd like.

"No bribes," Melody instructed. "Kids can smell you trying to suck up to them a million miles away. Plus, it'll piss off the ex-wife and you don't want to do that, either."

So, unarmed and a little scared, I arrived at Victor's house on a Saturday morning in late October, ready to face the firing squad of his children. I walked up the front steps of his house, taking deep breaths before I knocked on the door. "I got it, Dad!" a little boy's voice yelled from inside, and the door flung open. Max stood in front of me, his hand still on the doorknob. "Who are you?" he asked.

I gave him what I hoped was a friendly but not over-the-top kind of smile. "I'm your dad's friend Grace. I'm going to the pumpkin patch with you guys today." *Didn't Victor tell them I was coming? Maybe Max is just forgetful.*

He stared at me for what felt like a full minute before speaking again. "You're bigger than my mom," he said, and then spun around and raced through the living room and into the den, where I could hear the loud racket of cartoons.

Wonderful. I wasn't overweight by any means, though I was on the heavier side of normal according to my doctor's charts. Exercise wasn't high on my list of enjoyable activities, so I had a wide variety of Spanx to create the illusion of firm thighs and stomach, but overall, I felt pretty good about my body. Of course, I'd seen pictures of Kelli in Ava's bedroom. She was barely over five feet tall and almost as thin as her daughter, with disproportionately large breasts. (Fake, I suspected, since rarely does a petite woman sport such a substantial rack naturally, but there was no way to know for sure.) I was secure enough in my looks to not feel terribly intimidated by her beauty; men often commented on the appealing combination of my bright green eyes and wavy auburn hair, and Victor told me I was gorgeous every day. But there was no doubt about it. As a woman, there was no way to take "bigger" as a compliment.

I stepped through the doorway and Victor appeared from the hallway. "Sorry," he said with the sideways grin of his I loved. "He didn't mean to be rude."

"It's okay. I get it." I smiled and let him give me a quick kiss on the cheek. We'd agreed not to show any physical affection in front of the kids, but I fought the urge to throw myself into his arms and have him reassure me that everything about this day would go well. I peered over his shoulder. "Where's Ava?"

"Trying on a fifth outfit." He rolled his eyes. "I told her, it's a pumpkin patch, not a fashion show, but who am I to argue? You women change your clothes as often as you change your minds."

Max ran back into the living room from the kitchen, hopping in place with his feet together and his arms ramrod straight at his sides. "Dad! It's sunny! Can we play soccer before we go?" I smiled, thinking that Max was exactly as Victor had described him to me: "a jumping jack of a boy, with enough energy to power a small nation."

Victor walked over to his son and dropped into a squatting position so they were face-to-face. Max stopped jumping. "I don't think we have time, buddy," he said. "It's a little bit of a drive to

Snohomish and we don't want to wait too long. All the good pumpkins will be gone."

"Mom already *got* us pumpkins at the grocery store."

Victor threw a glance at me, then looked back to Max. "Well, this place doesn't *just* have pumpkins. It has a petting zoo and arts and crafts and caramel apples. Doesn't that sound like fun?"

"No," Max said. "Can I bring my DS? I want to play Mario Kart."

Victor sighed and stood back up. "In the car only."

Ava chose this moment to emerge from her bedroom, entering the living room with slow, deliberate steps. She wore slim-fit jeans, a blue windbreaker, and knee-high green rubber boots.

"Hi, Ava," I said brightly. "I'm Grace. It's so nice to finally meet you. Your dad has told me so much about you both."

She made brief eye contact with me and gave a short nod of acknowledgment before walking over to her father and hugging him tightly, burying her face into his stomach. Victor leaned down and kissed her on top of her head, his lips landing on one of the fluorescent orange hair clips she wore.

A few minutes later we loaded into Victor's SUV, both of us making idle conversation about pumpkins and the upcoming Halloween holiday.

I shifted in my seat to look at the children. "What costumes are you going to wear this year?" I asked them, figuring this was a neutral enough subject to get them to engage with me.

"Iron Man!" Max offered. "With real lasers on my hands!" He held his palms out at me, making pretend electronic shooting noises. "Pew! Pew!"

I laughed. "Awesome. I loved that movie."

"You did?" Max asked, an edge of doubt in his voice.

"Totally. Iron Man *rocks*." I grinned at him, and he grinned back.

"Pew! Pew!" he said, again pretending to shoot me. *Victory!*

"What about you, Ava?" Victor prodded, looking at his daughter in the rearview mirror. "What are you going to be for Halloween?"

Ava shrugged, staring out the window. "I don't know."

"It's next weekend," I said. "Do you have any ideas at all? Maybe we could help you figure something out."

She looked at me, pressing her lips together in a thin line, and shook her head. I sighed a little internally, wondering why she was so unresponsive. Had I already done or said something that bothered her? Maybe she simply hated me on principle, just because I was another woman, invading her time with her father. I could handle kids who were more like Max, open and mouthy.

Or maybe it was because he was a boy, and I was used to how my brother behaved when he was Max's age. I knew how to relate. Ava's silence made me extremely uncomfortable.

The afternoon went well, all things considered. I even got Ava to laugh when I did my impression of the llama that had spit at her dad over the petting zoo fence. Momentarily disregarding Melody's advice to avoid bribery, I bought them caramel apples covered in miniature chocolate chips and paid for the sepia photo of them with their dad dressed up in old western frontier clothes. Victor tried to get me to dress up and take the picture with them, but I felt like a family photo would be pushing things too far for a first meeting. I snapped many pictures of the three of them together that day, though, planning to put them together in a small album for both of the kids as a kind of thank-you for letting me join them. I went back to my condo after we returned to Victor's, even though at that point, I was already accustomed to spending almost every night at his place. There was no way I was going to freak the kids out by sleeping in their father's bed.

The next day, we went to brunch together at IHOP, then to the beach to collect shells before taking them to Kelli's house. She immediately seemed uncomfortable with my presence, even though Victor had prepared her by saying I would be there. I'd asked to meet her, thinking that if I were a mother and my ex-husband started dating someone, I'd certainly want to get to know the person spending time with my kids.

"What do you do for a living, Grace?" she asked me. Her voice wavered a bit as she spoke. Her tiny frame was clad in the tight black skirt and white blouse she wore to wait tables at her job. Both kids clung to her after being away from her for the weekend, and she wrapped her arms around their shoulders protectively.

"I already told you that," Victor interjected before I had a chance to answer her, his voice holding a twinge of annoyance I hadn't heard from him before.

"Do you have any kids?" Kelli continued, ignoring his remark.

I shook my head, and a brief, smug look flashed across her face. She tried to hide it with a quick smile, but it was too late—I'd seen it. I didn't understand why so many women seemed compelled to pit themselves against others who had simply chosen a different path. Stay-at-home moms against those who worked; women who breast-fed against those who chose to use formula; and my personal experience—women who had children against those who did not. Luckily, it wasn't the first time I'd faced this issue, so I gave my standard response to smooth her ruffled edges: "It must be amazing to be a mother."

She softened a little in that moment, when she

131

saw I wasn't intent on proving myself a better or more evolved woman because of my focus on my career. "It is amazing," she said, moving her gaze to Victor then, her eyes suddenly seeming darker and more intensely blue. "They're what keep me from falling apart."

Victor looked away. "We need to get going," he said. He smiled at his children and threw his arms out for one more hug. They complied, wrapping their arms around his neck until he pretended to choke. "Love you, monkeys. I'll talk with you this week."

"Love you, Dad!" Max hollered as he turned around and sped inside the house.

"Let me know how that algebra test goes, okay, kitten?" Victor said, and Ava nodded, shoving her face into his neck, inhaling deeply, as though she was trying to memorize his scent. Victor carefully extricated himself from her embrace, and she reluctantly followed her brother's path inside.

I smiled at Kelli. "It was so nice to finally meet you," I said, but she only nodded once, briefly, not taking her eyes off Victor. A moment later she whipped around and shut the door.

"Okay," I said a little shakily as we walked toward his car. "Did that go well or not? I couldn't tell."

Victor grimaced and shrugged. "Could've been worse," he said, reaching to take my hand. I opened my mouth, about to ask what he meant, but then closed it again, uncertain if at that point I really wanted to know.

Almost exactly a year later, as I heard the sharp slam of Ava's door, my gut churned thinking about the pain she and Max were facing. I was a little hurt that Victor asked me to leave the room when he told them about Kelli; I'd assumed we would do it together. It made sense, I supposed, that he wanted to do it alone, but I wished he had said something to me about it in the bedroom so I would have been prepared. So it didn't look to his children like he was dismissing me. Still, I'd heard every word from the den. They were devastated, and I had no idea how to help them through this. I had no idea how to get through it myself.

"Grace?" Victor called out from the hallway, pulling me from my thoughts. "What happened?" He must have heard Ava's door. His face appeared from around the corner a few seconds after his voice. He was pale and disheveled, as though he hadn't slept in weeks. I didn't want to tell him what his daughter had said. He had enough to handle; he didn't need a thirty-seven-year-old whining that she got her feelings hurt.

"Ava just needs some time in her room, I think," I finally answered him, sighing wearily. I couldn't believe the exhaustion rolling through my blood. Even my bones felt heavy.

His dark eyebrows furrowed and he frowned. "What did you *say* to her?"

"Nothing!" I snapped, trying to keep the defensiveness I felt out of my voice, but failing miserably. "She wants to be alone. She's traumatized, Victor. I'm not her mother and I'm certainly not a therapist. I don't know what I'm doing here."

The skin softened around his eyes and mouth. "Sorry." The word was a whisper. A ghost of an apology.

I nodded, holding my breath instead of speaking. It wasn't his fault. He didn't mean to accuse. He turned around, and a moment later, I heard another door quietly shut.

I blew out an enormous breath between pursed lips and leaned heavily against the back of the couch, pressing both of my palms to my forehead. It was obvious I was the intruder—a totally unwelcome guest. And this was supposed to be my new home. How would we build a life together after this? And then, a much worse thought, one I shoved back down the instant it echoed through my mind.

Maybe I shouldn't be here at all.

Kelli

Kelli was almost three months pregnant when she and Victor stood together in a small church and said their vows. Victor's mother, Eileen, was thrilled when Kelli asked her to be the matron of honor.

"Are you sure your parents can't come, dear?" Eileen asked as they shopped for a wedding dress. Eileen was a loving and kind woman, and while she was a little concerned that Victor and Kelli were marrying so young, she was as smitten with Kelli as her son had been. Eileen hadn't married again after Victor's father left them—she'd worked hard and raised Victor on her own.

"I'm sure," Kelli said, pulling a dress off the rack and holding it up for Eileen to see. "What about this one?"

"It's lovely, but maybe a touch too much lace here?" Eileen said, fingering the edge of the bodice. She looked at Kelli with the same warm gray eyes she'd passed on to Victor. "I just hope they don't regret missing all of this."

"They won't," Kelli said as she hung the dress back up. "We're not close." She hadn't spoken to her parents since leaving California and couldn't fathom having them in her life. They wouldn't have recognized her, anyway. She'd built a new version of herself since arriving in Seattle—bubbly and fun. She knew they'd be too much of a reminder of what went wrong, of the mistakes she'd made and the pain she'd suffered through. It was easier to simply tell people they were estranged.

"I'm sorry to hear that," Eileen said, giving Kelli a quick hug. When she pulled back, Eileen smiled at her. "Well, you have me now, so that's something."

Kelli smiled and nodded in return, imagining that Eileen would become the mother figure she'd always wanted. While it made Victor happy to see her spend time with his mom, he too expressed concern that Kelli never talked with her parents.

"They're your family," Victor said. "Don't you miss them?"

"Don't you miss your father?" Kelli retorted, knowing full well that Victor wanted nothing to do with the man who'd abandoned him. Her point hit home, and Victor let the subject go.

For the first few years, being married to Victor was everything she'd dreamed it would be. He couldn't wait to become a father. He placed headphones on Kelli's stomach every night, playing a wide variety of music for Ava—Talking Heads, Bach, and the Beatles. "We don't know what she likes yet," Victor told Kelli. "So we need to let her hear a little bit of everything."

He put his lips on her stomach, too, talking to their baby girl, telling her how much he couldn't wait to meet her. Kelli relished every kick and turn of Ava inside her body, calling her obstetrician a couple of times a week to make sure everything was okay. "She hasn't moved for almost eight hours," Kelli told the doctor once, waking him at three in the morning. "What if something's wrong with her?"

"She's sleeping, Kelli," her doctor said in a tired but patient tone. He was accustomed to the panic of first-time mothers. He knew how to talk them off the ledge. "If she doesn't move in the next couple of hours, then you can call me back, okay? Everything's fine. You have a very healthy baby girl on the way."

Kelli knew she was being paranoid, but she couldn't help it. This baby meant the world to her—being a mother, a wife, living the kind of life she'd always dreamed of having. She worked up until her eighth month, when her belly made it impossible to carry the heavy trays at the restaurant. "Is it all right if I stay home with her?" Kelli asked Victor. "Will we be okay?"

Victor smiled at her, reaching out to cup her belly. "It'll be a little tight, but I think we can make it work. I might have to work a few more shifts, though, to make ends meet."

She'd nodded, wanting nothing more than to spend hours every day cradling her baby girl, loving her, not letting her out of her sight. When her labor began, the doctor warned her it might be a long one, but Ava arrived after only four hours. Ava screamed atop Kelli's bare chest, and Kelli cried. Eileen, whom Kelli had asked to be in the room with them for the birth, wept, too, clutching Victor as they gazed upon this small miracle. They were a family.

Not long after Ava was born, Kelli found herself missing her mother; the longing to talk with her became a palpable ache in her chest. After a few weeks, she worked up the courage to call and tell her parents about their granddaughter. "She's perfect," Kelli said to her mother, who answered the phone. "Do you want—" Her voice broke on the words, so she had to start again. "Would you like to come see her?" She wondered what it would be like to share Ava with her parents. To see the joy and pride on their faces when they saw the beautiful life she had with Victor.

Her mother was quiet a moment. Kelli could hear her breathing, a lightly raspy sound, as though she was getting over a cold. "I think that might be too hard," she finally said. "And you know how your father doesn't like to travel."

As her mother spoke these words, the door that had cracked only slightly open inside Kelli slammed shut. It was a mistake to have called, a

138

mistake to believe that anything might have changed. As soon as she hung up the phone, Kelli swallowed her tears, pushed down her hurt, and turned her focus toward Ava. Toward her beautiful, perfect daughter whom Kelli knew she would love no matter what. She adored nursing, seeing her own blue eyes look back at hers, feeling the warmth of her daughter's body cocooned against her skin. Even though it thrilled Kelli that he wanted to be such an involved father, she was reluctant to let Victor change Ava's diapers or rock her to sleep. For the first year of Ava's life, Kelli was never away from her daughter —never left her with a sitter. Not even Eileen, who offered time and again to watch her grand-daughter. "You need to get out," she told Kelli. "Have an afternoon at the spa or lunch with your girlfriends."

"I can't stand to leave her," Kelli said, cupping Ava's dark head with her hand. "Why don't you stay for lunch and hold her while I make us something?" She didn't want her mother-in-law to think she didn't trust her. It wasn't that at all. There was something deeper inside Kelli that made it feel impossible to be away from Ava. Something she wasn't ready to explain.

Then one afternoon, when Ava was only thirteen months old, Victor called Kelli in a panic. "My mom had a stroke," he said. His words were jagged with tears. "I'm at the hospital."

"Oh no!" Kelli said. "Is she going to be all right?"

"No," he sobbed. "She died."

"Oh, honey," Kelli said, closing her eyes, suddenly regretting her unwillingness to let Eileen spend time alone with her granddaughter. "I'm so sorry." Hearing him weep like that unsettled Kelli. She didn't know how to manage that kind of grief—she was better practiced at pretending it didn't exist.

As Victor processed the loss of his mother, Kelli went about her days, attempting to work up the courage to chat with other mothers at the park, wanting to make friends, but she felt awkward and shy, worried they wouldn't like her because she was so young. They all seemed so confident with each other and their children—Kelli was afraid she wouldn't fit in.

Then one afternoon, a slightly chubby woman with dark messy hair sat down beside Kelli on the bench as Ava played. "I'm Diane," she said. "And that's Patrick." She pointed to a little boy a few years older than Ava, who was climbing on the monkey bars.

Kelli smiled gently and introduced herself. "We just bought a house over on Lilac Street," Diane explained. "I thought I'd bring Patrick to the park and check it out."

"Lilac Street?" Kelli said. "That's where we live. You bought the house next door to us!"

They'd only been in their house a few months; Eileen had left it to her and Victor in her will. A true gift, since there were only five years left on the mortgage.

"Well, what do you know?" Diane said. "I guess this friendship was meant to be."

Kelli smiled. Diane was plain—she didn't wear makeup and her gray sweatshirt had some kind of red stain on the arm—and Kelli liked her immediately. She reminded her a bit of Nancy, her best friend in ninth grade. She wondered briefly what had happened to Nancy but resigned herself to the idea that she'd likely never know. Nancy was another thing she had lost.

Now, though, having a friend next door helped the days go by much more quickly. Over the next few years, she and Diane spent almost every morning together, letting the children play, talking about their husbands, and gossiping about the other women they still saw at the park. Victor worked long hours at the restaurant, but Kelli did everything she could to give him a wonderful life. She cooked and cleaned and made sure his favorite beer was always in the fridge. She took long walks with Ava, staying in good enough shape to wear the lacy lingerie he loved. He adored her body; he touched her gently and was as focused on her pleasure as he was on his. They still wrapped around each other every night, murmuring about their dreams. "I think I might have an investor to open a restaurant next year," Victor told her one night when Ava was five.

"Really?" Kelli said, verging on the edge of sleep. "Who?"

Victor proceeded to tell her about a regular customer he'd gotten to know—an executive at Amazon who was looking to back a local business. "We went and looked at a space downtown today," Victor told her. "It's perfect. I can't wait to show it to you."

Kelli loved the space, too, and before she knew it, Victor had signed the paperwork and together, they began figuring out the design. It was just like they'd talked about that first night when he drove her home. They weren't just building a restaurant together—they were building a future. They were building the rest of their lives. Once Ava was in first grade the following year, Kelli imagined she'd work during the day at the Loft, helping Victor with their dream. She'd wait tables or serve as hostess. Whatever Victor wanted, she'd do. But just as Victor processed all the permits to begin renovation on the space, Kelli began feeling sick in the mornings, just as she had when she was nineteen. "Are you pregnant?" Victor asked her as Kelli stumbled out of the bathroom the morning they were supposed to meet with the general contractor.

"I think so," Kelli said, nodding. "I'm a few weeks late." She hadn't thought much of missing her period at first. She'd always been a little irregular, especially when her weight was down.

A flicker of panic sparked in Victor's gray eyes, but it disappeared just as suddenly. "Maybe it will be a boy," he said in a soft voice.

"I hope so," Kelli said just as Ava dashed into their bedroom from the hallway and jumped on the bed with Victor.

"Daddy!" she squealed, throwing her arms around his neck.

"Oomph!" Victor said as she hugged him. "Where's the fire, little girl?"

She pulled back and gave him a serious look. "There's no fire," she said. "But if there was, I call a fireman and then *stop! drop! and roll!* like my teacher taught me at school."

Victor kissed Ava's cheek. "Very good. How did you get to be such a smart girl?"

Ava shrugged. "I don't know. I just am."

Kelli smiled as she watched them together. She couldn't remember her father ever holding her so long or with so much affection. She joined them and gave Ava a kiss. "Guess what, honey?" she said. "Mama might have a baby in her tummy. You could be a big sister."

Ava was quiet a moment, then looked back and forth between her parents. "A *girl* baby?"

"Maybe," Victor said. "But it could be a boy."

"Yuck," Ava said, screwing up her pretty face. "If it is, can we take it back wherever you got it?" Kelli and Victor both laughed and curled up with their daughter on the bed.

A test soon confirmed that yes, in fact, Kelli was pregnant again. After she began feeling better, she continued to help Victor prepare the restaurant to launch. They lured Victor's best friend, Spencer, from the restaurant where they'd all worked, giving him a promotion from sous chef to executive chef, and together, the men designed the menu while Kelli worked on the décor. She was less panicky during this pregnancy. She knew what to expect. Max was born after another quick labor just a few days before the Loft was scheduled to open its doors. Money was getting tight, and Victor knew he'd have to spend more hours at the restaurant than he ever had at his previous job.

"I'll be fine," Kelli told him as he held their baby boy swaddled in a blue flannel blanket. "Diane can help out, and Ava's almost seven now. She can help, too." But then, inexplicably, right there in the hospital room, she began to cry, suddenly missing her mother more than she ever had before. She wanted a mother like Eileen—someone to nurture and help take care of her grandbabies. She wanted a mother who loved her deeply and uncontrol-lably, the way Kelli loved her own children. How could they not want to see her? Kelli wondered if they were simply relieved that she'd left so they wouldn't be reminded of what she put them through. She wondered if there'd ever be a time that they might want her back.

Seeing her tears, Victor visibly tensed. "Are you sure you'll be okay?"

A nurse entered just then, with Ava in tow. "It's just a hormone crash," she told Victor. "Totally normal." Kelli felt like it was something deeper, something more insidious, but she hoped the nurse was right.

Ava rushed over to Kelli's side, scrambling up onto the bed to cuddle her mother. "It's a girl, right?" she asked excitedly. They'd told her as soon as they'd had the ultrasound that she was going to have a baby brother, but she remained convinced that if she just hoped hard enough, she'd get the sister she wanted. "Aw, rats!" Ava said when Victor told her again that Max was a boy. She looked up to her mother, worried. "But you still love me. I'm still your favorite daughter."

"You sure are," Kelli said with a smile. She wiped at her cheeks to erase any evidence of her grief. "And Max is my favorite son."

"Huh." Ava shrugged. "What about Daddy?"

Kelli looked at Victor, still smiling. "Daddy is my favorite man in the world." Victor handed Max to her as though their son was a fragile piece of glass. The love she saw in his eyes would be enough, she decided, and at that moment, Kelli knew that after all she'd done wrong, this was as perfect a life as she would get.

Grace

After Victor went to comfort Ava and Max, I sat on the couch, staring at the wall above the fireplace, waiting. Waiting for what, I wasn't sure. Maybe to see if he asked me for help, though I didn't know what kind of help I might be. Clearly Ava wanted nothing to do with me, and on some level, I couldn't blame her. She'd just suffered the biggest loss of her life; a woman she only saw a couple of times a month certainly wouldn't be who she'd run to in search of emotional reassurance.

"Ava's always been a little hard to reach," Victor had told me one evening back in January. He'd just dropped the kids at their mother's house and I'd voiced my feeling that no matter what I did, Ava seemed determined not to like me.

"It takes time for her to warm up," Victor explained. He set his hand on top of mine. "Don't take it personally. It's about her, not you, okay? She'll get there."

I'd nodded, but really, it was impossible *not* to take it personally. Even though I reminded myself that she'd likely have treated any woman who dated her father this way, part of me worried that she sensed my trepidation around getting to know them and was simply keeping her distance.

Maybe I just needed to give her more time.

Now I lay on the couch while Victor went back and forth between his children's rooms, trying to comfort them as they both cried, and thought about the part I might play in their lives. My body tensed at the idea of being thrown into the daily demands of having them live with us—the home-work, the meals, the inevitable fighting. I wasn't sure I could do this, but I couldn't imagine running away, leaving my fiancé and his children to manage on their own in the midst of their grief. Maybe more importantly, I didn't *want* to. I wanted to be better than that.

I suddenly remembered a conversation I had with a woman I worked with in my late twenties. Her name was Barb, and she had just come back from maternity leave for her fourth child. She couldn't stop gushing about how much she loved having those three months off to be with her children.

"It doesn't overwhelm you?" I asked her. "Having four of them?" I thought about how hard it had been for me to help take care of just Sam by himself and I couldn't fathom doing it with three *other* children to worry about. In fact, the idea made me slightly queasy. I pictured babies rolling off the edge of couches, food splatters against the walls, toddlers racing out the front door and into the street before I could stop them.

Barb laughed at my question. "Sure it does.

When they're all screeching and demanding something from me and I feel like I might explode if one more of them makes a sound." She paused and gave me a dreamy smile. "But you really don't know what love is until you're a mother. You can't understand it until you've had a baby yourself, but it's the most intense feeling in the world. It makes every minute of the hard parts worth it."

I winced a little when she said this, as though she meant that a heart like mine was somehow defective because I hadn't had children. I didn't *think* of myself as less able to feel love. But her comments made me question myself and wonder if by missing out on motherhood, I was missing out on something that would make me a better person. Barb worked full-time and had four kids, so it wasn't as though she had to sacrifice her career just because she was a mother. I worked with countless women who managed their careers along with their families—it wasn't that it wasn't *possible* to do both; it was that I didn't think I *could*.

Melody seemed like the only person who really understood how I felt. "I think you either have the mommy gene or you don't," she told me once when we were discussing the loud ticking of her own biological clock. "It's probably like knowing if you're gay or not. You just *know*."

"Great," I said, laughing. "My brother got the

gay gene and I *didn't* get the maternal one. My poor mother." I knew my mom struggled with the idea that she likely was never going to be a grandmother, and ultimately, I felt responsible for depriving her of the experience. But even a severe case of daughter guilt wasn't enough to convince me I'd make a good mother. I'd also decided to try to work through my fears when I met Victor. And now that he was the only parent to Max and Ava, it wouldn't be fair for me to walk away. Not to me, not to Victor, and definitely not to the kids.

I glanced at the clock on the wall next to the bookcase. It was already ten; the hours had melted away. Victor was still with the kids—their cries were so raw, the sound reached in and squeezed the muscles in my chest. It made me think of my clients when they first came to Second Chances, grief wrenching them wide open. It was impossible to fathom the depths of their pain, and now it felt impossible to know Max and Ava's.

I rose from the couch and made my way to our bed, my body aching with fatigue. I took a long, hot shower, climbed beneath the covers, and tried to distract myself with some Jon Stewart while I waited for Victor. I didn't think I could sleep, but a while later, I woke to his gently shaking my shoulder, the television still on. "Do you mind moving to one of their rooms or on the couch?" he whispered. "I'm sorry, but I think they might sleep if they can be in bed with me."

I blinked a few times and glanced at the clock. *Midnight.* I nodded. "Of course," I said, my voice coming out like bits of gravel. I fumbled for the remote and turned off the TV. "Are you holding up okay?"

He shrugged. "I don't know." His voice was ragged. He'd been crying, too. "I'm just trying to be there for them. There's really nothing else I can do."

I righted myself on the edge of the bed and put my arms around him, resting my cheek on his shoulder. "I love you." I didn't know what else to say.

He pulled back and gave me a soft kiss. "I'm so glad you're here."

"Me too," I said, cringing a bit as I stood and made my way back to the couch, wondering if uttering those two tiny words had just turned me into a liar.

Ava

I couldn't breathe. I lay on my bed, tears slipping down my cheeks, my lungs swelling against my rib cage. *Breathe,* I told them, and they let the tiniest bit of air inside. *Mama is dead. Oh my god, she's dead.*

Daddy came into my room and lay down with

me. He pressed his body behind mine, wrapping a long arm over my chest and pushing his face into my neck. "I'm so sorry, baby girl," he whispered, his words muffled by my hair.

I shook my head, rubbing my face back and forth in my pillow. I wanted to scream at him to leave me alone, to go away and be with Grace. *Leave me alone, leave me alone.* The words beat a noisy rhythm in my head, but I couldn't say them. All I could see was Mama's face; all I could feel was the ache in my chest, the sharp stinging sensation of what seemed like a thousand tiny needles pricking my skin.

"I'm going to check on Max for a minute, okay, honey?" Dad said. His voice was frayed, like he might break down, too. I could hear my brother through the wall, the high-pitched, strangled edge of his cries. "I'll be right back."

I couldn't speak. There were no words. He shut the door quietly behind him and I opened my mouth wide, my insides twisting tighter and tighter. I wanted to scream. I felt desperate to get the pain out of my body, but no sound would come. Only tears.

She was gone. *Mama was gone.* She'd never hug me again, never tell me that I'm smart and pretty. A slideshow flashed through my brain, one image clicking after another: Mama climbing into bed with me at night, rubbing my back, whispering a lullaby in my ear to help me fall asleep. Mama standing in front of the stove, stirring the lemon chicken soup she made only when one of us was sick. Mama laughing, her mouth open wide and her blue eyes sparkling; Mama curled up in her bed, Max on one side, me on the other. Mama crying, telling us Daddy wasn't coming home anymore. Telling us we were on our own. Mama holding me this morning, saying she loved me so much.

"Mama," I cried, the word creaking out of my throat with blades attached to it, tearing at my flesh. "Please, Mama, *no*." How could she be gone? Here one minute and vanished the next? It wasn't true. It *couldn't* be. She was just *here*. She was here this *morning*. But something was wrong with her. She was dizzy and I let her convince me she was fine. I should have *known*. I should have sensed something was really wrong. There had to have been something I could have done. I could have made her go to the doctor. I could have told Diane she didn't feel well. But instead, I went to school. I didn't even kiss her good-bye when she dropped us off. I didn't want the other kids to see me and think I was a baby, like Max. Now she would never kiss me again. She wouldn't help me get ready for my first date or pick out my dress for the prom. She wouldn't take me to college or teach me how to use eyeliner like she'd promised she would once I turned sixteen. She wouldn't even *be* there when I turned sixteen. I'd be alone. *Motherless.* I felt like I was falling off a cliff. Down, down, down, flailing for a branch to hold on to. Something, *anything,* to save me.

This can't be true. The hospital made a mistake. I would have noticed if she was that sick. I would have known. I knew she wasn't happy that week, maybe even more withdrawn than usual, but she didn't look like she was *dying.* She'd been acting strange since Monday, when she picked us up from school, the black smudges beneath her eyes and red splotches across her face and neck evidence of her recent tears. Max didn't notice, but I did. The signs had become more familiar to me than her smile.

She drove us to his basketball practice at the Boys and Girls Club, and as we sat on the bleachers watching my brother run up and down the court with his friends, I took her hand in mine. "What's wrong?" I asked. She told me, sometimes, what was bothering her. That she was lonely or afraid that we didn't have enough money to pay the bills. Today, she kept quiet, but I kept prodding her.

"I just have a lot on my mind," she said. "I had a talk with your father today."

"What about?"

"Grown-up stuff," she said, and I couldn't help but roll my eyes a little. I'd been dealing with the fallout of her "grown-up stuff" with my dad for years now. Comforting her when she cried, making sure she got out of bed in the weeks after he moved out. It irritated me how she went back and forth between trying to be my mother and acting helpless. Strong one minute, then dissolving into tears the next. It made me jumpy, never knowing which version of her I'd get. I missed the mother she used to be, the one she'd been before Daddy left.

"He asked me not to tell you," she said, and my stomach flipped over. Even if she wasn't doing it on purpose, I hated it when she said things to make my dad look like the bad guy. Suddenly angry, I pulled my hand away from hers and concentrated on watching Max attempting to dribble. He bounced the ball off the tip of his tennis shoe and it shot across the court. "Don't worry, I got it!" he yelled, waving to his team-mates. He picked up the ball, tried to dribble, and bounced it off his shoe again. His coach started yelling at him to pass, but Max didn't listen. Instead, he raced after the ball, recovered it, and took a shot at the basket. "Nothing but net!" he hollered as the ball finally went through the hoop, then he did a little victory dance on the court. Watching him, I couldn't help but smile.

I wondered what it was Dad didn't want Mama to tell me, but it really could have been anything. I shot Bree a text message, "My mom's such a pain," and she texted back, "Mine 2."

Mama nudged me as I tried to text. "Hey," she said. "Are you *mad* at me?"

"No," I said, not looking at her. "Just watching Max."

"No, you're not. You're texting." She reached for my phone. "I want you to talk with me."

"*God,* Mom," I said, yanking my phone away so she couldn't get it. "I don't feel like talking, okay? Is that all *right* with you?" Her face crumpled and her eyes filled with tears, and I immediately felt horrible. I sighed and put my arm around her. "I'm sorry. I'm just tired."

She leaned her head on my shoulder and wiped her eyes. "Me too, baby girl. Me too."

Did she *know* she was sick, then? I wondered now, as I lay on my bed crying. Did she want Daddy to tell us instead of her, because he was better at handling those kinds of things? Maybe she knew she had something wrong with her as I sat with her on those hard bleachers. Maybe she wanted me to *make* her tell me, to coax it out of her like I'd done countless times before when she was upset. I'd let her down. I got irritated and ignored her. I should have told Daddy something was wrong. I should have called him and told him how upset she was, how she wasn't sleeping and how she still cried all the time. I didn't do any of this and now she was dead.

The pain suddenly inflated, pushing against the underside of my skin. I rolled around, trying to escape the mounting pressure inside me. "No, no, *no,*" I cried, and without warning, the ache exploded, slashing through the muscles in my chest and up out of my mouth. I screamed into my pillow, hot tears scalding my cheeks. I punched the wall, barely registering the hard smack of my knuckles against it, then hit it again. My cries raked against my throat, over and over, until finally, Daddy came rushing back in.

"Oh, Ava, sweetie," he said, wrapping himself back around me, trying to hold me still.

I struggled against him, wanting to pull away, but there was no point. He was too strong; he wouldn't let me go. "I'm here, honey," he said. "It's okay. Everything's going to be okay."

"No!" I screamed again, but he only held me tighter. I sobbed then, the pain seeping out of me, my body melting into my father's embrace, my mind still knowing he was wrong.

Knowing that no matter what he said, things would never be okay again.

Grace

In the morning, I didn't want to leave Victor alone to deal with the kids, but I also wasn't sure really what good—if any—I would be to him. Max had some Cocoa Puffs, but the rest of us didn't want to eat. We all carried dark luggage beneath our eyes and no one said much. Ava wouldn't even look at me. The kids watched noisy and distracting cartoons in the den, while Victor and I took some time to talk in our room. We sat on the bed, his hands wrapped around mine.

"I'm sorry I snapped at you last night," he said.

"It's okay." I gave him a tired smile. "Is there anything I can do?"

"I don't know." He sighed, and his eyes filled with tears. "The kids are just annihilated, Grace. I feel so helpless. I have to be here for them, but I also need to get over to their house and get them clothes, plus make all the arrangements. Kelli didn't want a funeral, but I was thinking we could just have a small gathering here at the house, maybe on Thursday? I also have to make sure the restaurant is covered for the next week, at least . . ."

His voice held a slightly panicked edge, so I held my hand up to stop him. "I can get their things. The kids need you here more than they need me." *Or want me.* I thought of Ava's angry words from the night before.

He looked doubtful. "Are you sure? It's not going to upset you?"

"I don't think so. Can you ask what they might want me to grab? Favorite clothes or whatever?" He nodded, and I felt a twinge of relief at having been given something to do. A thought struck me. "Have you called her parents?"

Victor nodded. "From the hospital, last night." He sighed. "I'm not sure her mother fully understood what I was saying. She didn't sound right, you know? Confused."

"Like how, confused?"

"Like not-mentally-all-there confused. Scattered confused. They're in their late seventies, I think, so maybe she's got some dementia or something?" I nodded, and he went on. "Anyway, they're not coming."

My jaw dropped. "Really?" He nodded again. I knew Kelli was estranged from her parents, but I still had a hard time trying to imagine the kind of people who'd never met their own grandchildren and now wouldn't give their only daughter enough respect to come say good-bye. "What *happened* between them and Kelli?" I asked. I'd never had reason to be curious about this issue before, but it suddenly seemed important to know. "What could have been so bad?"

"She didn't like to talk about it," Victor said with a heavy sigh. "They were pretty uptight and Kelli was more of a free spirit. It's what I liked about her."

My stomach twisted hearing him say this, but I ignored it as best as I could. He had been *married* to her; at one time, he loved her the same way he loved me now. He would need to talk about his feelings for her, and I needed to be a big enough person to understand this. I shook my head and tried to focus on what was important. "Okay, but it's their *daughter*."

"If they didn't make the trip when she was alive, why would they when she . . ." He swallowed, visibly choking on his next words. "When she's not." He cleared his throat.

"I guess so," I said. "But it's still pretty sad." Both sets of my grandparents lived on the East Coast, so Sam and I didn't get to see them much when we were growing up, but they always sent us birthday cards and Christmas presents. I always knew they loved me.

Victor nodded. "Anyway . . . how are *you* doing?" he asked, searching my face with his clear gray eyes. It seemed like such a small question for the enormity of our circumstances.

I shrugged and gave him a brief smile. "It doesn't matter how I'm doing. How are you? How are the kids?" I paused, knowing he was looking for a better answer than that. The problem was, I didn't have one. Everything inside me felt unhinged. I took a deep breath before speaking again. "I don't think it's easy for any of us right now. It's just devastating all around."

Victor sighed and took my hands in his. "I don't want you to be devastated. This was supposed to be such a huge weekend for us. Telling the kids about our engagement. And now . . ."

"Now things are different," I finished for him.

"But we're still engaged. We just don't tell the kids yet. That's all. We help them get through the roughest part of this first."

"That shouldn't be your job," he said quietly, looking back at me. "Listen. I know this wasn't part of our plan. The kids with us full-time, I mean. I'm a little overwhelmed by the prospect myself, so I'd understand if you didn't want to do it." His voice was low, his words deliberate.

I swallowed hard, wondering if my fear and confusion about the situation was obvious despite how hard I'd worked to disguise it. I decided the best thing I could do was be honest. "It is over-whelming. And I'd be lying if I said I wasn't a little apprehensive about dealing with all of this."

He suddenly looked scared, too, and in that moment, it felt like my choice was made. There was no way I could leave him. Not now. I reached a hand up and smoothed his hair back from his face. "I know you're tough, honey, but you can't be the rock for everyone. I'm here for you. I'm not going anywhere."

"Thank you for that," Victor said, and his eyes grew dark. "But I need to be very clear with you about something. You don't have to worry about taking care of the kids. They're *my* kids. *My* responsibility. Our life will be different because they're living here, of course. But our relation-ship—you and me—doesn't have to change.

Because I want you to be my partner, not their parent. Okay?"

I nodded once, briefly, allowing myself to become buoyed by his words. We kissed, and he went to talk with the children while I showered and dressed. I texted Melody and asked her if she could meet me at Kelli's to help me pack up the kids' things, and she immediately shot back an "Absolutely. Send me the address." I complied and then walked down the hallway to the kitchen, where Victor handed me two sheets of paper listing the things Max and Ava wanted me to bring: *Purple radio by bed,* Ava had written. *Orange paper clips. Conditioner in green bottle in the shower.* And then she went on to detail the multitude of clothing I would need to pack up. Max's list was easier: *Jeans,* it read. *Shirts with stuff on them. Red flashlight and my Iron Man Halloween costume. My mom's blue blanket off her bed.*

"Take as long as you need," Victor told me. "Call me if you have any questions."

My mother had left me a message earlier, returning my call from yesterday, so I slipped on my headset and called her back as I drove toward Kelli's house. She was likely in her garden, where she'd spent most of her time since she retired ten years ago and moved about ninety miles north of Seattle to Bellingham. I pictured the last time I had seen her in the small but lush yard outside of her tiny one-bedroom house—a beach shack on Lake Whatcom with white-washed cedar clap-boards. It was back in early September, at the beginning of a beautiful Indian summer, and the morning sun lit up the startling autumnal hues in her yard. At sixty-two, she was really just starting to show her age in the slight sag of the skin beneath her chin and the pronounced lines around her eyes and mouth. Still, she was a beautiful woman. Her frizzy reddish-gray curls were hidden beneath a wide-brimmed straw hat. She wore what she called her "mom uniform": stretchy blue jeans with an elastic waistband, a pink cotton button-down shirt, and lime-green work gloves.

I thought I could drive as I talked with her, but as the phone rang, it suddenly struck me that Ava would never be able to call Kelli like this in a moment of need. She could never reach out for her mother's comfort again. I had to pull over and park when she answered the phone, crying when I heard her voice.

"Mama," I said, and the tears started to fall. I couldn't remember the last time I'd used that particular endearment. She was always Mom or Mother. But not now. Not today.

"Sweetie, what's wrong?"

My throat convulsed as I tried to speak. "Kelli . . . Victor's ex-wife . . . she died."

"Oh *no!*" she said. "What *happened?*"

I filled her in on the little I knew. "I'm so worried she killed herself. Victor said she was pretty upset when he told her we're engaged."

"Grace," my mother said in a firm but gentle tone. "Honey. Don't get ahead of yourself. Okay? Can you promise me that?"

"Okay." She was right. We didn't have all the facts yet. It was silly to draw any conclusions at this point.

"What about the kids? How are *they* handling it?" She'd only met Max and Ava once, but I knew she looked forward to the possibility of becoming a surrogate grandmother when Victor and I decided to get married.

I told her what Ava said to me, tearing up again as I spoke. "She *hates* me."

"I don't think that's true, sweetie. But her heart is broken. And she's only thirteen. Think about how *you* were at that age."

"When you had Sam." I sniffled and wiped beneath my eyes with the back of my hand, happy I'd thought better of putting on any makeup.

"That's right. And that was hard enough for you to deal with. Put yourself in Ava's place. She's lashing out because she's hurting, Gracie. She's just lost the most important person in her *life*."

"I know. I totally get that. And I'm just *devastated* for her. And for Max, too. But I just don't know if I'm going to be any good for them, you know? What if I say or do the wrong thing and make things *worse?*" She didn't say anything, allowing me the space to go on. "I'm not used to feeling so powerless. I *manage* crisis situations—that's my job. And there's nothing I can do to manage this. They don't even *want* me there."

"You never know. Maybe that will change. You've told me before that most of your clients aren't always emotionally ready to accept the help you offer them, but they eventually come around, right?"

"Right, but . . ." I didn't know how to articulate my fears, to explain how deep they went within me. How fundamentally ill equipped I felt around children, even after spending ten years helping to take care of Sam.

We were both quiet a moment, listening to each other breathe. My tears began to slow down, and finally, she spoke again, so quietly I barely heard her. "Do you regret that you moved in with Victor?"

Leave it to my mother to ask the one question I didn't want to answer. Maybe she could read my mind or had some kind of other motherly psychic ability I wasn't aware of. I shook my head, even though she couldn't see me, pressing my lips together before speaking. "We were supposed to tell the kids about the engagement this weekend."

"I'm *so* sorry this is happening, sweetie."

"Me too." I half snorted, stifling another sob. "I hid the ring in my purse. This is so not how I pictured celebrating my engagement."

"Nothing is perfect, Grace," she said with a heavy sigh. "If there's one thing I learned being married to your father, it's that sometimes, you just have to make the best of the hand you're dealt."

He was late again. My eighth-grade graduation dance was about to start at the school gym, and if I was going to catch the last bus to get there, I needed to leave in the next ten minutes or I wasn't going to make it. I paced in our living room, waiting for my dad to get home from his shift at the garage. My hair was curled, my bangs were sprayed, and I was wearing a pair of acid-wash Guess jeans I'd found at Goodwill the week before. My mom had to work, so I had made sure that morning that my dad knew he needed to be home no later than six thirty.

"Of course," he said, giving my cheek a soft pinch with grease-stained fingers. "Don't want my girl to miss the big dance."

Now my baby brother, Sam, cooed at me from his playpen by the window, sucking on a bottle and staring up at the mobile that turned in lazy circles above him. He had been born seven months ago, and at the time, I was still a little horrified by the fact that my mother had gotten pregnant in the first place. I knew about sex, having read the educational book she had surreptitiously left on my bed when I was nine. This book also explained in great detail the unexpected hair that would soon sprout on my body, as well as the strange but imminent monthly event that somehow translated into my becoming a woman. I found the pencil sketches of boys' erections highly disturbing, and for months after seeing them, I tried not to glance at any of my male friends' crotches on the playground, lest I witness any such horror in person.

She told me about the baby after her first trimester, and six months after that, I held Sam in my skinny, shaking arms. With his cone-shaped head and swollen, slanted eyelids, he looked like a tiny purple, wrinkly alien. I had a hard time blanking out the fact that he'd shot out of my mother's vagina, a feat I imagined was akin to pulling a pot roast through one of my nostrils.

"You can help me with him," she said to me in the hospital. Her reddish curls were matted around her head like a wild woman's and she looked pale and weak, more tired than I'd ever seen. Her green eyes were half-closed. "Babysit when I'm not home."

I'd nodded at the time, my own red waves bouncing. I was excited, at first, at the prospect of helping my mother, completely unaware just how many hours a week my "helping" would translate into. I didn't know how to picture myself taking care of this mewling little creature; I'd always had more interest in my father's collection of Matchbox cars than the baby dolls people bought me—dolls that usually played the role of an enormous evil toddler who terrorized the racecar drivers on the speedway, threatening to smash them with her giant plastic feet. But I knew that after a month off, my mom planned to return to work at Macy's to help supplement my dad's job as a mechanic, so in the meantime, I enrolled in a Red Cross babysitting course. I learned CPR, the Heimlich maneuver, how to handle minor injuries, and techniques for remaining calm in case of emergency. The other girls in the class seemed to be taking it lightly—they were taking care of other people's children as a hobby, and for money. Not me. I studied my notes diligently—this was my baby brother I was going to be responsible for. I passed my final test with a perfect score.

During the day my mom took care of Sam, but most afternoons, as soon as I got home from school at three thirty, she had to leave for work. "I wish we could afford to hire someone else," she said, "but we just can't. Not now. I'm relying on you, okay? You can do it. Your dad will be home at six, and his bottles are in the fridge."

But tonight, it was already six forty-five and my dad wasn't home. I grabbed the phone and dialed the garage again. It rang and rang, until the answering machine picked up. That didn't mean he wasn't there. He could have been stuck under a car, trying to fix it so the customer wouldn't have to go the whole weekend without anything to drive. He could have been on his way, slowed down by traffic.

He could have been at the bar, playing poker.

"Hey, Gracie Mae," he'd say on the nights he came through the front door on time. He'd walk over to the refrigerator and pop the cap off a bottle of Budweiser. If Sam was awake and in his playpen, he'd lift him up, kiss him on his head, then proceed to the den, where he'd plop himself down in his brown leather recliner to holler out wrong answers for *Wheel of Fortune* and *Jeopardy!*

Other nights, he didn't come home until I'd given Sam his bath and gotten him down to sleep all on my own. "Stopped for a beer with Mike and Rodney," he'd say, reeking of cigarette smoke and fried food. "How'd our little man do?"

"Fine," I would always answer, keeping my eyes on my homework, knowing that stopping for a beer with his friends meant poker at the bar, and poker at the bar meant a fight with my mother later about how much money he'd lost. I tried not to listen to them from my bedroom, but the walls of our small house were thin.

"You have to stop this," my mother said in a low, angry tone after she came home. "You know we're barely making it. Since Sam was born, our health insurance alone is more than half your paycheck."

"I'm just blowing off a little steam," my dad said. "I'll stop, I promise." And for a while, he would. He'd come home every night, help me with the baby so I could finish my homework or even talk on the phone with a friend. But one night back at the poker table was all it took to lose enough to make my mother angry again, and for me to have it cemented in my mind that my mother had three children, not two.

I sighed now and didn't leave a message. That was it. He wasn't going to get here in time for me to catch the bus. I didn't have any other way to get to the school. All of the other kids had parents who drove them there, and the few friends I had I wasn't close enough to to call and ask for a ride. I wanted to go to the dance so badly my body almost ached. I wanted to stand next to Jeffrey Barber in the dark and wait for the DJ to play "Careless Whisper," then "accidentally" bump into him. I imagined his black curls and dark blue eyes, his smile as he would take my hand and lead me to the dance floor. I imagined his hands on my waist, the smell of his neck. I imagined what his lips might feel like on mine and every inch of my body grew warm.

"Dad, where *are* you?" I said aloud, to no one, then looked over at Sam, who was beginning to gurgle in a way that I recognized as the precursor to his starting to cry. Despite everything I'd learned about babies, I always felt a little scared when I was home alone with him, but I knew I didn't have a choice in the matter. He was my family, and it was my job to help take care of him.

I dialed the women's department at Macy's and asked the salesclerk who answered if my mother was around. "Gracie?" she said when she came on the line, the word coming out in a hurried breath. "Is Sam okay? What happened?" I wasn't supposed to call her while she was working unless it was an emergency.

"He's fine," I said. Across the room, as though on cue to prove me wrong, Sam started to cry. "But Dad's not home yet. I'm going to miss the dance."

"Oh, Grace. You scared me." She exhaled a long, tired-sounding breath. "Did you call the garage?"

"Yes. He's not answering."

"I'm sorry, sweetie. I know you really wanted to go." She paused a moment, listening. "Is that Sam?"

"Yesss," I said with a sigh, drawing out the word. *Who else would it be?*

"Why is he crying?"

"How should *I* know?"

"Watch your tone, young lady."

"Sorry," I mumbled, and then explained. "He just finished his bottle. He probably needs to be changed." While I'd learned the hard way to cover his tiny penis with another diaper before taking away the old one, changing Sam was far from one of my favorite responsibilities. I couldn't believe that something so small could produce something so completely disgusting—and so *much* of it. The pitch of his cries suddenly grew louder and a deep-seated, panicky ache clutched my insides. *I don't want to do this. Please. It's too hard. I don't want to be here.* "Can't you come home?" I said to my mother, pleading. "Can't you pretend you're sick or something?"

"I wish I could, but I have to work. There's a sale tonight and I'm the manager. I can't leave. You know that."

I was silent, feeling my blood rush in my ears. "I *hate* him," I finally whispered. She knew I meant my father. This was far from the first time he had let me down, and I doubted it would be the last.

"No, you don't," Mom said. "You're just disappointed." She paused. "I'm sorry, but I have to go. I'll talk with your dad tomorrow, okay? We'll get it figured out. Please take good care of your brother. I'm counting on you."

I hung up, staring at the phone, listening to the increasing pitch of my brother's wails. "This isn't fair," I said. "I *hate* it." Sam cried louder, and I took a deep breath, then made my way slowly over to him, hoping I could find a way to take his sadness away.

Ava

I wanted this to be like any other Saturday morning at my dad's house, knowing I'd go home the next day and see my mother. But it wasn't like any other day. Max and I had woken up in our Dad's bed, his long body in between us, and I felt the crackle of dried tears on my cheeks. *Mama,* I thought, and started to cry. It didn't feel real. I kept looking at Dad's front door, thinking she might come walking through it. My body ached with a strange pain—my muscles were tingly and tight beneath my skin. It was a feeling I'd never had before, a sensation I didn't know how to name. It almost was like I was floating just outside my body, tethered to it somehow but likely to drift off if I found a way to let go.

I didn't know anyone who didn't have a mother. A few kids at school were adopted and didn't know the mothers who'd given birth to them, but none of them didn't have a mother at all. Mama was who I went to for almost everything. When Bree made me mad or I felt like a teacher was being unfair. Who would I go to now? I closed my eyes and tried to hear her voice in my head—to remember what it felt like to have her thin arms around me and what she looked like when she laughed. All I could see was the image of her crying. All I could feel was the emptiness surrounding me now.

I thought about how she used to take me to the library every Saturday, letting me run my fingers over the spines of books, as though I could feel which stories needed a good home. She always checked out a stack of books, too, with titles like *The Price of Love* or *Forbidden Fruit* and with half-naked people on the covers. She didn't allow me to read them, but lately, when she wasn't home, I'd sneak into her bedroom and flip through the pages, blushing as I read the steamier chapters. Mama believed in love. She had loved our dad so much and I knew she wished he'd never left. I wished he'd never left, too. If he hadn't, maybe Mama would still be alive.

I sat on the couch with my brother, staring at the TV. It felt weird to just sit there watching cartoons, but we didn't know what else to do. Grace left to go pick up some of our stuff from Mama's house and my dad came into the den and turned the television off. When Dad sat down next to us, Max started crying almost right away, a quiet but blubbery noise. I reached over and took his hand in mine.

"I love you guys, you know that, right?" Dad said. He looked like he'd grown more lines on his face overnight and he hadn't showered or shaved. I wasn't used to seeing him with so many whiskers on his face. There were a lot of white ones; it made him look old. For some reason, that made me afraid.

Max and I both nodded. We had both cried so much last night, I couldn't believe it when more tears came now. My stomach hurt and my eyes were so swollen, it was almost hard to see out of them. Crying made it worse.

"I miss Mama," Max said. His voice crackled. "I don't want her to be dead."

"Me neither, buddy," Dad said. "I wish I could change it, but I can't. We'll just have to stick together and find a way through, okay? I'm not going anywhere. I'll be right here for you."

You left before, I thought. *You left and Mama couldn't handle it. You got a new life and a new girlfriend and now she's dead.* Panic suddenly gripped me. What if he died, too? What if he didn't want us to live there? What if *Grace* didn't want us? I felt wobbly inside, balancing atop the thinnest of threads, terrified I might make a wrong move and lose my father, too. Letting go of his hand, I wrapped my arm around my brother and he leaned against me, still crying softly.

"Ava?" Dad reached over and wiped my cheek with his fingers. "Do you remember anything from yesterday morning?"

I sniffled. "Like what?" Everything seemed blurry in my head, like a movie set on fast-forward. I wanted to press pause and then rewind so we could go back to yesterday, when Mama was still here.

"I don't know." He paused. "I guess if something happened that seemed out of the ordinary. If your mom acted differently than she normally would."

The moment she threw her palm flat against the wall flashed in my mind. "She got dizzy," I said. "She said it was because she had too much coffee, but I thought it was because she hasn't been sleeping. Or eating." I searched my dad's face. "Can that make you dizzy?"

He nodded. "Sometimes."

"What did the doctors say happened?" I asked, the muscles in my stomach twisting tighter with every breath I took. More tears swelled in my chest, trying to fight their way out.

Dad looked at Max and then back and me. "They're not really sure. All we know is that she lay down in her bed and then . . . her heart stopped."

"Did she have a heart 'ttack?" Max asked, sounding much younger than seven. He only talked like a baby when he was really upset.

"I don't know, Maximilian. I wish I did."

We were quiet a moment, then Max spoke again in a tiny voice. "What's going to happen to us now? Where will we go?"

Dad visibly tensed for a second, then relaxed.

"You'll stay here, of course. I'll take care of everything, I promise."

"What about the rest of my stuff?" Max asked.

"Who cares about your stuff, dummy," I snapped, pulling away from him, and my dad put his hand on my forearm, squeezing lightly. "Ava," he said.

I wouldn't look at him. If I did, I might cry again. I didn't want to be like her. I didn't want to cry too much. I gave him what I knew he wanted. "Sorry, Max. I didn't mean it." My dad offered me a grateful look, then turned to my brother.

"We'll get the rest of your stuff, kiddo. Maybe not all of it at once, but the important things, okay?"

"Okay," Max said, easily satisfied.

I swallowed. "What about Mom's stuff?"

Dad paused again, considering this. "I'll probably box most of it up and keep it in storage for you two, when you're older. Does that sound like a good idea?"

Both Max and I nodded, even though I couldn't imagine putting away all of Mama's things in a cold, dark storage room. I wanted to have them with me. I wanted to smell her perfume and wear her clothes; I wanted to wrap myself in the blanket she used to cuddle with me under on the living room couch. *I want her not to be dead.*

Dad smiled. "Okay then. That's what we'll do."

I stood up. "I'm going to my room." My dad

stood up, too, and Max turned the TV back on and picked up the controller for the Xbox. Dad and I walked together through the kitchen, where he pulled me into a long hug and kissed the top of my head, just like Mama used to. I felt my body tensing, wanting to pull away, but I wasn't sure why. I wasn't sure of anything.

In my bedroom, I picked up my cell phone and checked the text messages. There were six from Bree, asking why I had to leave class. I didn't know how I could say the words out loud. *My mother is dead.* I tried it once, whispering the words, and immediately felt like I was going to throw up, even though I hadn't eaten anything since the candy bar I'd sneaked from my closet yesterday afternoon.

I thought about what Dad had said—about how she might have died. There was no way she had a heart attack. She was only thirty-three. She didn't smoke cigarettes or eat too much fat, which is what our health teacher, Mrs. Goldberg, said were two of the big reasons people's hearts stopped working. She didn't go to the gym, but she said she ran around at the restaurant so much and didn't need to. She was skinny, but she always told us she was healthy.

But she was sad. She cried almost every day. She was losing too much weight. Last month Mrs. Goldberg had talked with us about how to look out for signs of depression in our friends and when to tell an adult if we thought that person might be in serious trouble. *Who do we tell when it's an adult who's in trouble?* I longed to ask. *Who do we tell when it's our mother?* I should have found someone. I should have done something to help her. I thought if I just did everything to keep her happy—if I helped clean the house and take care of Max and write out the checks for the bills—she would be okay. I didn't know there was something really wrong with her. Something bad enough to take her away.

My phone buzzed on the nightstand and my breath caught in my throat. I grabbed it and saw Bree's name on the caller ID. I let it ring two more times, almost letting it go to voice mail, before I decided to answer.

"Where the h-e-double-hockey-sticks have you *been?*" Bree demanded. "Why didn't you answer my texts?" My mouth was so dry, I had to swallow a couple of times to see if I could speak. "Ava? Are you okay? What's going on?"

"My mom . . ." I began, and then the tears came again. I only used the name "Mama" at home; it was what she liked us to call her. I called her "Mom" to everyone else. Unlike Max, I wasn't a baby. I swallowed, sniffed, and spoke again, barely a whisper. "My mom died."

"*What?!*" Bree said. "You're kidding, right?" I didn't say anything. "Oh, shit," she continued. "Oh shit, shit, shit. Of course you're not kidding. I'm sorry. That's like, the worst thing I've ever heard." She paused. "What *happened?*"

"I don't really know," I said, my voice tight as I tried not to lose it completely. "And my dad is acting all weird, like he isn't telling us something, and Grace is here and I *hate* her!" I let loose a shuddering sob and Bree remained silent until I spoke again. "I can't believe she's dead. I don't want her to be dead." Maybe if I kept saying the word, the fact that it was true would sink in.

"What do you think your dad isn't telling you?" Bree asked. Her voice was quiet, and for some reason, because she was calm, I felt the tiniest bit calmer, too.

I sniffled. "I'm not sure. I just feel it, you know?" It was funny how sometimes, when people talked, you could still hear all the words not being said. Sometimes they were louder than the ones that came out of their mouths.

Bree sighed. "Yeah, I know. Like when my dad was going to leave right after Christmas, and he and my mom pretended to be all in love in front of me when we opened our presents." She snorted softly. "Like we couldn't tell it was a big, stupid act."

"Right," I said. But I didn't feel like hearing about Bree and her family. I reached for a tissue from the box next to my bed so I could blow my nose. I sat on the edge of my bed, concentrating on the dark purple stitching of my comforter, staring at it until the pattern became wavy and I had to blink. "I've gotta go."

"Ava?"

"Yeah?"

"I'm really sorry about your mom."

"Thanks," I said, and hung up the phone.

Grace

As I neared Kelli's house, and after talking with my mom, I couldn't help but think more about my father. We'd never been especially close, even before Sam came along. He wasn't ever the kind of dad to snuggle with me on the couch or read to me, and it was my mom who taught me how to tie my shoes and ride my bike. He was the kind of dad who seemed bewildered that he was married with two kids—that he'd somehow stumbled into a life he never wanted to live. His body was there, but his mind was not; I'd always sensed that he would have preferred to be anywhere but with our family.

But however rocky our parents' marriage was, the end of it had shocked both my brother and me. I guess we assumed that after so many years of putting up with Dad, Mom had grown too weary and accustomed to his bad behavior to change anything between them. So even when she called me and said, "That's it. I'm done. Your great-aunt Rowena died and left me enough to retire on, and I'm not going to let your father piss it away on the poker table," there was a part of me that didn't believe her. She'd stayed with him through so much. But then she hired a lawyer, and Dad didn't know what hit him. He left the marriage quietly, as though he had expected the end would happen all along. He used the small payout from the inheritance Mom had received to immediately move to Las Vegas, where he eventually suffered a stroke and died a few years ago. Since I barely spoke with him, when he died the sense of loss was vague, like the misplacement of a pair of earrings you liked but had rarely pulled out of your jewelry box to wear.

Melody's car was already parked in front of Kelli's house when I pulled up. She sat on the front porch, clad in Levi's, a snug-fitting tie-dyed T-shirt, and running shoes. Her long blond hair was pulled into an *I Dream of Jeannie* ponytail on top of her head. She trotted down the steps and hugged me when I approached, and I found myself tearing up again.

Melody pulled back and searched my face with kindness in her brown eyes. "How *are* you?"

I shrugged. "Sad. Confused. A little pissed off."

She smiled. "Sounds about right. I was up baking all night," she said. "I had to do something. I was so worried about you. And the kids. I made two pound cakes and six dozen cookies. Oh, and three lasagnas."

"Good lord. What are you going to do with all that?"

"Send it home with you so you can put them in your freezer. You'll need something to feed the kids over the next couple of weeks. Victor's going to have too much going on and lord knows *you're* not going to cook."

I stuck my tongue out at her, grateful for her ability to make me smile. She glanced down at my left hand and immediately squealed. "Oh my god, let me see!" She snatched my hand and pulled it close to her face so she could admire the ring. I'd put it on in the car after talking with my mom, wanting to show it to my best friend. "Wow. Totally impressive rock, Mr. Hansen. I love the baguettes framing the center stone like that. It's gorgeous."

I allowed myself to feel a moment of giddiness in seeing my friend's reaction to my engagement. "It *is* gorgeous, isn't it? I love it."

"As well you should. That, my friend, is a ring from a man who obviously adores you. I will *attempt* to not be wickedly jealous." Melody was single but determined to get married and have at least two kids before she turned forty. She read countless how-to-find-your-soul-mate self-help books and tirelessly revised her online dating profile to try to attract the man who would make her rampant desire for motherhood come true. She scoured *What to Expect When You're Expecting* and parenting magazines so she would be prepared to immediately launch herself into the job when the right man came along. And yet, she didn't find him. She prepared for first dates the way athletes train for the Olympics, but those dates rarely blossomed into anything more than a temporary fling. I knew she was happy for me when I met Victor, but a little envious, too, the same way a friend who is trying to lose weight is happy when her best friend drops twenty pounds while still quietly bemoaning the wide span of her own hips. We were good enough friends that we could talk about how she felt and not let it become a problem between us, which was a relief. As a transplant to Seattle and with her parents still living in the small Iowa town where she grew up, I was the closest thing to family Melody had. She often spent the holidays with us and Sam had affectionately dubbed her his "bonus sister." I would never have done anything to hurt her.

Standing in Kelli's driveway, she winked at me now, then frowned a little as she watched me slip the ring off and put it back in the safety of my zippered wallet. "It's not about the ring," I said, hoping I sounded more convincing than I felt.

"Damn right, it's not," she agreed. A moment later, we ascended the front steps, and I was just putting the key Victor had given me into the lock when a woman's voice called out.

"Excuse me," she said. "What do you think you're doing?" I turned my head to see a short, slightly heavy woman with shoulder-length light brown hair chugging her way across the lawn. She wore jeans, a purple University of Washington sweatshirt, and tan slippers edged in faux fur.

I lifted a hand in greeting, realizing instantly who this was from the kids' description of their mother's best friend. *The woman who found Kelli.* "You must be Diane," I said. "I'm Grace, and this is Melody. We're just here to pick up a few things for the kids."

She looked me up and down, not even pretending to be subtle about it. "Grace," she repeated as she came to a stop at the bottom of the stairs. I assumed that since she and Kelli were friends, she'd heard my name at least a time or two, perhaps followed by a few choice descriptive expletives. After our first meeting, Kelli and I hadn't exactly bonded; her distaste for my presence in Victor's life continued to be an almost palpable thing. I'd done my best to ignore it on the rare occasions when we had to interact, but she hadn't made it easy.

Diane huffed a little bit now, trying to catch her breath. "Where's Victor?"

"He's with his children," Melody said, and I hoped that only I could hear the touch of annoyance in her words. Melody had a low tolerance for people who had a hard time grasping the obvious. I could almost hear the other—unspoken—sentence in Melody's head: *Where the hell* else *would he be? The Bahamas?*

"Oh. Okay." The edges of Diane's face softened, and I noticed that her eyes were red rimmed and swollen. *She's just lost her best friend,* I reminded myself. *She's in pain, too.* She sighed, then continued speaking. "I just saw you sitting out here and then the both of you trying to get into the house and I didn't know what to think." She tucked her hair behind her ears. "How are they?"

"Pretty much in shock, I think," I said. "Trying to understand what exactly happened."

Diane cocked a single eyebrow. "Didn't the doctors say anything to Victor?"

I wondered if Diane knew something we didn't. "They told him about the pills by her night-stand—"

"What?" Melody exclaimed, and I realized I hadn't known this when we'd talked last night, before Victor got home from the hospital.

"She took those for anxiety," Diane said quickly. "The prescription could have just run out. It doesn't mean anything."

"You're right," I said, resting my hand on Melody's arm, hoping she'd realize I didn't want

185

to get into this particular discussion right now. I'd tell her about my concerns later, not in front of Diane. "It doesn't. We're hoping the doctors will figure out exactly what happened, but Victor decided it was better not to mention the bottle or the pills to the kids."

Diane nodded slowly. "I suppose that's best." She paused. "Kelli told me you and Victor got engaged."

"We did."

She raised her eyebrows. "That was quick, wasn't it? You two haven't even been together a year yet."

I opened my mouth to respond, feeling my cheeks get hot, but Melody spoke for me. "Um, *actually* they've been together *over* a year. *Not* that it's really your business." I shot my friend a warning look.

"Sorry." Diane looked back and forth between Melody and me. "It's just that Kelli was pretty upset when Victor just dropped the news on her like that."

"I don't think he *dropped* it on her," I said, doing my best to keep my voice even. "He—*we* thought it would better if she knew before the kids. In case they had questions."

She tucked her hair behind her ears. "Have you *told* the kids?" I shook my head, hoping we were on the tail end of this conversation, but then she spoke again. "Will there be a funeral?"

"Just a small gathering at our house, I think. Maybe on Thursday. Victor said she wanted to be cremated."

"Well, let me know if I can do anything. She was a good friend to me." Her eyes filled until she blinked the tears away, then she glanced up to the front door. "I could help you pack up the kids' stuff, if you want. I know what they like, for the most part."

I held up the notes Victor had given me. "I think we're set. They made me a list." I smiled at her, trying to imagine how I'd feel if Melody had died. My stomach flipped over at the thought. "But thank you. I appreciate it. And I'm really so very sorry for your loss." I reached out and squeezed her arm this time.

"Thank you," she said with obvious surprise. She nodded again, a slightly pinched look on her face, then gestured toward the tan house next door. "That's me, if you change your mind."

"Thanks," Melody said, and we finally went our separate ways. We stepped through the door-way, and while I'd been to Kelli's house several times, it felt foreign to me now. Empty and sad, as though it somehow sensed that she'd never be returning. The entryway was thick with the scent of vanilla—Victor had told me about Kelli's tendency to overuse plug-in air fresheners, to the extent that he eventually developed allergies to them. Sunlight slid through the cracks in the drapes, highlighting the dust motes in the air.

"Well, this is slightly creepy," Melody said, glancing around the living room, a small space littered with kids' clothes, toys, and stacks of magazines. "Knowing she's never coming back here." She shuddered. "What do you think Victor will do with the house?"

"It was his mom's, but I imagine he'll still need to sell it." I took a deep breath. "We should get to work. Victor said there should be suitcases in the hall closet." We proceeded to our right, easily found several large black suitcases, and decided that each of us would pack up a child's room. "Can you do Ava's? I feel like she'll be happier if it's not me." I explained what Ava had said to me the night before and Melody sighed.

"Poor kid. She's angry and you're an easy target. She can't be mad at her mom for dying, so she's mad at you for still being alive. I think if she didn't care about you, she wouldn't trust you with *any* of her feelings, so in a way, it's a good sign for your relationship with her."

"I hadn't thought about it like that," I said, the weight in my chest suddenly feeling a tiny bit lighter. "You should totally be a therapist; you know that, right?"

She smiled, and we went our separate ways. Max's room smelled exactly like the one at our house did—eau de musty sweat socks. His walls were painted a bright blue and were littered with

Iron Man posters. He had an elaborate Lego city built in the corner and a gaming system hooked up to a small television at the foot of his race-car bed. I opened his dresser drawers, only to find bulging piles of unfolded and mismatched clothes —I'm sure being a single mom, Kelli chose to not make this a battle she waged with her son. I couldn't say I blamed her.

Now I sifted through each of Max's drawers, folding and packing as much as I could in the suitcase. I found his Iron Man costume in a wrinkled mound on the floor next to his bed—I wondered if he liked to sleep in it. I grabbed handfuls of underwear and a huge pile of mismatched socks and threw them in, too. His red flashlight was under the bed, something that I discovered only after crawling around and looking in every other nook and cranny of his room, including the back of his closet. I was still reaching for it, my butt in the air, when Melody spoke.

"I think I've got everything Ava wanted," she said, and then, seeing me on the floor, asked, "What the hell are you doing under there?"

I jerked back, knocking my wrist on the bottom of the bed frame as I pulled out the flashlight and held it high for her to see. I stood up and sighed. "Boys are messy."

She laughed, then paused. "Have you and Victor talked at all about what's going to happen with the kids?"

"This morning, a little bit." I told her what Victor had said and my promise to be there to support him.

She gave me a sidelong glance. "That's a lot to take on, Grace."

"I know," I said, sighing and lifting my eyes back to hers. "But what am I supposed to do? Abandon them? I won't do that. Not to mention the fact that I'm totally in love with Victor." My voice shook with the threat of tears.

She nodded but didn't appear entirely convinced. "Okay. Then I'll help however I can. Take step-parenting classes with you. Or go to a support group."

"Do they *have* support groups for women who are engaged to men whose ex-wives are dead and now have to help raise two kids?" I asked hopefully, only partially joking.

Melody laughed. "Probably not." She reached up to tighten her ponytail. "So, what's the deal with the pills?" I filled her in on what we knew —which wasn't much. She dropped onto Max's bed and let out a long breath. "Let me guess. You're worried you and Victor getting engaged had something to do with her committing suicide?" She paused. "*If* she did, that is."

I nodded. "My mom basically told me not to borrow trouble."

"She's right. You shouldn't. You've got enough to deal with right now, my friend. Let's cross that bridge when we come to it, shall we?"

I nodded again but couldn't let go of the worry that niggled at me. I was a big believer in going with my gut, and my gut was telling me there was more to this situation than I knew. My mother and Melody were right about one thing, though — there was nothing to be done about it until we knew for sure exactly how Kelli had died. I didn't even want to consider what might have been going through her mind if her death wasn't an accident—if she had swallowed those pills deliberately. I knew from Victor that over the years, her refusal to deal with her past made her emotionally unpredictable and maybe even a little unstable, but he'd never indicated she could be suicidal. If he'd suspected any possible danger, I had to believe he wouldn't have let her take care of their children. He would have intervened.

"Is there anything else we should grab?" Melody said, interrupting my thoughts as she popped back up to her feet.

"I need to get a blue blanket from Kelli's bed. It's on Max's list. Maybe you could get another suitcase and fill it up with some of Max's toys and whatever else from Ava's room she might like, so they'll have some more familiar things around? They have some things at our house, but not very much."

"Great idea," she said, and headed back down the hall while I made my way into Kelli's bedroom. The door was open, and when I stepped inside, I saw Kelli's girly personality spread all over the room in its powder-blue walls, yellow floral curtains, and white lace throw pillows. Every inch of space on the top of her dresser was covered in beauty products, and she had a tall jewelry case set next to the maple-hued vanity with its huge, circular mirror. Her closet door was open, too, as though she had dressed in haste and forgotten to close it. I wondered what her last thoughts were. Maybe she was thinking of watching a Friday-night DVD at home with the kids and what she might get accomplished while they were with us for the rest of the weekend. I must have been in my office when she took her last breath, when she'd crawled into bed after dropping the kids off at school. I was sitting at my desk, reviewing those client files, no idea that everything was about to change. My throat thickened at the realization that I would never know when my life would come to an end. How suddenly everything might be lost.

I coughed and pushed back my tears, trying to focus on the task at hand. My eyes moved further around the room and noticed the floor around the white wicker hamper in the corner was littered with lacy bits of underwear. A stack of books rested on the nightstand next to her unmade bed. There was no empty pill bottle; Diane must have given it to the medics who took her friend to the hospital so the doctors would know what she might have taken.

Curious to see what Kelli had been reading, I stepped over and looked at the book on top of the stack. *Healing After Loss*, the title proclaimed in bright red letters. *How to Let Go of the Pain and Reclaim Your Life.* She'd lost her relationship with her parents; she'd lost Victor. Was there something else?

As far as I had witnessed, Kelli and Victor's post-divorce relationship seemed mostly amicable. They had their moments of tension over the extra expenses around the kids that child support didn't cover, or when Victor had to switch around which weekend he could see them because of a commitment at the restaurant, but overall, they seemed to get along. But I hadn't been around the two of them together very much, so I didn't know for sure. Seeing this book on Kelli's nightstand now, three years after he'd moved out, I wondered if she regretted asking him to leave. I wondered if there were important things about their marriage that I didn't know.

I shook my head, as though my mind was an Etch A Sketch and I could simply erase my thoughts. Glancing over to the bed, I saw the fuzzy blue blanket I was sure Max meant for me to bring to him, and after grabbing it, I noticed several photo albums over on the bookshelves. I decided to bring the kids a stack of those, too, thinking it might comfort the kids to have pictures of their mom. Impulsively, I took a few of Kelli's sweaters out of her dresser for Ava to wear, too. Even if they didn't fit her, it still might feel like her mother's arms were around her.

Just as I was about to leave the room, I noticed another book lying on Kelli's bed. It must have been beneath the blanket. The cover was a deep burgundy and stood out against her white lace sheet like a square of spilled blood. Hesitating just a breath before setting what I already carried down on the floor, I stepped back over to her bed and picked up the book.

It was a hard, smooth cover, larger than a novel or textbook. I flipped it over in my hands, not surprised to see *San Luis Obispo Saints, 1993* in italics across the top. A yearbook. I turned the pages to find Kelli, starting with the freshman class. There she was: Kelli Reed. The picture was black and white, but I recognized her long, straight hair and closed-lipped smile. She'd been extremely pretty, even at what I guessed was fourteen. A little gawky maybe, but I could see the curve of her chest—not fake, it turned out, as this photo seemed to prove. Ava had mentioned that her mother had been a cheerleader in high school, but as I fanned through a few more pages looking for an image of the cheerleading squad, she was nowhere to be found in the pictures. I wondered if she just hadn't been on the team her first year. I looked at the front two pages of the book, and then the back, but they were totally blank. No signatures. No *"You are 2 Good 2 B 4gotten"* or *"Science lab sucked!"* Why would she have a yearbook but not ask anyone to sign it? Maybe she hadn't been popular enough, or maybe she was too shy. But even with all the time I spent taking care of Sam when I was in high school, at the end of the year I still had my classmates at least sign their names in my yearbook.

I glanced at the bookshelves again, thinking the other three yearbooks might be there and I could bring them along with the photo albums for Max and Ava to look through. But I didn't see any book spines similar to the one I held. Why had she been looking at this before she died?

"You done, Grace?" Melody called out, interrupting my thoughts. "I filled another suitcase and it weighs about six hundred pounds. I need help getting it out to the car."

Suddenly, the yearbook didn't matter. Tears stung the back of my throat when I considered stepping back into the house with Victor and the kids. The hollow grief in their eyes, the already weary expression on Victor's face. The story I'd written in my head of the kind of life I thought we would live had vanished. Now there were endless blank pages ahead, waiting to be filled. I suddenly felt the urge to hand everything over to Melody and let her deliver it all. However much I loved Victor and worried for Max and Ava, I wasn't sure I could go through this without losing myself completely. I wanted to be the type of selfless woman who faced this kind of drama head-on, but I wasn't sure I had it in me. I thought about my cramped but wonderfully peaceful condo and imagined myself within its walls again, sur-rounded by all my things. No real stress, no huge emotional disasters to clean up. *And no Victor, either,* I reminded myself. *No companionship. No acceptance. No love.*

"Coming," I responded, holding the albums and blanket close to my chest, looking around Kelli's room one last time. There was no question I would have to face this. Victor needed me. It didn't matter whether I felt ready or not.

Kelli

In the romance novels Kelli liked to read, the men were always handsome. They might be hard to reach at first—they might be in denial about how much they wanted to fall in love—but after they'd met and finally made love to the heroine, they always crumbled and admitted how they felt.

For two weeks after Kelli had lain down in the front seat of Jason's truck, she kept waiting for him to crumble. She saw him in the hallways; she smiled at him in algebra. But he barely spoke a word to her. When she tried to talk with him, he looked at his friends and snickered. He moved his seat away from hers when she passed him a note. *My parents grounded me for a month,* it said. *But it was worth it.* Hot tears flooded her eyes when she saw him toss the note around to his buddies. She didn't understand how he could *do* that when he loved her.

"He doesn't *love* you, Kel," Nancy told her as they stood next to each other in the bathroom, fixing their hair before heading to their next class. "He used you to get laid."

Kelli blushed. "He did *not*. He told me he loved me."

Nancy turned and frowned at her. "Please. Boys will say anything to get in your pants."

Kelli blamed herself. Maybe she didn't play hard-to-get long enough. She should have made him wait. She should have made him take her on a real date. The only place her parents would let her go was the library, so for the next few weeks, she went there after school and scoured back issues of *Cosmo* for articles about what to do to win Jason over. *Want to make him jealous?* one article said. *Flirt with his friends and he'll realize how much he cares.*

Perfect, Kelli thought. The following day, she approached Jason and his friends Rory and Mike at their table in the lunchroom. "Hi, Mike," Kelli said, purposely not looking at Jason. She knew she looked pretty—she'd borrowed a tight blue sweater from Nancy and a pair of Levi's that had been pegged at the ankles. Every curve on her body showed.

Mike, another tall boy who wasn't quite as handsome as Jason, smiled at her. "Hey, Kelli. What's up?"

"Not much," she said, lifting her shoulder and pushing out her chest. "I was thinking . . . do you maybe want to study together later? I could use some help with algebra."

Mike glanced over to Jason with a strange smirk on his face. "Sure," he said. "I've heard you are *lots* of fun to, uh, *'study'* with." Mike made invisible quote marks in the air, and seeing this, all three boys burst into laughter.

Kelli felt like she'd been punched in the stomach. She didn't know what to do. Her eyes burned with tears, and she looked over to Jason. "You *told* them?" she whispered. Her voice fractured as she spoke.

Jason lifted his jaw and shrugged. "Yeah, well, you're a church girl, right? You should have known better." They all laughed again and Kelli raced out of the lunchroom. She hid in the bathroom for the rest of the afternoon, crying.

When she got home, her father was standing in the living room, waiting for her. She stopped short, unused to seeing him before the bank closed at six o'clock. She knew her eyes were red, so she dropped her gaze to the floor, hoping he wouldn't notice. "Where's Mama?" she asked.

She felt his eyes on her. "She's in our bedroom. She got a call this afternoon from the school secretary. You weren't in any of your classes after lunch."

Kelli's stomach clenched and she looked up at him. She'd never skipped class before—she didn't even think about the fact that her parents would get a phone call. "Daddy—" she began, but he held up his palm to stop her.

"I don't want to hear it. You are a disappointment to me, young lady. You are a liar." He paused and pushed his black-rimmed glasses against the bridge of his nose. "Your behavior is unacceptable and you will be punished for it."

Kelli nodded, feeling the tears well up behind her eyes again. She longed to be able to ask him for help—to find comfort in her father's arms—but she knew it was pointless to hope for this. "How much longer am I grounded?" she asked quietly.

"Grounding you didn't work." He took a breath. "Go get the wooden spoon."

Kelli's breath caught in her throat. He'd only spanked Kelli a couple of times—once when she was four years old, after she had grabbed her mother's favorite crystal vase to admire it and accidentally dropped it to the floor, and then again when she was six and, in a fit of anger, cut off all the blossoms on her mother's roses. "Daddy," she said again. "Please. I promise it won't happen again."

He nodded, pressing his lips together into a white line before speaking. "You're right. It won't. And this time, you'll remember why. Get the spoon."

She was fourteen; he couldn't do this to her now . . . could he? "Mama?" she called out, and her father took a step toward her. Kelli took a step back.

"She agrees this is the proper punishment." He stared at his daughter. "Don't make me ask you again."

Kelli felt a wave of anger rise up inside her. She clenched her hands into fists at her sides and straightened her spine. *"No,"* she said. "I made a mistake. I was upset and crying in the bathroom and I lost track of time. I didn't do it on *purpose*." She knew he wouldn't ask why she was so upset. He didn't care about that. He only cared that she had broken a rule. He only cared how *he* felt, not her.

Her father's dark eyebrows raised. "You're lying."

"No, I'm not." Kelli saw her mother appear behind him. "Mama, it was an accident. I didn't mean to skip class. Tell him to stop this. *Please.*" She was so scared, her voice shook. She'd never stood up to him this way.

Her mother looked over to her father, then back to Kelli. "Thomas," she said. "Maybe it's too much."

Kelli's father turned toward her mother. "You called me at work. You *asked* me to come home and do this."

"Not to *hit* her," Kelli's mother said quietly. "Just to talk some sense into her." She put her hand on his arm. "I'm sorry. I should have just dealt with it myself."

Kelli's father's body visibly relaxed and she seized the opportunity. "I'm so sorry, Daddy. It will never, ever happen again. I promise." She began to cry, but neither of them moved to soothe her. After a moment, her parents left the room— her father out the front door to head back to work and her mother to the kitchen to start dinner. Kelli stood weeping in the living room long after they were gone, wondering if anyone in this world loved her at all.

Over the next couple of months, Kelli stayed quiet. She was quiet at school, quiet at home. She felt nauseous much of the time, tired in a way she'd never been before. All she wanted to do was sleep. She made polite conversation with her parents, accompanying them to church and attending youth group without a fight. She stayed as far away as possible from Jason—she even distanced herself from Nancy. Everyone in the school was talking about her—whispering about what she'd done. One boy cornered her at her locker and asked if she gave blow jobs in the front of trucks, too, and she wished she could simply close her eyes and disappear. She shut herself off from anything that might hurt her, and yet she cried every night in the dark, her face buried deep into her pillow. She wasn't sure what she wept for, but the tears came whether she understood them or not.

"You're losing weight," her mother remarked one morning as they sat at the table for breakfast. Her father had already left for work. Since the day she stood up to him, he'd barely spoken to her at all. It was like he'd have preferred that she didn't exist.

"I'm not hungry," Kelli said, swirling her spoon around in her cereal. "I feel a little sick."

Her mother reached over and placed the back of her hand against Kelli's forehead. "No fever," she said. "Have you been throwing up?"

Kelli shrugged. She had, in fact, just thrown up that morning. She'd been throwing up for weeks. Grief over all that had happened, she decided. Like one of the heroines in her novels—she was lovesick, devastated by how Jason had used her. How easily she had given herself away.

"Do you have your period?" her mother asked, her voice so soft Kelli could barely make out the words.

"No," Kelli answered, and then her breath froze. She looked at her mother, wide-eyed. "It hasn't come." *Oh no. Oh please. It couldn't be true. It was only once. It happened so fast.*

Her mother's face went gray and her shoulders slumped forward. She dropped her fork with a clatter. "For how long." A statement, not a question.

Kelli tried to remember the last time she'd needed the supplies in the blue box under the bathroom sink. It was before Jason. Before her world as she knew it began to fall apart.

Grace

When Melody and I got to the house, Victor was on the phone with the restaurant, talking with his head chef. I pictured Spencer standing in the gleaming, stainless steel kitchen of the Loft. He was the muscular man who'd saluted me the night Victor and I first met. During a conversation with him a few weeks later, I thought he looked more like he belonged in a wrestling arena than a restaurant, but he was actually an incredible cook, blending ingredients in a way that seemed to hypnotize customers into returning for more.

"What did you do?" I asked him once after sampling a particularly decadent cream of wild mushroom soup he'd made. "Sprinkle cocaine in this? It's totally addictive."

"No, ma'am," Spencer responded with a slow smile. "Only love." For a big man, he was soft-spoken and a little shy—the consummate gentle giant and an excellent reminder that a person's appearance doesn't define the truth of who they are.

"Ew," I joked. "Don't tell the health department that."

Now Melody and I unloaded all the food she had prepared the night before into the commercial upright freezer we kept in our garage, keeping out one lasagna and a container of cookies for us to eat today. After that, we put the suitcases in the kids' rooms and went to go talk with them while Victor finished his conversation with Spencer. I carried the blanket Max had requested and one of Kelli's sweaters for Ava. When we entered the den, I saw that they were sprawled out next to each other on the curved leather sectional, still in their pajamas. Their glassy eyes were glued to the huge flat-screen across the room, but the TV was off. They were staring at nothing. Ava was loosely holding Max's hand and seeing this unexpected act of tenderness toward her brother, I choked up again.

"Hey, guys," Melody said, stepping over to sit down next to Ava. "I'm so, so sorry to hear about your mom." She reached out and rubbed Ava's arm, and Ava jerked away. Melody didn't pull back after Ava's reaction; instead, she drew Ava closer and gave her an enormous hug. I expected Ava to yank herself out of Melody's arms—they'd only met a few times when Melody happened to stop by when the kids were with us for the weekend—but instead, Ava began to cry and softened into my friend's embrace. Melody held her close, rubbed her back, and pressed her cheek into the side of Ava's head.

Seeing this, Max leapt off the couch and threw himself at me, his skinny arms tight around my hips. I stumbled back a step, surprised by this sudden outpouring of affection, but then found my footing and dropped down to the floor and took him into a tight embrace, wrapping his mother's blanket around him. Neither child spoke a word, but Melody looked at me, tears brimming in her eyes. Ava looked over to me, too, and saw her mother's red sweater in my grasp. I held it out to her.

"I thought you might like to have this with you," I said, keeping one arm around Max, who was sniffling into my shoulder.

Ava hesitated, then slowly extricated herself from Melody's arms. She stared at her mother's sweater, an unreadable expression on her face. "That was her favorite," she whispered. "Dad bought it for her."

"Then you should definitely keep it." I smiled

gently, trying to ignore the slight twist in my stomach that arose with the picture of Victor and Kelli together. In normal circumstances, it wouldn't have bothered me, but after seeing that book in her room, I felt the tiniest bit insecure.

Ava lifted her eyes to mine, her bottom lip trembling as she took the sweater from me. "She might be coming back," she said, her voice slightly muffled as she held it over her nose and mouth. "Maybe the hospital made a mistake."

Max chose this moment to look up at me, his nose running, his blue eyes bright with tears. "That happens, right? I've seen it on TV. They think it's the person who died, but they're wrong."

I gave Melody a helpless look, and she stepped in. "I wish it worked that way, honey. But the doctors are sure it was your mom. I'm sorry." Both kids began crying again, and Melody and I held them close.

Victor rushed in from the kitchen, cell phone in hand. He stopped short when he saw us. I gave him the smallest of reassuring smiles and mouthed the words, *It's okay*. He nodded but still sank to the floor behind me, wrapping his own long arms around both me and his son. He pressed his damp cheek against mine and the heat from his body enveloped me.

As Victor held us, I experienced the briefest flicker of hope that I could do this. If I could be here now, in a painful moment like this, I could be here always. Maybe I would learn how to find my way through this *with* the kids instead of in spite of them. Maybe being a mother wasn't nearly as scary as I'd made it out to be.

Ava

With most things, there were rules about how to act. I knew how to be quiet and pay attention to my teachers when I was at school; I knew how to laugh with Bree and how to be sweet to my dad when I wanted something from him. I had no idea how to act now. Mama was dead and nothing else mattered. Not how I looked or what I did or didn't do. I could eat or not eat, cry or not cry, and nothing would change. *Brush your teeth,* my brain told me. *Walk down the hall. Sit at the table. Take a bite of toast.* I responded to these thoughts in slow motion—with stiff, stilted movements, like the Tin Man in *The Wizard of Oz* when he rusted up after it rained. My body tingled the same way my mouth does after a visit to the dentist. There, but not there. Moving, but numb. *Empty.*

We didn't have to go to school, so Max and I basically spent the entire week sitting around the house. I colored with him and read him his favorite stories, pointless forms of distraction that did little to make either of us feel better.

"How are you doing?" Dad asked us every day—usually more than once—and I didn't know how to answer him. How did he *think* we were doing? I couldn't have cried again if I tried. I was tired in a hollowed-out way I'd never been. We spent every night with Dad in his room, while Grace made a bed for herself on the living room couch. I don't think any of us were really getting much sleep. The minute I closed my eyes, Mama's face appeared and my pulse pounded noisily through my blood. I felt it throbbing in my head, my neck, my fingers—even my toes.

Now it was Thursday, the morning of the day everyone was coming to our house for some sort of weird gathering Dad wouldn't call a funeral but actually kind of was. I wanted to escape what I had to face today. I wanted to stay curled up in Dad's bed. He and Max had already gotten up—I was alone. Wrapping Mama's red sweater tightly around me, I brought my knees to my chest beneath the covers and closed my eyes again.

"Ava?" My dad's muffled voice came through the bedroom door. "Are you awake?"

I wondered what he'd do if I didn't answer. Or if I pitched a fit and refused to leave the room. I could scream and kick and bite him if he tried to make me go. Part of me wanted to find out what might happen if I did, but the other, smarter part of me answered him. "I'm up."

"People are going to be here soon and Grace has to get ready."

My eyes snapped open. I threw the covers off and rolled over onto my back. "*Okay,* Dad! I said, I'm *up.*" I didn't care that I was being sassy. He could punish me all he wanted and it wouldn't matter. Nothing could make me feel worse than I already did.

He didn't respond, so I figured he'd gone back down the hall to tell Grace she could have their room back. I wondered how she was feeling, being kicked out of my dad's bed. I wondered if she was angry we were taking up so much of his time. She'd given me lots of space this week, only speaking to me to offer bits of food or to ask if I wanted to go for a walk with her and Max, letting Dad be the one to tell us we should shower or put our cereal bowl in the sink. She spent the days talking on the phone with her assistant, working on her computer, and cleaning the house. She was quieter than usual, tiptoeing around, hugging and kissing my dad when she didn't think we were looking. Maybe she didn't know how to act, either.

There was a soft knock on the door, and Grace opened it a second later. She gave me a half smile when she saw me still lying in their bed. "Hey there," she said. "Is it okay if I get showered? You can stay in here awhile, if you want."

I nodded, and she closed the door behind her

after she entered. She was wearing black pajama pants with a loose purple T-shirt and her hair was a crazy mess around her face. She was about to go into their bathroom when I spoke up, my own voice surprising me. "Grace?"

She stopped, turned, and looked back at me. "Yeah?" She said the word softly, and with such tenderness, it almost made me cry. I had to force my jaw to stop trembling before I could speak.

"Do I *have* to be here today?"

Her mouth twitched into a quick frown. "I think it's probably best if you are. It gives you a chance to say good-bye."

I thought about this a moment. "But what if I don't want to?"

She sighed. "I get why you'd feel like that, sweetie. This all really sucks, doesn't it?"

I looked at her, eyebrows raised, shocked to have an adult speak so plainly, that someone who I'd been so mean to was being so nice to me. "Yeah, it does," I said. I sat up, pulled Mama's sweater closed, and dropped my gaze to the mattress. My insides were bound up in knots, but I knew I needed to apologize. "I don't really hate you, Grace. I don't know why I said that. I'm sorry." My voice shook, feeling disloyal to Mama, somehow, with every word. She'd been jealous of Grace, I knew. Jealous of her job; jealous that Daddy loved her. I'd understood that I wasn't supposed to like Grace, and yet, here she was while Mama was . . . gone. I didn't know how to feel.

"Ava, honey, look at me," she said. I did as she asked and gritted my teeth so I wouldn't cry. She wasn't smiling, but her green eyes were filled with kindness as she spoke. "I understand, okay? Sometimes we do and say things we don't mean when we're upset. So please don't worry about it. I care about you very much and I'm here for you however you need me to be."

I nodded briskly, grateful that she wasn't going to make a big deal out of it. If I had said something like that to Mama, I'd have been grounded for weeks. Grace smiled at me, then went into the bathroom. I lay there a while longer, oddly comforted by the sound of her getting ready—the water running, the hair dryer's low buzz. It reminded me of listening to Mama get "prettied up" for work. I decided to skip taking a shower and went to my bedroom to get dressed, pulling my hair into a tight ponytail to hide that it hadn't been washed. I looked in the mirror, reviewing the black skirt and blouse I wore with Mama's sweater. "Dress for yourself," she always told me. "What matters is how you feel in what you're wearing, not what anyone else thinks of it."

Crossing my arms over my chest, I rubbed my hands over my biceps. "I hope you can see me," I whispered. "I'm wearing this for you."

•••

Spencer was the first to arrive, looking handsome in a navy blue suit. His dark hair was
slicked back and he had a red kerchief tucked into
his breast pocket. He shook Dad's hand, then
pulled him into a one-armed hug, and they patted
each other's backs like they were trying to burp a
baby.

"Hey there, monkeys," he said to us, and Max
and I both gave him a little wave. We liked
Spencer. Whenever we visited the restaurant, he
made us a special garlic cheese toast and snuck
us bites of expensive desserts. "Can I help set
up?" he asked, looking around the living room.
Grace had kept the house so clean all week, it
barely looked like anybody lived there.

"I still need to move the dining room chairs in
here," Dad said. "So people will have a place to
sit."

"Let's do it," Spencer said, slapping his hands
together. They made their way into the other
room, and Max and I walked over to the couch
and dropped onto it together.

"What're *we* supposed to do?" Max whispered,
and I shrugged. There weren't going to be very
many people coming over—maybe Diane and her
son, Patrick, plus a couple of people from Mama's
work. Dad said her parents couldn't come
because their health wasn't good enough to travel.
I supposed if I knew them I'd have been upset,

but I honestly didn't know how to miss someone I'd never met.

Before I could answer my brother, Melody walked in through the front door wearing a simple black dress and matching ballet flats. Her hair was pulled into a bun at the base of her neck, which was encircled by a strand of pearls. She looked like a blond Audrey Hepburn. Grace gave her a big hug, then offered to take her coat. Spencer and my dad emerged from the dining room, each carrying a couple of chairs. Melody saw them, did a double take, then nudged Grace. "Who is *that?*" she whispered.

"Spencer," Grace said. At the sound of his name, Spencer set the chairs down and walked over to them. "This is my friend Melody," Grace continued. "Melody, this is Spencer. He's the chef at the Loft. The one whose food I'm always raving about?"

"Nice to meet you," Spencer said with a small smile, and held out his hand. Melody shook it and nodded, and I thought I caught her giving him a second glance after he'd already looked away.

"Ava, what're we supposed to *do?*" Max asked again, pulling at my sleeve. I yanked away from his touch.

"I don't *know!*" I snapped. His eyes glossed with tears and I immediately felt like crap for being mean to him. "Why don't you go eat something?" I suggested in a much nicer voice. "There's a ton

213

of food on the table." He shook his head, then leaned it against my arm. I sighed and took his hand in mine. His fingers were warm and sweaty, but I held on to them anyway. I knew he couldn't always help being a pain. He was only seven.

I felt Grace's eyes on me from across the room, then she made her way over to the couch. "I brought some of your mom's photo albums from her house, remember?" she said quietly. "Do you two want to look through them?"

I shrugged again, my stomach flipping over inside me. I'd forgotten about those albums, and suddenly, I wanted to do nothing else. Grace gave my arm a gentle touch before going into the den and returning with a stack of albums. She sat down in between Max and me, giving me one I didn't recognize from the top of the pile—it had a worn black vinyl cover and spiral edges.

I ran my palm over the front of the album and wondered why Mama hadn't shown it to me. She had stacks and stacks of albums from when Max and I were babies—I made fun of her for how many pictures she took of us just lying on a blanket on the floor, doing nothing. "What was so interesting about *that?*" I asked her, and she'd smile. "Every single little thing you did as a baby was like magic," she said. "I couldn't take my eyes off of you for a second. You were the best thing that ever happened to me."

Swallowing the lump in my throat, I opened the

album to the first page, and Max reached over Grace's lap to point at a picture of an unsmiling little girl who stood in front of a red brick house. She wore a plain, dark blue dress and her blond hair was pulled into a ponytail at her neck. What looked like dead shrubs grew up around her, right out of the dusty ground.

"Who's that?" Max asked.

I scrunched my eyes up to read the tiny letters written on the white edge of the photo—"Kelli, three years old," I said, then looked at Max. "It's Mama." I scanned the other photos on the two open pages, then flipped through a couple more, taking in the images in front of me. "These are all of Mama growing up." There were pictures of her standing with her mother—a wisp of a woman with dirty-blond hair and heavy lines across her forehead; an image or two of her father resting his large hand on her small shoulder. He was a tall, grim-looking man with blond, slicked-back hair and black-rimmed glasses. His white, short-sleeved shirt was buttoned all the way to the top, and the wobbly skin of his neck was pinched with a bow tie. There was Mama standing in front of a church in a long white dress, a lacy cap pinned in her hair, with the words, "Kelli, first communion," written on the picture's edge.

"She never showed us these before," Max said, and as he did, Dad approached us and sat down on the chair next to the couch.

"Never showed you what?" he asked.

Grace smiled at him. "One of the albums I brought from Kelli's house."

"It has pictures of Mama when she was little," Max said, and just as he did, my eyes landed on a picture of Mama that had "Kelli, 13," written in spidery script on its edge. We almost could have been twins, only Mama had blond hair and mine was dark. But our bodies were the same, slight and skinny, all elbows and knobby knees. She sat on a white wicker chair, holding a thick book in her lap. Her mouth was smiling, but her eyes were not. We turned a few more pages of the album, seeing more pictures of Mama around my age, looking unhappy and dark, and I thought about the pictures Bree and I took with our cell phones —goofy shots of both of us making faces or puckering our lips and pretending to be glamorous. There was nothing like that here. Maybe Mama had never had many friends. Maybe her life was just so miserable with her parents that she had to leave. There was something so plain about her in these pictures, so the opposite of the woman I watched spend an hour straightening her hair and carefully applying her makeup. The woman who wore tight blue jeans and knee-high, black leather boots.

"Why didn't she ever show us these?" I asked Dad, then swallowed to ease the cottony feel in my mouth. I kept my eyes on the album, afraid I might miss something if I looked away.

Dad sighed. "Probably because she didn't like talking about her past very much, honey. It was hard for her."

I turned another page, stopping short when I saw the last ten pages or so were blank. The pictures just stopped after the ones of her at fourteen. I finally looked over to my dad. "Did you ever see any from when she was in high school? When she was a cheerleader?"

Dad shook his head. "I don't think so, sweetie."

"But why would they just stop?" I asked. "You guys have tons from when you met and got married. And tons from when me and Max were babies. Why wouldn't she have any from when she was a teenager?"

"I guess because she didn't take any with her when she left California," he said. "Her parents probably still have them."

"But she has this one," I said, giving the album a little shake. "Why wouldn't she have taken those, too?"

"I don't know, Ava. Okay?" His voice held a sharp edge, one I'd heard him use on Mama more than once. Grace reached out to touch his hand. He took a couple of deep breaths, his face softening almost immediately when she touched him. I wondered why Mama never reached out to him like that when he was angry, instead of screaming or crying about how bad a husband he was. Maybe if she had, he'd never have left us.

He spoke again, more gently this time. "Sweetie, look. I understand you want to feel close to your mom right now. You want to know more about her. But there just isn't that much more to know. She and her parents just didn't get along. For all sorts of reasons." He paused and reached out to take my hand. "She didn't believe the same things they believed, and I think for them, that was bad enough for them to not want to see her anymore. When she left, she left everything behind. Pictures included. Maybe this album was all she could take with her."

I considered this, not quite believing he was telling me everything he knew. A panicky thought rose up inside me and I looked at him with wide eyes. "Could *I* ever do anything so bad that you'd not want to see me?"

"Never," he said quickly. "Not in a million years. No matter what you do, I will always be here for you, okay?"

"Okay," I said, allowing myself to be momentarily comforted. He and Grace got up when the doorbell rang, and a couple of people Mama worked with entered the house, staring at Max and me with such intense pity, I had to look away.

"Thanks for coming," Dad said to them. "Kelli would have appreciated it."

Max scooted closer to me and tried to take the

album out of my lap. "Hey!" I said, yanking it out of his reach. "Don't!"

"It's *my* turn," he whined.

"No. You'll get it . . . sticky."

"I will not!" He regarded his hands a moment, palms up, then began to lick his fingers.

"*Gross,* Max!" I said, loud enough for Grace to shoot me a brief warning look. "Knock it *off,*" I whispered.

He dropped his hands to his lap and wiped them on his pants. "I just want to look at it again," he pleaded. *"Please?"*

"Okay, but *I'm* holding it." He nodded, and I turned back to the first page, examining each image of my mother when she was a child. Over the next couple of hours, more people trickled in and out of the house, murmuring how sorry they were about Mama. I only nodded in response, not lifting my gaze to meet theirs. Not trusting myself to speak without crying.

After a while, Max got bored looking at the album and went to get something to eat. I still sat on the couch, trying to ignore everything that was going on around me. Dad checked on me; Grace did, too. I told them I was fine, unable to focus on anything but the album I held in my lap. But as the day went on, as most of the people finally left, it wasn't the pictures I found myself thinking about. It was the blank space of her high school years, the place where Mama just seemed to disappear.

Kelli

Whore.

The word repeated over and over in Kelli's mind as she curled up in the backseat of her parents' car. It was the word her father had used right before he slapped her across the face a few weeks ago, right after her mother told him his daughter was pregnant. Kelli had barely felt the sting of his hand on her skin. In fact, she barely felt anything at all. Not since her mother made her take the test to confirm what they feared. While she waited for them to decide what to do with her, Kelli went through the motions of her life—to school and church—like nothing had happened. Every time the secret rose up inside her, she swallowed it down, trying not to choke. But here was the truth: she was pregnant and her parents were sending her away. At that point, she didn't care. None of it mattered. Maybe she *was* a whore.

They'd asked who had done this to her, but she refused to tell them about Jason. "What about the baby?" she asked instead. "What will happen to her?" She didn't know why she assumed it was a girl; she just did.

Her parents ignored her question. "We'll say you were having trouble with your grades," her mother said. "We'll say this boarding school caters to young girls who need to focus on their studies."

"Where is it?" Kelli asked.

"A couple hours north of San Francisco," her mother told her. She went on to explain to Kelli that one of her friends from church had a drug-addicted daughter whom they'd sent there when she was sixteen. "She came back a year later and she was entirely changed."

Changed into what? Kelli wondered. She knew her parents were devastated. She knew they were angry and ashamed. They wanted her to be a clone of them, but no matter where she went, no matter what happened to her, she didn't think she could be. But even as part of her ached with guilt, another part was excited. The baby would love her. Kelli would never put her down. She'd kiss her baby's toes and sleep with her each night. She'd love her baby the way her parents had never loved her.

Her father pulled off the highway and onto a long gravel road with tall red cedars towering above them on both sides. Kelli almost asked how much further it was to the school, but then she saw a sign that read *New Pathways, 3 miles ahead*. Three miles was a long way, Kelli thought. The last town they'd seen was more than an hour ago, so it wouldn't be easy for students to try to run away. Not that Kelli planned to. She was almost happy to be tucked into the woods, far away from everyone and everything she'd ever known. It was almost as though she was being given a chance to start over.

A little while later, a large brick building loomed ahead of them. It was a perfectly plain gray box, three stories high with small square windows. Kelli was relieved to see several other girls sitting out on the lawn on blankets. Some of them were reading, others were talking—a few even had smiles on their faces. One of them was clearly pregnant, much further along than Kelli, who hadn't even begun to show yet.

Her father parked the car by the front steps, and the three of them sat in silence for a moment. "You should get your things," her father said. "The trunk is open."

"Aren't you going to come in with me?" Kelli asked, her words shaky and thin.

"We're not supposed to," her mother said. At least she had tears in her voice. "The director is expecting you in the front office. They'll get you settled."

"But when will I see you again?" Kelli asked. Neither of her parents responded. It was almost as if she had vanished. It was almost as though after what she'd done, she didn't exist to them at all.

Kelli quickly learned that most girls at New Pathways thought it little better than a prison. They all adhered to a strict schedule: showers at six, breakfast at seven, classes from seven thirty to three. Chores and homework for two hours, one hour of free time for a walk or to read on the lawn, dinner at six, lights out by nine. There were no more than thirty girls who lived there, but during her first month, Kelli wasn't openly welcomed by any of them. They nodded and said hello, but conversations never got much past "Please pass the rolls" at the dinner table. Most of the girls kept to themselves, plagued by their own set of secrets. None of them asked why she was there, and on some level, she was glad. She thought about the life growing within her, imagining that it would change who she was—make her a better, strong person. She needed to rest; she needed to focus on her schoolwork so she could get a good enough job to take care of her baby girl. Most of the time, she welcomed the structure the school required.

But one night, as she sat in the corner of the school's small dining room, slowly eating rubbery chicken and bland steamed broccoli, the reality of her situation sounded off in her brain, too loud to ignore: Jason used her. She was pregnant and alone and nobody—not even her parents—wanted her. They didn't even love her. They wouldn't have sent her away if they did. They would have kept her with them if she was worth anything at all.

Sorrow wrapped itself into a heavy chain

around her neck until it felt like she couldn't breathe. Tears stung her eyes as she choked down the last bite of food on her plate, then took her dishes to the kitchen.

Later, while the other girls watched television or listened to music, Kelli sat at the small wooden desk next to the narrow bed she slept upon and made a list of all the things she would need for her child. *Diapers, clothes, and bottles. Baby powder, blankets, and a crib.* She thought if she had a list, maybe she'd feel better, more capable of being a good mother. She tried to think of everything she'd seen in movies about babies but couldn't come up with much. She hoped when she and her child went home, her mother might help her. This would be her grandchild, after all. Her baby would change everything.

"Whatcha writing?" A voice popped through her thoughts and Kelli whipped around to see the pregnant girl, whose name she'd learned was Stella, standing in her doorway. Her mousy brown hair was twisted on top of her head in a messy bun and she wore stretchy pajama bottoms and a T-shirt that was too small to cover her stomach. Kelli could see her belly button and for some reason, that made her uncomfortable.

Kelli flipped the piece of paper over, even though Stella wouldn't have been able to see it. "Nothing. Homework."

Stella cocked her head and ran one palm over

her swollen belly. "Homework, huh? More like a letter to your boyfriend. That who knocked you up?"

"No!" Kelli exclaimed, a little shocked. She hadn't told anyone why she was there. "How did you know?"

"Your boobs. They're bigger than when you first got here. And you stomach's starting to pooch out a little, too." She gestured toward Kelli's bed. "Mind if I sit down? My feet are killing me."

"Sure," Kelli said, tucking the sheet of paper into her folder before turning around to face Stella. "Is that because of the baby? Your feet hurting, I mean?"

Stella groaned as she carefully lowered herself to the bed, putting one hand down flat on the mattress so she didn't fall right over. "Yeah. I'm all swollen and achy. And fat. It sucks."

"Are you scared?" Kelli asked, strangely exhilarated to finally be talking about this with someone who might understand how she'd been feeling. She was a little freaked out thinking about the fact that she actually had a whole other body growing inside her. The only conversation she'd had about her pregnancy since getting here was with the director, who told her if she tried to sneak her boyfriend in the school for sex, she'd regret it, and with the doctor whom she'd met with once for a checkup, who told her to eat

Tums if she got heartburn and make sure to take the prenatal vitamins he gave her.

"Sort of," Stella said. "Are you?"

Kelli nodded, trying to keep her bottom lip from trembling. She'd never been so afraid of anything. Remembering how Jason being inside her had hurt, she couldn't fathom the kind of pain having a *baby* would bring. She pictured sweat and blood and screaming and instantly, fear spread like hot tar inside her chest. "What else does it feel like?" she asked Stella, hoping she might learn some-thing that would ease her concerns.

"Well, some of it's pretty cool. When the baby moves and everything? It's kind of like having an alien inside you." Though that wasn't especially reassuring, Kelli nodded and waited to hear more. Stella sighed. "I have to pee like, every ten minutes, too. Which sucks. And my boobs hurt. And my back."

So much for reassurance, Kelli thought. "When are you due?"

"Any day now," Stella said. "I can't wait to get this thing out of me."

Kelli froze at her choice of words. "You don't want to keep it?"

Stella scrunched up her face and shook her head. "Are you nuts? No way. It was totally a mistake, but my parents wouldn't sign off on the abortion, so here I am. It's going to be adopted by some couple in L.A."

Kelli couldn't imagine giving her child up so easily. "Did you get to meet them? Are they good people?"

Stella shrugged. "They don't let us meet the parents. They just take the baby." Her eyes became shiny and she looked out the window into the dark night. "I can't wait to get back home. My boyfriend and I are gonna get a house together. He's the manager at the gas station and he's going to take care of me 'til I turn sixteen and can get a job."

"What about your parents?"

"They don't want me to come back." She looked back at Kelli. "What about yours?"

"I don't know . . ." Kelli said, trailing off. "They didn't want to talk to me about what was going to happen. They just . . . sent me here." Her voice cracked and she swallowed to try to keep the tears back. "I just want my baby, you know?"

"Your parents didn't send you here so you could keep it," Stella said. "All the girls have to give up their babies. That's the whole point. They hide your secret from the world, and you get to go back and pretend nothing happened. It's a win-win. Your parents aren't embarrassed by what a little slut you were, and your life isn't ruined before you're eighteen."

"I'm not a slut," Kelli whispered. Her father's voice lingered in her mind . . . *Whore.*

Stella shrugged again. "Whatever. So you loved

the guy and it was all meaningful. I love my boyfriend, too, but it doesn't mean I'm ready to be a mother."

"Are all the girls pregnant here?" Kelli asked. Maybe they just weren't showing, like Kelli.

"Nah. Some of them, yes. But most are just wild and their parents sent them here to stop drinking or whatever. It's like military school for us. Only without the uniforms. Or the boys." She yawned. "Okay, well, I'm wiped. I need to go to bed. Nice talking with you."

"You too." Kelli watched Stella's laborious rise from the bed, dread gripping her as she wondered how she could stop what was going to happen. How she'd manage to keep the doctors from taking her baby away.

Grace

"I've totally got a handle on things," Tanya assured me the morning after Kelli's memorial. I'd called throughout the week to see how everything was going at the office, a little worried about being away from our clients. But so far, according to Tanya, everything seemed to be rolling along fine without me. "Stephanie came in for a few hours yesterday to organize the on-call schedule for the counselors," Tanya said. "She also finished reviewing the files of the women getting ready to transition out of the safe houses. We're all good."

"You're an angel," I said, picturing her sitting at her desk.

Tanya snickered into the phone. "Yeah, some angel."

"You are," I said insistently, thinking of how she somehow juggled the demands of single motherhood and remained an ideal professional. Granted, she had a built-in caregiver in her mother, who moved from South Carolina to help take care of her two toddlers after Tanya left one of our safe houses. Having that kind of support certainly made her life infinitely more manageable. But however much I loved my own mother, I certainly wouldn't have wanted her to live with us.

We hung up just as there was a knock on the door. I stumbled my way over from the couch and opened it to see Melody bearing a cardboard box. "Good morning! I come bearing a vat of white bean chicken chili, sausage marinara, and three freezer bags of precooked chicken breasts."

"Oh, hello," I said with a laugh, holding out my hand and pretending to introduce myself. "I'm not sure if you know me. I'm Grace, and I live with a man who owns a restaurant? I'm pretty sure we're not going to starve."

"I can't help it," she said. "You know I'm compulsive. Where can I put it?"

"The freezer in the garage would be great," I said. "Thank you."

She set her purse on the entryway table and carried the box into the garage, where I heard her open the freezer and rummage around a bit, presumably finding space for all she'd brought. I walked into the kitchen and poured us each a cup of coffee, carrying them back into the living room, where she now stood waiting for me. She gratefully accepted the mug I handed her, then looked at me sternly. "I only have an hour before my first client, but I wanted to see how you're doing after yesterday." She eyed the sheets and my pillow. "Still on couch duty, eh?" she said.

I nodded and took a sip of my drink, then pushed my bedding to the floor so we could sit down. "The kids need to be near him right now." I understood this, of course, but my back was starting to get a little resentful of the arrangement. And honestly, I was a little bit lonely.

She glanced down the hallway. "They're in bed? It's almost nine o'clock."

"They probably need the sleep. I think the memorial wore them out."

"It wore *me* out," Melody said as we both lowered to the couch. "And I didn't even do anything. I can't even imagine how they're feeling."

I nudged her softly with my foot. "You seemed to be having a fine time talking with Spencer." I'd watched Melody shadow Spencer yesterday, helping him replenish the table and make sure the coffeepot was kept full; I saw them chatting, their heads leaning in toward each other. I'd recognized the smile she gave him, the smile that said, "Welcome, I'm available. Please, ask me more."

"Who, me?" She looked at me over the top of her coffee mug and fluttered her eyelashes. I nudged her again, a little harder this time, and she laughed. "Okay, okay. I did have a good time chatting with him. I can't believe you never introduced us before! He's totally my type."

I shrugged. "I guess I never made the connection. He's so quiet and you're so . . ."

"What?" It was her turn to nudge me. "I'm so *what?*"

I grinned. "Energetic?"

"Ha! That's just a nice way to say 'spastic.' " She exhaled and smiled at me. "We're going out tonight. After he gets done at the restaurant."

"That's great, Mel. I'm happy for you." I *was* happy for my friend, but I couldn't help but release a tiny, dejected sigh, too.

"Okay. Then why do you sound like you want to slit your wrists?" She cringed. "Oh, wow. Sorry. Bad choice of words."

I gave her a half smile. "No worries. I just feel like I've been holding my breath all week, you know?" She nodded. "I'm ready to get into some kind of routine. All this sitting around the house is making me crazy." I missed my office; I missed my clients. I missed feeling like each moment had a purpose, that the things I did made a difference. Here, with Victor and the kids, I couldn't gauge how much I mattered.

"Maybe you need to get back to work?" she suggested.

"Maybe. I've been taking care of e-mails and a few phone calls, but that's about it." As I spoke, Victor stumbled into the room. He wore plaid pajama bottoms and a white T-shirt and his dark hair was twisted in multiple cowlicks around his head, which usually meant he'd tossed and turned all night.

"Hey, handsome," Melody said. "I hate to drink and run, but I have to get to the spa and prep for the day." She stood up and walked over to Victor, landing a kiss on his cheek. "If you talk to Spencer, tell him how great I am, okay?"

"You got it." Victor smiled at her, then walked over and sat down next to me. I fingered the empty spot on my left ring finger, feeling a twinge of sadness with the touch. Victor noticed the movement and lifted my hand up to kiss the same spot.

"All right, lovebirds," Melody said. "Catch you later." She waved as she headed out the door.

"Sorry," Victor said after she was gone. He still held my hand. "I know this is rough on us."

"I just miss you," I said, squeezing his long fingers. "That's all."

He sighed. "I miss you, too. We'll try them in their beds tonight, okay? A regular routine will be good for them, but the counselor said we just have to let them go through whatever they need to, you know. Try to accommodate where we can."

"Of course." I nodded, and he kissed me again, his full lips lingering on mine for a moment longer this time, the tip of his tongue brushing against mine. I groaned and pushed him. "Go away. You're making it worse."

He groaned, too. "Aww. You drive me crazy, woman."

"Crazier, you mean?" I teased him.

"Ha ha," he said. "So funny I forgot to laugh." We both giggled at our stupid inside joke. One time I'd told him I felt silly in a dress I'd picked out to wear to dinner, and he'd said, "Sillier, you mean," with a wink. From then on, any opportunity we had to make a similar goofy jab, we took it. It felt so good to laugh with him now—to feel that spark of love and connection during what had been such a dark time.

I didn't want to ruin it, but I suddenly thought about the yearbook I'd found in Kelli's bedroom. We'd been so focused on the kids, I hadn't wanted to bring it up earlier in the week. "Hey, honey?" I began, then told him about the signature-free pages, how I didn't see any others from the rest of her high school years.

Victor listened, his eyes intent on mine. "Okay. So what are you asking, exactly?"

"Well, don't you think it's kind of weird that her photo albums and her yearbooks stop when she was a freshman? Especially since she said she was a cheerleader . . . right?" I paused. "Did you ever see any other yearbooks? Or pictures of her as a cheerleader?"

"No," he said, drawing out the word. "But I don't see how it matters. It doesn't change anything." His toned was clipped, as though he didn't want to be discussing this with me.

"Of course not," I said quickly. "I was just thinking for the kids . . . you know. For them to have a clearer picture of who their mother was. Having her other yearbooks or other photo albums during that time might be good for them. Make them feel more connected to her, you know?" I didn't say I wanted to find out what had happened to her back then, that I wondered if it might somehow help explain how she died. Because if she *did* commit suicide and it was something from her past that led her down that dark road, it would mean that my getting engaged to Victor hadn't. It would mean her dying wasn't partially my fault.

He pondered this a moment, then leaned over to kiss me again. "I'll see what I can do."

I didn't know what he meant by that, exactly, but I took it as a good sign that I hadn't made him

234

angry. I put my hands at the back of his neck and prolonged the kiss, teasing him a bit this time by running one hand down his smooth chest to the waistband of his sweats and slipping it under the elastic.

"Oh god," he said, slowly pulling away. "Now you're just playing dirty."

"I thought you *liked* it when I played dirty."

He gave a good-natured growl and finally went to the kitchen to make his own coffee. I threw myself back down on the couch, thinking of how before Kelli died, Victor and I made a point of having plenty of sex during the week when the kids were gone, so on the weekends they were with us, we could focus on them without the distraction of our raging hormones. Now I wondered how we'd ever manage to be naked together again. I knew couples with kids figured it out, but I'd heard from most of my other married girlfriends that sex went downhill after the kids arrived. I suffered a pang of guilt for even thinking of such a shallow thing considering our current circum-stances—*What, the kids move in and you're not going to make love to me any-more?* I realized how immature and whiny the thought sounded. Still, I couldn't imagine losing that physical connection with Victor and was willing to put up a fight to keep it.

The kids got up a few minutes later and I showered while Victor fed them breakfast. Neither of them said very much, though Max gave me an unexpected hug as I passed him in the hallway back toward the kitchen. "Good morning," he mumbled.

I hugged him in return, rubbing his back. I smiled at this spontaneous show of affection, a little surprised by the intense rush of tenderness that filled me.

"Hey, buddy," I said. "Going to take a shower?" He nodded, and I continued into the kitchen, where Victor and Ava were sitting at the counter, looking through the photo albums again, and I wondered if our brief conversation earlier had inspired him to do this with her. A tear rolled down Ava's cheek and Victor reached over to wipe it away with the edge of his thumb, then leaned over and kissed her on top of her head.

It touched me, seeing him comfort his daughter like this. Being the kind of father I'd always wished mine had been to me. It struck me that Ava and I had something in common—being forced to grow up at thirteen, well before the time that we should have had to. Me because of the birth of Sam, needing to help take care of him, and Ava because of the death of her mother. I thought about what my father might have been like if my mother had died, leaving him alone with Sam and me. I imagined the wild grief I would have felt in losing her—the one grounding force in my life, the one person I knew I could always count on—and I simply couldn't conjure a picture of my father sitting with me as Victor sat with Ava now. I suddenly felt better than I had all week, believing that the four of us just might make a family yet.

"Hey, Ava," I said, and she jumped a little, as though just noticing I'd entered the room. "I was thinking about going to the mall and doing a little shopping. Are you interested?" I didn't really have a reason to shop—I just thought it was something Ava might actually want to do. Something that could momentarily distract her from her pain.

Ava shrugged. "Not really."

Victor looked at me and mouthed the word "sorry," and I gave him a brief nod in return, despite my ego's suffering another quick hit. "Well," he said. "I think I'm going to head over to your mom's place and pick up the rest of your clothes. Grace will hang out with you guys here, okay?"

I flashed him a quick look, a little bothered that he hadn't asked if I'd be fine with staying with them—maybe I'd want to go into the office; maybe I actually did want to go to the mall—but I swallowed the feeling as quickly as it rose up inside me. We were a team now. I had to remember that. We had to back each other up.

"I want to go with you," Ava said, pushing her stool out from the breakfast bar, but Victor shook his head and put out a hand to stop her.

"No, honey. It's too soon."

"Too soon to be in my own house?" Ava said, lifting her chin. "Too soon to pick out what clothes I want to have with me?"

Victor sighed. "I'll pack up your whole dresser and closet."

"But I want to go to my *house*," Ava said.

"This is your house now," Victor said. "I don't want you going back there."

Ava's mouth dropped open. "Not *ever?*"

Victor shook his head. "There's no reason to. I'll bring you a few boxes of your mom's stuff, too, okay? So you can have it here?"

Ava's face flushed scarlet and she slammed her mother's album shut. "You just want to pretend she never existed!" she said, her voice getting louder with each word. "You're *glad* she's dead so you don't have to deal with her!"

"Ava," I said, trying to calm her. "I don't think your dad feels that way at all."

She glared at me, blue eyes flashing. "How would *you* know?" she snarled, and I could feel the weight of her contempt from across the room. I thought about her apology yesterday and wondered if she'd only been trying to placate me. Maybe this, right now, the way she was looking at me with utter disdain, was how she really felt.

"That's not true and you know it," Victor said

to her, apparently choosing to ignore the way she'd just spoken to me. The edge in his voice was back. I wanted to reach out and calm him, to warn him to not go to this place with Ava so soon. I didn't know when he'd decided against letting the kids go back to their mother's house. He hadn't dis-cussed it with me. It was a little extreme, I thought, to deny her the opportunity to see it again. I wondered what he was trying to protect her from. But this wasn't the time for me to question him, especially not in front of Ava. I looked back and forth between them, and I was struck by the similarities in their stances: back straight, shoulders back, jaw set.

"I don't know *anything* anymore!" Ava said in a pitch so high it sent shivers up my spine. She pulled the album to her chest and pushed past her father, running down the hall to her bedroom. The door slammed and I gave Victor a supportive smile.

"I'm thinking that's a sound we'll have to get used to," I said, hoping I could make him laugh. Hoping we could go back to that place on the couch where we were just an hour ago. Playful, teasing, affectionate. The way we used to be. But his expression remained grim and he strode past me as Ava just had, leaving me to stand in the kitchen all alone.

Ava

The moment I walked into homeroom on Monday morning, everyone went silent. Even Mrs. Philips stared at me as I stood in the threshold, holding my backpack across my chest like it was an inflatable life vest. "Ava," she finally said, "welcome back."

I'd spent extra time getting ready that morning, carefully brushing and straightening my hair, applying and reapplying a little mascara and blush until I was happy with the result. I picked out my best pair of jeans and a red tank top to wear under Mama's sweater, hoping that if I at least *looked* normal, everyone would assume that I was fine and leave me alone. The last thing I wanted to deal with was people telling me how sorry they were about Mama, how horrible it was that she had died. Like I needed reminding of *that.*

I gave Mrs. Philips a brief nod and kept my gaze glued to the wooden floor as I made my way to my desk by the window. It was too quiet. I wanted the chatter of the other kids to distract me from the thoughts that spun in my head. My dad had spent the weekend packing up Mama's house and bringing Max and me the rest of our stuff. He even brought over a few boxes of Mama's things—her clothes and books, mostly. He put a few boxes up in the attic, saying they were for Max and me to have later, when we grew up, then gave me a couple of boxes to go through. I let him put them in my room but shoved them into a corner after he left. I didn't feel ready to see what was inside. My anger was barbed and bitter in my mouth. I still couldn't believe he didn't let me go with him. I also couldn't believe he thought he could make me stay away.

Now, in class, I dropped my backpack to the floor, slid into my seat, and tried to focus on what Mrs. Philips was saying about next week's quiz on balancing equations, wishing this wasn't the one class Bree and I didn't share. Whitney sat one row and one seat behind me; I could feel her blue eyes boring into the back of my head. *I won't look at you. I won't.*

"Psst," Whitney whispered. "Ava." I lifted my chin and squinted my eyes like I was trying to focus on the board. "Hey, Ava!" She said my name again. "What happened to your mom?"

My skin prickled and I tried to ignore her. *Please, just leave me alone.*

"Did she really have a heart attack?" she asked, and finally, Mrs. Philips noticed she was talking.

"Whitney, can you come up here and solve for *x* in this problem, please? And explain as you go, too, so the rest of the class can follow along."

Whitney smiled sweetly at our teacher. "I would, Mrs. Philips, but I'm *so* upset about Ava's mother, I don't think I can. Isn't it just a *tragedy?*"

I whipped around and glared at her. "Don't. You. *Talk* about her." I growled the words, a little surprised at the sharp spike of my pulse, the urge I felt to haul off and smack her. An image rose in my mind: the quick sting of my open palm against her cheek, the shock and tears in her eyes. *The satisfaction of wiping that smug look right off her pretty face.*

"Ava, turn around, please," Mrs. Philips said. I complied, then she directed her attention back to Whitney. "Nice try, but no luck. Get on up here."

Whitney sighed and did what she was asked. She got the problem wrong, and when she returned to her seat, she bared her teeth at me. "So happy you're back," she said, her tone laced with sarcasm.

"So happy you're a *bitch,*" I murmured quietly, but still loud enough that Whitney would be sure to hear.

"Wow, you're such a *badass!*" Bree exclaimed later when I told her what I'd said to Whitney. We were walking together toward her house, which was only a few blocks from school. Dad had been waiting for me and Max in the parking lot when school was over, but I told him I wanted to go over to Bree's.

"I don't know," he said slowly as my brother scrambled into the back of the car.

"Dad!" Max said. "My friends made me a card and they all *signed* it." He held up a huge piece of folded white card stock, covered in scribbled names and, inexplicably, a few odd drawings of robots. *He's so stupid. Does a crappy card really make up for the fact that Mama is dead?*

Dad twisted his head toward the backseat. "That's nice, buddy. Very thoughtful."

I shot Max an evil glance and he stuck his tongue out at me. Ignoring him, I turned my attention back to what I was trying to accomplish. "Dad, please? I haven't spent any time with her in over a week. I need my best friend." I gave him my most convincing innocent smile, hoping he'd give in. I knew he felt bad about our fight. All weekend he'd tried to bribe me with offers of ice cream and to go through Mama's boxes with me, but I didn't give in. Now I figured if I asked something as small as going to Bree's, he'd see it as me forgiving him, which was exactly what I wanted him to believe.

"Will her mom be there?" he asked. *He's faltering. He's going to say yes.*

"Of course," I lied. My dad didn't know that Mama always called Bree's mom, Jackie, to make *sure* she was going to be there. He didn't have us with him often enough to understand that's what he should do. All I knew was I had to be back at her house by six thirty, when he'd come pick me up. That gave me three hours to get to Mama's house and back. If I was outside Bree's house waiting for him, he'd never know what I'd done.

Now I shrugged as Bree congratulated me on putting Whitney in her place. "She deserved it. I'm tired of her always pushing me around." I took a deep breath and released it, knowing what I was going to say next might upset my friend. "So, hey. I think I might try out for the dance team after all." I looked at her, carefully watching for her reaction.

She stopped in her tracks and swung her head around to look at me. "What? *Why?*"

I stopped walking, too, and sighed. I figured she'd freak out on me. "I just do. I think it might be fun."

"You just got done saying what a bitch Whitney is, and now you want to hang out with her and her minions?" Bree asked, shaking her head. "That's *crazy*."

"It is *not*," I snapped. "I don't care about Whitney. And I won't be 'hanging out' with her." I made invisible quotes with my fingers around the words, then dropped my arms to my sides. "My mom was a cheerleader, you know? She liked to dance. Maybe I'd be *good* at it." I felt the sting of tears in the back of my throat, and I swallowed hard to repress them. I didn't want to cry. It was only my first day back at school and I was already exhausted of everyone staring at me. It wasn't just Whitney—I saw other people whispering as I walked by them in the hallway, trying not to make eye contact. I just wanted to find a way to be *normal* again.

Her expression softened after I said this. "Okay," she said. "I get it." I was grateful she didn't push the subject. We started walking but didn't talk until we got to her house.

"What time is the bus?" I asked as we entered. I couldn't believe just she and her mom lived there in this huge house on the bluff overlooking downtown Seattle. Bree said her mom wouldn't marry her boyfriend because that would mean her dad would be able to stop paying alimony to her and she'd have to get a job. I thought that was pretty awful of Jackie, but I didn't say this to Bree, even though she probably already knew it was true. It was okay for me to say bad things about my parents or for her to say bad things about hers, but it wasn't cool for either of us to say it about each other's. Those were just the rules, and both Bree and I understood them.

"Four ten," she said. "The number fifty-five goes right past your mom's, right?"

I nodded. I'd taken that bus a few times on my own to come to Bree's. She glanced at the clock. "Let me feed the cats and then we should get going."

A few minutes later we headed out the door,

Bree making sure to set the alarm. It was only a short bus ride through the West Seattle Junction to get to my mom's tiny house at the top of Genesee Hill. It was a gray day; the clouds hung low in the sky, and it looked like it might rain. The edges of the leaves in our neighborhood had just started to turn red, like they had witnessed something they shouldn't have and were blushing. My muscles began to jitter as we walked from the bus stop to the front door. I checked for Diane's car, happy to see it wasn't in her driveway, so she wouldn't see us go inside. The last thing I needed was for her to call my dad and tell him I was here.

Taking a deep breath, I pulled my key out of my pocket and unlocked the front door. I looked at Bree. "Ready?"

She nodded and blew out a hot breath; her glasses a little steamed up from the moisture in the air. She wore one of her dad's plaid flannel shirts and a pair of jeans with holes in the knees, and carried her dark green backpack, in case there was anything we'd need to take with us.

Inside, the air was the same temperature as it was outside and had a strange, stale smell, like it had been much longer than a week that we'd been gone. All the lights were off, but there was enough daylight coming in through the front window that we could see. Everything looked just like I remembered—I couldn't even tell that

Dad had been there to pack up some of our things. The brown leather couch in the living room was covered with Mama's favorite pillows; the coffee table was strewn with an assortment of Max's action figures and several of my books. Our school pictures were on the mantel, and a pile of unfolded laundry was in a basket on the floor. I could see the plate that Mama had put the toast she had made me on still resting on the kitchen counter, and it made me want to cry. Why hadn't I eaten it?

Bree dropped her backpack to the floor. "What should we look for?"

"I don't know," I whispered, trying to control my breathing. "Let's check out her room, I guess?" The idea of seeing her bed, where I knew her body had been when she died, made me feel sick. *Maybe this wasn't such a great idea. Maybe we should just go.* Suddenly, a gripping sense of panic filled me. I couldn't afford to make my father angry by being here when he'd forbidden me to come. I couldn't afford to lose him, too.

But Bree was already walking down the hall, and before I knew it, I followed her. When I entered, I averted my gaze from the bed. Mama was everywhere in that room. After Daddy left us, she decorated it in blues, yellows, and lace—all of her favorite colors and fabrics. "We don't need him, do we, love?" she asked as I watched her roll the fresh paint on the walls. "We'll be just fine. We're strong women, you and me."

I'd nodded, a heavy, sinking feeling in my belly. I *did* need my daddy, and I wasn't so sure that Mama was strong. Strong people didn't cry over the littlest things, like when the microwave broke or when the bank closed before she got there to deposit her tips.

Now, standing in Mama's bedroom with Bree, I realized a little of what I'd been feeling over the last week was relief that I didn't have to take care of those tasks for Mama anymore. I wouldn't have to help her pay bills or call the plumber for her when the toilet broke. A wave of guilt washed over me with this thought, as though I could somehow hurt Mama by thinking it.

"Ava?" Bree said, jarring me back to the present. "Can I turn on her computer?"

"It's still here?" I said, surprised that my dad hadn't packed it up, too. I could tell he'd been in her closet—the door was open and all her clothes were gone. Seeing this brought up a fresh round of tears pricking my eyes—memories of Mama letting me play dress-up in her clothes, trying on her high heels, pretending one of her pretty slips was a ball gown. Impromptu fashion shows in her bedroom, helping her decide which outfit she should wear. Empty hangers were all that remained—ghostly reminders that she was gone.

"Yep," Bree said, motioning toward the desk by the window. "It's right there."

"Okay then," I said, taking another deep breath to keep from crying. "But here . . . let me." I took a couple of steps and sat down on the bench in front of Mama's desk. Bree sat down next to me. We waited for the laptop to boot up, then I pushed the right buttons on it and clicked on the icon to bring up a history of the websites my mom had visited. There weren't many—she didn't have a Facebook or Twitter account and she didn't like to shop online.

"Bank of America," I read aloud as I skimmed my finger down the list. "Google; Greg Morton, PI; Tracy Lemmings, PI." I paused, dropped my hand to the desk, and looked at her. "There are like ten PI websites."

"PI?" she repeated. "What's that?"

"Let's find out," I said, looking back to the screen and clicking on one of the links.

" 'Tracy Lemmings, Private Investigator,' " I read aloud. " 'We guarantee a discreet investigation to suit any of your personal or professional needs.' "

"Why would your mom need a private investigator?" Bree asked.

I blew a long breath out between my lips. "I have no idea." She shot me a sidelong glance, her eyebrows slightly raised. "Really, Bree. I don't *know*."

She sighed. "Well, let's look at all the sites and see if there's a theme."

"A theme?"

"Yeah. Like if they specialize in a certain area or something, you know?"

I nodded. "Good idea." I clicked through all of the websites, but each of them offered a variety of services: surveillance on a cheating spouse, searching for runaway or missing children and long-lost relatives, suspicious insurance claims— the list went on and on. There was no way to know what she would have hired them to do for her.

"Let's look at her e-mail," Bree suggested. "Maybe she sent something to one of the investigators."

I nodded again, then typed in the password to my mom's e-mail account: a combination of my and Max's birthdays. I'd helped her create it because she didn't know how to do it on her own.

"All right, then," I said. "Let's see." I typed a few keystrokes and then used the mouse to sort the e-mails by who they were from. "There's a lot to Diane," I said, peering at the screen. She read for a minute, and I did, too. Most of the e-mails were about meeting for coffee or about fights Diane was having with her husband.

"I don't see anything to a private investigator," Bree said. "Do you?"

I shook my head. "What about other people? Maybe there are some from my grandparents."

I ran a search for the names "Thomas" and "Ruth" and nothing came up. I tried again with

"Mother" and "Father," "Dad" and "Mom." Nothing came up. "Do you think they'd even *have* a computer?" Bree asked.

I considered this point. "Probably not," I said with a sigh. Finding out what happened between Mama and her parents might turn out to be more difficult than I thought. I didn't even know what I was looking for, really, since I couldn't imagine parents who didn't love their child like I knew mine loved me. Even with how mad I was at my dad right now, I knew he loved me. I scrolled further down the screen, past old e-mails between Mama and Dad. My belly did flip-flops thinking what it was I might discover, but something inside me pushed to keep going, so I ignored the gnawing sensation in my chest that told me I should shut the machine down and just leave. I opened one dated three years ago, right after my dad moved out, and Bree and I started reading:

Kelli,
You know I love our kids, and I wish that I could find a way to make it work, but I just don't think it's possible. I'll file the paperwork this week. I've tried so hard to understand everything you've gone through, but I'm done trying to force you to deal with it. I'm done with it all.

You don't have to worry about anything— I'll take care of it. You can stay in the house with the kids; I'll get another place nearby. I'll want to see them as much as I can, of course, but I do think you'll have to go back to work. I'll talk with Steve and see if you can have your old job back waiting tables. The money's good, and you'd have insurance.

"Why would your dad help her get a job when he was leaving her?" Bree asked, moving her gaze from the screen over to me. "That doesn't make sense."

"He took care of her," I said, just above a whisper. "She always said he promised to take care of her and then he just went away." I read the rest of the e-mail.

We made two beautiful children together, and whatever happened with us, I know that we were meant to be together, even if it wasn't forever. I know we were together so they would be ours.

That was all it said. He didn't even sign his name. Bree dropped back against her chair, then spoke quietly. "Do you want to keep looking?"

I shook my head. I felt deflated, suddenly not caring about anything else I might find. I didn't know why I thought coming here would help me feel better. What I was looking for—what I *really* cared about—was gone. But I couldn't tell Bree that. I couldn't say that I'd held a tiny flicker of hope that I'd walk into this house and Mama would be here. "Baby," she'd say, holding out her arms to me. "Everything's okay. It was all just a bad dream. I was sick, and I couldn't come home." A coma, I imagined. Like on a soap opera. A coma so deep even the doctors wouldn't know she was still alive.

"Are you sure?" Bree said, snapping me back to the moment. Back to where Daddy had left us and Mama was dead. "You don't want to get anything else?"

I shook my head again. "Not now. I can't." My palms were sweaty and my heart threw itself over and over against the inside of my chest.

"Okay." Bree sighed. "I'm sorry, Ava."

"Whatever," I said, shutting down the computer. "Let's just go." My voice trembled and the words didn't come out hard and strong, the way I wanted them to. I stood up and turned around, this time forcing myself to look at the spot where Mama had died. Her blue comforter was crumpled the way I'd seen it a hundred times before, pulled back like she might come back and climb beneath it at any moment. I could smell her all around me—the faint scent of her sweet perfume. Above her bed, she'd framed a stick-figure drawing of our family I'd made for her in third grade: Daddy tall in the middle, his hair sticking out like porcupine quills; Mama standing in a pink dress next to him. Me holding Daddy's hand, and Max holding Mama's. It was a beautiful day in that picture, the sun a bright yellow ball in the impossibly blue sky. We all had smiles on our faces, not a care in the world. It was the way I saw us back then, when we were all still together. Back before the family I knew—the family I'd thought would always be mine—tore at its seams and finally fell apart.

They were fighting again. I shoved my head beneath my pillow and tried not to listen, but it was impossible. Their anger was so big, so powerful, it pushed through the walls of our house. I imagined it was black, thick, and heavy, like storm clouds brewing in the sky. My bedroom was right next to theirs; I couldn't ignore it.

Dad had come home late, way after Max and I went to bed. I woke up once to the sound of Mama crying, then once more when I heard their bedroom door slam. "I can't do this anymore!" my dad yelled. "If you can't handle how much I have to work to take care of you, then there's nothing I can do! You're a grown woman, for Christ's sake! You need to start acting like one." His voice was twisted in a way I'd never heard before.

"*I* need to grow up?" Mama shrieked. "*I* do? Who's the one who's never with his children?" She paused for a minute, and I hoped it might all be over, but then she started again. "That's you,

Victor. *You.* Don't think I don't know what's going on here. Don't think I haven't seen."

Seen what? I wondered, sitting up in my bed, switching on the small lamp on the nightstand, then pulling my blankets up to my neck. Dad had been gone more and more. One night last week he hadn't come home at all. He told Mama he had so much work to do, he slept over at the restaurant, but I knew Mama didn't believe him. He had a couch in his office there, so I didn't know why she thought he wasn't telling the truth.

"You haven't seen *anything,*" my dad said. It sounded like he was spitting the words. "You're too busy feeling sorry for yourself. I'm sorry your parents disowned you. I'm sorry you can't get over it! I'm done with it. *No more,* do you understand? I'm *done.*"

"Fine!" Mama screamed. "You have somewhere you'd rather be? Go! Get the hell out of my house!"

I cringed, my stomach starting to hurt worse than it ever had before. I didn't understand what Mama was saying. Where else would Daddy want to be?

I heard drawers slamming shut, Mama still crying. The door of my room slowly opened and I held my breath, thinking it might be Daddy, but it was only Max. He had one hand on the doorknob and his worn yellow blanket in the other. His eyes were wide; his bottom lip trembled. He

255

was only four. "Come here," I whispered, lifting up my blanket and scooting closer to the wall. He tiptoed over to my bed and climbed in. His body was warm, but he was shaking.

After a moment, he put his head against my chest and started to cry. "Shh," I said, slipping one arm around him, and together, we waited for morning to come.

Grace

"Grace?" Max's voice crept into my dreams and tickled me awake. He put his small hand on my shoulder and gave it a gentle shake. Victor wasn't home yet; it was a few weeks after Kelli's death, and he had started working later hours at the restaurant to make up for the time he spent taking care of the kids in the afternoons. Last night, he'd called at eleven to say he had to finish the wine order and wouldn't be home until well after the bar closed.

"What's wrong, sweetie?" I asked Max. "It's so late." *Or so early.* I forced myself to open my eyes and look at the clock. Two twenty-three. *Ugh. Definitely early.*

"I wet the bed," he whispered. "I'm sorry. I didn't mean it." He started to cry. "I had too much milk last night after dinner and I'm not supposed to and I had a bad dream and I wet the bed!" He began to sob in earnest, and I spun upright, steadying myself on the mattress with one arm and reaching out to him with the other, rubbing his back. The front of his jammies were soaked and cold. I tried not to gasp as a waft of ammonia hit me.

"Hey now. Of course you didn't mean it. Don't worry. We'll take care of it."

He clenched his eyes shut and shook his head rapidly back and forth, not seeming to hear me through his tears. "Mama always says not to but I forgot 'cause I was just so thirsty!"

I wanted to cry, too, hearing him refer to her in the present tense—as though she were still alive. "Max, honey," I said, dropping into a squat so we were eye level with each other. "I didn't know that, so it's nobody's fault. Okay?" I pushed his damp hair back from his face and gave him a quick kiss on the forehead. "It's only an accident. We just need to go get you some new sheets and new PJ's, right? Everything's going to be okay."

"No it's not!" he shrieked. He stamped his foot. "Not it's not, no it's *not!*"

"Max," I said again, trying to keep my voice level, but feeling my heart rate begin to rise. "Ava is sleeping. I need you to try to be quiet." I glanced at the doorway, willing Victor to walk through it. I wasn't sure how to handle this on my own.

"No!" he screeched, and began to sob. "I want

Mama!" he cried, and suddenly swung his arm out, knocking my alarm clock to the hardwood floor with a clatter.

"Max!" I grabbed his arms so he wouldn't lash out at anything else.

"Did he wet the bed?" Ava said as she entered the room. So much for not waking her. Max yanked away from me, ran over to his sister, and pressed his face into her side. I straightened my spine and nodded. She frowned. "You shouldn't let him have milk after dinner."

Before I could stop myself, I shot her an angry look. "I realize that *now,* Ava," I snapped. Things had still been a little tense between us since the day she'd fought with Victor over going back to Kelli's house. I kept my distance, trying to give her the space she seemed to need. Apparently, it hadn't helped.

She rolled her eyes and wouldn't meet my gaze. "C'mon, Max. Can you help me strip off your sheets? And then we'll clean you up a little and get you back to sleep." He nodded slowly and sniffled away his tears.

"Let me help you, too," I said, taking a step toward them, but Ava held up a hand to stop me.

"It's fine. I've got it." They left the room, and after I listened to the murmur of their voices against the backdrop of running water, less than ten minutes later it was quiet again.

Once curled back up under the covers, though,

I couldn't sleep. I thought of everything I didn't know about Max and Ava—all the things that were as natural to Kelli as breath. And while so far there was little tangible demand on me with the kids around, I felt oddly strained. When we were all home, everything became focused around what they needed, their schedule. I couldn't help but feel a little bit backed into a corner by the continuous noise—of the TV, their loud video games, and Max, who seemed literally incapable of moving through the house without slamming a door or stomping his feet against the hardwood floors. Accustomed to silence—maybe infused with a little music or the occasional reality TV show—I jumped at every sound he made. Ava—unlike tonight—most of the time was quiet and withdrawn. On some level, that was almost more disconcerting than Max's constant over-the-top energy level and need for interaction. The counselor at the hospital told Victor that kids tend to process things more internally, and we should watch out for their grief coming out in other ways.

"What kind of ways?" I'd asked him, a little panicked by the thought of what their behavior might entail. I suddenly envisioned Max purposely throwing baseballs through our windows or Ava coming home with a tattoo.

Victor had shrugged. "She didn't really say."

"How's the schedule working out?" Melody asked one evening when she'd come over to our house and Victor and the kids weren't home yet. She and I sat at the dining room table, nibbling at a plate of cheese, flatbread, and fruit she'd brought over, sipping at a small glass of crisp Chardonnay.

I shrugged, crunching on the bite in my mouth before speaking. "Victor says it's going okay. It's only for a couple of hours when he picks them up from school, and then I take over so he can go do the dinner shift."

"Isn't having to leave the restaurant and then go back later pretty stressful for him?"

I took a swallow of wine. "Are you saying I should change *my* schedule and go pick them up from school, so he can have a break?" The sudden defensiveness in my tone surprised even me.

She dropped back against her chair, eyebrows raised. "Wow. I'm pretty sure that's not what I said, Grace."

I sighed and reached out a hand to squeeze hers. "Oh god, I'm sorry. It's just been so hard seeing how tired he is, and I feel guilty, like I should be doing more, you know?"

"I get it," she said, squeezing my hand in return before pulling away. "But your job is important, too, and it's not exactly conducive to bringing children with you, right?"

"I know. But if I'm going to marry him, isn't that part of the deal?" Melody didn't answer, so I went on. "And now Ava wants to try out for the dance team and Victor isn't sure he can manage getting Max to basketball at the Boys and Girls Club *and* getting her to practice. He already had to give up his Tae Kwon Do classes because he just couldn't fit them in." I sighed. "Jesus. Listen to me. Bitch, bitch, bitch. Can we talk about something else, please? What's happening with you? How are things with Spencer?"

She sat back against her chair with a dreamy expression on her face. Her brown eyes lit up as she told me how he'd been calling her every day since their first dinner date and how the massage she gave him ended in a highly unprofessional manner.

I laughed when she told me this. "I thought you said that was against the masseuse's professional code of ethics or something."

She shrugged her shoulders. "It was an accident!"

"Oh," I said with a snort, "I see. Your hands just *accidentally* massaged his penis?"

"No!" she said, still laughing. "He rolled over onto his back and there it was, beneath the sheet. I didn't mean to do it. The opportunity just sort of . . . *presented* itself." She wiggled her eyebrows. "In a *big* way. If you know what I mean."

I rolled my eyes and shook my head, chuckling. "Okay, I so did *not* need to know that." I paused, thrilled to feel such a sense of lightness in this moment, laughing with my best friend. "Do you think it might be serious?"

She pressed her lips together and nodded briskly. "He's just the gentlest man I've ever met. He doesn't talk a lot, but when he does, it's genuine and totally honest, you know?" She paused. "Did you know he was a foster child?" I shook my head, and she continued. "He told me he learned he was more likely to get adopted if he seemed quiet and well behaved, so it just stuck with him to be like that. But he never *was* adopted, and he really, really wants to have kids, so he can give them the kind of life he never had." She sighed. "Isn't that the sweetest thing you've ever heard?"

"It's very sweet. And fits right in with your plans, huh?"

She stared out the window a moment before responding. "I'm trying not to have any plans this time. No agenda. Just appreciating what I like about him, which is a lot. We'll just see how things go."

We chatted more about how she wasn't going home to Iowa for Thanksgiving or Christmas this year, even though her parents were begging her to. She booked more stressed out clients during the holiday season and they tended to tip her extremely well as a bonus, so she decided she couldn't afford to be gone.

"You'll spend them with us, then, I hope?" I said. "You and Spencer."

She smiled. "That would be great." Holding up

her wineglass, she tilted it toward mine for a toast. "To good friends," she said.

"To friends," I echoed. "The family you get to choose."

Thankfully, Sam and his boyfriend, Wade, offered to host Thanksgiving at their house in Magnolia. We'd sort of overlooked Halloween, since neither of the kids expressed interest in celebrating anything so soon after their mother's death. Thanksgiving would be the first holiday we'd be spending as a family, and Victor and I were happy to hand the organizing over to Sam and his partner.

It was wonderful to see my brother in such a loving relationship, since his first couple of boyfriends had a hard time with the concept of monogamy. Then Wade showed up at the AIDS center as a support person for a mutual friend who'd recently been diagnosed as HIV positive, and sparks flew. Almost two years later, they were still going strong.

"Can we bring anything?" I asked Sam the Saturday afternoon before the actual holiday.

"Well, you know Wade is an absolute *beast* in the kitchen," Sam said. "But if you want to bring some kind of appetizer for us to munch on while he cooks, and maybe a dessert, that would be great. Tell the ankle biters I'm looking forward to it."

I hung up the phone and smiled at Ava, who was

sitting at the dining room table painting her fingernails bright orange. Max was having a play-date at a friend's house and Victor was at the restaurant to make sure everything was organized for the holiday rush.

"Sam says he's looking forward to seeing you two on Thanksgiving," I said. She didn't respond but gave the barest shrug of her shoulders. I tried again. "Is there anything you like to eat every year? Something we could make to bring?"

She looked up, then, her eyes wide. "My mom always made the best pumpkin cream cheese Bundt cake."

Buoyed by the fact that she'd actually spoken to me in a normal tone of voice, I seized the opportunity. "Well, why don't we do that, then? We can go to the store and get what we need."

She gave me a doubtful look. "Maybe we should wait for my dad." She was thinking, I was sure, about my tendency to avoid the kitchen.

I stood up. "I think we should just do it. I actually do know how to cook, it's just not my favorite thing." Maybe this was all we needed to get over the tension between us. I'd been holding back, not wanting to push, waiting for her to reach out to me, when it was me, as the adult, who needed to reach out to her.

Ava nodded slowly, her expression lightening the slightest bit. "But we don't have the recipe. It's at my mom's house."

My spirits fell. "Are you sure? Your dad didn't bring her cookbooks back with him?"

Ava slowly shook her head. "I don't think so." She stared at me, wary, waiting to see what I'd do.

"Well," I finally said. "Do you still have the key? We can go pick it up and come right back." She nodded, and I swallowed the apprehension I felt in going against Victor's wishes, rationalizing that we'd only be at the house for a minute or two, just to grab the recipe. "We'll have to be quick, though, okay? Like *ninja* quick."

She granted me a small smile and less than twenty minutes later, we pulled up in front of Kelli's house. I turned to look at her as we took off our seat belts. "Are you sure you're okay to do this?"

She nodded again and we headed inside. There was a small pile of mail on the entryway table— Victor had asked Diane to put it in the house for him to pick up. He knew he needed to get the house completely cleared out so he could get it listed for sale, but he'd been so busy, he hadn't found the time. I also suspected that because it had been his mom's, it was possible he'd have a hard time letting it go.

Ava walked slowly into the kitchen, and I followed behind her, watching for signs that being in her mother's house was too much for her to handle, but she seemed to be okay.

"Do you know where it is?" I asked her.

"Yep," Ava said, reaching to the left of the stove, where there was a shelf filled with various sizes and shapes of cookbooks. She pulled down a small one and opened it, flipping through the pages until she looked up and smiled. "Here it is. It's all covered with splatters." Her eyes began to fill with tears and she quickly looked away.

I could almost see the memories flashing through her mind—in the kitchen with her mother, laughing together as they baked. A thought struck me. "Ava, you know how the pictures in your mom's photo albums kind of stopped after she was fourteen?" She nodded but still didn't look at me. "Well, do you happen to know where she kept her yearbooks from high school? Did she ever show them to you?"

She snapped her gaze back to me and her eyes were free of any tears. "No, I never saw them. I don't know where they are." She paused, tilting her head to one side. "Why?"

I didn't want to tell her about the yearbook I'd found, since Victor had never brought the issue back up after our talk the day of the memorial. It was bad enough I had brought Ava here when he had specifically instructed her not to come.

"No reason, really," I said. "Just curious." I glanced at my watch. "We should probably go so we have time to make the cake before your dad gets home."

"Are you going to tell him we came here?"

"Yes," I said, though inside I wanted to say no. "I'll just explain about needing the recipe and he'll understand." This time, she followed me into the living room. She stopped in front of the table by the front door, grabbed a pile of letters, and began to thumb through them.

"Are you expecting something?" I asked. "We should take them with us, so your dad can make sure any bills get paid." Not seeming to hear me, Ava set the bulk of the mail back down, held on to a single envelope, and then tore it open. "Ava. That's not yours."

"It's from a doctor in California," she said, ignoring me. "Why would she get a letter from there?" She read it out loud, quickly. " 'Dear Ms. Hansen: I'm sorry to inform you that I do not have you listed as a patient in 1993 or 1994. I wish you luck in finding whatever it is you're looking for. Sincerely, Dr. Brian Stiles.'" Ava looked at me. "Do you think she was sick back then? Do you think it might have had something to do with what happened to her?"

"I don't know, honey," I said. "Maybe we can ask your dad, okay? Maybe he knows." I doubted that was true. Victor had made it clear to me that Kelli didn't like to talk about the specifics of her past. But after I did some quick math in my head, I realized that 1993 and 1994 would have been her freshman and sophomore years of high school, right when the hole in her life appeared.

My mind flipped through possibilities and landed on one that made the most sense: If she had suffered from depression, maybe her parents sought treatment for her and she was looking for her medical history. Not being in contact with them, she might not have known—or remembered —the doctor's name. I smiled at Ava, gently taking the letter from her hand and slipping it into my purse. "Let's go, okay? We can talk about it with your dad later."

On the way home, we made another quick stop at the grocery store to pick up the ingredients we needed for the cake. Soon we were back in the kitchen, and I was happy to focus on something other than Kelli's past. "Okay," I said. "What do we do first?"

"I don't know," Ava said quietly. "My mom always made this. I just watched." She was obviously distracted by the letter we'd found at Kelli's house. I was, too, but I was also determined to finish what I'd started with her— to bake her mother's cake.

I hesitated. She wasn't going to make this easy on me. "Well, let's look at the recipe, then. What does it say?"

She leaned over the cookbook and told me we needed to cream the butter, cream cheese, and sugar until it was fluffy. I grabbed the three cubes of butter and two packages of cream cheese from the refrigerator with feigned confidence. I really wasn't a baker—in a pinch, I could do decent tacos, spaghetti, or meatloaf—but I couldn't stop and call Melody or Victor for help now. "Here," I said, "you unwrap these and put them in the mixer while I measure out the sugar."

Ava complied and put the cubes in the mixer. I added the sugar and turned the machine on, horrified by the sudden *thunk-thunk*ing noise it made. "That butter's pretty hard, huh?" I said.

Ava gave me a pointed look. "It never made that sound when my mom made it."

Of course it didn't. I sighed internally and kept a bright smile on my face. "Now, what do we add?" Eggs came next, the recipe said, and over the next five minutes, we added the rest of the ingredients to the mixer according to the instructions on the page.

" 'The batter should be light and creamy,' " Ava read, then looked at the gloppy mess in the bowl. Hard little bits of butter and white cream cheese chunks floated to the surface; the batter looked about as appetizing as spoiled milk. "I don't think this is right," she said.

"Let's bake it and see what happens," I said. "Maybe the clumpy bits melt and disappear when it's in the oven?"

She looked at me, one eyebrow raised, but handed me the buttered Bundt pan, and I poured the mixture in, then slid it into the preheated oven. "Voilà! We did it." Half an hour later, when the timer went off, I pulled the cake out of the oven. It was a hard, dark brown, and lumpy mess. "Well, at least it *smells* good," Ava said, and we both looked at each other, then burst out laughing.

Just then, we heard the front door open. "Dad!" Ava yelled, scooting into the living room. "You'll never guess what Grace did! She tried to *bake!*"

I followed her and saw Victor hugging his daughter. He looked up and smiled when he saw me, his eyes lighting up in a way they hadn't for over a month.

" 'Tried' is definitely the operative word," I said. "I think it's more of a science experiment than a cake."

Ava looked up at her father, craning her neck. "The batter was *gross,*" she said, and I chuckled.

"*Really* gross," I said, agreeing with her. "We'll make another one on Wednesday, okay? Maybe your dad will be kind enough to give us some helpful hints."

"I can do that," Victor said, still smiling. He looked down at Ava. "I need to talk with Grace, honey. Can you give us a minute alone?"

Ava's smile vanished as she let go of Victor and walked down the hall to her bedroom. I waited until I heard her door click closed, then looked at him, concerned. There was no way he could have known that I'd taken Ava to Kelli's house. It had to be something else. "What's up?"

He sighed, pulling off his coat and hanging it

in the closet by the front door. "Spencer slipped in the kitchen a little while ago and landed hard on the cement floor. I'm pretty sure he broke his arm."

"Oh no!" I said. "Did he go to the hospital?"

"He's there now," Victor said. "And I'm down my head chef for Thanksgiving."

I felt something in my belly drop down a notch and realized the last thing I needed to do right then was tell him where Ava and I had gone. It would only give him more to worry about. "What does that mean?"

"It means I'm screwed. I gave a lot of people the holiday off and there's no one else to cover. Spencer was supposed to manage all the catering we're sending out plus the reservations we have for dinner tomorrow. Now I'll have to do it all."

I didn't respond right away. I thought of the huge pile of work I needed to get done before Monday —the client files I needed to review, the budget that needed tweaking before the end of the year. I had hoped to make some headway on it before the holiday weekend, so Victor and I could actually enjoy some time together. A tiny thread of irrita-tion shot through my veins, but then an idea struck me. "Can't you hire someone to cover for him temporarily?"

He shook his head. "There's not enough time. And even if I hired someone next week, I'd have to be there to train them on the menu, anyway, which is really more work than just biting the bullet and doing it myself."

I thought about how Victor would have to run the restaurant at night on his own until after New Year's, and the holidays were his busiest season, when he needed to make enough money to make it through the leaner times. From Thanksgiving on last year, he'd worked fourteen-hour days, six days a week—I was lucky to see him at all. And now, with the kids to manage on top of the restaurant, I couldn't fathom how he'd make it work. It was doubtful he would hire someone to babysit the kids—I'd suggested this right after the kids had moved in, thinking an after-school nanny would alleviate the pressure he was feeling to be with them when they weren't in school, but he'd nixed the idea. "They need *me*," he told me. "Not some stranger. I don't want them to feel like I'm shoving them off on someone else. Like they're somehow inconveniencing me." I understood what he was saying, but now, considering the circumstances, it seemed like a good time to reevaluate. Kids had caregivers other than their parents all the time. I knew from years of being in HR the challenges parents faced in the work-place—rare was the family who didn't employ the help of day care or a nanny to enable both parents to be at their jobs. But there was something deeper in Victor driving him to be so completely hands-on with the kids. He was worried after the loss of their mother that if he hired a babysitter, they might feel he didn't want to be with them.

"Couldn't the kids be alone for a few hours after school?" I suggested now. "I was already taking care of Sam when I was Ava's age."

"And you enjoyed that so much, right?" he said, raising a single eyebrow. I was silent, so he went on. "Christ. If Spence really is totally out of commission, I'll need to rework my whole schedule. I'm not sure how I'm going to pull it off."

"You'll figure it out," I said, wishing I were entirely convinced that he would.

Ava

I sat on my bed, staring at the boxes of my mother's things. They were clothes, mostly, plus some of the romance books she loved to read. Daddy didn't know that Mama hadn't let me read them, but now I wanted to—more than just the sex parts. I wanted to better understand what she saw in them. I'd asked her once and all she'd said was, "Hope, baby girl. They give me hope."

Now I listened as Dad talked with Grace in the living room, their voices low enough that I couldn't hear what they were saying, even if I pressed my ear up against the door. Dad had that weird, strained look on his face when he walked through the front door, and even though he laughed when I told him about the cake, I could tell he was stressed out about something. I wondered if Grace had already told him that she'd taken me to Mama's to get the recipe; I wondered if she told him about Dr. Stiles's letter. I couldn't stop thinking that Mama knew she was sick. Maybe she had some kind of horrible disease that she never told us about. Maybe she'd been so sick that she missed the last three years of high school. But if that were true, why would she tell me that she was a cheerleader? My stomach began to hurt, thinking that she might have lied to me. Thinking that she hadn't been a cheerleader at all. I wondered if she'd been looking at a private investigator to help her find the doctor. I wondered whether she'd still be alive if she'd found the right one.

I thought back to the times *I'd* been sick, when I had a fever and needed to stay home from school. Before he'd leave for work in the morning, Daddy would make me peppermint tea and cinnamon toast, bringing it into my room on a tray. "Daddy's medicine has arrived," he'd tell me. "It's magic, you know."

I'd smile and take a small sip of the tea. "Feel better already, don't you?" he'd say, cupping my cheek in his palm.

"Yes," I said, nodding. "Thank you, Daddy."

"I love you, kitten." He gave me a hug, then Mama would kiss him before he walked out the door. "You've got the best mama in the world," he'd say, and Mama would smile and look at him with so much love, it almost made me jealous. I didn't understand what could have happened to make that kind of love go away.

A little while later, after Max came home from his playdate, Dad sat us down in the living room to explain that he was going to miss Thanksgiving dinner with us this year. "There's no one to cook if I'm not there," he said. "And if no one cooks, all the families who were depending on my restaurant to make their dinner won't be able to eat."

"What about *your* family?" I said. "We depend on you, too."

Dad's eyes closed, and he grimaced. "I know, baby. But I'll see you later that night, and we'll have some of your mom's dessert that you and Grace will make, okay? I'll go over the recipe with her so you two can get it perfect this time. That will be our special celebration that no one else gets to have."

I shot Grace a quick, sidewise glance as he said this, wondering again if he knew where we'd gone. Grace furrowed her eyebrows and gave her head a brief shake, and I understood that she hadn't told him yet. It felt a little strange, sharing a small secret with Grace, just as it had felt weird to actually enjoy hanging out with her earlier.

"It's not fair," I said. "Why can't someone else just do it for you?"

"It has to be me, Ava," Victor said. "Things have been a little slow at the restaurant and I need to make sure everything runs smoothly so maybe we'll get more customers. Times are a little tight for everyone right now, and this is just something I have to do to make sure the restaurant keeps going. Okay?"

"It's not going to close, is it?" Max asked. "You're not going to lose your job?" I felt a little frantic considering this, wondering if having us move in was costing Dad money he didn't have.

Dad reached over and mussed Max's hair. "No, buddy. But people aren't going out to eat as much as they used to so it's really important I keep all of my regular customers happy." Max nodded, and Dad kept talking. "Okay, then. I want you two to be on your best behavior at Sam and Wade's house, please." He looked pointedly at Max. "No burping."

"What if I have to fart?" Max asked with a mischievous grin.

Dad sighed. "You run to the bathroom. No bodily functions in public, do you understand?"

Max nodded, but his eyes twinkled, and I wondered if he was capable of following Dad's instructions at someone else's house when he couldn't follow them at home.

• • •

Walking into the gym on Monday afternoon was probably one of the scariest things I'd ever done. There were five members of the dance squad sitting at a long table on the far side of the basketball court, clad in their tight red sweaters and short skirts. Mrs. McClain stood next to them, and another group of girls—girls like me —sat in a small circle on the floor, waiting for their turn to be called. Tryouts usually happened in September at the start of school, but Sarah Winston's mother got a new job and they had to move to Portland, so her spot was open, plus there was a rumor Mrs. McClain might open a few more. The more I thought about it, the more fun it sounded like it would be. I'd get to dance for assemblies and sports events; I'd even get to ride the bus with the boys for away games. I wondered if Skyler Kenton would notice if I joined the team. He was probably the cutest boy in eighth grade—I liked his crooked smile and shaggy black hair. My second day back to school after the week Max and I were gone, he'd come up to me in the hallway by my locker and gave me a hug. "Sorry about your mom," he said, and then walked away before I could even say thank you.

"He *totally* likes you," Bree whispered in my ear. She'd been standing right next to me when it happened.

"He does not," I said. "He's just being nice." I

looked around for Bree now, wondering if she'd come to watch me try out. She wasn't there.

"You're really going to *do* this?" she'd asked me earlier that day. I knew she was having a hard time with the idea of me doing something with the "popular" girls, but I couldn't let that change my mind.

"You could try out too, you know," I suggested. I told her how there might be more than one opening. "We could do it together."

"Uh-uh," she said, shaking her head. "No way. I look like I'm having a seizure when I try to dance." She paused. "But it's cool that you want to. Your mom would be proud."

Would she? I wondered. *What if she thought a smart girl wouldn't worry about dance team?* People had told Mama being pretty was all she had. I asked her once why Daddy wanted her to marry him. She'd looked at me and said, "Because men like pretty things."

Now I walked slowly, heel to toe, over to the five other girls waiting their turn to dance. Lisa Brown was the only one who smiled at me; the others tilted their heads together, whispering. *Are they talking about me? The girl whose mother died?* I didn't want to be that girl. I smoothed my hair and rubbed my lips together—I'd stopped in the bathroom to swipe on some lipstick and old mascara I had hidden in my locker. I'd practiced at home in my bedroom in front of the mirror, and I thought the routine I'd come up with was actually pretty good. I was wearing red stretchy shorts and a white T-shirt, cinched in the back with a rubber band so it wouldn't ride up when I was dancing.

I glanced over to the bleachers, where a few women sat together—mothers of the other girls, I supposed, and the hollow space inside my chest suddenly seemed to expand. I kept wanting to feel normal, but reminders that Mama was gone were everywhere—at home, and now at school.

I sat down next to Lisa and crossed my legs. "Hey," I said. "Good luck."

She smiled and tightened her ponytail. "You look really pretty," she said.

"Thanks," I said, blushing. "You too."

"Is your mom here?" Lisa asked, and then her hand flew to cover her mouth. "Oh *god*. I'm *so* sorry. I didn't even think . . . god. That was such a stupid thing to say." Her chin trembled as she spoke, and I knew she hadn't meant to hurt my feelings.

I pushed my lips together and shook my head, trying not to let the tears that stung the back of my eyes fall. "That's okay," I said, taking a deep breath with the words.

She put her hand on my arm. "I'm really sorry."

"Don't worry about it." I looked away from her toward the bleachers and was shocked to see Grace and Max finding a place to sit. Max caught my gaze with his own and began to jump up and down. "Hi, Ava!" he yelled. "We're here to watch you dance! Do it like this!" He did a little shimmy, wiggled his butt, and flapped his bent arms like a chicken.

"Oh my *god,*" I whispered under my breath.

"What?" Lisa asked, but then looked in Max's direction and laughed. "Oh. He's so cute."

"You don't have to *live* with him," I said. Grace waved at me, too, then gently pulled Max to sit down next to her. She must have left work early to be there—I'd told my dad I'd find a ride home after the audition, but I guessed because he was going to be at the restaurant more, Grace would be the one to drive Max and me around.

Mrs. McClain's loud clap startled me from across the court. "Okay, girls. Settle down. We need to get started." She smiled at those of us sitting on the floor. "I've decided that we're going to open up three positions on the team instead of just one, so we'll have an even eight and can take on some more complex routines." She consulted the clipboard she held, then looked back at us. "Does anyone want to go first?" All of us glanced at each other, but no one spoke up. "All right, then. Ava, how about you?"

My face went red, but I nodded and rose from the floor, clutching the CD I'd brought with me. I figured I might as well get it over with. I handed the CD to Mrs. McClain and she put it in the small player that sat on the table. Whitney smiled at me as I positioned myself in front of everyone, but it was a forced, sharp-edged motion. "Let's see what you can do," Mrs. McClain said, and I closed my eyes, gripping my hands into fists. I pictured Mama in our living room, turning the stereo up. I saw her arms flailing and hips swaying in perfect rhythm with the music. "Come on, baby," she'd say. "Let's *dance!*"

The music started—Katy Perry's "California Gurls"—and my eyes snapped open. I threw my arms above my head and smiled as wide as I could, losing myself in the song, in the movement, in the memory of dancing with my mother. It was almost as though I could feel her next to me, laughing and giggling, and in that moment, I felt happy for the first time since she died.

A brief flicker of joy washed through me as the song ended, and I could hear Grace and Max calling my name and clapping. Mrs. McClain was smiling, as were the other dance team members who sat at the table. All but Whitney of course, who leaned back with her arms crossed and a scowl on her face. I didn't care. Breathing hard, I smiled back at Mrs. McClain and took my seat again on the floor next to Lisa.

"Wow," she said. "Where did you learn to do that?"

"My mom taught me," I said, thinking that maybe in her own way, she'd shown up for the audition after all.

Kelli

The eight months Kelli spent at New Pathways went more quickly than any others had in her life. Each day, she followed the expected schedule —she did the best she could in class; she took her prenatal vitamins and marveled at the bubbly movement of her daughter inside her. "Is it a girl?" she asked the doctor when she saw him in her fifth month for an ultrasound.

"We don't tell you that," he said as he wiped the cold jelly off her stomach. "The ultrasound is only performed to make sure the child is developing properly."

Kelli didn't understand why she couldn't know the sex of her own baby. "Is she, then? Developing properly?"

"She looks fine," the doctor said, then looked guiltily away, realizing that he'd just told Kelli exactly what she wanted to know.

A girl. She marveled at the thought. *I'm having a girl.* Her fifteenth birthday came and went with no word from her parents, but she didn't care. She wrote them a letter, telling them about their granddaughter—Rebecca Ruth, she said she would call her. Both holy names—both strong and beautiful like she knew her daughter would be. She couldn't imagine that they'd actually make her give Rebecca away. They would come to the hospital to see her and everything would change. They didn't write back, but Kelli didn't let that deter her from her course. Her grades went up; she felt stronger and happier than she ever had before, feeling her baby growing inside her. She was still a little scared, but Kelli had to believe that the day Rebecca was born, she, too, would be born again.

The pain was like a hot knife slicing through her belly. Her back muscles froze into a tight band, her heart pounded, and her abdomen seized. The gush of warm liquid between her legs woke her in the night, and while she was afraid of what she was about to go through, Kelli was thrilled. Rebecca would be here soon.

After the contraction had passed, Kelli quickly got dressed and shuffled down the stairs to the night counselor's office. "The baby's coming," she said as another searing cramp gripped her body. It almost brought her to her knees.

The counselor, a larger woman with limp black hair and a seemingly permanent pinched expression on her doughy face, opened the door and looked at Kelli like she'd done something wrong. "Is your bag packed?" Kelli nodded. "Okay," the counselor said. "I'll call your parents and meet you out front."

Kelli smiled at the thought of seeing her family

again. She couldn't help but believe that Rebecca would be what allowed all of them to forgive each other. Kelli could forgive them for sending her away and they could forgive her for what she'd done. It might not be the easiest thing, but the love they'd have for Rebecca would heal them all.

The ride to the hospital was silent, except for Kelli's moans as the pain got worse. "I feel like I'm going to die," she gasped, holding her hard belly and trying to remember to breathe.

"You won't," the counselor said with a sigh. Her annoyance at being woken in the middle of the night was clear. Kelli felt like she was somehow offensive with her giant belly and swollen ankles, as though her sin had affected this woman on a personal level. But she couldn't worry about that now. The only thing that mattered was Rebecca.

The counselor got Kelli into the emergency room, where Kelli was already preregistered, then waited to leave until a nurse came and wheeled Kelli down the hall to her room. After helping her change into a hospital gown, the nurse wrapped what looked like an enormous belt around Kelli's stomach and put an automatic blood pressure cuff on her right bicep. There were beeping machines next to her bed and with every pain that zipped through her body, Kelli's fear began to worsen.

"Will you tell me when my parents get here?" she asked the nurse in a small voice. "Please?"

The nurse patted Kelli's arm. "Sure thing,

doll. I'm Francine, and I'll be taking care of you."

"Thank you," Kelli said, realizing this was the first show of affection she had experienced in months, and it came from a complete stranger. The tears started to fall as another contraction wrapped its jaws around her and clamped down, hard. "Oh my god!" she cried out. "Please help me! *Please*."

Francine held her hand tight. "Breathe, baby. You just have to remember to breathe. Short ones, like this." She demonstrated, and Kelli tried to mimic her, but the pain was too much. She felt like she was being ripped in two.

On and on the contractions went, cycling through her body. After about two hours, Kelli vomited. "Can I have some water, please?" she asked Francine, who only gave her ice chips. Kelli kept her eyes on the door, positive her mother would walk through it at any moment. But more time passed, five hours, and then eight, and still, her parents didn't come.

"Why aren't they here?" she sobbed, leaning against Francine's chest. "I don't understand how they can do this to me!"

"Shh, now," Francine said. "You're not the first girl from that school to go through this alone and you won't be the last. Your parents have done the best they can, I'm sure, and being here right now just isn't part of that. You'll be fine, Kelli. Everything's going to be fine."

With sweat pouring off her body and racked by another contraction, Kelli didn't believe her. She screamed for her mother; she wept as Rebecca tried to push her way out of her body. "Her heart rate's down," Francine told her. "And yours is going up, which is making us a little worried about a condition called preeclampsia, so I'm going to give you a shot of something called labetalol." She quickly administered the shot as Kelli continued to cry. Francine patted her arm. "The doctor'll be in any minute to deliver. The baby might have the cord around her neck, so we need to get her out, quick."

Panic joined the blazing pain in Kelli's body. "Don't let anything happen to my baby," she cried.

The doctor entered her room, clad in blue scrubs and wearing a mask over his face. He made her put her feet in the stirrups and checked if she was dilated enough to start pushing. "Get her out of me," Kelli moaned. Her head felt fuzzy and disconnected; the world blurred around her. "Please. I can't do this anymore."

Francine stood next to her and wrapped an arm around Kelli's shoulders. "You can, and you will," she said. "Now, with the next contraction, we need you to push. Bear down, hard."

Kelli cried, but she couldn't tell if her eyes were stinging because of sweat or tears. When the next wave of pain washed over her, she took a deep breath and did as Francine had asked.

Over and over she pushed, feeling her daughter's head move inside her, wanting nothing but relief from the extraordinary pressure, nothing but to get this baby into the world. "You're almost there," Francine said. "One more good push and her head will be out."

"What about the cord?" Kelli sobbed. She felt dizzy and weak. She was certain she was going to die. "Can she breathe? Is she going to be okay?"

"She'll be fine," the doctor said. "Just push, now, and it will all be over. Make it a good one."

Kelli groaned and sat up when the pain started again. She pushed with everything in her, holding on to the hope of finally being able to hold her baby in her arms. And then, with one huge rush of relief, the pressure stopped and there was the high, thin noise of her daughter's cries. "Is she okay?" Kelli asked, trying to look down and see Rebecca's face. She had to hold her. She had to look her baby girl in the eyes.

"You just lie back," Francine said, giving her a pill to take with a small glass of water. "This will help you rest. The doctors need to see her now."

Kelli took the pill and downed the glass of water in one gulp, watching as the doctor carried a tiny bundle in his hands over to the lit bassinet across the room. Straining, Kelli tried to sit up but didn't have the energy. Against her will, her eyes began to flutter. She'd never felt this kind of fatigue. She let the sound of her baby's cries be her lullaby and even though she fought it, Kelli closed her eyes and fell fast asleep.

"Kelli?" Her mother's voice woke her. Kelli almost didn't recognize it, it had been so long since she'd heard it.

"Mama?" Kelli said, groggy from sleep and the medication the nurse had given her. "Where's Rebecca? Where's my baby?" She forced her eyes open and though her vision was blurry, she saw her mother standing next to her and her father at the foot of the bed. Kelli looked over to the bassinet, but it was empty. The light above it was turned off.

"Lie still," her mother said. "You need your rest."

Kelli struggled to sit up, trying to prop herself on her elbows, but the pain in her pelvis made her gasp and drop back to the mattress. "I don't *want* to rest. Where is she? Please, Mama. Please. Bring her to me."

Her father took a couple of steps and picked up a small stack of papers on the tray next to Kelli's bed. "Here," he said. "You need to sign these for the hospital." He put a pen in her hand and Kelli signed on the pages where he told her to sign, thinking of nothing else but Rebecca. When she was done, he looked at Kelli's mother with his lips puckered into a sour expression.

"Please," Kelli said again. "I need to see my baby."

Kelli's mother looked at her father, who shook his head. They stared at each other a moment, glanced at the door, then Kelli's mother finally gave a brief nod.

"What?" Kelli asked, looking back and forth between them. "Where is she?"

"She didn't make it," he said. "The child died." He said it the same way he might have said the furnace broke or the sky was blue.

"No!" Kelli screamed, a wild, angry noise. The sound came from somewhere deep inside her body, dark and primal. "You're *lying!* She was just *here.* I *saw* her." Sobs overtook her and she clawed at her mother's arms. "Please. No. Bring her to me. I need to see her."

"It's not a good idea to see her now," her father said. "We'll gather your things and take you home later today. The doctor said your blood pressure came back down so you're fine to travel. The school will send the rest of your clothes."

"I don't want to go home!" Kelli screamed. "I want Rebecca!"

"She's gone," her mother said, weeping. "I'm sorry, but there's nothing more we can do."

Grace

Holiday traffic was light on Thanksgiving morning, and it didn't take long to arrive at Sam and Wade's house. They lived in a Frank Lloyd Wright–esque rambler on a bluff overlooking the Puget Sound. Wade was extremely successful in his financial advising career, and after they dated for a year or so, he had happily asked Sam to move in with him.

"They live in a glass house," Max remarked as we walked up the front steps. Ava pushed past him to be the first at the door, causing her brother to stumble. "Hey!" he said, but she only shot him a dirty look.

"Please stop it, you two," I said wearily, trying not to drop the store-bought tray of veggies and hummus dip I'd picked up last night. They'd already argued that morning over who got to carry their mother's cake, which I resolved by telling them to take turns; Max carried it from our house to the car, and Ava carried it now.

"I didn't *do* anything!" Max said. "It was *her!*"

I sighed, hoping their bickering wasn't a sign about how the day was going to go. I decided to ignore it and attempted to change the subject. "I'd sure hate to have to clean all those windows. Wouldn't you, Ava?"

"Who cares," she muttered, but loud enough for me to hear. I had to tense my jaw to keep from snapping at her like I had the night Max wet the bed. I wondered if I got under my mom's skin the way Ava seemed to with me. I don't remember doing it deliberately, so I tried to give her the benefit of the doubt. Maybe right now, she couldn't help it. With the weight of losing Kelli, she was dealing with pain I'd never faced.

"Well, look who's here!" my mother exclaimed when she opened the front door. "Ava, Max, it's good to see you!" They had met last spring, not long after I'd moved in with Victor, when we'd taken the kids up to Bellingham for the day.

The kids greeted her politely and we all shuffled inside. "I hear you made the dance team, Ava," my mom said, taking the veggie tray from my hands. "That's wonderful."

"Thank you," Ava mumbled, keeping her eyes to the floor as she set the cake on the small table by the front door.

My mom gave me a slightly worried look and I responded with the smallest of shrugs. "All right," she said, "come join us in the kitchen when you get settled in." She returned to the kitchen, and I took a moment to breathe in the rich aroma of roasting turkey and sage. I glanced around the living room, unable to imagine living in a space so devoid of any warmth. Every piece of furniture was sharply lined and square—even the couch appeared to have hard edges instead of welcoming cushions. Their tables were glass and shiny chrome; the art on the walls was Cubist.

Melody arrived as we were all taking off our coats and putting them in the hallway closet. I gave her a quick hug. "Where's Spencer?" I asked.

"The doctor said as long as he promises not to try to lift anything, he can be at work. I guess he's going to expedite the orders or something while Victor cooks?"

"But I wanted to sign his cast," Max said with a small pout. "I was going to draw a picture on it for him!"

Ava put her arm around her brother's shoulders. "It's okay," she said, sounding more like a mother than a sister as she comforted him. "We can do it at the restaurant another day, all right?"

Max nodded, then leaned against her and wrapped his skinny arms around her slender waist. It amazed me how quickly they could go from arguing to affection with each other; I wished I could predict which direction they'd turn.

Melody smiled at them. "Are you guys ready for dinner? I'm starving. How about you?"

Max nodded, but Ava said, "Not really. My stomach kind of hurts."

"Do you feel sick, honey?" I asked. "I think I

have some Tums in my purse." I started to rummage through my black leather bag. She did look a little pale.

"Not that kind of sick. But do you have any Tylenol? My head kind of hurts, too." She grasped her forehead with her free hand and winced. Maybe that's why she was snotty—she didn't feel well.

"Let me check," I said. "If I don't, I'm sure Sam and Wade do."

As though on cue, Sam stepped out of the kitchen to welcome us. "Gracie!" he said. "Melody! And kidlets!" He smiled at the kids, who waved at him. "So great to finally meet you."

"You too," Ava said. At least she was being polite to him.

"I like your hair," Max said solemnly. "It's very fiery."

"Well, thank you, Max," Sam said with a laugh. He ran his fingers through his close-cropped red curls. "Okay. Sorry to greet and run, but I'd better go see if Wade needs anything. The man would be *lost* without me." He grabbed the cake from the table where Ava had set it down, then headed back into the kitchen.

"Come on," I said as I pulled out the small bottle of Tylenol I had in my purse. "Let's get you something to drink to wash this down with." We followed my brother through the arched doorway and when we entered, I saw my mother seated at the breakfast bar, sipping at a glass of white wine while Wade and Sam stood at the counter, chopping vegetables.

"Hey, Grace," Wade said, turning to look at us while continuing to work. "I'm Wade," he said, smiling, to Max and Ava. They both waved again and gave him a small smile in return, still seeming a little uncomfortable. I couldn't blame them, really. Having them there without Victor made me a little uncomfortable, too.

"I'm supervising," my mom said. "Would you like to join me?"

"I will," Melody said. She walked over and sat down on the other bar stool at the counter.

"In a minute." I looked at Max and Ava, who were now hand in hand. "Is water good, Ava? Or maybe some Sprite to help settle your stomach?"

"Water, please," Ava said, her manners toward me seeming to return. She really did look peaked —a little green around the edges. I hoped it wasn't anything serious.

My mother furrowed her brow a bit and took a sip of her wine. "Everything okay?"

"She's not feeling a hundred percent," I said, reaching for a glass from the cupboard. I filled it from the dispenser in the front of the refrigerator, then handed it to Ava, along with a couple of Tylenols.

She released her brother's hand and accepted them gratefully. "Thanks."

"Want to help me put these potatoes in the water, Max?" Sam asked.

"Okay," Max said, taking a couple of steps toward the counter.

"Do you want a glass of wine, Grace?" Wade asked.

"Maybe with dinner," I said. For now, I poured myself a glass of water, too.

"I'm sorry that Victor couldn't make it," my mom said. Her tone was carefully measured.

"He's sorry to miss it," I said in an equally measured tone, not wanting to get in a big discussion about my relationship circumstances right before dinner, especially not in front of the kids. We'd talked earlier in the week, and I'd relayed a bit of the stress I was feeling getting used to having the kids with us full-time, so I knew she'd be carefully observing us today, gathering her own opinions.

"We are too," Wade said, blowing me a kiss. "I'd hug you, doll," he said, "but I'm covered in gravy." He was a handsome man with slightly thinning blond hair, extremely fit and well dressed. Today, he wore a red apron over his loose-cut Levi's and Ed Hardy T-shirt, and a pair of Buddy Holly–type glasses.

"You're such a slob," Sam said. "I don't know why I put up with you."

Wade leaned over to give him a quick peck on the cheek. "Because you can't help yourself."

"Grace," Ava said in a tightly strung voice. "Where's the bathroom?"

"Down the hall," Sam answered for me, nodding toward the entryway that led out of the kitchen. "Second door on the left."

"Thanks," she said, and quickly turned around, walking in a stiff, strange motion. I felt a twinge of concern in my own stomach, wondering if she had some kind of a virus or if it was just the stress of facing the first major holiday without her mother. With Victor's having to be at the restaurant, she could have been feeling even more abandoned.

"Poor thing," Melody said, reaching for a carrot from the veggie tray Sam had set out in front of them. "I hope she's okay."

"Me too," I said, leaning against the wall behind me and taking a sip from my glass.

Sam gave Max a little nudge with his elbow. "So, tell me, Max," he said as he cut potatoes into inch-wide cubes. "Is there anything you're especially grateful for this year?"

I held my breath, wondering if this was a loaded question for my brother to ask. Kelli had died just over a month ago—I wasn't sure if there was anything Max *would* be grateful for right now. I suddenly worried he'd lose it, like he had the night he wet the bed.

But Max, who had been scooping up pieces of cubed potato and dropping them into a silver pan filled with water, simply paused a moment before answering. "Well," he said in a matter-of-fact tone, "I'm pretty grateful that Grace isn't cooking this dinner."

"Ha!" Sam said, patting Max on the back. "Me too!"

"Me too!" my mom and Melody chimed in unison.

"Hey now!" I protested, though I was laughing. "Be *nice!*"

We all chatted for a few minutes, making small talk about how business was going at the Loft and how many new clients Melody had during the holiday season. I kept glancing in the direction Ava had gone, waiting for her to return, but she didn't. "I'm going to check on her," I said, placing my glass on the speckled granite countertop. I made my way down the dark hallway, stopping in front of the bathroom door. A thin sliver of light glowed beneath it and I heard the quiet but still audible sound of Ava's crying.

"Sweetie?" I said, knocking softly. "What's wrong? Did you get sick?"

"No," Ava said. Her words were muffled by the door and her tears. "Please go away."

"I can't," I said quietly, placing my palm flat against the door. "I'm worried about you." I paused. "Is it just being here without your dad? I'm sure you're missing your mom so much today, too. It's totally normal to be sad—"

"It's not *that!*" she cried out as she flung open the door, leaving me standing with my palm in the empty air. Her eyes were swollen and she was still very pale. I dropped my hand and reached out to smooth her hair from her face.

"Then what is it?" I asked, attempting to keep my tone low and calm.

She dropped her chin down, shaking her head back and forth. "I don't want to tell you."

As I considered her symptoms, a realization clicked in my mind. Headache, stomachache, pale skin, and now hiding in the bathroom. "Did you get your period?" I asked in a soft voice, so no one else would hear. She was the right age for it, and as far as I knew, she hadn't gotten it yet. If she had, I was pretty sure I would have seen the evidence in the bathroom over the last year.

Max chose this moment to pop his head around the corner from the kitchen. "Did she *barf?*" he called out, and I had to repress a giggle.

"No!" Ava snapped, and reached to close the door in my face, but I stopped her by stepping through the threshold.

"We'll be out in a few minutes, Max," I said. "Can you ask Melody to come talk with me, please?"

"Okay!" he said, and disappeared.

I looked back at Ava, who had dropped down to sit on the edge of the bathtub, her face in her hands. Her shoulders shook as she cried. "I miss my mom," she said.

The muscles in my throat tensed hearing the pain in her voice. I closed the door behind me and put the toilet lid down so I could sit, too. "I know you do, honey. I'm so sorry. This is all so hard." I paused. "What do you miss most about her?"

She looked at me hesitantly. "I don't know how to say it. I just miss her. She's supposed to be here for me. To help me. And she just *left*."

"What was your favorite thing to do with her? Cook?"

Ava shook her head. "Dance, I guess. She liked to dance."

"Ah. So that's why you're so good at it." Her wanting to join the team suddenly made more sense.

"I miss her so much. I want her to come *back*." Her shoulders began to shake and I reached over and put my hand on the top of her thigh, rubbing lightly. I wanted to hug her, but it felt like there was an invisible shield between us. I didn't want to push my luck and have an already fragile link shatter.

I was quiet for a few minutes, just letting her cry. Letting her miss her mother without my trying to make her feel better, which I knew was a pointless endeavor. Like the women I worked with, who came to us with not just broken bones but grief-ridden souls, Ava needed to let the pain out. All I could do was bear witness to her sorrow so she wouldn't have to work through it on her own.

When she finally quieted, I spoke again, knowing we needed to deal with the more practical issue at hand. "Are you bleeding a lot or just a little?"

"Just a little." Her voice was small. "I just put some toilet paper—"

"Good," I said, gently cutting her off. I remember being *horrified* having to discuss anything related to my body with my mother, so I wanted to save her from having to explain the details. "I don't have any supplies with me, so hopefully Melody will. I'm pretty sure Sam and Wade don't keep any around. But we can always make a run to the store, okay? Everything will be fine."

She gave a short groan. "This is so *embarrassing*."

"I know," I said, reaching out to rub her back. She wore her mother's red sweater with a black skirt, as she had the day of Kelli's memorial. "I think every girl gets embarrassed when it happens. I remember when I got *my* first period. I was twelve, wearing white jeans, *and* I was at school."

She looked at me with wide eyes. "Really?" Her hand flew to cover her mouth, then dropped it again. "What did you *do?*"

"I ran to the bathroom and my teacher sent the school nurse in to help me."

"That's *awful*. I would have *died*."

I chuckled. "I felt that way at the time, too, but I got over it. Eventually." She gave me a small smile and I felt such an overwhelming wave of fondness for her in that moment, I almost began crying myself. But then there was a soft knock on the door, and Melody opened it.

"So *this* is where the party is!" she said. "Why didn't I get an invite?"

"Do you have any tampons?" I asked her in a low voice, and understanding quickly blossomed across her face. She nodded.

She took a step toward Ava and leaned down to hug her. "Welcome to the club, darlin'." She returned less than a minute later with her purse in hand, then pulled out a small blue box and placed it on the counter next to the sink. I stood up, too.

"I'll be right outside, if you need help," I said. Melody moved into the hallway and I started to follow her, but then Ava spoke again.

"Grace?"

I stopped and turned to look at her. "Do you want me to stay?"

She pressed her lips together and shook her dark head. "No. I'll be fine. But . . . thank you."

"You're welcome, honey," I said, giving her a warm smile before rejoining the rest of my family, suddenly feeling like I had a whole new reason to give thanks.

Ava

When we got home from Thanksgiving dinner, I went straight to my room. I couldn't believe I got my period and Mama wasn't there to help me— it made me feel like I'd lost her all over again.

But Grace was there. She was actually really *nice* to me, which just made me feel more confused. When she talked with me in the bathroom that night, I felt protected and safe. Understood. Grace calmed me down, she made me laugh, and thinking about her now, I could feel Mama's disapproval hanging in the air around me, thick enough to make it hard to breathe.

After I'd shut the door and flipped on the light in my bedroom, I walked directly over to the boxes of Mama's things. If she couldn't be here today, maybe at least I could feel close to her by touching the books she'd held in her hands, smelling the clothes that she sprayed with her perfume. With a deep intake of breath, I yanked the cardboard top open and looked inside. Books were stacked together tightly; I picked one of them up, flipping through the pages before setting it aside and picking up another. I didn't know what I thought I'd find. It would have been easy if she kept a journal, spilling out all of her secrets onto the page, but I was pretty sure if she had, Dad wouldn't have given it to me. I should have looked for one the day Bree and I were at her house. And soon, he'd hire movers to pack up the rest of the house. Everything would be gone— every trace of my mother erased. I opened the second box, pulled out a wad of Mama's clothes, and pressed them to my face. I breathed the scent of her in and a few tears squeezed out of the corners of my eyes.

I reached back into the box to see what else my dad had packed. I pulled out another book, this one called *Healing After Loss*. I vaguely remembered her reading this as she lay in bed, underlining passages and making notes in the margins. I fanned through the pages slowly, looking at the sentences she'd marked up: *You can let go of the pain,* one of them read. *You can choose to stop hurting, to release it like a tree releases a leaf from a branch.* Reading this, I snorted, rolled my eyes, and picked up my cell phone to call Bree.

"Guess what?" I said. "I got my period." We'd both been wondering which one of us it would happen to first and each promised to let the other know the minute it happened.

"Wow, really?" She waited a beat. "Is it . . . weird?"

"Yeah," I said. "But not too bad." She didn't ask anything more about it, probably sensing I didn't really want to get into the details. Bree was good like that. "What're you up to?" I asked, and she sighed.

"Hiding in the bathroom. My dad's in the kitchen with the Blond Hose Beast," she said, referring to her father's gum-cracking girlfriend. "She's feeding him whipped cream off her *fingers*." She made a gagging sound. "How about you?"

"Just looking through some of my mom's things. You won't *believe* the crap she was reading." I told her about the stupid leaf sentence.

"What did she lose, do you think?" Bree asked. "Your dad?"

"I don't know. Maybe." I flipped through a few more pages, seeing her notes of *Yes! This is me!* in the margins next to certain passages. "None of this makes any sense." I threw the book down on my bed, and my eyes caught the corner of a piece of paper sticking out of the pages in the back. "Hold on a second," I said to Bree. I pulled the slip of paper carefully out from the book, a tiny swirl of excitement in my belly. Maybe it was a clue. Maybe it would tell me what I needed to know. It was small, the size of a bookmark, and only had a few words scratched on it in Mama's handwriting. *"She's gone,"* I read aloud to Bree, *"but still, I feel her. I miss her so much."*

"What?" Bree said. "Are you talking about your mom?"

I explained the slip of paper in the book, then read the words aloud to her again. "What do you think it means?" I asked her.

"Heck if I know," Bree said. "This whole thing just keeps getting more confusing." I'd told Bree about the letter from the doctor, but now, reading this note, it seemed like she might have been looking for a woman, not a man. But that didn't mean it couldn't be a doctor, I supposed. Mama wouldn't *miss* a doctor, though. It really didn't make any sense.

I ran my fingers over the words Mama had written. "I have to figure out who she was looking for."

"Okay, but how?" Bree asked.

I took a deep breath. "I need to call my grandparents. They know what happened."

"Yeah, but will they talk with you?" Bree sounded doubtful. "They've never even met you."

"I know, but I have to at least try, right?" I was suddenly determined. "I'll call you back." We hung up, and before I lost my nerve, I scrolled through my list of contacts until I came to the one I'd labeled "Grandparents." I'd dialed their number once before Mama had died, after she'd called them and ended up crying, thinking I could talk with them and get them to stop making Mama so sad. But I hadn't pressed send, too afraid to hear their voices. Too worried that they'd make me cry, too. I programmed the number into my phone, though, just in case I worked up the courage to try again.

Moving my thumb over the send button, I closed my eyes, took a deep breath, then pushed it a little harder than I probably had to. I wondered if they'd answer, and if they did, what exactly it was I wanted to say. I thought about the things my English teacher taught me to consider when doing research for something I had to write: *Who? What? When? Where? Why?* That last one, *that* was the real question. The only one I really needed to know.

The phone rang six times before someone picked up. "Hello?" A woman's voice, frail and crackly. *My grandmother.*

"Hi . . ." I faltered, unsure how, exactly, to begin this conversation. "Happy Thanksgiving." *God, that was a stupid thing to say.*

"Who is this?" She almost sounded scared, and I couldn't understand why. Then I remembered that Dad told us she was a little confused, that sometimes this happened to people as they got older. I hoped she wasn't too old to remember what I needed to know.

"It's Ava," I said. "I'm . . . I'm your grand-daughter." I waited a moment and when she didn't respond, I continued. "I'm just calling to see . . . to see if you can help me." That seemed like the easiest way to put it. Other questions screamed in my mind: *Why didn't you ever come see us?*

Why didn't you even care when Mama died? What kind of a mother are *you?*

"Help you how?" Her voice was still shaky, so I tried to keep mine steady.

"Well," I began, "I have a photo album. One of Mama's from when she was a little girl."

"I don't know how I can help you with that," she said, interrupting me.

"The pictures stop when she turned fourteen," I said quickly, afraid she might just hang up the phone. "I just want to know why. Do you have some you could send me? And maybe her yearbooks, too? From when she was a cheerleader in high school."

"She was never a cheerleader," she said. Her words were suddenly sharp. "And I'm sorry, but I don't have any pictures to send you."

What? Mama lied *to me? Why would she* do *that?* My bottom lip trembled. I didn't want to cry. I wanted to be strong. Just long enough for her mother to tell me what I needed to know. I tensed the muscles in my face and tried again. "There's something else," I said. "A letter from a doctor. I think she was looking for the one who took care of her when she was fourteen." I paused and took in a small breath. "Was she sick?"

"No." She whispered the word.

"Then why would she be looking for her doctor? Why wouldn't she just ask you?"

"She did ask me. I don't remember his name."

"Okay . . ." I tried again. "Are you sure you can't just send me her yearbooks, anyway? I really want to know more about her."

"She didn't have any except her freshman year. She went away for a while that spring, to an all-girls school so she could focus on her studies." She cleared her throat. "When she came home, she decided she wanted to go to the community college for her GED."

An all-girls school? I wondered if she was remembering that wrong. I took a deep breath. "Where was it? Can you at least tell me that?"

She sighed and waited several breaths before answering. "It was called New Pathways." She coughed, a loud, startling sound. "I have to go now. My husband is calling me." *Her husband. Not "your grandfather."*

"Wait," I said, my voice flooding with tears. I gripped the phone tighter. "Please. I don't understand why this is so *hard*. Why you won't just *talk* to me. I miss Mama so much. Don't you miss her, too?" My chin trembled as I waited for her to respond. She was Mama's *mother*—how could she not care about what happened to her?

"Of course I do," she said softly. "Of course. But it's in the past, and some things are better left forgotten. You'll understand that when you're older."

"But—" I began, only to have her cut me off again.

"I'd change it all if I could," she said. She sounded like she was about to cry. "But your mother made her choices and we made ours. It's too late now."

"It's *not* too late!" I said, pleading. "You can help me. *Please*."

"No," she said, "I can't." And then she hung up the phone.

"Damn it!" I said, throwing my cell to the other end of my bed. I tried to process the short conversation. *She was never a cheerleader. She never wore a blue and yellow uniform or was captain of the squad.* She told me that story again and again, and every time, it was a lie. What else had she lied to me about?

I suddenly felt shakier than ever, more lost than I ever had before. I didn't know what to believe about Mama. I wondered if her mother wasn't remembering right. If she had lied to me just to get me off the phone or if what Dad said about her being confused was true.

My head swam with questions. The more I thought about what had just happened, the more angry I became. It wasn't *fair* that Daddy left us. It wasn't *fair* that I had to take care of Mama for so long; it wasn't *fair* that she might have lied to me, that everything I ever believed about her might have been wrong. It wasn't *fair* that she died and I was left with Grace, who might have been nice enough, but she was not—nor would she ever be—my mother. Hot tears seared my eyes and I took a couple of shuddering breaths so no one would hear me. I was tired of crying, tired of feeling so sad. I just wanted everything to go back to the way it used to be.

A few minutes later, I had calmed down just enough to reach for my phone again, planning to call Bree back and tell her everything my grandmother had said, when there was a huge crash in Max's room. This was immediately followed by the siren sound of his screaming his head off. Grateful to finally be distracted from my own dark thoughts, I leapt off the bed and ran down the hall, anxious to see what my brother had done.

Grace

After we got back from Sam's house, I waited in the living room for Victor to come home. The kids were in their bedrooms—Max was playing with the Wii system Victor had brought from Kelli's house and Ava was talking on the phone, to Bree, I assumed. I sat in the relative quiet, flipping the pages of the book I'd picked up on how children process their grief. It talked about how some would shut down completely, coping only by pretending that nothing had changed. They might go about their daily lives as they always had—

going to school, spending time with their friends, trying to have fun. They wouldn't want to talk about their parent's death; they wouldn't cry or get angry with the surviving parent. At least Max and Ava weren't shutting me out. I felt buoyed by the moment Ava and I had shared in the bathroom earlier. Hopefully, she'd remember that I tried to comfort her. Maybe after some time, we'd find a way to be friends.

I really *wasn't* trying to replace Kelli, but I was happy I could be there for Ava. I wondered if Kelli really would have chosen to end her life, knowing she would miss such important milestones with her daughter. If she would have believed her circumstances were so dark that the only solution to them was death.

I thought about the letter from the doctor I'd kept in my purse, after finding it at her house with Ava. I still hadn't told Victor we'd gone to get the recipe there—with his work hours and having the kids around us, the timing just hadn't been right. I felt a little guilty, and afraid, now, too, I supposed, that he'd be even more angry that I'd waited to tell him. We'd never kept secrets from each other before—at least, not as far as I knew. There were things he didn't know, but they were little things, like how much I spent to get my hair colored and cut each month, or about the entire bag of choco-late I finished off each week, the one I kept hidden in my desk at work. But he still hadn't talked with me about the weird fact that Kelli's freshman yearbook was absent any signatures. He hadn't "looked into it" like he said he would. Not that it was a huge deal, but if it might help explain whether or not Kelli purposely ended her own life—if there was something so devastating in her past that might have led her to that leaping-off place—I didn't see why he wouldn't be anxious to find out for sure. Maybe I could do a little dig-ging, but I wondered if Victor's avoidance of it meant that he knew more about Kelli's past than he wanted to admit. I wondered if he was keeping secrets from me, too.

My curiosity overwhelmed me and I got up, walked over to my purse, and pulled out the letter. *Dr. Brian Stiles.* It was a handwritten note on a blank sheet of paper. I found it a little strange that he hadn't typed it on letterhead, but the script was slanted and slightly shaky; maybe he was retired. I could Google him, I decided, find out what kind of doctor he was. Maybe that would tell me why Kelli had contacted him.

A moment later, I was at the dining room table, drumming my fingers on the top of my thighs, waiting for my laptop to fire up. *Maybe I shouldn't be doing this without telling Victor first.* But I knew if I did tell him, he'd brush me off. I couldn't help but feel if I figured out what happened to Kelli as a teenager, it might give us some clue about how she died.

Straightening in my seat, I opened up the browser and typed in the doctor's name and address. His website was at the top of the results list and showed his credentials as an ob-gyn. *Oh my god. Maybe* that's *why her parents disowned her, why her yearbook is blank, and why the pictures in her albums stop when she was fourteen. Maybe she got pregnant.*

I sat back against my chair and released a heavy sigh. If she had a baby, what had happened to it? Did she give it up for adoption? And if that were true, why wouldn't she have told Victor about it? Had her parents made her so ashamed that she held on to that secret for all those years? I did a quick calculation in my head, figuring that if Kelli had the baby when she was fifteen, and Kelli was thirty-three when she died, the child would be eighteen now. I wondered if Kelli had contacted this doctor, trying to find her baby. Maybe she *did* find her child and he or she didn't want anything to do with Kelli, and *that's* what led her to take too many pills. If, in fact, that was what she'd done. Maybe she was devastated by an entirely different sense of loss.

My spinning thoughts were interrupted by a sudden, huge crash down the hall, followed by the sound of Max's bloodcurdling screams. Forgetting about Kelli entirely, I raced to his bedroom, passing Ava on the way, and threw open his door to find him jumping up and down on the Wii remote. The white box that had been next to the small television on his desk was on the floor, too, cracked wide open, wires and circuit board exposed.

"Damn it!" Max screamed. Spittle flew from his lips with the words. His brown hair stood out in uneven tufts across his head, and he stared at me with wide, angry blue eyes, breathing hard. "Crap!"

"Stop it, Max!" I said loudly, rushing over to pull him off the remote. "What happened?"

He tried to yank away from my grasp, but I held tight. "It's a stupid game. I *hate* it!" He began crying, his small shoulders quaking. Fat tears rolled down his flushed cheeks and he pulled away from me. This time I let him go, following him over to his bed, where he threw himself face-first into his pillow and pounded the mattress with his fists.

I sat on the edge of the bed and put my palm flat on his back. Not rubbing, not trying to comfort. Just letting him know I was there, the way I used to with Sam. "Why is the game stupid?" I asked quietly. Adrenaline shot through my veins and I tried to take a few unobtrusive deep breaths.

"Because it *is*," was his mumbled reply.

Ava appeared in the doorway and leaned against the doorjamb with her arms crossed. She still wore her mother's red sweater but had changed out of the black skirt she'd worn to Sam's house and into her plaid flannel pajama bottoms. "He's mad because he sucks," she said simply. "He always gets mad when he doesn't win."

Max rolled over, glanced wildly around his bed, then grabbed his hardback copy of *Harry Potter and the Sorcerer's Stone* from his nightstand and chucked it across the room, missing his sister only by a couple of feet. "I do not!" he screamed. "Why don't you just shut *up?*"

I grabbed his arm again. "Max! That was totally unacceptable. Do you understand me? You could have really hurt your sister." Then I turned my gaze to Ava. "And you. Don't say your brother sucks."

"Whatever," Ava said, and rolled her eyes, which looked a little swollen. Had she been crying? She looked more angry than sad—as if she'd walked into her brother's room already primed for a fight. *What the hell?* Just a few moments before, I'd been thinking how our relationship might be turning a corner, and now this? I knew adolescents could be unpredictable —I remember throwing a few nightmare hissy fits when I was thirteen, too—but this seemed extreme.

"I don't *care* if I hurt her!" Max shrieked, his face burning scarlet, the tears still falling.

"You're such a little shit!" Ava yelled.

"Max! Ava!" I said, letting go of Max and

standing up in the middle of the room. "Both of you knock it off *right now!* Do you hear me?" I was yelling, too, and breathing hard.

Ava looked at me, now the lift of her chin and defiance in her narrowed eyes making her seem much older than she was. I remember giving that same look to my father when he'd try to tell me what I should do. *Screw you,* it said.

"You're not my mom," she said. Her voice was low and full of spite. "I don't have to do anything you say."

"I'm the adult here, young lady, and you will do *exactly* what I say." Even though I felt unsure, I lowered my tone to match hers, the same strategy I used to employ as an HR executive when mouthy employees tried to steamroll over me. I refused to allow this little girl to believe she intimidated me in any way.

At this point, I heard the front door open and shut. "Hey, guys," Victor called out. "I'm home!" He appeared behind Ava a moment later, and she whipped around to bury her face against him. Her shoulders shook, and I couldn't help but think she was faking her tears to look like a victim. Max pushed past me and threw his arms around his father's waist, too. Victor gave me a confused, imploring look, his hands rubbing his children's backs. "Hey now," he said. "What's all of this? What happened?"

"Max threw a tantrum and trashed the Wii," I

said tiredly, gesturing to the mess of cracked plastic and wiring on the floor. "Then he and Ava started fighting and he threw a book at her."

"Grace *yelled* at us, Dad," Ava said. Her tone had shifted from spiteful to sorrowful. "Max and I were trying to work it out."

"That's not what happened, Ava, and you know it," I said. "Victor? Can we go talk about this in the other room?"

He moved his eyes to the shattered Wii box and then to me. I couldn't read his expression. "I'll come talk with you in a little bit," he said. "Let me handle this, first."

"But—" I began, but Victor cut me off.

"Grace. I've got it handled, okay?"

I stared at him, and a pain in my chest began radiating out through the rest of my body, a feeling I couldn't immediately name. It wasn't anger. It wasn't fear. I took slow, deliberate steps across the room, careful to edge my way around Victor and the kids without touching any of them. I waited for him to reach out, to put his hand on my arm or give me a reassuring look. But he didn't make eye contact and made no move to touch me, either.

Back in our bedroom, I sat in the chair at the end of our bed and reached into my purse. I pulled out the engagement ring I still kept with me, and even wore when I wasn't around the kids. Tears filled my eyes, and it was only then that it finally struck me what the prickly sensation in my body actually was.

In a moment where Victor and I should have stood united, a moment when I needed him to back me up, the feeling that coursed through my veins was something I never believed he would cause. The feeling I felt was betrayal.

I pretended to be asleep when Victor came to bed a while later. I listened to him undress in the dark, take a quick shower to wash off the scent of the restaurant from his skin, then felt the pressure of his weight on the other side of the mattress as he climbed beneath the covers. Again, he made no move to touch me; he only said my name once, quietly. I lay immobile, turned away from him, regulating my breath so it appeared I was asleep. I knew we needed to talk, but honestly, I was so hurt, I didn't know what I'd say to him that wouldn't cause more damage than it would heal.

"Grace?" he said again, louder this time. I released a heavy sigh. There was no way I could pretend I hadn't heard him.

"What." The word shot out of me like a bullet.

"I heard from the doctor tonight. Kelli's toxicology report came back and he thought I'd want to know the results."

I rolled over to look at him, temporarily forgetting my anger. I could barely see him in the dark, just the shadowy outline of his long body, the sharp angles of his face. "He called you on Thanksgiving?" Victor nodded. "Okay, so?" I prodded, still furious with him, but letting my curiosity get the better of me.

"He said she died of a sudden ventricular tachycardia. A heart attack, basically."

"We already *knew* that." I couldn't tell if he was being purposely evasive or just struggling to find a way to say what he needed to say. I was too irritated to care.

"Right, but now we know it was caused by the medication she was taking."

"Victor," I said, past the point of any patience with him. "Did she commit suicide or not?"

He sighed. "There's no way to know for sure. The doctor said her electrolytes were completely out of whack, probably because she wasn't eating. She was on the verge of anorexia, I guess, which completely screws up how your body processes things." He swallowed once before continuing. "So the meds she was taking built up in her system to the point where they became toxic to her."

I thought about this a moment. "Is there any way for him to tell how many pills she had taken that morning?"

Victor shook his head. "Not an exact dosage. But the levels in her blood were higher than they should have been, so she was probably taking more than the prescribed dose for a while. It's more the combination of that and her system being too broken down to handle it, I guess. Her heart just gave up." He sighed. "I don't know what to tell the kids. Ava keeps asking."

"You can't tell them the truth?"

"That their mom was a pill-popping anorexic? That's a *great* idea."

I knew I needed to confess my trip to Kelli's house with Ava and explain the possibility that she might have given up a baby for adoption, but his tone slammed a door shut inside me. My cheeks warmed and I gritted my teeth to keep from telling him to fuck off. "*Jesus,* Victor," I said instead. "I wasn't suggesting you should say it like *that*." I rolled back over and pulled the covers up to my neck. This conversation was over. "I'm tired, okay? Good night."

He didn't respond, but soon, his breath fell into a slow, deep rhythm, and I knew he was asleep. Frustration crackled through my body, keeping me awake. I knew his first loyalty lay with his children, and rightly so. And yet. The way he'd spoken to me—dismissed me, really. Like anything I had to say was irrelevant. I gnawed on this thought, tossing and turning for most of the night, wondering how we would get through this situation, questioning whether or not I could.

Around four thirty, I finally gave up any pretense of being able to sleep, got up, and took a shower. Victor woke up at six to find me already dressed and sitting in my armchair in the corner of our bedroom, reviewing one of the client files I'd brought home from work. He propped himself up on his elbows and gave me a small smile. "Hey. You're up early."

"Yep. I figured I might as well get a jump-start on my day."

He cocked his head to one side. "It's a holiday weekend. You're going into work?"

I bobbed my head once. "For a little while, before you need to get back to the restaurant. I need to get some things done now, since I'm assuming you'll need me to take care of the kids in the afternoons, so you can be at work?" He hadn't asked specifically, but I understood that with Spencer's broken arm I would need to take over much of what Victor would normally do for the kids because of his longer hours on the job. I'd need to alter my work schedule so I could pick them up from school. I'd need to get Ava to dance squad practice and Max to basketball. At this point, I didn't see any alternative but to do whatever had to be done. There was no reason the kids should suffer just because their dad was being a jerk.

"Yes," he said slowly. "If that's okay with you."

"Of course. Ava got her period when we were at Sam's house," I told him. Despite how angry I was, I felt like this was something he should know. Everything else—everything about Kelli's past—could wait.

"Really?" His eyebrows raised. "Is she okay?"

I nodded. "I think so. But don't talk with her about it, okay? Unless she brings it up. You'll just embarrass her."

"I get it," he said. "Thank you for being there for her."

"You're welcome."

He was silent a moment, assessing the business-like edge to my words. "Are you okay? I know last night was stressful. Finding out all of that stuff about Kelli. And the kids, arguing like that. That's the way it goes with them sometimes."

That's the way it goes when you coddle them and don't even bother hearing the adult's side of the story. Of course, I didn't say this. "I'm fine," I said instead.

He sat up. "Oh yeah, you definitely *sound* fine. Not pissed at me or anything." His words were lightly teasing, but I was in no mood.

"You can't ask me to help you take care of them and then not trust me to make good decisions," I said softly, planning for that to be all I had to say about what had happened last night in Max's room. I stood up and shoved the file into my briefcase. "And I'm sorry about the news about Kelli. I'm sure you'll figure out the right thing to tell the kids." I kept my tone cool. He obviously wasn't interested in my input, so I'd decided I wouldn't give him any.

He waited a moment before answering, staring

at me. When he finally did, his tone matched mine. "Okay. Thank you."

I lifted my gaze to him briefly, and at the sight of the hurt in his eyes, my anger eased just the tiniest bit. "I love you," I said. And then, for the first time since moving in with him, I left the house without kissing Victor good-bye.

Ava

Dad and Grace were fighting. It wasn't a loud fight. It wasn't the kind he and Mama used to have, the kind where their words reached inside me and Max and gripped us with icy fear. It was the quiet, moving-around-each-other-like-there-was-an-invisible-wall-between-them kind of fight. The kind where they didn't speak to each other unless they had to, and when they did, their voices were stretched at the seams. I couldn't decide which kind of argument was worse.

Dad spent all of his time at the restaurant, coming home late over the holiday weekend, the same way he had when Mama and he were still together. I felt a strange sense of panic fluttering around inside me, just like I had in the months before he'd left us three years ago. I felt bad about lying to him about what had happened in Max's room, but I was afraid if I told him the truth, it would only make things worse. I didn't

323

want to say anything to him that might make him regret having Max and me living with him.

"Do you think Grace might leave?" Bree asked me in the locker room after school. It was the first week of December and she was keeping me company while I changed for dance team practice. After finding out Mama had never been a cheerleader, I thought about quitting, but then decided it was something I liked enough that I wanted to do it anyway.

I pulled my T-shirt over my head and looked at Bree. "I don't know," I said. "I don't think so. It's probably just a fight." I hadn't thought about the fact that it could be Grace who left us, and was a little surprised to feel worried that she might. "Are you going to stay and watch practice?"

Bree shook her head and stood up. "Nah. I'm gonna head home. Have fun." She wiggled her fingers at me, then headed out the side door that led to the parking lot.

Just as I entered the short hallway that led from the locker rooms to the gym, Skyler Kenton appeared. He jerked his head to the side, moving his swath of black hair out of his eyes. "Hey," he said with a smile.

"Hey," I said, suddenly glad I'd taken the time to put on a little mascara and lip gloss. I reached up and smoothed my ponytail, hoping he didn't think my knees were too knobby.

He took a couple of steps toward me. "You made the dance team, huh?"

I nodded and gave him a shy smile. "Yeah."

"I heard you're pretty good at it."

"Really?" I said, cocking my head to one side. "Who said that?"

"Lisa. And like, four other girls on the team. They were talking about it in the lunchroom."

"Not Whitney, I bet."

He grinned. "Nah, not Whitney. But she's kind of a bitch, so who cares what she thinks." I giggled, thinking how much I wanted to tell Mama that he was finally talking with me. I'd had a crush on him since last year, when I watched him help Max learn how to dribble a basketball on the playground. But Mama was gone, and the giggle in my throat suddenly morphed into a potential sob.

"So, maybe I'll see you at the games?" I nodded, not trusting myself to speak. "Cool," he said, reaching out his arm and letting his hand rub the outside of my arm. "Talk to you later, then?"

"Sure," I said, the word squeaking out of me. I watched him saunter down the hallway toward the exit. *Skyler Kenton just totally touched my arm!* I was not the kind of girl he usually talked to. Losing Mama had turned me into some kind of strange celebrity, and most of the time, I hated it. The looks people gave me, full of fascination and pity, made me want to scream. But now, here

Skyler was, suddenly touching my arm. I sighed, a strange sort of fluttering feeling in my stomach, and went to join all of the other girls in the gym.

Lisa smiled and waved at me as I approached the group, who were sitting in a circle around Mrs. McClain. Happy that Lisa had made the team, too, I sat down next to her, cross-legged, giving Whitney a closed-lipped smile when she tried to look like she wasn't going to make eye contact with me. *Whatever. Let her be mad.* The other girls were talking and laughing—a few others even smiled at me. It felt good to be part of a group.

Mrs. McClain clapped her hands to get our attention. "Okay, girls. Before we get started with practice, let me hand out the details about our new uniforms! The one we picked is on page forty-two, and you can go online and order it in your size. They tend to run a little small, so keep that in mind." She gave a stack of catalogs to Lisa, who took one and handed it to me. I flipped to the right page, saw the red and white sleeveless top with matching pleated skirt, and liked it immediately. Then I glanced at the pricing chart and let out a little gasp. Lisa nudged me.

"You okay?" she asked, and I nodded, even though I wasn't.

"I just didn't know the uniform would be so expensive," I whispered. I didn't *have* two hundred dollars. I *maybe* had a little over one hundred in the bank account my mom had opened for me, but Dad hadn't been giving us an allowance since we moved in with him. I knew he was already stressed out about having enough business at the restaurant and I didn't want to make things worse by asking him for money. I definitely wasn't going to ask Grace.

"Ava?" Mrs. McClain said. "Anything the matter?" I hadn't noticed that all the other girls had already stood up. Everyone was looking at me. Whitney stood with a hand on her jutted-out hip and gave me a quick roll of her eyes.

"No, I'm good," I said, dropping the catalog to the ground, and joined the rest of my team in the center of the floor.

Grace was late picking me up. Mrs. McClain waited with me outside of the gym, and when Grace's car finally pulled into the parking lot, I climbed into the front seat without saying a word, shoved my backpack and gym bag to the floor, and crossed my arms over my chest.

"Sorry I'm late," Grace said to Mrs. McClain as she used the driver's-side controls to open my window. "Max's basketball practice ran a little bit longer than I expected."

"Hi, Mrs. McClain!" Max called out from the backseat, where he was sucking down water out of a bottle.

She smiled at him and waved, then looked

back at Grace. "I understand," she said. "But if you can possibly help it, we try not to make late pickups a habit."

Grace nodded, but her cheeks flushed pink. "Right. Absolutely. It certainly wasn't intentional." She closed the window and gave a loud sigh. Usually she would ask me about my day and how the squad's new routine was going, but she didn't even look at me as she pulled away from the curb. I figured she must still have been mad at me about what happened in Max's room on Thanksgiving, but I didn't know how to say I was sorry to her without getting in trouble for lying to Dad. So instead, I kept my mouth shut, matching her silence with my own.

As Grace drove us home, I clutched the uniform catalog, thinking about the rest of what Mrs. McClain had said during practice, telling us about the away games, how we had to pay for our own food and drinks and for what it cost to ride the bus. The other girls on the team didn't even blink hearing how much money it would take to be a part of the team, but none of them were scholar-ship students like me. I couldn't bear the thought of having to quit because I didn't have enough money. I didn't need to give Whitney another reason to make fun of me.

When we got home, Grace put her stuff down and went into the kitchen to warm up dinner. Max followed her, and I sat in the living room, staring at my homework. My thoughts strayed to the slip of paper Mama had stuck in that book. I turned her scribbled words over and over again in my mind, convinced the person she'd lost was why she'd looked into private investigators, but there was no way to know who that person was. I wanted to talk with my dad about it, but after the way he reacted when I asked a simple question about pictures from when Mama was in high school, I was pretty sure he wouldn't help me figure it all out. I was also pretty sure he'd have been pissed I called Mama's parents, for all the good it had done me.

New Pathways. I hadn't had time to look it up yet. I glanced over at Grace's laptop on the table —it was on, as usual. "Hey, Grace?" I called out. "Is it okay if I look something up on your computer real quick? It's for my homework tonight."

"Of course," she said. "Do you need any help?"

"No, I've got it." I walked over to the table and sat down, glancing quickly toward the entry to the kitchen, hoping Max wouldn't join me. I opened the browser and typed in "New Pathways school, California," and waited for the results to show up. There were about ten listed, but as I clicked on the links, I realized that most of them weren't girls-only, so I added that into my search words. The only link that came up was in an online news article, listing the school as one of the many private schools that had closed in the late 1990s due to lack of funding.

"Shit," I whispered under my breath. It didn't have a website or a list of teachers I could contact, but the article said it had been a small boarding school for troubled girls. How had Mama been troubled? I thought about asking Grace exactly what "troubled girls" might mean, but I hadn't told her about my conversation with my grand-mother, even though she'd been the one to ask me about Mama's yearbooks. I wasn't sure why she was interested in what happened to Mama in high school, but I felt weird talking about it with her. I also felt weird because I was pretty sure she still hadn't told my dad that we'd gone to Mama's house.

The ringtone on Grace's cell jolted me out of my thoughts. "Ava?" she said, her voice carrying from the kitchen. "Can you grab that for me, please? I'm expecting a call from work and I'm afraid if I stop stirring this pasta, it'll burn."

"Okay," I answered, closing down the browser before heading over to the entry table where Grace's purse lay. She told me once that she had her phone set to something like twelve rings before it went to voice mail so she'd be sure not to miss important calls from her clients. Which was nice enough, I guess, but annoying when that weird salsa-dancing ringtone went on forever. Opening the purse, I stuck my hand inside to rummage for her phone but instead came up with her slim, black wallet. I was about to put it back but then hesitated when an idea hit me. *My dance uniform.* I took a deep breath, knowing even thinking about stealing was wrong but feeling desperate enough to consider it. Grace might not even notice, I reasoned.

The phone rang again. I glanced toward the kitchen to make sure she wasn't waltzing through the doorway into the living room to check on me, then I opened her wallet up. There was a stack of twenties in the space behind her checkbook. There were so many, she probably didn't keep track. With what I already had in the bank, I only needed five. In a swift movement, and before I could change my mind, I slipped them out of the wallet and into my back pocket, then grabbed the phone and ran it into the kitchen.

Grace stood in front of the stove, stirring the pot. Max kneeled on a chair next to the counter, tearing up lettuce and throwing it into a bowl. "Slow-poke," he said, and I screwed up my face at him.

Ignoring Max's teasing, Grace put her hand out, but just as I gave the cell to her, it stopped ringing. "Oh well," she said with a small shrug as she set the phone on the counter. She glanced at the screen. "Looks like it was just a telemarketer, anyway."

"Sorry," I said, bending my right arm so I could slide my hand into my back pocket. I fingered the bills I'd just put there, feeling a hard knot of guilt in my stomach, knowing that apology was for so much more than just the missed call.

Taking that money from Grace made me feel guilty, yes. But getting away with it also made me feel brave enough to sneak just a tiny bit more out of her purse when she was in the shower the next morning—this time taking a few fives and ones, figuring she'd be less likely to notice those being gone. I planned on ordering my uniform and saving the rest to help pay for away trips. And then maybe I could ask my dad if I could work in the restaurant a little, just sweeping the floors or wiping down tables, and I would slip the money back into Grace's purse and she'd never realize what I'd done. I convinced myself that it wasn't really *stealing* if you planned on giving the money back.

When I got to school, I asked Bree to skip our last class and go to my mom's house again. I wanted to see if there was anything else that might help me figure out why she'd written that doctor. But most of all, why she'd lied to me. Why she'd lied to everyone.

"Are you sure this is a good idea?" Bree asked as we walked down the street to the house. It was a cold and drizzly December day, and she'd been a little hesitant to leave early, afraid we'd get caught, but finally gave in after I'd begged her to come with me.

"I'm sure," I said.

"What are we going to say when the school calls our parents?" We both knew that any absence that wasn't preapproved by a parent resulted in an immediate phone call from the secretary to our homes, inquiring where we'd been.

"We'll just say I got really upset about my mom," I told her. "And you took me into the bathroom and talked with me to help me feel better and I was crying so hard for so long we didn't realize we'd missed class until the bell rang." It was a little astounding how easily the lie came to me. "No one can prove we weren't there the whole time. It's not like they have cameras in the bathroom. Okay?"

"Okay," she said, not sounding entirely convinced.

"We might find something about New Pathways," I said. Bree already knew about my conversation with my grandmother, and earlier I'd told her about the online search I'd done for the school.

"It was an all-girls school, right?" Bree said. I nodded. "Maybe your mom was missing a friend she made there?"

"I don't know . . ." I said, trailing off. I didn't know what to think about the scrap of paper I'd found with Mama's writing: *She's gone, but still, I feel her. I miss her so much.*

"Oh my *god!*" Bree said, stopping in the middle of the sidewalk and grabbing my arm.

"What?" I asked, pushing my hair away from my face.

"Oh no. No *way*." She looked at me with wide eyes. "What if she fell *in love* with another girl? What if her parents found out and *that's* why they wanted nothing to do with her? That would *totally* make sense. They're super religious, right?"

"Right," I said slowly. "But why would they send her there in the first place?"

"Maybe it was like our school, small and private with good teachers, and they just wanted her to have the best education. Isn't that what your grandma said? And then she met a girl and like, *experimented* with her, and that was the end of it for her and her parents. Like they couldn't deal with it or something."

I nodded, my thoughts racing, unable to process what this all meant. "But she loved my dad. I *know* she did. How could she be in love with a girl and then get married and have kids with him?"

Bree shrugged and we started walking again, turning the corner that led to my old house. "Maybe that's part of why they got divorced? And why she was looking at private investigators after your dad left. She could've been trying to find the person she wrote that note about."

"It's possible, I guess." We approached the house, and a weird feeling began to form in the pit of my stomach. I didn't like thinking about

Mama this way. I wanted to remember her as I knew her. I wondered if maybe I shouldn't have been trying to find out about her past at all.

"What else could it be?" Bree said. "I mean, what else would make her parents flip out like that and totally disown her? It had to be something big, right? Her being a lesbian is pretty big."

"My mom was *so* not a lesbian!" I said with more force than I'd intended.

Bree's shoulders curled as she looked away from me. "God, *sorry.*"

I sighed again and reached out to touch her hand. "No, *I'm* sorry. I just . . ." I paused, struggling with how to verbalize everything that was spinning inside my head. "It's just that we don't know for sure that's what happened." She nodded, and we walked up the front steps. I put my key in the lock when suddenly, the sound of my name stopped me from turning it.

"Ava?" It was Diane. *Shit.* I hadn't thought about her being home. Bree grabbed my arm again and squeezed as Mama's friend made her way across the lawn and to the front porch.

"Hey, Diane," I said with a big smile, hoping if I acted like my being there was totally normal, she wouldn't tell my dad.

She stopped at the bottom of the stairs and looked up at us. "What are you doing here? Shouldn't you be at school?"

"It's a half day," I lied, which, apparently, I was

getting good at doing. "Teacher's conferences or something like that." I tilted my head toward Bree. "We're just picking up some of my stuff."

Diane gave me a strange look. "I thought Grace and your dad had already done that."

"Most of it," I said. "But they forgot a few things. My mom's things, actually. I sort of want to have more of them with me, you know?"

"Of course," Diane said, pushing back her frizzy brown hair from her face. Bree's grip lessened on my arm. "Do you need some help? I could drive you home."

"It's not much, really. Thanks, Diane. I appreciate it." I turned toward the door, hoping she'd take the hint and leave us alone, but she spoke again.

"So . . . are things okay at home? Have your dad and Grace set a date for the wedding?" she asked, and everything inside me went cold. Diane went on. "I know your mom was pretty upset about the engagement when she found out, but I think she would have eventually come around, don't you?"

Bree dug her fingers into my arm so deeply I was sure she'd leave a bruise. *Dad and Grace were engaged? And Mama knew about it?* I took a deep breath and lied to Diane again. "Sure. It's fine. They haven't set a date." My voice felt brittle enough to snap in two. I gave Diane a smile. "We should probably hurry up. Grace is expecting me back soon."

"Okay," Diane said with a short wave. "I'll leave you to it. Nice to see you, honey. I've missed having you next door."

"Nice to see you, too," I said, and finally, Bree and I were able to slip inside the house. I reached for the light switch, but when I flipped it, nothing happened. My dad must have had the power turned off so he wouldn't have to pay the bill.

"Oh my *god*," Bree exclaimed. "Your dad's engaged? And he didn't even *tell* you?"

"I guess so." My entire body tingled like my foot does when it falls asleep. "And my mom knew." I suddenly pictured Mama at Max's basketball practice the week she died. How upset she was after talking with Dad, how I had to wait for him to tell me whatever it was that was bothering her. At the time, I hadn't paid much attention to it, but now it totally made sense. She knew Grace and Dad were engaged and she was devastated. I suspected that part of her always hoped she and Dad would get back together— the same way Max and I used to whisper about it right after he left. I remembered another night, just a few weeks before she died, when I'd found her sitting in her closet, sobbing so hard it gave her the hiccups. I'd dropped to the floor and wrapped my arms around her. "What's wrong, Mama?" I asked, and she just kept shaking her head.

"It's hopeless," she cried, her eyes so swollen I

337

could barely see them. "I'm hopeless. Nobody wants me."

I held her tighter as she shuddered, panic rushing through me. "I want you," I said. "Max does, too."

"Not your dad, though," she sobbed. "Not my parents." She let loose a deep, keening cry, one so aching and raw it gave me the chills. "Oh *god*. I can't *do* this anymore."

"Mama, you're going to be okay," I said. "Everything's going to be fine." I wanted her to believe those words. I wanted to believe them myself. After she'd cried a while longer, I helped her crawl back into bed and tucked the covers around us both. Her head was on my chest and I smoothed her hair back from her face again and again, the same way she had done for me more times than I could count. I convinced myself she was fine, that it was just another one of her bad spells.

But now, another thought struck me, one more terrible than any I'd had since the night Daddy told us Mama was dead. I looked at Bree, my eyes shiny with tears. "What if she was so upset she didn't want to live anymore? What if that's the reason no one will tell us how she died?"

Understanding blossomed across Bree's face, immediately followed by a look of horror. "Like maybe she *killed* herself, you mean?"

I nodded, pressing my hand over my mouth.

Bree was the only person I'd told about how much Mama cried, how many things I had to do to help take care of her. I knew she was depressed, even when she tried to hide it behind bright smiles and chirpy laughter. Maybe she hadn't been sick at all. Maybe she just didn't want to be alive anymore. Maybe Max and I were just too much work for her to handle and when she found out that Grace and Dad were engaged, it finally convinced her he'd never come back to her. Maybe she just gave up. And maybe it was my fault because I told her she'd be fine.

I dropped my hand back to my side, not wanting to think about any of this. I couldn't stand to consider that I'd failed Mama—that she'd been asking me for help all along and I let her down. I wanted to relieve the sharp, biting pain in my chest. I'd always known it was possible my dad would want to marry Grace, but it was always distant, in the future, like the idea that I'd someday go to college or get married myself. I thought about everything nice Grace had done since we met her, suddenly convinced she was manipu-lating me the entire time, trying to impress my dad so they could get engaged. She didn't really *like* being with us. I'd seen the tension etched across her face since Mama died. I knew that having us around wasn't part of her plan. We were a burden, a means of getting what she really wanted all to herself—my dad. I tried to remember the last time he had come into my room on a Saturday morning to tickle me awake and came up empty. He stayed in bed with Grace now, and Max and I got up on our own and poured ourselves bowls of cereal. I didn't understand how he could choose her over us—how anything could be more important to him than just being my dad.

"If Grace thinks I'm going to call her 'Mom,' she's out of her *mind*," I said, gritting my teeth.

"But you do *kind* of like her, right?" Bree asked. Her words were halting and unsure. I could tell she was trying not to make me mad.

"No," I said again, unable to hide my annoyance. "I put *up* with her. There's a big difference." This wasn't exactly true. I'd been feeling grateful to have her around. Yet every time I moved a step closer to Grace, I could almost feel Mama's hands on me, trying to hold me back from the woman Dad loved.

Bree sighed. "Okay. If you say so."

She didn't believe me. She didn't understand that Dad brought Grace around so *he* didn't have to be there. So he could spend all his time at the restaurant and leave us all alone . . . again. "How would *you* feel if your dad married the Blond Hose Beast?" I asked her. "If you had to call her your mom?"

Bree snorted. "Well, *first* of all, I would *never* call her that, even if she tried to make me. Which she wouldn't, because she hates the idea of being old enough to be anyone's mother."

"Yeah, but—" I began, only to have her cut me off.

"And *second,* you can't even *begin* to compare Grace against the girls my dad falls in lust with. He just keeps replacing my mom with a younger, trashier version of her." Talking about her parents that way, Bree's voice was almost as bitter as mine had been just a moment before.

I didn't argue with her, knowing she was just repeating the same words she'd heard her mother say about her father's many girlfriends. "I just don't want them to get married," I said quietly. "I just want my life to go back to the way it used to be."

Bree sighed. "But you know that it can't . . . right?"

I didn't answer her. Instead, I looked around the living room, which was illuminated only by the muted gray light from the front window. It didn't look any different than it had when Grace and I came to get Mama's cake recipe—Dad hadn't had time to hire movers to pack up the rest of our stuff. It didn't seem to matter now, why I'd come here today. What mattered was the fact that every grown-up in my life seemed to lie to me. What mattered was that outside of Bree, I didn't think there was anyone left I could possibly trust.

Kelli

My baby is dead. In the months that followed her brief stay at the hospital, Kelli turned this phrase over and over in her mind. The memory of her baby's thin cry pierced through her lungs, making it feel impossible to breathe. They never let her see Rebecca. She never got to say good-bye.

None of the doctors or other nurses talked with her about what happened; when they came into Kelli's room at the hospital, her parents spoke with them in low tones, shielding Kelli from having to deal with any of it. Her father brought more paperwork for Kelli to sign. She scribbled her name and didn't ask why.

"This is all for the best," Francine said when she wheeled Kelli out to her parents' car. "It's hard, but you'll get over it, I promise."

Get over *it?* Kelli thought. *Is she* insane? She didn't respond, not knowing what to say to a person who believed that a baby's death could ever be for the best.

Once home, Kelli immediately entombed herself in her bedroom. She rolled around beneath the covers, forcing herself to sleep the days away. She felt too broken and vacant to do anything else.

"You need to eat," her mother said one evening, about two months after they'd brought Kelli back. She held a tray with chicken soup and saltine crackers.

"No," Kelli said, the word muffled by her pillow. Her blond hair was greasy and had begun to fall out in thick clumps. Her body was wasting away. When she looked in the mirror, she could see the xylophone of her rib cage and the sharp knobs of her joints pushing against her skin. She drank water, barely nibbled at the food her mother brought her, and slept. That was all she could manage.

Her mother would not be deterred. She set the tray on the dresser and came over to sit on Kelli's bed. "Everything will be okay. You'll forget soon. You can start over."

"Not without her," Kelli said. "Not without Rebecca."

"You have to let her go," her mother answered. "She wasn't meant to stay with you. You made a mistake. A horrible mistake. And God is giving you another chance."

Kelli rolled to look at her mother, blinking at the sudden influx of light. "I *hate* God," she said. "I *hate* Him."

Her mother looked as though Kelli had slapped her. She closed her eyes and took a deep breath before speaking again. "You're angry. I understand that. I've been angry with Him, too."

This got Kelli's attention. "You have?"

Her mother nodded. "When I believed I couldn't get pregnant. Being a mother is all I ever wanted, and when it didn't happen for so many years, I blamed God. I cried and yelled and turned my back on Him." She gave Kelli a small smile. "It wasn't until I accepted the fact that I wasn't in charge of what happened in my life that He gave me you." She reached out and touched Kelli's cheek. "We can't fathom what God's plans are for us, we simply have to accept them and do the best we can. You need to go back to school. You need to get your life back on the right path."

"I'm not going back there." Kelli shook her head. She didn't care what her mother said about God; she wanted nothing to do with Him. She also couldn't imagine facing Jason or Nancy, or anyone else for that matter. She felt a thousand years old, distant from them in a way that could never be lessened. She'd lost her child, and there was no way any of the kids she knew would understand that. Her parents had strictly forbidden her from telling anyone where she'd been or what had happened to her. The weight of this secret was like a stone inside her. It felt malignant.

"You need your diploma," her mother said.

"Then I'll get a GED," Kelli answered. "I'll find a job and take whatever tests I need to take. I'm *not* going back to school."

A few weeks later, when Kelli still wouldn't leave her bedroom for more than a brief trip to the bathroom, her parents relented and registered Kelli for the necessary classes at the local community college. "Only if you eat something," her father told her. "Only if you get out of bed every day. This nonsense has gone on long enough."

Nonsense? Kelli thought. *My baby dying is nonsense?* "What if I had died when I was born?" she asked him, surprised by her brazenness. "How would *you* feel?"

He held her gaze for a moment, and she looked for a small crack in his usually impenetrable exterior, but he didn't look away, didn't drop his eyes to the floor, ashamed. "I would accept it as God's will," he said. "I'd find a way to move on."

Something shut down inside her as he spoke those words, something that severed any feelings she might have had left for him. She blamed her parents for her baby's death. She blamed them for sending her away, for letting the shame they felt be more important than their grandchild. Even if Rebecca hadn't died, they would have tried to make Kelli give her up for adoption. Kelli would never understand why they seemed to hate her so much. That they hated her was the only explanation for how they treated her.

It was in that moment that she began to plan how to flee her parents' world, and it was the thought of running away that fueled her to finally get out of bed. She began to eat more; she went to her general education classes at the college, relishing the anonymity the large campus gave her. When she turned sixteen, she applied for a cashier's position at the local pizza place, and after a few months, the manager promoted her to waiting on tables.

On her first day as a server, a pretty girl named Serena trained Kelli. Serena took one look at Kelli's black pants and white button-down blouse and said, "Oh, honey. You won't make one red cent wearing that getup. These college boys want to think they might get lucky. The more you make them think that, the more beer they buy and the bigger the tips you get." She winked, reached over to pull Kelli's blouse out of her pants, and tied it into a knot over her belly button. Then she unbuttoned the top until her bra was almost exposed. "There. Much better. You need a short black skirt, too, okay? With knee-high boots. Trust me."

Kelli took her advice and was stunned by the amount of money she made. She decided that her beauty was her only real commodity. No one could blame her for using it. She was asked out constantly, and after a while, she began to say yes, giving in to her need to be held, to feel like someone loved her even if it was only for the night.

"You're using protection, aren't you?" Serena asked her one evening, after she'd watched Kelli give a handsome boy with black hair her phone number. Kelli blushed but nodded. She insisted on condoms—she'd learned that much, at least.

Her life fell into a simple routine. She went to class in the mornings, studied all afternoon at the library, then worked five nights a week. "Will you join us for church?" her mother asked every Sunday morning. She and her parents moved around each other in wide circles; Kelli was home only to sleep and shower. She kept her grades high, her room clean, and her laundry done, determined to avoid their finding any more fault with her than they already had.

"No, thank you," Kelli always responded, and her mother didn't force the issue, perhaps understanding it was a battle she'd already lost.

One Friday night after she'd been home almost a year, Kelli was in the middle of setting a large pepperoni with olives in front of a customer when a noisy group of teenagers came in. She saw Nancy before Nancy saw her. Her old friend hadn't changed—her jeans were too tight and her black hair was teased a little too much. Kelli scanned the other faces, worried Jason might be among them, but then she realized he'd likely graduated. As she approached their table, Nancy looked up and widened her brown eyes. "Hey," she said, shifting around in her chair.

"Hey," Kelli said, giving her a small, uncomfortable smile.

"You work here now, huh?" Nancy asked. Kelli nodded, and Nancy looked around, as though assessing the restaurant's value. "That's cool. How was the school you went to?" The tone of her voice made Kelli uncomfortable, as though Nancy might know the real reason her parents had sent her away.

"It was good," Kelli said. "It sort of inspired me to get my GED at the college instead of coming back to high school. I can't wait to get away from this town." She paused, watching her friend bob her head. "How are you?"

"Great. I'm great." Nancy looked around to her other friends—people Kelli vaguely recognized but had a hard time naming. Part of her wished she could just sit down with them, feel like a normal teenager again. But when Nancy didn't introduce her, Kelli grabbed her notepad and pen, under-standing that she was not going to be invited back into this fold. She just didn't fit.

"You guys ready to order?" she said, silently pinning her thoughts on the day she'd turn eighteen. The day she'd finally be able to make her escape.

Grace

"So, we're on track for finishing up next year's budget," I told my staff members, standing in front of them in the conference room for our weekly meeting. "But we need to talk about beefing up our crisis line coverage over the holidays, because we all know violent incidents tend to increase this time of year." Everyone nodded in agreement. "Anything else we should be thinking about doing?"

"Is there any way we can afford having a full-time staffer at the ERs?" Helen, one of my counselors, asked. "Maybe work with the major hospitals and see if they'd be amenable to it? It just seems like by the time we get there, the victim has disappeared and it's too late to help them."

I considered this, drumming my fingers on the table in front of me. "I don't think we could hire anyone new right now, but that is a great idea. They have social workers, but they're typically spread too thin to handle every domestic violence case that comes through the door. Maybe we could have you guys rotate one day a week there, working remotely?" Helen and several other counselors nodded, so I glanced over to Tanya. "Can you set up a few meetings for me with the managing nurses at all the major ERs? If I can get them to help me campaign, we'll have better luck with the hospital board letting us in." She nodded and made a few notes on the pad in front of her.

"All right, then," I said. "What else? More ideas?" Before anyone could respond, my cell phone rang. A quick glance at the screen told me it was the kids' school, and I immediately felt my pulse quicken, thinking maybe one of them was sick and I'd have to cut my day off even earlier than usual. Grabbing the phone, I apologized to everyone for the interruption and gestured for Tanya to continue the meeting without me. "This is Grace McAllister," I said, then reluctantly left the room.

"I don't care what the *reason* was," I said to Ava as we pulled into the driveway of our house later that evening after taking Max to basketball and picking her up at the school. "You don't skip class. *Ever*. If you're upset, you go to the office and talk to the counselor. Not Bree, okay?" Victor hadn't answered his cell, so the school had called me. Ava's explanation to her teachers about crying in the bathroom with Bree *seemed* plausible, but the pout on Ava's face now reeked more of annoy-ance at getting caught than grief over her mother's death.

"I wish you'd stop telling me what to do," Ava said under her breath.

"Excuse me?" I said. "What was that?"

She snapped her head around to face me. "I *said,* I wish you'd stop telling me what to do."

I took a deep breath, trying to keep my cool but failing miserably. "Well, *I* wish you'd stop being so disrespectful. It's totally unacceptable and I'm a little bit sick of it." What the hell was going *on* with her? I wondered if her increasing bad attitude was grief-driven or hormonal, but at that point, I really didn't care.

"Whatever," she muttered as she flung open the car door and stomped inside, carrying her backpack over one shoulder.

"She's cranky, huh, Grace?" Max said, piping up from the backseat with what I was sure he thought was helpful commentary.

"I think so, buddy," I said with a heavy sigh. I dreaded the thought of telling Victor that she'd skipped class. Though I assumed he'd believe that she'd been in the bathroom, crying; I wasn't so sure this was true. But voicing my suspicions probably wasn't the best idea. Even though I knew in my gut that we should have, Victor and I hadn't yet talked about what happened in Max's room. A week after the blowup, we were still walking a bit on eggshells with each other, exceedingly polite and seemingly going through the motions of our relationship. We slept in the same bed, but we didn't make love; we talked logistics about drop-offs and pickups with the kids, and how things were going at the restaurant with Spencer's reduced capacity.

Over lunch earlier in the week, I'd talked over my reluctance to confront Victor with Sam, but he'd been less than sympathetic. "Sorry," he said, "but I'm pretty sure you need to stop talking with me about it and talk with your fiancé. What are you so afraid of?"

I shrugged and threw my gaze to the salad in front of me. "I'm not sure. Maybe I should just try to rise above it, you know? It just feels so immature, telling him I need him to choose me over his kids."

Sam sighed. "You're not asking him to do that. You're asking him to show a united front. To let the kids know that you two are a cohesive unit, not something they can divide and conquer."

"That's a good way to put it," I mused. "Hey. I have an idea. Why don't you just talk with Victor *for* me?"

"No, thank you," Sam said sweetly as he twirled the fettuccine he'd ordered on his fork before taking a bite. He waved his utensil in the air like a conductor in front of an orchestra. "This kind of bullshit is just another reason why Wade and I won't be adopting."

"I didn't know you'd even talked about it."

"We talked about *not* doing it. Same thing, I suppose. He's too old, anyway." I laughed. Wade was only thirty-two, eight years older than my brother, five years younger than me. But things were apparently different in "gay years," as Sam once explained to me. "You have to add another six months for every year he's been alive. So thirty-two is really forty-eight."

"Where do you come *up* with this stuff?" I'd asked him.

"It's in the Gay Lifestyle Handbook," he'd joked, and I laughed again.

"You have to talk with Victor about how you're feeling," he said now. "It won't get resolved until you do."

I let loose a heavy sigh. "You sound like Melody."

"She's a smart girl."

I took a sip of my iced tea. "I just don't know how to approach it, you know? He's going to be defensive because they're his kids. He's going to take their side."

"And where does that leave you?" Sam asked. "The wicked stepmonster?" He paused and rolled his eyes. "Please. Don't martyr yourself, Grace. If you can't be honest about how you feel with the man you're going to marry, then maybe you shouldn't be marrying him."

I knew on some level my brother was right, but as he spoke those words, I couldn't help but be filled with a horrifying sense of panic. If I couldn't make things work with Victor, maybe I couldn't make them work with anyone.

Now Max and I followed Ava inside. She was

standing in the entryway taking off her backpack. Max dropped his backpack by the front door right next to her, then they ran off to fight over who got the shower first. "I call first!" Max yelled as he peeled off his T-shirt midrun. Everything between them was a competition. It was exhausting to witness the continuous one-upmanship—which one of them got the first shower, who had the biggest piece of pizza. The list of potential rivalries between them was endless.

Ava ran past him, shoving him into the wall. "I don't *think* so!" she said.

"Hey. Don't push your brother like that," I said, already irritated from my encounter with her in the car.

"He was in my way," Ava said. "I can't help it if he's slow."

"You can help yourself from pushing him, though. So knock it off. Please." I added the last word as an afterthought, hoping that maybe if I showed her a little respect, I might get some in return.

No such luck. She didn't respond and instead propelled her way into the bathroom and slammed the door. Max began crying and came running toward me. "She's so mean," he said. "Why is she so *mean?*"

I sighed and pulled him toward me into a hug. "She's a teenager, honey. It's part of the territory." What I was really thinking was: *Good question.*

Max sniffled against my stomach, rubbing his nose on me. "Well, I'm never going to be that mean. Not ever."

"I think that's a lofty goal. But we all do mean things sometimes—it's just part of being human. As you grow up, you hopefully learn to control it more, and try to treat people how you'd like them to treat you, you know?"

"I try that with her and it doesn't work. She's just *mean*."

I rubbed the top of his head, feeling the warmth and sweat from all the exercise he'd done at basketball. "How about you go grab some of your art stuff and we can draw together at the table?"

He looked up to me, pushing his chin into the flesh of my belly. "Are you a good drawer?"

"Not really. But maybe you can help me?" He nodded and raced off to the den, where we kept pads of paper and various markers in a drawer. I carried the grocery bags to the kitchen and pulled out the dinner we'd eat when they'd both finished cleaning up. Food, homework, then me trying to get at least three client files reviewed before midnight, when Victor would get home. I glanced over to the front door, where the kids had dropped their backpacks, and saw the edges of their gym shorts peeking out from the open zippers. They'd need to be washed tonight, so they were ready for practice tomorrow. Better to get them started now, so I didn't forget.

I pulled Max's clothing out first, and once again found myself baffled as to how he could stain it so thoroughly when he'd only worn it indoors. What was that, chocolate on the cuff of his shorts? Or was it blood? In the utility room off the kitchen, I sprayed the edges down with heavy-duty detergent, letting it lie flat on top of the washing machine to soak a bit while I headed back to the entryway to get Ava's gym clothes, too.

"I'm ready, Grace!" Max called out from the dining room.

"Be right there," I said. "Why don't you get everything set up for us?"

"Okay!" he replied. I smiled to myself, thinking that it was almost as though the tantrum he'd had over the Wii released something inside him that he'd been pushing down. I wondered if this was what the counselor at their school had meant—kids process grief differently. His anger hadn't been about the game at all, but destroying it was how he expressed his pain over his mother's death. Still, I was a little worried it wouldn't be the last time he blew up like that.

Ava had a separate gym bag, so I kneeled down next to it and stuck my hand inside, pulling out two pairs of tiny spandex shorts that maybe could have covered one of my ass cheeks. I didn't see her T-shirts, so I opened up another zippered compartment inside her bag and rooted around a bit until I found them. I felt another small wad of material, which I assumed was her sports bra, and pulled it out as well, setting it on the floor. An edge of something green sticking out from the bra caught my eye, and at first I thought it was just the tag, but after a second look, my mind registered what it was.

Money.

As far as I knew, Victor hadn't given her any cash. I felt something drop down a notch inside me. I slowly unraveled the bra and saw that the bills were folded into a small square. I picked it up and straightened them out, counting as I went —just over a hundred dollars. Five twenties and a few ones and fives. I'd suspected that the money I used to pay for the groceries that afternoon was short of what I'd taken out of the bank earlier in the week, but I figured I'd simply spent it and not remembered, as I often did when I used cash instead of my debit card. I wanted to believe that's what happened. I didn't want this to be true. I didn't want to be the one finding out what Ava had done. More than anything, I didn't want to tell Victor his daughter was a thief.

Just as I began to stand up, I realized the shower had stopped running. Ava came rushing up behind me, trying to snatch the money from my hand. "What are you *doing?*" she yelled. "That's mine! You don't have any right to go through my stuff!" Her hair hung in wet little snakes around her face, and she had already changed into pajama pants and her mother's red sweater.

I yanked the money out of her reach. "I have every right!" My teeth ground against each other, and the squeak inside my mouth caused me to shiver. "You took this from my purse, didn't you? Or are you stealing from someone else?"

She stared at me, her blue eyes narrowed. "I didn't steal *anything*. I don't know what you're talking about."

I shook my head, my lips pressed together before I spoke again, trying to control the anger I felt. "Then how did the money get into your backpack? Tell me that. Did it just magically grow legs and climb in there itself?"

"How should I know?" she said, spitting the words. "I don't keep track of your *crap*. Maybe Max put it there."

"I did not!" Max screamed. He'd apparently heard us yelling and came to investigate just in time to hear his sister accuse him. "You take that *back!* And I saw you stealing money from Grace's purse! Just this morning. You didn't see me 'cause I was hiding behind the door, but I watched you do it while she was in the shower."

Ava stormed toward him, her fists clenched. "You shut the hell up!"

"Ava!" I said, moving to grab her with my one free hand. She twisted out of my reach and lunged at her brother, tackling him. They both landed on the hardwood floor, and Max screamed. Ava straddled him, drawing her arm back, but I managed to pull her off before she was able to hit him.

"Let *go* of me!" she screamed as she struggled to get out of my grasp, but I held her beneath her armpits and dragged her away from Max. "I *hate* you! Why don't you just *go away?* We don't need you here! Everything was *fine* until you came along. I bet you're happy my mom is dead so you can have my dad all to yourself! I know you're *engaged!* I know you've been *lying* to us this whole time!"

I dropped her to the floor—it wasn't far, just a few inches—but she shrieked as though I'd thrown her against the wall. I tried to catch my breath. *How did she find out about the engagement? Did she find my ring? Did Victor tell her and not share it with me?* I shook my head, unable to process enough of what was going on to question her. I took a step over to Max, who lay curled up on the floor in a ball, his legs and arms drawn into himself. "Max? Honey?" I said. "Are you okay?"

He shook his head and mumbled something through his tears.

"What, sweetie?" I asked.

"He's fine!" Ava spat through her own tears. "He's a big faker so he gets all the attention."

I whipped my head around to glare at her. "You. Go to your room. *Now.*"

"No!" she yelled, her face crunched up in a wild mess of anger, sadness, and fear. I hated that it was me making her feel that way, but I couldn't help what she had done. I didn't want to be dealing with this at all, but there I was, smack-dab in the middle of it.

"Now!" I bellowed, and she cringed at the noise, sobbing as she slowly pulled herself to a standing position and staggered down the hall like she'd been shot.

Max's cries increased, and I was suddenly concerned that Ava had really hurt him. "Max," I said, trying again. "I need to see if you're okay. I won't touch you if you don't want me to, but I just need to know that you're not bleeding any-where. Does it feel like anything is bleeding?"

"My *heart* is bleeding!" he cried, and my eyes stung with grief for all this little boy had suffered through. His parents' divorce, his mother's death, and a sister who at times seemed hell-bent on making his life miserable. He slowly unfurled his body, and I searched for any signs of blood. Not seeing any, I breathed a sigh of relief.

"Where does it hurt most?" I asked him, and he held out his left hand. His pinkie finger was swollen and looked as though he may have landed on it when Ava leapt at him. I was afraid it might be broken. "Let's get some ice on that, okay? Can you go sit on the couch in the den and I'll come bring it to you? We might want to tape it to your other finger, too, just to keep you from knocking it against stuff and making it hurt worse."

Max nodded and began a labored walk to the den while I went into the kitchen to grab an ice pack from the freezer and the white bandage tape from the first aid kit in the cupboard. The roasted chicken I'd bought was getting cold, but I couldn't think straight enough to worry about dinner. I didn't want to see the look on Victor's face when I told him that not only had his daughter cut class, she was stealing from me and had violently attacked her brother.

"Grace?" Max called out. "Are you coming?"

I pulled out the first aid kit from the cupboard by the sink and took a deep breath before answering. "I'll be right there," I said, and, though I hated to admit it, fought the quiet urge to run away.

Ava didn't emerge from her bedroom for the rest of the night. I thought about going to talk with her, but I was too angry and I knew whatever I said would only make the situation worse. After I gently wrapped up Max's finger, put ice on it, and gave him a dose of children's ibuprofen for the pain, I fed him some dinner and read him several chapters of *Harry Potter and the Sorcerer's Stone* until he began nodding off on the couch. I carried him to his bed, breathing in the nutty scent of his skin—he never did take a shower—his arms wrapped around my neck and his cheek resting against my chest, remembering doing this with Sam. "Night, Mama," Max mumbled as I tucked the covers around him, making sure he had Kelli's blue blanket tucked up around his chin.

The muscles in my chest clenched hearing him call me that name, and I knew he was already asleep, halfway between reality and dreamland, a place where his mother might still have been alive for him. Sam had called me "Mama" a few times when I took care of him, and I made sure to clarify that I was Sissy, not his mother. I didn't know what I was to Max and Ava. There was no label for the role I played in their lives. I was simply Grace, the woman standing where their mother should rightfully have been.

I turned off the overhead light in Max's room and shut the door behind me. There was still a sliver of light coming from beneath Ava's door, but it was quiet, and I wondered if she had cried herself to sleep. Knowing it would likely be better if I left her alone, I still couldn't stop myself from gently tapping on her door and listening for a response. When there wasn't one, I inched it open, cringing as the hinges squeaked. My eyes traveled the room, and there was Ava, curled up on her bed, her mother's red sweater wrapped tightly around her, enveloping her like a chrysalis. I wondered what kind of transformation was taking place inside her, how she would survive this astoundingly painful loss. I took in her deep, even breaths, and while I was still angry, I felt an enormous swell of compassion. Afraid I might wake her, I silently left the room, turning the light off behind me.

Victor was surprised to see me awake when he came home. I sat on the couch in the den, waiting for him, thinking it was the furthest point away from the kids' rooms, knowing that however this talk went, it wasn't going to be quiet. "Hey, baby," he said. He strode over and leaned down to give me a quick kiss.

I reached up and pulled him down next to me. I took a deep breath, wanting to find a way to reconnect with him before hitting him with our conversation. "How was work?"

He gave me a tired smile and I noticed that the crinkles around his eyes seemed to have grown deeper over the past couple of weeks. "It was good. We had over a hundred and fifty tables move through for dinner, and all of them bought a ton of wine."

I'd learned enough about the restaurant business in the last year to know that beverages—wine and cocktails, especially—were where the biggest profit margin lay, typically 80 percent, so this was good news, considering the recent struggle Victor had been facing with the Loft's sales. I whistled, a low sound. "Impressive.

Anyone throwing drinks at pain-in-the-ass jocks?"

He chuckled. "No, baby. You're still one of a kind." He put his arm around me and I cuddled into him, relishing the heat off his body and breathing in his scent, which, tonight, was a comforting mix of onion, garlic, and slightly musky male sweat. I rested my head on his chest and listened to the slow thumping rhythm of his heart, letting it soothe me. Just the sheer act of making physical contact with Victor brought me a peace I hadn't felt all week.

"I've missed you," I said quietly. "I'm sorry I've been so distant."

He dropped a kiss on the top of my head. "I've missed you, too. I wasn't really sure what was going on, but it seemed like you needed some space. So I gave it to you."

I sighed and decided to ease into the topic. "I think I'm just learning how to do this step-parenting thing. I know you said I'm your partner and not the kids' parent, but the truth is, with you gone so much, I have to be."

"I know you do. And I appreciate it more than you realize." He paused and pulled out of our embrace. "But it won't be forever, Grace. Spencer will be back full-time and we can find a better way to manage things."

"I know," I said, taking another deep breath, well aware that I needed to forge ahead with the conversation about the issues we were having even though it would be easier not to. It would be easier to reminisce about how we were at the beginning of our romance, how he cooked for me, how we could talk for hours or spend an entire Sunday in bed. The memories would warm us from the inside out, our hands would begin to wander, Victor would kiss me, and everything would be right with our world again. But I knew that reality would set back in, and the problems that loomed heavy above us would still be there, needing to be discussed. Better to get it over with now. "But can we still talk a minute?" I asked.

He squinted. "About?"

"The kids," I said. "I just don't want to feel like some ignorant babysitter who can't handle things that come up when I'm with them." I paused, fearful to continue but knowing I had to. "Like the other night, when Max broke the Wii? You didn't even stop to hear my side of things. You just took Ava at her word, and she was lying to you."

I felt him immediately tense and pull away. I sat up and looked at him with what I hoped he knew was love. His expression suddenly turned hard, his lips drawn into a firm, straight line. Anger flashed in his gray eyes. "Did you just call my daughter a liar?"

"No," I said, drawing the word out slowly. "I said she lied *to* you—once."

"I don't see the difference." He shifted away,

scooting to the other corner of the couch and folding his arms across his chest.

There was a sudden, cold ache in my belly, followed by a warm flash of rage in my chest. I didn't want to fight with Victor. I didn't want to make things worse but decided there was no point to stopping now. "I also got a call from the school today," I said, telling him about Ava skipping class and then the money I found in her gym bag.

"There has to be some kind of explanation," Victor said after I'd finished talking. He slowly shook his head. "Maybe she skipped class—all kids do that at one time or another—but there's no *way* she stole from you."

"Max saw her taking money from my purse this morning," I said quietly. I reached out and squeezed his hand, but he yanked it away. A shadow passed over his face and I knew we had entered dangerous territory.

"Max is *always* trying to get his sister in trouble. They try to get *each other* in trouble, for god's sake. It's the way things are with siblings. We have to take it with a grain of salt, or they're going to pit us against each other and totally manipulate things. You have to be smarter than that."

I tried not to respond to the subtle but definitive shift he'd made from "we" to "you," indicating that it was me being stupid. Blatantly separating us. "I realize they tattle, but tonight was different.

Ava lunged at Max and almost broke his finger. She attacked him, Victor. I'm worried about her."

He gave me a hard stare. "Brothers and sisters fight, Grace. I know you were older than Sam so maybe you didn't, but it's totally normal."

"Stealing is not normal." I paused. "I was talking with Melody about it—"

"Wait," Victor interrupted. "You told Melody about this?"

"Yes. I needed someone to talk to. You were at work."

He threw his hands into the air and stood up, taking a couple of steps away from the couch. "Great! She'll tell Spencer and he'll want to talk with me about something he never should have known about. Thanks a lot."

I took a deep breath, knowing that Victor was on the defensive and not wanting to anger him further, but getting Ava the help she needed was more important than how things ended up between her father and me. "She's acting out," I said. "And stealing could just be the beginning."

"What are you saying? That she's going to turn into some kind of delinquent? Her *mother* just died. You need to cut her a little slack."

I stared at him a moment, trying to steady my rattling pulse. "I cut her *plenty* of slack. When she rolls her eyes at me or talks down to me, I let it slide. She's upset, I get that. She's in pain, and she's obviously not managing it well. She also knows we're engaged. Did you tell her?"

"Of course not. Did you?"

"No." I paused. "Maybe Kelli did. Or Diane."

"She hasn't *seen* Diane."

I thought about telling him then about my trip to Kelli's house with Ava. Maybe she'd gone back there without our knowing. Maybe, as Melody and I had, she'd run into Diane, who'd assumed we'd already told the kids. I opened my mouth to confess all, to tell him everything, but the cold, hard look on his face stopped me. "However she found out doesn't matter," I said instead. "I'm worried about her. Maybe we need to get her into counseling."

"Suddenly you're the parenting expert around here?" The disdain in his words was clear.

"I've spent more time at it than you," I shot back, and immediately wished I'd kept my mouth shut. It was a low blow, and I knew it. He worried about how little time he'd spent with the kids when he was still married to Kelli, and now how overwhelmed he felt having them with us full-time. But that didn't change the truth—that with the ten years I spent taking care of Sam, it was likely I was the more experienced of us two.

Victor's face closed up, his eyes a hard wall as he looked at me. "Look. I'm tired. You're tired. We're going to end up saying things we don't mean. You're choosing a bad time to talk about this."

"There *is* no other time, Victor! We never *see* each other."

"Jesus!" he said, reaching up to rake his fingers through his hair. "Can you quit complaining about things for five minutes, please? I know things are rough. I know this isn't the life you expected! Okay? I get it. But if we're going to stay together, we have to learn how to find our way through hard times, too. And accusing my daughter of being a thief isn't helping anything."

I stared at him, my eyes filling with tears. I tried to tell myself all of this was only temporary, like a television station announcing it was having technical difficulties. Our regularly scheduled program—or, in this case, our previously scheduled life—would eventually resume. But it seemed there was no use in trying to get him to understand. He was going to protect Ava no matter what.

Seeing my tears, his expression softened. "I'm sorry." He took a step toward me and reached out his hand, but I moved so he couldn't touch me. He sighed, then dropped back down to the couch. "I didn't mean to snap at you," he said. "I'm just so exhausted. I love the kids so much, but I've never really done the full-time father thing before. Kelli always took care of them."

"I know," I said quietly. "I get that this is all hard for you, too."

"It is," he said. "I was used to the schedule we

had, you know?" He shook his head. "God, it makes me sound like such a horrible person, but after I finally left Kelli, I was relieved to get my life back. She sucked so much out of me. I didn't realize how much until I was gone."

"You're not a horrible person," I said.

"Thanks, but it feels like I am." He gave me a weak smile. "Honestly, honey, I thought handling their fight without you was better, so you wouldn't have to bother with it. I guess I was trying to shield you from the stress out of pure habit, the way I always had to shield Kelli. I didn't give you enough credit, but that was about me, not you." He sighed. "I'm sorry. I'm just trying to find my way through this. And I'm scared . . ." He trailed off, dropping his gaze to his lap.

"Of what?" I asked him, feeling my hurt ease as he expressed his vulnerability. He was just as afraid as I was. Unsure of himself as a father, worried how to handle bringing me into his children's lives.

He chuckled softly, still not looking at me. "More like what am I *not* scared of," he said. "I'm scared I'm not a good enough father for Max and Ava. I'm scared I'm like my *own* father —that somehow having his blood run through my veins might make me too weak to help my children through their pain." He finally raised his eyes and met my own. "But that's scared me for years. What scares me now is that I might lose you. That you might give up on me and having this life together. That I'm too screwed up for any woman to want to be with at all." He whispered that last sentence, as though admitting it to himself for the first time. It struck me then how similar Victor's insecurities were to mine.

"Kelli loved me," Victor continued. "But it was in such a needy way, you know? I always felt like I wasn't enough for her, no matter what I did, no matter how much I took care of her. And then *you* came along, so independent, and I thought, *Wow. Here's a woman who can be my partner. We can take care of each* other. But now I'm messing that all up, too."

"You're not messing anything up." I felt how much he cared for me, how much he needed someone to be there for him.

He hesitated a moment before leaning over and lowering his head into my lap. "I'm sorry," he said again. "I love you."

I ran my fingers through his thick, dark hair, feeling the warmth of his scalp and the wet of his tears on the top of my thighs. Filled with a deep sense of tenderness, I suddenly couldn't imagine doing anything but staying there. "I love you, too," I said. I would tell him what I suspected about Kelli's past later. Now wasn't the time.

"I'll talk with her, okay, Grace? I'll ask her what happened and we'll go from there."

Ava

I woke up the morning after Grace found the money in my backpack with swollen eyes and a sick feeling in my stomach. I couldn't believe the way she'd yelled at me—no matter what I'd done, Mama had *never* talked to me like that.

Mama. I closed my eyes and all I could see was her face hovering over me. "Wake up, love," she'd say. "Time to greet this beautiful day." If I concentrated hard enough, I could almost feel her breath on my cheek as she kissed me awake; I could smell the faint echo of her strawberry shampoo. "I miss you," I whispered into my pillow. The muscles in my throat thickened, the way they always did when I allowed myself to think about her too long. "I want you to come back."

My mind strayed to one of my favorite memories of her, before Dad had left: curling up on the living room couch and reading her favorite cookbooks with her. She'd read the recipes aloud, like a story, and I could almost taste the meals she described. "One cup of basmati rice," she read. "Cook in coconut milk instead of water, add chopped Thai basil and a chunk of ginger for spice."

I loved times like this alone with Mama. Max

was at a friend's house and it was just us two. "Your dad loves Thai food," she told me. "Shall we surprise him? You can help me stir the rice and make the peanut sauce, okay? We'll even pick up some chopsticks at the dollar store."

She kissed the top of my head, and I nodded, snuggling closer to her as she flipped through the pages. Later, in the kitchen, after we'd picked up everything we needed to make dinner, Mama turned up the radio and danced around, using a ladle as a microphone. She grabbed me from my stool and made me dance with her, spinning around in circles until we both were giggling and dizzy. Daddy walked in from work just then and joined us, his long arms around Mama and me both. "My favorite girls," he said, laughing.

"Ava?" My dad's voice came through my bedroom door, snapping me out of that happy, remembered moment. The hinges squeaked as he entered, and I pulled the covers up over my head, turning onto my side to face the wall. He sat down on the edge of the mattress, the weight of him rolling me onto my back and pulling the covers off of my face. I wasn't his favorite girl now. That much I knew for sure. "Kitten, look at me, please. We need to talk."

"I don't *feel* like talking," I said, keeping my eyes glued to the ceiling. I was terrified he was going to yell at me too, since I was positive that Grace had told him what I'd done.

"Did you take the money from Grace's purse?" he asked. "Tell me the truth. Lying is only going to make things worse."

Nothing could get *worse.* My eyes filled and I pressed my lips together, hard, and bobbed my head once.

He sighed and ran his fingers through his hair, a gesture I'd begun to notice he only did when he was tense. "Can you tell me why?" I shrugged. "Ava." He sounded drained. "Please."

"I needed it for dance team. We have to pay for uniforms and away trips and the bus." I paused to take a heaving breath, finally looking over to him. He stared at me, his gray eyes dark and unreadable. "Do you hate me now?" My voice shook.

"Oh, honey," he said, reaching out and cupping my face with his hand. "Of course not. I'm just worried about you. Stealing is wrong—I know you know that." He pulled his hand back. "Why didn't you just ask me for the money?"

"I didn't want to bother you," I said in a small voice. "I just . . . you know. Mama used to give us an allowance, and if we needed money we asked her and I just didn't know how to talk with you about it. You're so busy and stressed out from the restaurant and you said people aren't eating out as much as they used to, so I was afraid having us live here was already costing you enough money. I didn't want to make things worse."

"Sweet girl, you can ask me for anything. I should have thought about an allowance, but you're right. I've been busy. We'll figure that out, okay?"

I nodded. *Maybe he isn't going to yell. Maybe I can talk my way out of what I did.* "I'm sorry," I said, and I realized this was true. I felt awful. I still felt a flicker of anger, but this time it was toward Dad instead of Grace. If he'd been a better husband to Mama, if he had never left us, none of this would have been happening. He never would have *met* Grace. And Mama would still have been alive. And even though I thought this, I was too afraid to speak the words out loud.

Dad pulled his hand from my face and set it on my hip, patting it once. "I'm glad you're sorry. But it's Grace who needs to hear that. Do you understand me?" I nodded. There was no way around it. I was going to have to apologize to her. "And one more thing," he continued. "How did you find out that we're engaged? Did your mom tell you?"

I shook my head, pressing my lips together. "I ran into Diane. She brought it up like I'd already know." I hoped he wouldn't ask me *where* I'd run into her; I was in enough trouble, and his finding out I'd gone back to Mama's house definitely wouldn't go over well. I gave him a reproachful look. "Why didn't *you* tell us?"

Dad sighed and rubbed my leg. "We were going

to, the weekend right after I proposed to her." He paused. "But then your mom died, sweetie, and we just didn't think it was the right time. You had enough to deal with."

I pulled myself up, tucked my legs to one side, and sat against the wall. "Diane said Mama was really upset."

Dad nodded. "She was. But your mom got upset about things pretty easily . . . right? You remember that, don't you?"

I didn't want to think about how easily Mama got upset. "Do you think . . ." I faltered, not knowing how to ask what it was I wanted to know. I swallowed, trying to push down the lump in my throat. "Is that how she died? Did she . . . ?" I searched his face with pleading eyes, hoping he would tell me the truth. I needed to know if she *chose* to leave us.

"Did she kill herself, you mean?" Dad said quietly. I nodded, and he shook his head. "The doctor said her heart stopped because of a combination of things. She wasn't eating well and her body's systems were beaten down. When she added in the medicine she took to help her sleep, her heart just couldn't take it."

"But . . . did she take too *much* of it?" I asked, and he froze a moment, his gray eyes cloudy. I could almost hear the debate in his head over what to tell me.

"There's no way for us to know for sure," he

finally said. "And that's the truth, Ava. That's what the doctor told me. We don't know what happened. I wish we did."

"She was really sad, Daddy," I said. The corners of my mouth dipped downward and my chin began to quiver. "She was crying all of the time and I didn't know what to do." I told him about how little she slept and ate, how I found her hysterical on the floor of her closet. "It's my *fault* she's dead. I should have told you. I should have asked for help."

Dad pulled me into his arms and I pressed my cheek against his strong chest. "Oh, Ava. None of this is your fault. *None* of it." I pulled away, sniffling. A few tears ran down my cheeks in hot streams. He looked at me intently, his hands gripping my arms. "Your mom was a grown-up, and no matter what, if she needed help, it was her responsibility to ask for it. I'm sorry I didn't see how bad things had gotten with her. I wish I had paid more attention."

"*I* wish you'd never left her," I whispered, dropping my gaze from his. "I wish you'd stayed because then maybe she wouldn't be dead." Terror gripped its icy fingers around my stomach as I spoke those words, but I couldn't hold them back.

Dad briefly closed his eyes, and when he opened them, they were shiny with tears. "Sometimes I wish I'd stayed, too. Leaving was the hardest decision I'd ever made. But the problems your mom had ran much deeper than just my relationship with her. And she refused to get help with them. She wouldn't see a counselor or talk about her past. I hoped that if I left, if she had to start taking care of herself without me doing everything for her, she might finally deal with her issues."

"But she *didn't*," I said, starting to cry again. "She just got worse. And then you got engaged and she *died*." I sobbed the last word, and Dad reached over to try to pull me into another hug, but I stiffened, forcing myself to stop crying. I didn't want him to think I was like Mama. I wanted him to believe I was stronger than that. I longed to tell him everything I'd found out about Mama—how she'd never been a cheer-leader and how her parents sent her away to the all-girls school—but in doing so, I'd have to tell him *how* I'd found it out, and I was terrified of how he'd react.

"I'm sorry you're hurting, honey. I wish I could fix everything for you." Dad wiped at his eyes with the tips of his fingers. "I'm not going to punish you for taking the money because I know things are really rough right now. But none of that is an excuse for that kind of behavior, okay? I expect better of you."

"I know," I whispered, wishing he could fix everything, too.

Kelli

Kelli didn't set out to lie about her past. At first, she thought she could just outrun it. The moment she'd saved enough money, she left the tomb of her parents' house and decided not to look back.

"You don't love me," she told them. Her voice shook. "There's no point in staying here." She waited for them to argue with her; she looked to her mother to stand up and beg her not to leave, but instead, they both were quiet, their shoulders curled forward, just as they had been the day they dropped her off at New Pathways. As though they were relieved to see her go.

She bought a bus ticket to San Francisco, thinking she'd find a hostel to live in for a while, but then ended up renting a room in a huge house near the marina. The landlord was a skinny, balding man in his forties who'd stared too long at Kelli's breasts for her to be comfortable, but when he implied he'd lower her rent if she went out on a date with him, she complied. The sex was quick and painless. It made her feel ill to do it, but it gave her what she needed at the time, and she told herself that was all that mattered.

After she got settled in her small room, she

found a job cleaning houses and relished the hard work, which tired her to the point of almost falling asleep in the bowl of ramen noodles that typically served as her evening meal. She didn't talk much to the other tenants, until one day she was sitting on the front porch, reading one of the romances she'd borrowed from the library, and another woman sat down in the other white wicker chair.

"Beautiful day," she said. She was older and heavyset, with limp brown hair and bright pink lipstick.

"It is," Kelli agreed, setting her book in her lap.

"You getting settled in okay?" She paused. "Burt sure seems to like you."

Kelli picked her book back up, staring at the words as they blurred on the pages. She hated that anyone noticed he visited her room. Most of all, she hated that she let him.

"Ah, honey," the woman said. "I don't mean no harm." She stuck out her hand. "I'm Wendy."

Kelli only hesitated a moment before shaking Wendy's hand and introducing herself.

"You're just cute as a button, aren't you?" Wendy said. "Like a cheerleader."

"I *was* a cheerleader," Kelli said, the lie popping out of her mouth before she'd even realized she had the thought.

Sitting on that porch with Wendy in the late

afternoon sun, Kelli spun a tale of her tryouts and ultimately being named captain of the team. *I love to dance,* Kelli told herself. *It's just a little white lie.* Over the next six months, she began opening up more to the people she talked to— always referring to her high school years as being the best of her life. She made up details about the color of her uniform—royal blue with yellow braided trim on the sweater. She talked about the complicated routines she and her friends put together that were the talk of the whole school. She deflected questions about her parents, saying only that they were old-fashioned and didn't approve of Kelli's trying to make it in the world on her own. She told herself the story of the life she wished she'd lived—and eventually, she began to believe it was true.

At night, though, reality spun its web around her and sticky memories clogged her mind. She dreamed of painful spasms in her abdomen, tangible enough to wake her and make her gasp in pain. She heard her baby's weak cries, the searing moment when the nurse took her away. "The doctors need to see her now," the nurse said. She never got to hold her baby. She never was able to tell her her name.

Reliving this moment, dark, aching emptiness felt like it might split Kelli wide open. She squeezed her eyes shut, curled fetal, and rocked her body back and forth, back and forth, the way she never was able to rock her baby girl.

She took a second job bagging groceries at a local store, trying to keep herself busy so she didn't have too much time to think, but then one night when she came home, she found Wendy sitting on the porch with another woman, who was holding a little girl.

"Hey, Kelli," Wendy said as Kelli walked up the front steps. "This is Jenna and her daughter, Macy. They just moved into 2-B."

"Hi," Jenna said. She looked like she was trying to channel the 1950s, with her cat-eye glasses, yellow cardigan, and full, rose-patterned skirt. She looked down at her daughter. "Can you say hi, Macy?"

"Hi!" the little girl chirped. She appeared to be about three years old and had her mother's fine, practically white-blond hair and blue eyes. She thrust out the stuffed gray kitten she held in her lap toward Kelli. "Chuck!" she said, and Jenna laughed.

"I don't know where she came up with that name." She nuzzled Macy's neck, and the little girl shrieked with laughter and held Chuck tightly to her chest.

"Mama, don't *tickle!*"

Kelli couldn't speak. She watched Jenna hold this child who could have easily been Rebecca. Her daughter would have had Kelli's hair and her blue eyes . . . wouldn't she? Or would she have looked more like Jason? Her throat closed as she was reminded of what she'd never know, the child she'd never see.

"Kelli?" Wendy prompted. "Are you okay?"

"What?" Kelli said, realizing she hadn't responded to the introduction. "Oh, sorry. I'm so tired." She forced herself to smile at Jenna. "Nice to meet you." She looked at Macy, who was twirling a lock of her mother's hair around a stubby finger. "She's beautiful." She hoped she didn't sound as close to crying as she felt.

"Thanks," Jenna said. "We think so."

"We?" Kelli said, keeping her eyes on Macy, who smiled shyly back at her. *Oh, my heart,* she thought.

"Jenna's husband works the night shift over at the hospital," Wendy said. "He's going to be a doctor."

"Oh," Kelli said as a sharp pang of jealousy began to knit itself together in her chest. *Jenna couldn't be much older than me, and look at all she has. Look at her daughter. It isn't fair.* "Well, good night," she said, and quickly made her way to the safety of her room.

Over the next few weeks, Kelli tried to avoid seeing Jenna and her family in the building. She stopped hanging out with Wendy on the front porch. The times she came home to find Jenna playing with Macy in the front yard, it was all Kelli could do to keep from dissolving into tears right there on the sidewalk. She held her breath as she walked by, unable to look at this beautiful little girl.

"Hi, Kelli!" Jenna said one sunny but humid Saturday afternoon. She was running through the sprinkler with Macy, who wore a tiny pink and white polka-dotted bikini and matching hot-pink sunglasses. "Want to join us?"

Kelli shook her head and kept on walking, accidentally colliding with Burt as she raced up the front steps. "Whoa there, missy!" he said. "Where's the fire?" He stank of alcohol and cigarettes; his white T-shirt had a brown stain on the sleeve. "Rent's due Monday. Want some company?" He leered at her, and Kelli had to hold back the bile in her throat. She heard her father's voice: *Whore.*

That was it. She needed to leave San Francisco. She couldn't stay there a minute longer. Her past was nipping at her heels. She pushed past Burt and ran down the hall. "Hey!" he said. "Where you goin'?"

"I'm leaving," she called out over her shoulder. "Moving out." She was on a week-to-week lease; she didn't need to give him notice.

"Wait a minute! You still owe me for this week. At the *full* rate!"

Kelli grabbed her suitcase from the closet and opened the lining where she kept her cash. Burt appeared in her doorway. "You hear me?" he bellowed, and she practically threw a stack of bills at him.

"There," she said, her voice breaking. "Now, please, just leave me alone." She slammed the door in his face and began to pack her bag. She would start again. She'd create the best version of herself, only showing people the bright, happy side of who she was. She'd work hard, fall in love, and maybe even have a family of her own.

When the taxi she called arrived, she strode out to the street, keeping her eyes on the ground, not answering when Jenna and Macy asked her where she was going. She climbed in the backseat of the yellow cab and told the driver where to take her.

Twenty minutes later, she was at the bus station and she stood in front of a bulletin board, wondering where she should go. A brochure caught her eye, a picture of the Space Needle and a snow-capped mountain against a dazzlingly blue sky. *Seattle.* All Kelli knew about the city was how wet it was always supposed to be, and so she closed her eyes and imagined the clouds, the lush green grass, wondering whether if she lived there long enough, all that rain might finally wash her sins away.

Grace

December was generally a dark month in Seattle, and along with everything else that was happening, I couldn't help but think it was contributing to my foul mood. It was the Monday morning after Victor and I fought over Ava's stealing, and I'd arrived at the office early to catch up on some of the work that was piling up. I had client files to review, grant requests to compose, but instead of accomplishing any of that, I sat at my desk, staring out the window at the cloud-laden sky.

"Okay," Tanya said when she entered my office to bring me a stack of checks to sign. She gave me a stern look and tucked her thick mane of curls behind her ears. "What's up with you?"

I averted my eyes from her and forced a short laugh. "Nothing. Just feeling a little overwhelmed by the workload."

"I don't think so." She peered at me. "Something going on with Victor and the kids?"

I kept my eyes on my computer screen and my fingers poised on the keyboard, thinking about how easily I'd been frustrated by Ava's poor behavior, how a better, more loving woman wouldn't have been. "I just don't think I'm very good at this mothering thing," I said. Tears pricked my eyes as I spoke those words. It was hard to admit, even to myself, but over the years I did question whether there was something fundamentally wrong with me because of my decision to not have kids. I talked a good game —blaming the years I spent taking care of my brother, citing my drive to have a career and the insecurity around whether I could be a good mother—but deep in my belly there was a seed of doubt that any of this was true. Maybe the consensus about women who weren't naturally maternal was true—I was heartless. Or, at the very least, the heart I *did* have wasn't built for the kind of selfless existence motherhood demands. Maybe I just wasn't cut out to share my life. Maybe I'd be better off on my own.

Tanya gave her head a quick shake, and her springy black curls bounced. "You don't give yourself enough credit." She smiled at me thoughtfully. "Do you remember when we first met at the thrift shop? I'd been living at the safe house for about a week with my kids, and Stephanie brought me in to fold clothes with you. You weren't the boss yet, just volunteering your time."

"I remember." I pictured Tanya the first time I saw her. She was barely a shadow of the bright woman sitting before me now. Her face bore the evidence of a man's fury in a mottled mess of purple and black bruises against her dark skin. Her brown eyes were lifeless; she looked at me, bewildered, like a prisoner who had suddenly been set free and didn't know what to do with her newfound liberty.

"Well," she said now, "then you'll remember how you sat with me for hours, just listening and letting me cry. I think we managed to fold about three shirts. You were so calm and collected. You held my hand and you told me over and over again that I didn't have to live the way I'd been living anymore. You told me I was stronger than I knew. You said I could be anything I wanted to be, and the way that you said it with such conviction, I believed it might be true." Her full bottom lip trembled as she spoke. "You may not get all gushy about your *feelings,* but if I've learned anything over the past couple of years, it's that any fool can learn to talk a good game about how they feel. It takes real strength to show up and prove it." She paused. "You hear me? You understand what I'm saying? Love is a *verb.*"

My own lip trembled then, and I nodded, too afraid that if I spoke I'd burst into tears. "Thank you," I finally whispered.

Tanya smiled and picked up the file next to her. "You're welcome. Now, let's get you to work!"

"Yes, ma'am," I said with a smile, and she went back to her desk, quietly closing my door behind her. For the next few hours, I poured myself into writing the proposal that, if approved by the state, would bring Second Chances almost half its operating funds for the next fiscal year. I described the women we helped, their desperation and fear; how our counselors worked with them to build their confidence and a support system that would keep them from ever going back to their abusive partners. Putting the words on the page, I felt better than I had in a month. *This* I was good at. This was where my talents were—helping these women. Running this organization in a way that made me proud.

As I was typing up a list of all the different services we provide for our clients, I went into great detail about how many of the women who came to Second Chances were without family in the immediate area—how their abusers isolated them both emotionally and physically. Often-times we'd have to do a nationwide search to locate relatives our clients could connect with for support, and it suddenly struck me that I could utilize those resources to confirm if Kelli actually *did* have a baby in high school. In fact, we'd even had a few women who'd given up babies for adoption and asked our assistance in finding them. But before I could do this for Kelli, I needed to make sure I wasn't headed down the completely wrong path.

I opened my Internet browser and did a quick

search to bring up the California census website. Our staff had access to databases that included all births and deaths for every state so we could find out if the women had surviving family members. I could run a search for California and see if any babies were born under Kelli's maiden name during 1993 or 1994. That would at least be a place to start. "Hey, Tanya?" I called out through my open office door. "Can you help me with something for a minute?"

She appeared a moment later, notepad and pen in hand. "What's up?"

I turned the monitor of my computer so she could see it. "I need to log in to Vitalsearch for California and I can't remember my password."

She strode across the room and came around behind my desk, then leaned over and typed in the right combination of keystrokes. The site opened up and she straightened, smiling at me. "Do we have a client looking for family there? The counselors usually tell me before you."

"This is a little more personal," I said, then explained to her about the doctor's letter and my suspicions about Kelli.

"Wow," she said. "What does Victor say about all of this?"

I lifted one shoulder and looked away from her, focusing my eyes on the screen. "I haven't exactly told him yet."

"Uh-oh," she said. "That's not good."

I sighed, drumming my fingers on my desk. "I *know*. I just feel like it'll be better to talk with him once I find out something for sure, either way. Right?" I looked at her again, eyebrows raised, hoping she'd agree with me.

"How long have you *not* told him?" Tanya asked, and my hope vanished.

"Too long." I sighed again and leaned forward, quickly clicking on the links that would lead me to the birth databases for the time frame I was interested in reviewing. Tanya pulled up a chair and sat next to me. I typed in the words "Baby Reed" for both 1993 and 1994, then waited to see the results. There were over four hundred babies with that last name born in California during those years.

"You'll have to narrow your search by county," Tanya said. "Where did she live?"

"San Luis Obispo, I think." I ran another quick search and confirmed that the city was located in the county of the same name. The result this time was zero.

"Well, so much for that idea," I said.

"Hold on," Tanya said. "Maybe her parents sent her somewhere else to have the baby? If it was such a big secret, then that would make sense, right?"

I smiled at her. "You're a genius."

"True," she said. "But don't worry. I won't let it go to my head."

I chuckled and brought up a map of California, noting there were fifty-eight counties in the state. "I don't know where to start."

"Try San Francisco and Sonoma," Tanya suggested, so I typed in Sonoma first, thinking we'd get fewer results because of its smaller population. I was right—there were only ten. I had to click through six "Baby Reed"s before I looked at the screen and my stomach flipped over. "Mother, Kelli," I read aloud. "Father, unknown."

"Well, there you go," Tanya said. "Finding out about the adoption won't be as easy as this, you know. Especially if it was closed."

"I know, but her baby would be eighteen now, so maybe he—or she—is looking for Kelli."

"You could start by posting her name on the international reunion registry, if you want. That worked well for Laurel, remember? She found her birth mother pretty quickly that way."

"I think I'd better talk with Victor first," I said. "I've been keeping it from him long enough."

A few hours later, I arrived at the Loft to pick up the kids after their respective activities. In what I was sure was his attempt to make up with me, Victor had left the restaurant early so he could do that afternoon's shuffle between basketball and dance practice. I wrestled with a vague sense of anxiety as I waved at the servers who were sitting at a table folding black cloth napkins, wondering how seeing Victor would feel after the way we'd left things the night before. And now that I needed to confess I'd been rooting around in Kelli's past, I worried that I was about to erase any progress we'd made.

I walked toward the kitchen, surprised when I entered the swinging doors to see both Melody and Spencer standing there. My best friend hurried over to hug me, and I glanced over at Max and Ava, who were sitting in the chef's-table booth, where Victor and I had shared our first meal. Ava was leaning over Max's schoolwork, looking like she was trying to explain something to him.

"Hey, you," Melody said. "I was just dropping Spencer off."

I must have appeared confused, so Victor explained. "His physical therapist said he can be out of the sling a few hours a day, so I asked if he would come in at night to help expedite and close things up. No heavy lifting or cooking, of course, but I thought it might help if I came home a few hours earlier." He searched my face, his expression hopeful.

The tension in my chest relaxed a bit hearing this, knowing our argument had spurred him to this kind of action. "That's great," I said, still feeling like a bit of my guard was up. We still had the issue of Ava's stealing to deal with, so I wasn't ready to forgive him completely. Of course, I had my own transgressions to admit and I was fairly sure he wasn't going to be happy with me, either. "Have they eaten?" I asked Victor.

He nodded. "They helped me prep first, but I just fed them so you won't have to worry about making dinner." He was trying, that much I knew for sure.

Melody squeezed my hand. "Want some company tonight? My boyfriend is busy for a few hours and I don't have any clients, so I can come hang out."

"Boyfriend?" I said before I could help myself. I threw a glance over to Spencer, who blushed furiously but smiled. Melody laughed and walked over to stand next to him, giving him a quick peck on his cheek.

"Can I see you a second?" Victor asked me. "Before you go?"

I nodded, and he glanced over to his actual prep cook, Rory. "I'll be right back," he said, and we walked together to his small office in the back of the building. The space was a mess of paper and boxes of wine; his desk was covered in seating charts and half-drunk glasses of water.

"You need a house cleaner," I said, trying to keep the air light between us. This was not the time to delve into our problems, in earshot of the kids and his entire staff.

He blew a long breath out between his lips, making a puttering sound. "I need a lot of things," he said. "To get my head out of my ass, for one."

I laughed out loud at his unexpected pronouncement, clapping my hand over my mouth. He reached over and gently clasped his long fingers around my wrist, pulling my hand away. "Don't cover your smile. It's one of the things I love most about you." He paused but didn't let go of my wrist, running his index finger back and forth over the sensitive skin at the base of my palm, causing me to shiver. "I talked with Ava this morning."

"Oh?" Again, I tried to keep my tone light.

"She admitted she took the money. She needed it for her dance uniform and she was afraid to ask me because I've been so stressed. She shouldn't have taken it, of course, but I can't help but feel like it's partially my fault for not remembering they'd need an allowance." He shook his head, and I could see the guilt he felt scribbled across his face. I had to remember that I wasn't the only one in this situation struggling with feelings of inadequacy. "I'm sorry I reacted the way I did, Grace. I just couldn't believe that my little girl would do something like that."

"I know," I said gently, my fears beginning to evaporate. We could find a way to make this all work out.

"We can talk about it more later, if you want,

but I told her she has to apologize to you, okay? So you need to let me know if she doesn't, and we'll deal with it when I get home." I nodded, and he pulled me to him, his long arms tucked tightly around me, his chin resting on the top of my head. "I love you so much, Grace. Please forgive me."

I hugged him tighter and then pulled back enough to look up at him. "Of course I forgive you. We just have to make sure we stay on the same team."

"I told you on our first date I don't get sports analogies," he said with a wink, then inched his face toward mine. The kiss was soft and sweet, long and slow, and it awoke something in me I hadn't felt since before Kelli died. Having children around, I'd realized, was arousal's kryptonite.

When he finally pulled away, I had to catch my breath. He pressed his hips against me and groaned. "Okay. You should go, or I'm going to be in danger of violating a few health codes right here in this office."

I laughed, and he held my hand as we walked back into the kitchen to face the kids.

Melody told me she had to run to the bank and deposit a check before coming over to our house, so the kids and I climbed into the car and headed home. The drive was quiet. Max hummed along with the radio, but other than a couple of perfunctory answers to my questions about how his day at school had been, he wasn't his usual chatty self. He raced inside after I parked the car in our driveway, but Ava sat still in the backseat. I trusted that Victor actually had talked with her, but I wasn't going to be the one to bring up what she'd done. "Everything okay?" I asked her. "Do you need help carrying your bag?"

She shook her head, staring at her lap. I turned to look at her and saw that she was clasping her hands together so tightly, her knuckles were white and she was digging her fingernails into her skin. The tips of her nails were ragged, and the edges were lined in blood, as though she'd been gnawing on her cuticles. "Ava, honey, don't do that," I said as gently as possible, feeling the same rush of tenderness toward her as the other night when I'd watched her sleeping.

"I'm sorry I stole from you, Grace," she whispered. "I just . . ." She trailed off and took a deep breath before continuing. "I needed to pay for my dance uniform and I didn't know how to ask for it, and the money was there in your wallet and I just took it. I'm so sorry. I know it was really, really wrong." Her voice broke on her last word, and I felt my throat swell.

"I forgive you, Ava. We all make bad choices sometimes . . . me included." She nodded, so I went on. "But I also need to say that I'm a little concerned about how you jumped on Max. You could have really hurt him."

"I know," she whispered. "I don't even remember doing it, really. I just remember being mad." She paused, looking up at me with wide eyes.

"What is it?" I asked, sensing there was something else she wanted to say.

"I just . . ." she began, and bit her bottom lip.

"You can tell me, whatever it is," I said. "I want you to be able to talk with me."

"I called my grandparents last week," she said softly. "On Thanksgiving. After we found that letter from the doctor?"

"Okay . . ." I tensed slightly, wondering what else she had been hiding from us. "Did they talk with you?"

She nodded. "My grandma did, a little. I asked her if she could send more pictures or the rest of Mama's yearbooks and she said there weren't any." Her voice began to shake. "She said Mama was never a cheerleader. That they sent her away to a school for troubled girls. She said it was better to forget the past."

"Ava," I said, drawing her name out. Everything she was saying made sense with what I'd confirmed earlier—that Kelli had gotten pregnant and was sent away to have the baby. I couldn't tell Ava this, of course, not without talking to Victor first. "I think we need to tell your dad about *all* of this. I never told him about going to your mom's house to get the recipe or finding the letter, which was totally not the right thing to do. And now with you talking to your grandparents . . ." I sighed. "We need to tell him the truth."

"He's going to be mad at me, though." Ava's voice trembled again.

"Because you called your grandparents?"

She shook her head. "No. Because going to my mom's house with you wasn't the first time I went there after she died. It wasn't the last, either." She explained how she and Bree had gone through her mother's computer and found a list of private investigators and, as I'd suspected, how Diane let it slip about me and Victor being engaged when they visited Kelli's house again. "I'm *so* sorrSy I lied, Grace."

"It's okay," I said, reaching my hand through the space between the front seats to squeeze hers. "I think your dad will understand. None of us are perfect." I paused. "And no matter what happened in your mom's past, she loved you and Max very, very much."

"I loved her, too," Ava whispered.

"I know you did, sweetie," I said. "I have no doubt she knew that much was true."

Kelli

Kelli tried not to be worried about how dizzy she felt. She didn't want Ava—who'd noticed it that morning—to worry, either. As it was, Kelli put her daughter through too much. She knew she relied on Ava to do the things Kelli should have been doing herself—paying the bills, cleaning the house, making sure Max brushed his teeth and didn't wear the same pair of boxers two days in a row. She'd been such a good mother when Victor was still with them. She knew she'd taken excellent care of her children then, but now she felt scattered and loose. God, she loved them. She needed to get help.

After dropping them at school, she drove home, blinking rapidly to clear her vision. She was shaky and nauseous and wondered if she should go straight to her doctor's office. What would she say, exactly? That she was heartsick? That every time she thought about Rebecca, her body rebelled and wouldn't allow her to eat? Seeing Ava about to enter high school had started to bring everything back. She was terrified that her daughter would make the same mistakes she had, but she didn't know how to talk with Ava about it without telling her the truth about what she'd done. When she did manage to sleep, she dreamed of her lost child. Her thin cries, the gaping, empty wound she'd left in Kelli's body. She dreamed of the pain, but also of her first daughter's kicks inside her, of the potential life that God had simply erased.

As she pulled into her driveway, her phone rang. "Hey, Diane," she said, trying to sound normal.

"Hey! Are we on for eleven?" It was their ritual, coffee and gossip at the kitchen table on the days Kelli didn't have to work the lunch shift.

"I don't know . . . I didn't sleep last night."

"Again? Honey, get thee to the doctor. I'm worried about you."

"I'm fine," Kelli said, unable to keep the exhaustion she felt from the words.

"Um, I'm pretty sure you're not." Diane paused. "Are you eating?"

Kelli was silent, and her friend sighed. "What's going on with you? Is it Victor's engagement?"

Kelli hesitated, wondering how to put all her jumbled feelings into words. "I'm just . . . sad." Her voice finally broke. "I can't stop thinking about Rebecca," she whispered.

"Oh, sweetie," Diane said. "Have you thought any more about hiring a private investigator?" Her friend had been the one to suggest that Kelli try to find the doctor who delivered her daughter. She said that if Kelli found out the details of exactly what happened that day, she might be able to finally move on.

"I can't afford it," Kelli answered with a heaving breath. "And what if it doesn't make a difference? What if I'm just always going to be . . . broken?"

"You're not *broken,* Kelli. You've suffered through some seriously painful circumstances in your life. You've lost a lot. But you also have two gorgeous children who need you. I know it's hard, but maybe you can try to stop focusing so much on the past and look at what's right in front of you."

Kelli was quiet a moment, sniffling back her tears. "Okay," she finally said. "I'll try. But I think for now, the best I can do is sleep for a while. Can I take a rain check on coffee?"

"Yes. I'll come check on you later. But if you don't make an appointment with your doctor next week, I'm going to drag you there again. And that's not just a threat, it's a promise."

Kelli laughed, grateful for the support of her friend, one of the very few people she'd told about losing Rebecca. They hung up and Kelli made her way into the house, forgetting to lock the front door behind her. She stumbled her way to the bedroom, past the kitchen, where she glanced at the toast she'd made for Ava, thinking that maybe she should try to eat it herself, but even the thought of taking a bite made her stomach roil, so she continued down the hall.

Once safely ensconced in her bedroom, Kelli stripped down to her bra and underwear, amazed that even with all the weight she'd lost, her chest size hadn't diminished. She remembered how Jason first touched her there . . . how enamored she'd been with the thought that he might love her. Tears flooded her eyes again as she thought back to the girl she'd been, so naïve, so alone.

Spurred by this memory, Kelli made her way into her closet and dug behind a stack of boxes, pulling out the two things—other than clothes— that she had taken with her when she left her parents' house: a photo album, which she'd taken from her mother's dresser, and her freshman yearbook, which her mother had given her even though Kelli had been at New Pathways when it came out.

Now she ran her hands over both of them, thinking it was finally time for Max and Ava to see a little of who she was growing up. Maybe then Kelli could work up the courage to tell them the truth about what happened between she and her parents, why they still wanted nothing to do with her.

Climbing into her bed, Kelli closed her eyes for a few minutes, feeling waves of exhaustion swelling throughout her body. She didn't know if a doctor would be able to help her. But Diane was right—her children needed her. Something had to change.

She forced herself to flip through the pages of the album. She saw the misery behind her blue eyes. She saw a child trying to appear happy when inside, she was slowly withering away. Her parents appeared even older than she remembered them, and she imagined them now, in their late seventies, frail and cold. She wondered if they were as miserable without her as she had been without them. Family was family, after all. She didn't understand how they could simply erase her from their life, because no matter how hard she had tried to let go of them, they popped up in her mind at the most unexpected moments —while she washed the dishes or served a man at the restaurant who was wearing a bow tie like her father's.

Her heart fluttered unevenly as she shut the album and turned the pages of her yearbook. How young everyone was, how inexperienced. Looking at her own picture, she couldn't fathom that that child had climbed into Jason's truck and let him do the things she'd allowed him to do. How desperate she'd been for love. She wondered if Ava ever felt that way and again, Kelli knew she needed to step up and start being the kind of mother Ava could be proud of.

But first, Kelli thought, *I need to sleep.* She closed the yearbook and set it next to her on the bed, thinking she might show the kids that one first. She took the album, got up, and tucked it onto the shelf next to the ones of Max and Ava, knowing it might take her a bit longer to let them see their grandparents and explain why the pictures of her just stopped at fourteen.

There was a painful, sudden buzzing in her head, and the room began to spin around her. She threw an arm out to grasp the edge of the bookcase so she wouldn't fall over. Staggering back to her bed, she opened the bottle that she kept in the nightstand drawer and popped the remaining three pills in her mouth. The doctor had told her they would reduce her anxiety and insomnia, and Kelli figured that since she had an abundance of both of those things, taking more than the prescribed dose was okay, just as long as the kids weren't around when she did it. She'd sleep the day away, waking in time to pick them up from school. She set her alarm, just to be sure. Max didn't have basketball that night and Ava usually wanted to stay home on the Fridays before she went to her dad's house. They'd put on some music, make homemade pizza together, and later, watch a movie. Kelli would tuck her children in, telling them just how much she loved them, how everything would be just fine.

Kelli pulled the blue comforter up to her neck, snuggling into its warmth, letting the drugs course through her system and gradually calm her mind. Her parents had told her she simply needed to begin again. And so, with that thought, with the hope that she could find the strength to shape her life into whatever she wanted it to be, Kelli closed her eyes and waited for sleep to finally come.

Ava

I was nervous the whole next morning, especially as I sat in social studies, totally unable to focus on the quiz Mrs. Philips had passed out at the beginning of class. I hadn't studied at all; in fact, I'd failed to turn in three of the last four assignments, so I knew even trying to answer the questions was pointless. School didn't seem important right now, especially knowing that Grace and I were going to sit down with Dad tonight and tell him everything we'd done. Me more than Grace, I supposed. She'd kept the secret from him about taking me to Mama's house, but it was me who'd snuck back there two other times and me who called my grandparents without saying a word about it. He had already forgiven me for taking the money from Grace's purse, but I was pretty sure that I wouldn't get off as easily for lying to him and sneaking around behind his back.

I was *especially* worried that once he found out the reason I'd done it all in the first place—to find out more about Mama's past—that would be the end of it. I'd never discover what *actually* happened to her. I pictured how Dad would look when I confessed—the deep cut of his frown, his dark eyebrows cinched together over his nose, the disapproving shadow hanging in his eyes— and was certain he'd instantly forbid me from doing anything else that might explain why her parents sent her away.

It made my stomach clench to think that I'd never find out why Mama's parents disowned her, who it was she'd written about missing in that note, or why she contacted Dr. Stiles. How could I live my entire life *not* knowing? I felt a deep-seated pang for Mama then, sharp enough to steal my breath. Tears welled up in my eyes, and even as I tried to fight them, images of her floated in front of me. She was supposed to *be* here for me in moments like this. Moments when I felt lost and scared, unsure of what steps to take. *Tell me what to do,* I thought. *Please. Help me.*

I waited. I wasn't sure what, exactly, I was expecting to happen, but there were no voices in my head, no eerie response from wherever she might have gone. But then suddenly, a seed of an idea took root in my mind, and during the last few minutes of class, as I marked down a random assortment of answers on the quiz, I started to piece together a plan, knowing exactly what had to happen next.

In the lunchroom, Bree was sitting alone at our usual table, picking through a pile of French fries to find her favorite extra-crispy ones. I hurried over and straddled the bench.

"Hey," she said, taking a sip of her chocolate milk. "What's up?" She knew Grace was making me talk with my dad tonight and was a little worried that meant she would get in trouble, too.

"I want to go to California and see my grand-parents," I said, then quickly explained why. "After my dad finds out what I've been up to, there's no *way* he'll let me keep trying to find out more about my mom . . . right?" She nodded, and I continued. "If I don't go now, I'll never be able to. It's the only way."

Bree didn't look convinced. "Can't you just *call* them again? Why do you have to go all the way *down* there?"

"*Because,* Bree. My grandma barely spoke to me when I called before. If I just show up, there's no way she can ignore me. What's she going to do, shut the door in my face?" I swallowed the fear that that might be *exactly* what she would do. I paused, waiting for my friend to say something, but she didn't, so I forged ahead with what I needed to ask her. "So, I was wondering if I could borrow some money for a bus ticket. I'll pay you back, I promise."

"I don't know," Bree said slowly. "Your dad is

already going to be mad at you. I don't think taking off to California is going to help."

"Then *you* shouldn't go to California," I snapped, then immediately felt bad for it. "I'm sorry. God. I'm so sorry." I waited, but she was still quiet, stung, I was sure, by my sharp words. "Bree," I started again, my voice cracking on her name. "You're my best friend. Please. I don't have anyone else to ask."

"Okay," Bree said, releasing a heavy sigh. "When do you want to go?"

"Now. I don't have dance squad today and Max is going to Logan's house this afternoon so Grace will be looking for me outside the school right at three thirty. I need to be out of the house by then."

She hesitated a moment, shredding the napkin she held, then spoke again. "*We* need to be out of the house, you mean."

I smiled, trying to keep my bottom lip from trembling, then threw my arms around her. "You're coming with me?"

"Umph!" she said, surprised by my embrace. "Yeah. You think I'd let you do something as crazy as this on your own?"

I shook my head, digging my face into her neck, unable to hold back my tears. After a moment, I managed to calm down, then pulled back. "Sorry," I said.

"What for? Having feelings? Please. At least I

know you haven't turned into one of those dance-team fembots."

I laughed, and we made our way to our lockers, deciding that it was probably easier to sneak off campus when everyone was still at lunch and most of our teachers were in their lounge eating, too. Slinging our backpacks over our shoulders, we tried to look casual as we strolled through the only exit that led to the street and was completely out of the office's view. A couple of other kids stood outside, laughing and talking, and suddenly, Bree froze in place, grabbing my arm. "Skyler at ten o'clock," she said, and I looked up to see him break off from his group of friends and start walking toward us just as we were about to dash across the last part of the playground.

"Hey," he said as he approached. He leaned in and gave me an arm-around-the-shoulder hug—the only kind of hugging allowed at our school between boys and girls. Nothing below the waist could touch—it made me blush a little when I thought about why.

"Hey," I said, a little dizzied by how good he smelled. I tried to sound relaxed, like it was totally normal for Bree and me to be hanging out on the edge of the school grounds. The last thing I needed was for him to ask us where we were going. "How are you?"

"Good." He gave me a crooked grin, flipping his bangs out of his eyes with a jerk of his head.

"But I totally bit it on that social studies quiz."

"Yeah, me too." I stole a glance at Bree, who attempted to appear extremely interested in her fingernails.

Skyler shoved his hands into the front pockets of his low-slung jeans. "I was thinking, maybe you might want to study together sometime? In the library or something?"

I smiled, relieved to see him blush, that he was nervous to talk with me, too. "Sure," I said, nodding.

He grinned again. "Okay. Cool. So, I'll text you?" He pulled his cell phone out from one of his pockets, I gave him my number, and he walked away.

"Oh. My. *God,*" Bree said, giving me a playful smack on the arm as we checked for any teachers in the immediate vicinity. None were around.

"I know, right?" I said, unable to keep a huge smile off of my face, momentarily distracted from what we were about to do. "That's kind of like a date?"

"Totally!" Bree squealed. We shot down the street as fast as we could, our backpacks bouncing. My heart raced, not just because we were running, but because of the anxiety pounding through my blood. If we got caught, I was going to get in serious trouble.

But as we turned the corner that led to Bree's house, I realized that going to California wasn't *about* me. It wasn't even about Dad. It was about Mama. About finishing what she had started. It was about facing her parents and finally hearing the truth.

Grace

"Ava, where are you?" I said, leaving a message on her cell phone. At three thirty, I'd pulled into my usual parking spot by the flagpole, but after ten minutes of waiting to see her familiar dark head and purple-checkered backpack come out of the school, she was nowhere to be found. "Call me right back, okay?" I shot her a quick text, too, suspecting she was more likely to check that than her voice mail.

I strode into the front office. "Excuse me," I said to the same gray-haired secretary whom I spoke with the day Kelli died. "Did you happen to see Ava pass by on her way out?"

She raised her thin, penciled-on eyebrows. "I was just about to leave a message for Mr. Hansen," she said, looking down at me over the top of her red-framed glasses. "Neither Ava nor Bree were in their classes after lunch." She paused. "Again."

Part of me wanted to wipe that judgmental scowl right off of her face, but I was too irritated with Ava to bother. I knew she was nervous about talking to her dad, but it hadn't crossed my mind that she'd actually run away from doing it. I tried to drill into all of my clients the knowledge that most of the things we worry about never happen, that the stories we tell ourselves about how awful a particular moment in time might be are often much worse than what actually ends up happening. I should have said as much to Ava.

I waved at the secretary, then called Victor as I hurried back out of the building to my car. "Have you heard from Ava?" I asked him.

"No," he said over the loud clang of pots and pans in the background. "Should I have? I thought you were picking her up."

I sighed. "I thought so, too, but she and Bree skipped their afternoon classes. She's not here and she's not answering her phone."

"Are you kidding me?"

"I wish I were," I said.

"What about Max?"

I reminded him about the playdate at Logan's, then told him I'd meet him at the house. Maybe Ava had simply gone home early. But when I arrived and ran inside to check her bedroom, it was empty. Her closet was open, and her black suitcase—the one I'd filled with her things from her mother's house—was missing. "Damn it, Ava," I muttered, then turned around and headed back down the hall. I checked the bathroom, the den, the living room, the kitchen, the garage . . . she wasn't there. She wasn't anywhere. My heart began to pound.

Victor showed up just as I was in the middle of sending Ava another text message. "Is she here?" he asked. He was still wearing his black chef's jacket and had a smudge of some kind of red sauce on his face.

I shook my head. "I checked the whole house. Her suitcase is gone, honey."

He dropped his arms to his sides. "*What?* Where do you think she went? Bree's?"

I nodded, quickly calling her friend's number. No answer there, either. I left another message and then hung up, frustrated, but also starting to feel scared. A thought struck me. "Maybe she went to Kelli's?"

Victor nodded, his lips pressed together. His gray eyes were frantic. "Good idea. Let's go." He scratched out a quick note and left it on the entryway table, telling her to stay put and call us immediately if she came home.

In the car, I sent Ava yet another text message: "Honey, we're so worried about you. Please, tell us where you are." I was a little surprised by the intensity of my own feelings in that moment— the sharp sense of icy dread thudding through my body not knowing where she was, wondering if she was in danger. *Is* this *how it feels to be a*

414

mother? Every cell of my body overwhelmed with fear that something terrible might have happened to her? I was terrified she wasn't answering not because she wouldn't, but because she *couldn't*. That someone had grabbed her and thrown away her phone. My mind spun with a thousand atrocities that could happen to a pretty runaway girl. *To Ava.* Ava, who was vulnerable and hurting, who might be feeling desperate enough to get into a car with a stranger. I flashed on ugly visions of her lying on the side of the road, her body broken and bruised. *Raped.* The thought made me feel like I might vomit.

"Why the hell would she *do* this?" Victor asked. "What is going on with her?"

"I'm sure she was nervous about talking with you tonight," I said. I'd told Victor that after her apology to me, Ava and I needed to talk with him about a few things. "She probably just wanted to go somewhere to think."

"Think about what?" he asked. Taking a deep breath, I explained how I had taken Ava over to Kelli's house for the recipe before Thanksgiving, and how we'd found the letter from the doctor Kelli had contacted.

"That's it?" he asked when I'd finished talking. "Why didn't you just *tell* me?"

"I should have. But then you came home and told me about Spencer breaking his arm, and things just got so busy and we were both distracted. There was never a right time." I paused and looked over to him. "I'm sorry. I should have said something right away."

He bobbed his head and changed lanes, trying to edge his way around a blue Honda. While the distance between our house and Kelli's wasn't far, with all the traffic on California Avenue, it could take up to twenty minutes to get there. "Okay," he said as he slowed to a stop at an intersection, "but there's no way she took off because she was afraid of telling me that." He honked at the cars in front of us, who were taking their time going through the light after it changed. "C'mon!" he yelled. "It's not gonna get any greener!"

"There's more," I said, and then quickly detailed everything else Ava was going to tell him about lying to him, skipping class, and sneaking over to her mother's house, trying to find out more about Kelli's past. Considering the circumstances, I figured he needed to know and it didn't matter that it was me who told him and not Ava. He shook his head as he listened, gripping the steering wheel until his knuckles went white. I reached over and put my hand on top of his leg; the muscles were rigid under my touch. He didn't say a word, but I could see the tendons working along his jawline as he clenched his teeth.

My stomach flipped over, at this point a little fearful of how he'd react to the rest of what I had done but knowing I needed to tell him everything.

"So, after Ava and I found that letter from the doctor Kelli contacted, I did a little digging on my own. When I realized he was an OB, I suspected the reason the photo album went blank when she was fourteen was because she might have gotten pregnant. But I also suspected that maybe she'd given up the baby for adoption."

"She didn't," Victor said slowly. "It died."

What? I blinked a few times, the gears inside my head grinding to a stop as I processed the impact of his words. "Hold on. You *knew* she got pregnant?" I swung my gaze to meet his. "I specifically *asked* you what drove Kelli and her parents apart and you lied to me?"

He shot me a dubious look as he finally entered Kelli's neighborhood. "And how is that different from you taking my daughter to her mother's house and then keeping it from me?"

"It's *totally* different," I said. "You knew exactly what *might* have led Kelli to kill herself. I was terrified that she might have done it because of our engagement . . . that it was possible I'd somehow contributed to her death by simply being with you, and you deliberately *lied* to me. You never asked me outright if I'd taken Ava to her mom's house."

"Because I didn't have a *reason* to!" He slammed on the brakes so he wouldn't miss the turn onto the right street.

I jumped at the anger in his tone, still

unaccustomed to Victor's losing his temper with me. Seeing my reaction, he continued in a slightly calmer voice. "By your logic, lying by omission is not as bad as lying outright? Is that what you're saying?"

"Yes!" I sighed then, realizing I was being a little ridiculous, considering he was right. I hadn't been totally honest with him, either. "Look. We're stressed out right now and I really don't want to fight. I understand why you didn't tell Ava, but me? *That* I don't get."

"I was just trying to honor Kelli's wishes. I felt like it was the least I could do for her after she died. She was intensely private about the whole thing and I knew she wouldn't want the death of her baby to be a subject of discussion." He paused and threw me a sideways look as he pulled up in front of Kelli's house. "And I didn't *know* you thought our engagement might have had something to do with how she died. You never *said* anything."

I took a deep breath and then exhaled slowly. Again, he was right. And what mattered now was finding Ava, not what was happening between us. "I'm sorry," I said as we got out of the car. He nodded and reached for my hand, and we raced up the steps.

Victor unlocked the front door. "Ava?" we both called out, walking through every room but coming up empty. The air was stagnant and cold and I shivered. She wasn't there. Victor tried calling her again, but she didn't pick up. I called Bree and sent Ava another text, but again got no reply from either of them. We locked the door and headed back to the car.

"It's starting to rain," Victor said once we were in our seats and he'd restarted the engine. *"Damn it."* He pounded the dash with his fist. I reached over and laced my fingers through his. He squeezed my hand and the long look we gave each other said more than anything either of us could have articulated. He held my gaze for another moment before speaking again. "Where else could she be?"

"This might sound a little nuts, but do you think she'd try to get to California?" I asked. "To see her grandparents? She called them on Thanksgiving." I paused, realizing I'd forgotten to tell him this.

"Jesus," Victor said, pulling away from the curb. "Is there anything else I should know?"

I cleared my throat. "Well . . . possibly. I know you said Kelli's baby died, but I checked the census database in Sonoma county, and it listed a Baby Reed born to Kelli Reed in 1994. The father was unknown."

"Okay. And?" Victor glanced over at me, eyebrows raised, as he drove us out of Kelli's neighborhood.

"So, if the baby had *died,* it would have been

listed right next to the birth information. Like on a tombstone. But it wasn't."

Understanding blossomed across his face. "Are you saying . . . ?" He trailed off and blinked a couple of times. "That Kelli *lied?* That her baby is alive?"

I shook my head. "We don't know that she lied. Maybe the baby was given up for adoption, and her parents didn't want anyone to know so they made her *say* it didn't survive? It's clear they hid the pregnancy by sending her away." I shrugged. "Talking with them is probably the only way to know for sure. If they'll tell you."

He looked over his left shoulder and pushed hard on the brakes before yanking the car back to the curb. "You drive. I'll call them."

We switched places, leaving the car running. "Where do you think we should go?" I asked. "The bus station? That'd be the cheapest way to travel, right? She could have asked Bree for money, which is probably why neither of them are answering their phones. They're probably together." I hoped this was right. I hoped she wasn't stupid enough to try to hitchhike. Again, horrible images flashed through my mind and I blinked to try to erase them. *Please, let her be okay.*

I pulled back into traffic as he dialed Kelli's parents. The rain was coming down fairly hard now, the drops pelting the car like a thousand tiny hammers. Thunder rumbled, and a moment later, a blaze of lightning followed. It was only a little past four thirty, but the charcoal clouds darkened the air around us.

"Ruth?" Victor said after he'd dialed Kelli's parents. "It's Victor." He paused. "That's right, Kelli's husband." He gave me an apologetic look, but I waved it away, knowing what he meant. "My daughter, Ava, the one who called you a few weeks ago? She's missing." He paused again and grabbed the door handle as I took an especially sharp corner. "Well, it *does* concern you, actually, because we think she's on her way down there."

He went on to explain that he knew about Kelli's first daughter and that we suspected she hadn't died. He listened for a moment or two as we crested the West Seattle Bridge and I made my way over to the First Avenue exit toward downtown. "No, Ruth. The baby *didn't* die. I don't know whether you told Kelli she had to lie or just made her believe that her daughter had died, but either way, that child is eighteen years old now, and we are going to find her, with or without your help." He took a heaving breath, trying to keep his composure. "Now, here's the deal. My daughter disappeared and I'm not one goddamned thing like you and your husband . . . I'm not *happy* she's gone. She is only thirteen years old and she needs us. She's confused and worried and scared and probably feels like her whole world has fallen in on her." His tone escalated, louder with every word. "Her mother—your *daughter*—just *died*. Do you understand that? Do you have any feelings about that at all? When you didn't come to the funeral, I figured it was for the best, so Max and Ava wouldn't be exposed to the people who'd made their mother's life so miserable. I gave you a pass, but now I realize that I shouldn't have. I need you to tell me the truth, please. Tell me what happened to Kelli's baby. You owe Ava that much. You owe it to your *daughter!*" He practically shouted this last sentence.

Victor listened a little longer, still breathing hard, and I reached over and rubbed the top of his thigh. He put his hand over mine just as we arrived at the bus station. I scanned the crowd on the sidewalk for Ava and Bree, but the sea of umbrellas and dark raincoats made it impossible to discern any faces.

A moment later, Victor hung up the phone. "What did she say?" I asked, turning off the engine.

"You were right," Victor said. "Kelli's daughter didn't die, but her parents told her she did. They arranged a closed adoption through a private lawyer."

"What?" I said with a small gasp. "How did they manage that without Kelli knowing?"

"She said something about Kelli signing papers

and not realizing what they were. Everyone at the hospital just assumed she knew she was giving the baby up."

"Oh my *god,* that's *awful.* Poor Kelli. I wonder if she knew the truth."

"I have no idea," he said. He froze for a moment and looked at me with cavernous fear in his eyes. "What if Ava's not here? What if we don't find her?" His voice was stretched thin.

I reached out again and linked my fingers through his. "Then we'll call the police. We'll call the National Guard. We *will* find her, Victor." He nodded again, desperate to believe me, and together, we made our way out into the cold, dark rain.

Ava

We went to Bree's house first. I watched as she packed a small bag, filling it with clothes and her toiletries. She even grabbed her bathing suit.

"We're not going on *vacation,*" I said, my arms crossed over my chest as I stood in her bedroom, waiting for her. We had to hurry so we could get to the bank, then to my dad's house and onto the bus that would take us downtown.

She grinned. "It's California, isn't it? You never know."

I shook my head, my heart racing, thinking about what it would be like, showing up at my grandparents' house. I'd found their address a few weeks ago in one of the boxes Dad had brought back from Mama's house, though I still couldn't help but worry they might refuse to talk with me. What would Bree and I do then? We'd be hundreds of miles away from Seattle with nowhere to stay. I wasn't even sure if we'd be able to pay for a hotel room; I was afraid we might be too young.

"Hey," Bree said, interrupting my thoughts. "I'm ready." She tilted her head, tucking a wisp of hair behind her ear. "You okay?"

"Yeah," I said, releasing a huge breath I hadn't realized I'd been holding. "Let's go."

An hour later, Bree had withdrawn six hundred dollars from the bank, and we had stopped at my dad's house so I could pack a bag, too. Not knowing how long we'd be gone, I didn't know how much to bring, so I just filled one of Mama's small black suitcases with a pile of underwear, jeans, and tops. I thought about writing Dad a note, just so he wouldn't worry too much, but I decided it was probably better not to leave any kind of hint about where we'd gone. I cringed as I thought about how my dad would react when he realized I'd run away, how worried and angry he'd be, but I forced myself to stop. I was going to California for Mama. This was my last chance to find out what happened to her, why her parents had sent her away. Dad would be so grateful when I came home, he'd forgive me right away for everything I'd done. I'd become the kind of daughter he'd brag about to his friends. I wouldn't lie or skip school or be rude to Grace. We could have a fresh start.

It was three o'clock by the time we were finally ready to lock up the house and head downtown. From the bus stop around the corner, it only took twenty-five minutes to get to the corner of Eighth and Stewart, about a block away from the Greyhound station. Bree looked up the address on her smartphone and confirmed the next bus from Seattle to San Francisco wasn't until six, so we had plenty of time. "We'll have to transfer in San Francisco to another bus that will take us to San Luis Obispo," she said as we walked down the street from the bus stop. "This is going to be a *long* trip."

"How long?" I asked, my belly twisting a little. Maybe this wasn't such a great idea. What had been so clear to me just hours before suddenly seemed ridiculous. Getting on a bus with a bunch of strangers and riding hundreds of miles to see the grandparents who hadn't given a damn about me or Max. About their own *daughter*.

"Almost a whole day," she said, and again, I briefly considered turning around and just heading back home. But once inside the station,

Bree and I pushed our way through the masses and dropped onto one of the benches, trying to hold our breath against the stink of body odor, which was worse than in our school gym after the boys played dodgeball.

"Should we buy our tickets?" Bree asked, but I shook my head.

"Maybe we should wait a little bit," I said. Seeing the look on her face, I quickly added, "Just until the line goes down."

"Okay," she said, drawing out the word. We sat together for about an hour, watching the people around us, whispering comments back and forth about how they looked or what they said to each other. The walls were tiled, so every noise was echoed and loud; people squabbled over which bus they should take to get to their destination on time and who remembered the snacks. A couple of guys next to us fought about whether or not they'd packed enough weed for the trip, and Bree rolled her eyes at me, mouthing the word "stoners."

Just as I was about to tell Bree that this was a stupid idea and we should probably just go, my eyes flew to the main doors as a rush of travelers came inside, shaking off their umbrellas. I saw Grace before she saw me. She wore jeans and a black jacket, and her red hair was in a wild, wet mess around her face. My dad was right behind her.

"Look," I said, nudging Bree with my elbow. She turned her head toward the door, then looked back to me and smiled.

"Should we make a run for it?" she asked, only partially teasing.

I pressed my lips together and shook my head, slowly standing up. Grace scanned the room and when her eyes landed on me, her hand flew to cover her mouth. I waved, unsure if I should feel terrified or relieved that they'd found me so easily. Grace turned to my dad and pointed to me. They raced over, and as soon as Dad was close enough, he grabbed me hard, lifting me off of the ground.

"Oh, Ava, thank god you're safe," he said, pressing his mouth against the side of my head. His voice was ragged, edged in tears. He pulled back, dropped me slowly back down, and cupped my face in his hands. "We were so worried. What the hell were you *thinking?*"

I blinked away my tears and looked over to Grace. She gave me a small smile and ran her hand down the side of my arm. "Are you guys okay?"

"We're fine," I said, turning my head to glance at Bree, and Dad dropped his hands from my face. "I'm sorry." I took a deep breath. "How did you find us?"

"We checked your mom's house, then thought you might try to go to see your grandparents," Grace said. "The bus seemed like the cheapest way to get there and you guys are too young to buy a plane ticket on your own."

"Do you have any idea what could have *happened* to you here?" my dad demanded. "Or on a bus to another state? I don't even want to *think* about it, Ava. I can't believe you'd do this."

My bottom lip quivered. "I'm *sorry*," I said again, dropping my gaze to the ground. "I just knew after I told you I lied to you and skipped school and went to Mama's house and called her parents, you'd make me stop trying to find out what *happened* to her." I looked up at him again, suddenly panicked, realizing everything I'd just confessed, terrified of what he might say next.

Seeing the distress on my face, his own expression shifted from one of anger to one of understanding. "Grace told me everything, honey." His voice was gentle, and for some reason, that just made me want to cry more. "If this was so important to you, why didn't you talk with me about it?"

"I *tried* to and you wouldn't even let me go to Mama's *house!*" I blurted, then sucked in a rough breath. Grace took a step toward me, but Dad put his hand on her shoulder so she'd stay back.

"You're right," he said, bobbing his head softly, seemingly urging me to continue, so I went on.

"I was so *angry* at you," I said, then threw my gaze over to Grace. "At you, too." Her expression didn't change, but she nodded the same way Dad had, keeping her eyes on me. I took another deep breath, not caring that we were in the middle of the bus station and a few people around us were starting to stare. "And you know what else? I'm *still* angry at Mama, because she lied. She lied and now she's gone and it's *not right* for me to feel this way about her. I want to know what happened so I can stop being so mad. I don't want to hate her. I want to understand why she kept secrets from me. I want to know why everyone thinks it's okay to keep *lying* to me!"

I lost control then. Sobs racked my body and Grace rushed over, put her arms around me, and pulled me to her. Her body was soft and yielding, her embrace so different than Mama's, her touch solid and reassuring. Mama's always seemed to drain something *from* me. Slowly, I slid my arms around Grace and held on tight, my tears wetting the front of her jacket. Dad put his hand on my back, rubbing it; Bree stood next to him, tears in her eyes, too. Grace stroked my hair back from my face and all I could think was how I used to do the same thing for Mama when she cried. After Dad left us, how often I'd wished Mama had it in her to still do it for me.

I melted into Grace, finally letting myself give in to the fact that she wasn't a horrible person trying to take my daddy away. I'd tried to hate her, I'd tried to make her the bad guy, but she'd shown me that she cared about me, and even when I was just awful to her, when I'd been downright rude, she didn't leave.

After a few minutes, my tears finally began to subside and I looked up to see Daddy with tears in his eyes, too. "I'm so sorry you've been carrying that all around, Ava," he said. "I'm sorry that I didn't let you go to your mother's house when you wanted to. I thought I was protecting you, but I can see that I was wrong."

I couldn't believe I was the one who'd made the mistakes and here he was, apologizing. He took a deep, shuddering breath and looked at Grace, then back over to me. "I'm also sorry I didn't tell you more about when your mom was a teenager. She made me swear not to. I thought I was doing the right thing, doing what she asked. I thought it would hurt you too much to hear the truth."

I pulled back from Grace, wiping at my eyes with the back of my hand. I looked at Bree, who frowned at me and gave a short shrug. I turned my eyes back to Dad. "What's the truth? What didn't she want me to know?"

He hesitated a moment, dropped his chin down, and gave me a stern look. "If I tell you, you have to wait and let me tell Max, okay? When he's a little bit older. I *will* tell him, but I think right now, it might be too much." I nodded, and Grace nodded, too, as though he were asking the same thing of her. He took a deep breath before speaking again. "Your mom got pregnant when she was fourteen, Ava. And her parents were so ashamed of her, they sent her away."

"Oh my god," I said, and I heard Bree gasp, too. The small bits of information I already knew suddenly made sense. "She *did?* Why wouldn't Mama talk about it? Why wouldn't she want us to know?"

"She was ashamed, honey. She tried to push it all down and pretend it had never happened. And when a person does that long enough, all that grief can start coming out in unhealthy ways. I begged her over and over to get help. But she wouldn't."

"What happened to the baby?" Bree asked, and my dad shot a surprised glance over to her, as though he'd forgotten she was there, then looked to Grace.

"She was most likely adopted," Grace said in a calm voice. "We don't know any of the details, really."

"*She?* I have a *sister?*" I asked, forgetting my tears. "Can we look for her?"

Grace and Dad looked at each other again, as though they were trying to decide. "Dad," I said, pleading. *"Please."*

Grace gave a slight nod, and Dad sighed. "Okay," he said. "Yes. But I don't want you to get your hopes up too high, honey. Because she might not even know she's adopted. Or even if she does, she might not *want* to meet her birth family. We'd have to respect that."

"Okay," I said, knowing he was right, but still excited at the prospect of getting to know a sibling I never knew I had. I could tell her all of the good things about Mama . . . and then, maybe someday, I could share some of the harder stuff with her, too.

My dad reached over to hug me again and kissed the top of my head. "I love you, Ava. We're going to find our way through this. But no more lying and sneaking around. No running away. Do you understand me?"

I nodded, tearing up again. "Can I talk with Grace alone for a minute?"

"Sure." He gave me another squeeze, then grabbed my suitcase. "Come on, Bree," he said. "I'll buy you a soda."

Grace and I watched them walk toward the small concession stand, Bree looking like a toddler next to my dad. Grace turned to me and released a long breath. "Want to sit? I'm wiped."

We moved to a nearby bench, not saying anything for what felt like a few minutes. "So you told Dad everything, huh?" I finally said. "Even about us going to Mama's house for the recipe?"

"Yep. When you took off, I didn't really have a choice."

"I get it," I said, barely lifting my shoulders. "It was kind of easier that way, I guess?"

"Maybe for *you!*" she said with a smile and a nudge.

"Sorry," I said, laughing. "You're right." I looked down to my lap, unable to meet her gaze. "I didn't mean to disappear like that. I just . . . everything with my dad . . ." I trailed off, trying to find the words to express what was going through my mind.

"It's all right," she said gently. "I understand how you've been feeling maybe better than you think." I gave her a quizzical look, and she smiled. "I was your age when Sam was born . . . did you know that?" I shook my head. I knew her brother was younger than her, but not *that* much younger.

She nodded and then went on. "Well, I was. And my dad wasn't like yours. He was pretty reckless. He didn't care about being a father, and because my mom had to work nights and weekends to help support us, I was responsible for taking care of my brother when she wasn't there." She hesitated a moment before continuing. "I know that it's not exactly the same thing, and I know you've been through so much more than I could even imagine, but I do know how it is to feel like a grown-up in some ways and still be a kid. It pulls you in different directions. Makes you feel sort of imbalanced. When I was thirteen I just wanted to be with my friends, you know?" She paused. "But here's the thing. It was really hard for me to take on all that responsibility, just like I'm sure it was hard for you to take care of your mom so much. We did it because we *had* to. But now you and Max are with us, and we want you to enjoy being kids."

"I *still* want to help find my sister," I said, but the words were soft, padded with relief. Grace seemed to understand more about me than anyone else ever had. Maybe even more than Mama. And while I felt a little guilty having this thought, part of me hoped that Mama would be *happy* I had someone there for me now that she couldn't be. Someone I could talk to when I was worried or sad, someone who could never replace her but might make me feel less alone.

"Of course," she said, then we were quiet for another minute. I knew I had to hurry up and say what was on my mind before I chickened out. "Grace?"

"Yeah?"

"I'm actually glad you're going to marry my dad," I said. "You make him really happy."

She reached over and put her arm around me. I stiffened at first, even after our hug, still not accustomed to letting her show me affection, but then I relaxed into her body, feeling her warmth, the confidence behind her touch. "He makes me happy, too," she said. "When he's not driving me nuts." She jiggled me a little to let me know she was joking and we both laughed.

"I promise I'll try to stop being such a pain," I said. "I've made everything so hard on you."

"It's not all your fault, Ava. I'm not exactly perfect, either. After your mom died, I was really scared about helping to take care of you guys."

"Really?" I couldn't imagine Grace being scared of anything.

"Really," she said, nodding. "Things have been tough for *all* of us, but I kept thinking I was making it worse."

I suddenly wanted to reassure her, too. "You were actually really nice. Even when I was being mean to you."

"Ha!" she said. "Yelling is not exactly nice."

I shrugged, remembering the few times she had yelled at me, for fighting with Max and taking money from her purse; I probably deserved it. "Neither is lying and stealing." I looked at her, tears blurring my vision. "That's not the kind of person I want to be, Grace. I hope you give me another chance."

She hesitated only a moment before leaning over and hugging me again. "I hope you'll give me one, too," she whispered, and then together, we stood up and walked over to meet my dad, both of us ready to let him take us home.

Acknowledgments

Some books come more easily than others, and I might not have finished this one without the support of several amazing people.

From the beginning, Greer Hendricks, my brilliant editor at Atria Books, sensed the kind of story I was *trying* to write and page by page (sometimes word by word!) helped me coax it into place. Sarah Cantin, a talented editor in her own right, shared vital and personal insight on a key aspect of the story—I cannot thank her enough.

As always, thanks to Victoria Sanders, the most resourceful, encouraging, and hysterically funny agent a girl could have, who calmly navigated my fits of insecurity and made me believe in myself all over again. I am beyond lucky to have her in my corner. Thanks also to Victoria's team: Chris Kepner and Bernadette Baker-Baughman, for everything you do for us crazy artistic types!

My deepest gratitude to the other amazing people at Atria who make this writing life of mine possible—to name only a few: Judith Curr, Chris Lloreda, Paul Olsewski, Lisa Sciambra, Hilary Tisman, Carole Schwindeller, and Aja Pollock. I'm grateful for the entire sales team at Atria, who work tirelessly to help get my books out into the world, and for the art department for creating such stunning, affecting covers.

Special thanks to Cristina Suarez, my extraordinary publicist at Atria, for cheerleading, enthusiasm, and her general fabulousness. Also, for incredibly tasty No Bake Makery treats! Can't wait for your cookbook!

I'm indebted to Tina Skilton, my dearest friend, who read and listened to me gnash my teeth over this manuscript more times than either of us could count. Laura Meehan provided me with keen editorial input, enthusiastic moral support, and perhaps more important, many adorable pictures of her sweet baby Noah's gorgeously cherubic face. (Laura, I'd drive with you through questionable areas of San Francisco anytime.) Thanks also to Laura Schilling, for listening to me babble on about the plot and brainstorming with me about soap operas and secrets.

For early reads and immensely valuable feedback, thanks to Stacey Harrington, Liz Ward, Laura Webb, and Beth Mellone. And for one of the most enjoyable, hysterical lunches ever, as well as stunning professional support, thanks to Pennie Ianniciello, Shana Lind, and Melissa Medeiros McMeekin.

Friends are the family you choose, and I couldn't write without the love and support of mine: Sally Cote, Sherrie Stockland, Carmen Bowen, Loretta McCann, Cheryl Baulig, Belinda

Malek, Brad and Deanna Martin, Rachael Brownell, Allison Ellersick, Jerrilyn Harvey, Kristie Miller Cobb, Robin Hart, Kurt Jensen, Kristin Cleary, Kelly Angel, Greg and Sue Bateman, Curt and Tracey Hugo, Wendy Bailey, Denise Brandon, and oh so many others, I can't list them here. I love you.

Thanks to the amazing book bloggers who have embraced my stories and helped share them with new readers—I am so grateful for you. To every reader who takes the time to write a review or tell someone about my books, to those who write me about how a story has affected them, I cannot thank you enough. Also, to my friends and fellow writers on Facebook, Twitter, and Goodreads—I appreciate you all so much!

To my mother, Claudia Weisz, who first encouraged me to put pen to page—thank you. (Who knew I could turn being a drama queen into a profession?) For hugs, cuddles, and never failing to make me laugh, thanks to my children— Scarlett and Miles, and to my bonus daughter, Anna.

And finally, to my best friend, my husband, and my partner in crime . . . thank you, Stephan, for building this life with me and gently cradling a heart like mine.

A Readers Club Guide

Questions and Topics for Discussion

1. Consider the two epigraphs that Hatvany opens the novel with. How do they frame the novel? How do you interpret the title, *Heart Like Mine*, in relation to these two quotations?

2. On the surface, Kelli and Grace are very different characters. What do they share? How do their upbringings shape the kinds of women they become?

3. *Heart Like Mine* is narrated by the three women in Victor's life—but we never hear from him directly. As a group, discuss your impressions of Victor. How does each narrator present a different side of him?

4. While family dynamics are at the heart of this novel, friendships are also integral to these characters' lives. Discuss the role of female friendship. What do Kelli, Grace, and Ava each get from a friend that they can't get from a significant other or a family member? How do you experience this in your own life?

5. How are mothers and fathers portrayed differently in the novel? What do you think the author is saying about the significance of each parental figure in a child's life?

6. Shortly after Kelli dies, Grace admits, *"However much I loved Victor and worried for Max and Ava, I wasn't sure I could go through this without losing myself completely"* (page 195-6). Could you empathize with her in this moment? Did you agree with her when she later concluded, *"It didn't matter whether I felt ready or not"*?

7. Discuss the ways that Max expresses his grief over losing his mom. How do they differ from the ways that Ava shows her sadness? What methods does each child use to try to cope with Kelli's death?

8. A pivotal moment in the novel occurs on page 121, when Victor asks Grace to leave the room before he tells Max and Ava that their mother died. Did you think this was the right thing for him to do for his children? Why or why not?

9. Consider Grace's coworker's comment about how having children changes you: *"But you really don't know what love is until you're a mother. You can't understand it until you've*

had a baby yourself, but it's the most intense feeling in the world" (page 148). Do you agree with this? Do you think Grace comes to share this belief?

10. On page 94, Ava thinks, *"I also thought it was weird that Mama was always telling me how pretty I was, but then practically in the next breath, she insisted being smart was more important."* Based on what you learned about Kelli's past over the course of the novel, how can you explain this apparent contradiction?

11. How does Ava's relationship with her father change after Kelli's death? What did you think about her comment on page 378 that *"I didn't want him to think I was like Mama. I wanted him to believe I was stronger than that"*?

12. Ava recalls her parents fighting about how much Victor was working at the restaurant. Did you side with either Kelli or Victor while you were reading these scenes?

13. Do you believe that maternal instincts are innate, or do you think that they are acquired? What do you think the novel is saying about the ways that mothering is either a learned skill or a natural ability?

Enhance Your Book Club

1. Amy Hatvany is the author of three other novels: *Best Kept Secret*, *Outside the Lines*, and *The Language of Sisters*. Consider reading one of these titles as a group, and then compare and contrast the ways that Hatvany represents family in each book.

2. Choose one of the novel's narrators, and pick a scene that you think captures their unique perspective. Now, attempt to rewrite the scene—this time, from a different character's point of view.

3. Some of Ava's favorite memories of Kelli involve cooking, and preparing a favorite recipe is one of the ways that Ava and Grace begin to bond. For your next meeting, have every member bring in a recipe that has significance to them and tell the story behind it. You might even make copies of each recipe so that every member leaves with a collection of new recipes to try.

About the Author

Amy Hatvany is the author of *Outside the Lines*, *Best Kept Secret*, and *The Language of Sisters*. She lives in Seattle with her family. To learn more, visit www.amyhatvany.com

Center Point Large Print
600 Brooks Road / PO Box 1
Thorndike ME 04986-0001 USA

(207) 568-3717

US & Canada:
1 800 929-9108
www.centerpointlargeprint.com